WHEN I CAST
YOUR SHADOW

✳ ✳ ✳ ✳ ✳ ✳ ✳

* * * * * * * * *

WHEN I CAST YOUR SHADOW

* * * * * * * * *

SARAH PORTER

TOR TEEN

A TOM DOHERTY ASSOCIATES BOOK
NEW YORK

WHEN I CAST YOUR SHADOW

Copyright © 2017 by Sarah Porter

A Tor Teen Book
Published by Tom Doherty Associates
175 Fifth Avenue
New York, NY 10010

www.tor-forge.com

Tor® is a registered trademark of Macmillan Publishing Group, LLC.

The Library of Congress Cataloging-in-Publication Data is available upon request.

ISBN 978-0-7653-8056-2 (hardcover)
ISBN 978-0-7653-9756-0 (ebook)

Our books may be purchased in bulk for promotional, educational, or business use.
Please contact your local bookseller or the Macmillan Corporate and Premium
Sales Department at 1-800-221-7945, extension 5442, or by email at
MacmillanSpecialMarkets@macmillan.com.

First Edition: September 2017

Printed in the United States of America

0 9 8 7 6 5 4 3 2 1

For those who live with ghosts

WHEN I CAST
YOUR SHADOW

* * * * * *

RUBY

✳ ✳ ✳ ✳ ✳

There it is again: in the middle of the black river a pale arm sweeps up and then curves down with a splash. Someone is swimming out there, and I know with all my heart who it must be. "Dashiell?" I say, but my voice clings in the nearby air. He doesn't hear me.

I've been here before, I think. Only once or twice, and never for longer than it took to catch the first glimpse of his back, wandering far away from me along the shore. It's always so dark here, the river so viscous and slow, its surface shoving in jellied wrinkles at the stones. But this time nothing happens to pull me away from this place and I see him again and again: the broad line of his shoulders parting the water, his face like a blurry moon.

"Dashiell!" I call. "It's me, it's your Ruby-Ru! Please come back."

And thank God, he must hear me now, because he laughs—I'd know that laugh anywhere—and rolls onto his back. I can see the pale arch of his bare chest, his streaming arms. He's still far away but the sound waves must have shifted somehow, because I can hear every tiny stir of his feet in the water.

"You shouldn't be swimming out there, should you, Dash?

That water doesn't look healthy." I know there's something I have to explain to him, that it's urgent, but I can't think of the right way to put it. "Dash, I think you don't understand? This is a really unusual opportunity for you. I mean, people don't just get chances to come back to life? And if you keep taking so many risks, it might seem like you don't appreciate it."

The shape of his body shifts into an arrowhead; he's traveling *away* from me. My throat thickens at the sight.

"If you want me to get a second chance, Ruby Slippers, then you're going to have to come to me. Swim out here and we'll discuss it."

That water looks so sickening, though: somber and gluey. "No! Dash, *please* come back here. Please don't do anything crazy. I don't think you understand how much we've missed you. And now—you have this chance, and you won't even listen to me!"

How can I find the words for what's happening to him? Dashiell died, that much I'm sure of, and now by some wild, sweet, improbable fluke he can have one more try at being alive—if he'll only care enough to take it. I don't know how I know that, but the truth of it is diamond-hard and sharp inside my chest. Out of all the people in the world who've ever died and been mourned, of course Dashiell would be the one who gets such an incredible opportunity. But how do I make him take it seriously?

"It wasn't fair, Dash. The way you died. It was a mistake and it wasn't fair to anyone, and maybe that's *why*—"

"Oh, pah, Ruby-Ru. You can't still be such a child, can you, that you'd suppose *fairness* could come crawling into a place like this? Swim out to me, and I can explain things to you without shouting."

No one is shouting. He's so far in the distance that I can barely make out the disturbance of his rising arms, but we can hear each other perfectly. I can feel him smiling at me across the water, and I don't know why I'm so afraid, why my heart tumbles featherlight inside me.

"Why can't you come to me? You don't know what it's been like, Dash. Without you. It's like—everything I thought was solid is hollowed out."

Everyone in our family is afraid of everything; I can *feel* Dash thinking that. I can feel him thinking that I'm just like our father, a man who was always cowering away from his own son, looking at his brilliant face with hunted eyes. Because the fire that was in Dash could burn anything, everything. But that never frightened *me,* and I won't let Dash think it scares me now.

"If you really want me back," Dash says, "you're going to have to prove it, Miss Slippers. Come get me."

With Dashiell you always have to prove everything, again and again, and nothing you can do is ever enough. You can't just *tell* him you love him, because he'll smile and play with your hair and say how absurd you are for thinking that words could be enough to make it true. I look at the black swirls inches from my feet, frilled with light shining from no moon.

"If I swim out there, then do you *promise* you'll come home with me?"

The water coils with anticipation; it could be the grease exuded from daydreams gone bad. I take a step forward and it sucks at my shoes.

"Oh, Ru-Ru, of course I do. Come for me now, and I'll follow you back like a little lost lamb. If you'd only been paying attention, you'd know that I've always been truthful with you."

I always paid attention to him; how can he not know that? Whenever I saw him I'd concentrate as hard as I could, trying to memorize the exact shapes the sunlight made on his face, every nuance of his voice, because I always knew that someday we might lose him for good. The water is up past my ankles now, and my shadow on its surface looks like a hole. Waiting to take me in.

"You won't believe the view out here, Ru-Ru. It's distance like you've never seen it before! *That* much black, *that* much emptiness. Ah, the night sky when I was alive was positively middling by comparison."

Something skids beneath my foot and I stumble in, thigh-deep now. That water will ruin my dress but I'm not about to take it off, not when Dashiell might see me. Besides, I can't imagine what could be hidden under that slick surface: things shimmying and almost alive.

"Ah, and here we go. I knew I could count on you, sweetest Ru. But you should consider how severely our father would forbid you from doing any such thing. He'd say you should leave me where I am, and good riddance. You wouldn't want to do anything he'd disapprove of, would you, Ruby Slippers?"

"Dad misses you, too," I say. "He just pretends not to. Dashiell, we all want you to come home, so much. And I'm—" *I'm coming for you, because I have to. Because you won't give me any other choice, but it's cruel of you to make me do this.* I can't say that, though. The water is at my throat now and I stumble forward, flailing. I can hear Dashiell's harsh laugh. I know I have to kick—I'm usually an okay swimmer, even if I don't look like I should be—but at first I can't get my feet up to the surface.

"I can see our Earth!" Dashiell calls. "Still very far away, but it appears to be flying closer at precipitous speed. Do you realize, Ru-Ru, that everything I'm seeing now is coming from you? Left to our own devices, the dead can't envision for beans."

I've got the best rhythm going that I can, though I have to tug my arms free of the water at every stroke. I can't tell if I've just left the shore, or if I've been swimming for hours. "Dash? I can't see you anymore. Where—"

"Not so much farther now, Ruby-Ru. You're doing just fine."

All I see are the dark folds and my own hands struggling against them. But Dash's voice still rings in both my ears; he could be inches away to either side, or right behind me.

"Dash? Wherever I go I keep thinking I'm about to see you, or that I've just missed you somehow. Like, that you got off the train one second before I got on, and I missed you in the crowd? Because it was so, so wrong what happened to you. You were going to be okay. You were clean."

"Ah, but technically I'm much cleaner since I've been dead, Ru-Ru. There's no clean like sloughing off your body completely, is there? If you bring me back now, I'll be sullied again by the whole sticky mess of carnality, blood and guts and hunger and desire. If *clean* is what you want for me, you might reconsider. Death works better for that than shampoo."

"But don't you miss us?" I can't tell if I'm moving forward anymore. I could be twisting in place, surrounded by night-colored walls. God, I'm going to sink before I find him. "Don't you miss *me*?"

Then I smack into something warm and slippery. Bare skin. I flush and try to jerk away, but Dashiell is there, his wavy strawberry-gold hair bright against the dimness. He's gripping me hard by my wrists and smiling. And he's completely naked.

"Poor little Ruby-Ru," Dashiell lilts. His face is silvery-gold, as gorgeous as ever, but with something sickly in the way it shines. "You've been so brave, but you don't grasp the consequences of your actions, do you? I'm sorry for what you'll have to go through, now. I don't suppose there's anything I can say that will make this easier for you."

And then I'm jolted out of myself, and I watch while Dashiell slides his hands to my shoulders. I watch while he shoves my head under the surface. The thrust catches me in the middle of an inhalation and water floods my throat before I know what's happening. I feel the cold pouring into my lungs, and at the same time I observe it all from a distance: a dumpy sixteen-year-old girl kicking desperately below me.

I'm not really struggling that hard, though, and as I watch myself I know why: I don't want to hurt him. Not my adored brother, not when he's finally been returned to me. Not when he's been through so much pain already.

"Ruby Slippers," Dashiell muses while he drowns me. "She slipped under the rug, she disappeared from view. Oh, where have you gone, Ruby-Ru, Ruby-Ru?"

My dark blond hair boils on the surface. I can see my own fingers starting to go limp, wet white commas drifting on the black sea.

"Dashiell," I say. "Dashiell, I love you so much! How could you do this to me?"

I don't know if he'll hear me. I don't know if I have a voice anymore, or a face, or a heart. The girl I was is bobbing below the surface. Dashiell jiggles me up and down experimentally, checking to make sure I'm dead.

"How could I do this? Ah, Ru, what kind of a question is that?" Dashiell tips his head and smiles, thinking it over. "I did it because there's no place like home."

I'm awake, I'm awake, and those are not horrible black waves sticking to me but my drenched sheets. I'm awake and breath is heaving into my lungs. This is my pretty robin's-egg blue bedroom in our pretty brownstone on Carroll Street, and Dashiell was buried almost two months ago, and even if I dream about him every single night it doesn't change the fact that I stood on the sweating September grass and dropped dirt on his coffin while my knees buckled.

This dream felt different, though, and not only because it was so terrible. It was somehow much *deeper* than my usual nightmare: the recurring one where Dashiell sits on my bed holding a syringe, and I know that if he shoots up again he'll die. In that dream I always know that we're getting a miraculous chance to change what happened, because the way he died was just too stupid and senseless and he was way too young and talented and amazing. Then he smiles at me and shoves the syringe into his arm while I beg, *Not this time, Dash, not again.*

I've been waking up every morning gasping and sobbing, my hands thrashing at the air as I try to grab him, stop him, before it's too late.

That nightmare is bad enough, but this was so much worse.

Because it felt like I had dreamed my way into a more powerful part of my mind. Because during the dream I completely believed it was real, and bringing Dash back to life was an actual *possibility*, and now I'm shivering from the memory of how an idea so absolutely insane felt so true. Because, no matter how bad my dreams get, Dashiell's never murdered me in one of them before. And because I'm sick with myself: it's awful of me, disloyal, to even *dream* about Dashiell doing anything so cruel.

I'm still clutching my blankets, trying to forget the sensation of those gummy waves closing around my head, so I don't notice right away that my door is open.

Everett is standing there watching me. My twin. Darker hair and a big sloppy mouth instead of my small one, but basically the same degree of podgy, unattractive, and socially hopeless. We were IVF babies, meaning our parents really wanted *one* of us—they paid a whole heap of money to get one of us— but then after three years of doctors and hormone shots it turned out to be a twofer and they were stuck with more than they'd planned on. Considering that their first child six years earlier was Dashiell, so beautiful and enchanting from the moment he was born, it's impossible to imagine that we didn't come as a disappointment.

The strain proved to be too much for their marriage, though they were never tactless enough to tell us so in so many words. But one time when she was visiting New York I overheard our mother tell our dad that she'd felt stifled by living with him, or maybe with us. She even told me to my face once that we'd *clarified* her feelings for her, and helped her realize what she really wanted out of life, and somehow she expected me not to recognize what that meant: *Not* you, *Ruby. Not you and your brother.*

Or maybe she knew I'd get it, and she didn't care that much. She's one of those people who treats *just being honest* as an excuse for being hurtful.

Now she contrives to be so very far away, and having such a fabulous life, that no one could reasonably expect her to remember we exist. And she usually doesn't.

"I heard you scream," Everett says. "It was Dash again?"

"Dash," I say. "Yeah. But it's getting worse, Ever."

"Every night? And I still haven't dreamed about him once? It's like he doesn't even care about seeing me again. He only wants to talk to you."

Suddenly I know I can't tell Everett what Dashiell did to me. Maybe *I* know now that what happened wasn't connected to reality, but what if Ever blames Dash anyway? "You don't want these dreams. They're horrible."

"I do want them, though. I mean, I want *something*. Because—I know it's not rational—but every night? Don't you start to wonder sometimes if that's really him? Like, if he's trying to get a message to you?"

"Ever, these are dreams. As in, they are not real. As in, I'm talking to something in my head, but it is not actually Dashiell. I think it's important for us to be clear about that?" I stare at him. "I can't believe you're making me *say* this."

"Do *you* believe that?" Everett asks. "I mean, believe it for real? You're not just trying to talk yourself into it?"

"I *have* to believe it! Ever, don't—thinking like this will make us both go crazy!"

If I let myself believe in Dash's dream-visit, if I imagine that his spirit truly came to me last night, then I would also have to believe in my own dream-murder. That's a line I can't cross. The real Dashiell wasn't an easy person to deal with, and I'm not pretending he was, but he wouldn't have done *that*.

Everybody else has always been way too ready to believe the worst about Dash, so that means it's up to me to remember him the way he *really* was. To fight for his memory.

He seemed like he loved me, at least a little. Like, in direct proportion to how lovable I actually am. It wasn't his fault that he got all the looks and glamour and charisma, so there was hardly any left over for Ever and me. It wasn't Dashiell's fault that he was the one who everybody wanted either to be or to sleep with. So since he was just inherently way more lovable than I am, it was natural that I loved him more than he was ever going to love me back. I didn't have any problem with that then, and I don't now.

It made sense. Everything made sense except the part where he OD'd six months *after* he kicked heroin.

Everett is still watching me. "It was just a dream, Ever," I say again, and my voice comes out rough. "You're supposed to be so realistic, remember? Superstitious stuff like this is totally beneath you. You are the *last* person who should start believing in ghosts. Right?"

"Fine," he says, and turns his back on me. "At least I don't read my stupid horoscope." I get up and shut the door, just a little too hard.

I'm still mad at Everett for saying those things, actually, especially since he's made it his job to be skeptical and detached all the time. So why did he have to let me down and start believing in something so utterly berserk—our dead brother coming to me in a dream, seriously?—and right at the moment when I have to pour all my strength into convincing myself there's no way it could be true?

Dash wouldn't hurt me. Not on purpose. Not like that. It's a ridiculous idea.

When I'm showered and dressed, I pull on the cherry-red, patent-leather Doc Martens Dashiell bought me the last time I saw him, just three days before he died. *Ruby slippers for you, my sweet Ruby-Ru.*

And I do it to remind myself of just how wonderful he really was.

EVERETT

✴ ✴ ✴ ✴ ✴

Here's an exercise. You pick something to stare at—anything you want, maybe the streaky red reflection of Ruby's boot on the steel dishwasher—and you just keep staring. After a while you can feel yourself turning into the thing you're staring at: that smudge of red. After a while you can completely stop being yourself. Then you're not *real* anymore, and neither is anyone else. Then you feel, as absolute truth, that nothing and no one matters. That the people who think they're so important are just deluded fools.

So Dad has noticed Ruby's boots, and he's scowling, and there's going to be another fight? Oh well. I'm out of it. I'm not anything at all.

Reality exists somewhere, maybe, but it's not where everybody thinks it is. Not in this kitchen. Not in my bowl of yogurt and granola. Not in this *family*.

Dashiell taught me that. He said that was what the drugs gave him. Transcendence. He said, *Once you walk out of your own mind, Never-Ever, there's no going back. You'll never forget what a joke it all is. You look back at everything you were so worked up about and you know it's just a clutter of figments. Shiny little fragments of who-cares.*

Figments, I tell myself. *Dad-figment is going to have a figment-fit at sister-figment, but no one is here to care.*

"I'd throw those boots in the garbage," the man known as Dad is saying, "except that it would provide you with an opportunity to frame yourself as the victim, Ruby. I have to say, Dashiell had a real gift for Pavlovian conditioning: he'd withhold and reject and insult you, so when he finally gave you *something* it assumed an outsized significance. How many pairs of shoes have I bought for you without it meaning anything to you at all?"

I mess up then. I start being Everett again enough to worry about how Ruby's taking it, and I look at her. She's sitting across from me, not eating, her hands gripping the edge of the kitchen table. Red eyes, swollen nose, her mouth all bent up. But she won't let herself cry. *She's not real,* I tell myself. *Ruby is not even an actual thing.* I can't totally believe it, though. She is my sister, and my twin.

I messed up. I'm sorry. I can't stop myself from caring about her.

I, I, I. What a disaster. No matter how hard I try, I can't keep the *I* out of my mind for long.

"You can afford to buy shoes," Ruby says. "Dashiell got me these with his very first paycheck from the gallery, and it wasn't much money at all, and he didn't have anything himself. His own shoes had these huge holes in the soles, and he had to wear them to *work* like that. Because you wouldn't help him!"

"Giving Dashiell money would not have helped him," our

dad says. Very flat, very dead, like he's talking about a complete stranger. "Nothing would help him. That's what you can't see, Ruby. He was fatally flawed. Quite literally. There was darkness in him that was bound to kill him, no matter what anyone did. I'm only grateful that he didn't take anyone else with him."

I stare at the granola lumps sinking into white yogurt. Down and down. Little pocks in white. I should be nothing but those little pocks, sinking and sinking. But my exercise isn't working now.

"He was amazing!" Ruby shouts. "He was the most brilliant person ever! And he had so many ideas, and everyone who met him loved him." That's it; she can't keep herself from crying. If Dashiell was here he'd make fun of her until she snapped out of it. But our dad doesn't know how to do that.

"He was a monster. Immensely selfish, callous, destructive, and manipulative. The fact that he had some superficial charm only made that worse. Ruby, if you can't see that, you'll never be free of him."

Ruby pouts. I know what the problem is: she can't totally deny that Dashiell could be a jerk a lot of the time. "Geniuses aren't supposed to be nice," she says at last. "Everyone knows that."

Our dad laughs. He laughs in a way that shows exactly where Dashiell got his laugh from. Ruby's looking at him like she wants to beat his face in. Her ratty blue dress with the big flowers and her hair full of plastic butterflies make it hard to take her seriously. Her face is a blazing pink blob. I wish I could laugh at her too. But I know her too well for that: if there's anything about Ruby that's *real*, it's how angry she gets.

"Ruby . . ." I finally say. She doesn't look at me. It's like rage is tied around her in big knots and she can't move. "Ruby Slippers," I say, to get her attention. "Ruby-Ru!"

"You will *not* call her that in my house!" It's the first time our dad has raised his voice. So *something* gets to him after all. "Everett, do you understand me?"

Ruby smiles. Back in the game, even with a tear still dripping down her fat shiny cheek. "Sorry, Dad. What isn't Never-Ever supposed to call me?"

She drags her hand across the table, then knocks twice.

Morse code. Dash, dot, dot. The letter D. And Dash-Dot-Dot was our private name for him, just like he had his personal names for us that we didn't ever use for each other. Not until this morning.

Never-Ever. Ruby Slippers. Normally a name is just sounds, but Dashiell made it seem like our names had infinitely deep meanings. Like they had power.

For a few seconds our dad looks like he's about to lose it. Then he kind of smoothes himself over and goes flat again. "Even if Dashiell had been a genius, it wouldn't have redeemed him. But he wasn't even close. You have far more potential than he did, Ruby."

Dash, dot, dot, goes Ruby's hand again. Messing with him. But self-control is one thing our dad has in truckloads, and he ignores her.

"Believe me, I wish it were different. It isn't natural or comfortable for a parent to think in these terms about his own child. But I've had to acknowledge that it would have been much better if Dashiell had never been born."

Ruby's hand stops and she stares at him. Her face goes sickly white and she stands up. I can't believe it, either. "How can you *say* that?"

"I can say it because it would have been better for Everett. And for you, Ruby. And the two of you are what matters to me now."

Ruby picks up a vase from the table and weighs it in her hand. It's a fancy handmade glass thing, clear blue-gray with white globs. Our dad looks at her, then at the vase, then back into her eyes. Like he knows what's coming and he's decided not to care.

"Say that again," Ruby tells him.

"Certainly. Even worse than the pathetic tragedy that was Dashiell's life, Ruby, is the tragedy of how you and Everett romanticize him. Even *dead* your brother is still a menace to you, because as long as you cherish these deluded views of him, there's always the risk that you'll succumb to his influence. Is that plain enough? If I had been able to see into the future twenty-two years ago then I would have done anything, absolutely anything, to save you both from that. Now go on. Throw it. I'm waiting."

Ruby puts the vase back down. Very carefully. "Anything," she repeats dully. "You mean like infanticide?"

"It would have been a great kindness," our dad says. "For Dashiell especially."

Ruby leaves the room. Not stomping, not banging doors. She just slips away, which is worse, because it means she's skipped over flipping out and gone straight to ice.

This is what I get, then, for screwing up and letting myself be Everett again. Letting myself feel what *Everett* feels.

I get the most intolerable thing I've ever seen.

"Why don't you go after her, Everett?" Dad asks. "I don't

think she'll be speaking to me for several days. And she needs someone now."

I stare at him. He's an old man, as old as some kids' grand-fathers. Silver hair, glasses, blue shirt, and that polite, stiff look on his face. He could retire already but he loves his work too much; today is Saturday but he's going off to the hospital and he won't be home until late.

"You could have gotten away with it, right?" I say. "If you had murdered Dashiell?" He's a neurosurgeon. He must know the best ways to not get caught. My chest feels wide and empty, like I don't weigh anything anymore. I almost decide to tell him about the dreams Ruby's been having—he doesn't know, and maybe he wouldn't have said those things if he *knew*—but then I think of how furious she would be if I did that.

"That's beside the point." He shrugs. "But very probably."

"There was a point?" I can't hear Ruby crying, but I hope she is. I hope she's not too frozen for that. "There was a *point* to your saying that to her?"

"I told Ruby exactly what she needed to hear. Of course I was aware that it would hurt her. There are times when pain is necessary, Everett. This was one of them."

"Like surgery," I say. I'm still staring at him. He has flat gray eyes, and they shine. I still don't really get what he thinks he was doing, but I know he was trying to do *something*. He would never say so, but I know Ruby is his favorite. He hates how in-tense she gets but he also sort of admires it, and he wouldn't be that mean to her for no reason.

He'd never tell *me* that I had "far more potential" than Dashi-ell did. Just as one example. I'd be the nerdish slacker who won't amount to much. The one where you have to say, *I love and support you just the way you are, Everett,* in an exaggeratedly patient voice, and then look off. Ruby would be *achievement-oriented* and *able to handle considerable responsibility.*

"For surgery we have anesthesia, Everett. With the body we can suspend feeling and no harm is done. But we don't have that luxury with the mind." He pauses, mulling it over. "Anesthetize the mind, and you wind up with someone like Dashiell."

People almost never believe things because they're objectively true. They just believe in whatever made-up reality hurts them the least. So that's what I'm thinking while our dad is talking: like, that maybe hating Dash so much is the only way he has to hold off the pain of what happened.

RUBY

* * * * *

It's a gray day and the trees up and down Carroll Street are cinnamon and singed tangerine. When the wind surges they all rock and shudder together, and I want to smash the window with my bare fists and reach out for them and ask them to take me away from here forever. Ruby Slippers is my true name, the name for the secret version of me that Dashiell knew and that I know too: the *me* that is too big and wild and free to fit in any room, or in my school, or especially in what other people think I am. No one is going to tell me I can't use my real name. *You will* not *call her that in my house!*

I hear sharp steps heading out the front door. Dad is heading to work and I wish he'd stay gone.

Because it's like Dad doesn't just want to go back in time and kill Dashiell. He also wants to kill the *me* that Dashiell knew was in there, even if I look like some dumb pink rabbit and act like a straight-A good girl who writes teen-angst poetry, and the adults all smile behind their hands and say, *Isn't it just adorable that she's so mad?* Because they know I'll never actually do anything about it. Or they think they know that.

Maybe Dashiell died at twenty-two, but at least he didn't

spend his life doing and being exactly what other people wanted him to be. At least he had the balls to piss everyone off. He didn't just obey them like some docile little weakling and live up to their lame expectations.

My head drifts over and I see my boots again, the boots that started the whole fight because I'm presumptuous enough to love my own brother. And suddenly I'm back in the memory so intensely that my blue walls and bird-print curtains are wiped away and I'm listening to the doorbell ringing again, somehow knowing it was Dashiell although it'd been weeks since he'd even texted me . . .

"Well, hi. Look at Miss Slippers, at the door in two seconds just like she's been waiting for me all along. Have you?" I noticed right away how healthy he looked, how his skin was clear again and his hair was shiny lush strawberry-gold and he wasn't so scrawny anymore. Tall and gray-eyed and gorgeous as usual, but in a much better way now. It was obvious that he'd managed to keep off the drugs, so when he sort of shoved me back from the doorway and wrestled me into an off-balance hug I didn't mind. I wasn't supposed to let him in the house—*under no conditions, Ruby!*—but if he was clean it *had* to be okay. He even smelled better, without that sneaking rotten stink he'd had before. "I just got paid from my new job at the gallery. Wanna see how much of my check we can blow into ectoplasm? You and me, Ruby-Ru?"

It was a Sunday but he didn't even ask if our dad and Everett were home. They weren't, but how did Dash know that? He was pulling back my hair to make me look at him like I was the only person in the world he'd ever wanted to see. I couldn't hide how happy I was. "Don't you think you should save it?"

"Oh, pah! Don't tell me my Ruby Slippers, my sweet lady of slip-sliding away, has gone and turned into an uptight old woman so soon? Let's go run through the streets. Let's make candy boats and sail them down the river." He was softly pushing me, buffeting me around the head, and I was glad I was laughing so hard because that way he wouldn't realize that I was also crying a little. "Or we can make paper boats out of your damned homework. Come on, maiden fair. Get your shoes and let's go!"

I reached to grab my sneakers off the hallway floor, but Dash was still bopping me around too much. "I'm trying!"

Dashiell twirled me so fast I completely lost my sense of direction and flopped against the wall.

"Oh, *trying, trying*. Here I come to rescue you from this vile nest of bourgeois propriety, Ru-Ru, and all you can say is that you're trying?" He was partly kidding, because that was Dashiell's way: to talk through strange shining layers of joking and poetry, so that you had to guess what he was really saying. He straightened the picture I'd knocked sideways and helped me to a chair, smiling slyly. "Let's go get ice cream. I've heard it does simply marvelous things for your coordination."

I was lacing my sneakers as fast as I could.

And then we were out and I barely managed to lock the door before Dash was tugging me down the steps—we live in the top two floors of our brownstone and rent out the bottom apartment—and we were charging up the street like a pack of wolves was after us—and for the rest of that day he stayed with me, his arm locked around my shoulder as we walked so that people we passed looked around in disbelief, that such a handsome boy was out with such a homely girl. He told me about the ways his life was changing, how excited he was, how glad to be free from his addiction, and I knew in my heart that the horrible part was finally over.

We walked to Dumbo and got lost in a big art installation made of nets, and then Dashiell insisted that we had to buy construction paper and tape to make boats, and we went to the park and the boats we patched together were ridiculous flowery multicolored things that swirled and floundered in the East River, and someone yelled at us for littering but we didn't care.

And then we went on the merry-go-round that sits like a jewel in its faceted glass house. Manhattan loomed on the far side of the river, and every time we went around I watched Dashiell's reflection stretched out on the glass, smeared and distorted so that it looked like some angelic golden tower had appeared on the New York skyline: a tower with a face. When it was over we got in line again, and rode again, our crystal reflections flying over the river and streaking through the sky.

Then we went for ice cream, just like he'd said—only when I asked for a cone he ordered two enormous sundaes—and sat at an outdoor table where we could watch the ferries skimming through blue ripples. While we were eating he grabbed my chin and turned my head at different angles, inspecting me. "You know, Ruby-Ru, your face isn't so bad. You'll grow up to be a reasonably pretty woman, even if no one can see it yet."

"I know how I look, Dash-Dot-Dot, and if I ever forget there are a ton of boys at my school who just love to remind me. You don't need to try and make me feel better about it. At least I'm smart, and I'd rather be a smart dogface than a beautiful moron any day."

"Oh, but I would never try to make you feel *better* about anything, Miss Slippers. I'd be happy to make you feel downright suicidal if honesty required it." He was smiling really sweetly while he said it, though, still tipping my head around. "Now, your goal should be to become just pretty enough that people can fall in love with you, but not so beautiful that everyone fools themselves into thinking they love you when they actually hate your guts."

I knew right away what he had to be talking about. "You mean like you."

"I mean like me, Ruby Slippers. Never has a man been so despised by so many people who profess to feel the most uncontrollable adoration for him. Why, even my own family!"

That shocked me. "Who are you talking about?"

"Well, not Dad, obviously. He hates me with a perfect lack of ambiguity. I'll give him credit, Ru. The man never pretends anything different." I knew that Dashiell had stolen almost fifteen thousand dollars from our dad, mostly by using his credit cards to buy things he could sell for drug money, but it seemed cruel to bring that up right when Dash was getting better. And anyway that wasn't what mattered then.

"Then who do you mean? Mom? I think you're the only one of us she actually cares about!" I didn't want to say it, but I had to. "Dash, you know how much I love you, right? You would never think that about me?"

He took a slow bite of ice cream and licked the fudge off his spoon, gazing at me speculatively. "Well that's an extravagant claim, Ruby-Ru. How am I supposed to know if you love me? Love me, that is, without some contrary treacherous feeling lurking below the surface? You haven't turned against me *yet*, but who knows if you will one day?"

"Dash, I *always* stand up for you, and I always—" *I always miss you so much that it feels like my heart is leaking blood, maybe just a trickle, but real blood, whenever you stay away and ignore us for long.*

"Love is one of those things that proves itself over time, Miss Slippers. From that perspective you're too young to say you love anybody. Sixteen? For God's sake, girl, what *is* that? You haven't lived long enough yet to *demonstrate* love. We'll just have to wait and find out."

"Dashiell . . ." My eyes were getting hot and my face felt swollen. I knew it was making me look repulsive.

"This isn't a discussion worth having, Ruby Slippers. Now stop before you ruin our perfect day together." He swatted me, but gently, and got up and chucked his half-eaten sundae in the garbage. "Ugh. Enough of that. Recent studies have shown that hot fudge induces excessive mawkishness in adolescent girls. We should go for cocktails instead. Let's get you plastered. An excellent antidote!"

I'd been about to sob but that made me laugh instead. "Who do you think is going to serve me *cocktails*?"

"My ID should be enough to cover both of us, surely. It is an *official* New York State license-to-persistently-exist, after all. Now ditch that gunk and let's go."

He dragged me to an amazing dark bar, all rippling mahogany and mirrors sliced up and arranged into glittering sinuous patterns, but the bartender wasn't convinced that one driver's license was enough and we got kicked out after a pretty short argument. It would have been embarrassing except that Dashiell was so funny about it that I kept cracking up, which probably didn't help persuade anybody that I was twenty-one. And then we were wandering up Smith Street in the sunset, not sure where to go next, and I started to dread the moment when Dashiell would remember that he had something better to do, or actually everything better to do, and tell me to get myself home.

And that was when I saw my boots in the shoe store's window. The air was just shifting toward blue and their red burst through it, blasted all the other colors in the world into shards, and gleamed at me. I felt like huge crimson roses were expanding through my chest. I felt like those boots were meant for me.

Dashiell watched my expression change as I saw them. "I almost forgot. We have some important shopping to do, don't we, Ru-Ru?"

I hesitated. "I might have enough money left from baby-sitting. But it's at home."

"Oh, pah," Dashiell said, and seized my wrist. The door chimed as we went in, Dashiell strutting and me bobbing along behind him like a toy on a string.

"We're about to close," the salesgirl snapped. Then she got a better look at Dash and her gaze went soft.

"We know what we want," Dashiell told her. "We'll be out of here before you can blink. Your shoe size, Miss Slippers?" He put his arm around me while the salesgirl went to fetch the boots and I made myself sit straight, though all I wanted was to bury my face in his shoulder and beg him to come home and never leave us again. Maybe I already had a bad feeling and I just couldn't let myself be consciously aware of it. Maybe on some hidden level I was afraid for him.

The boots came and I laced them up. I could see them flashing at me out of the mirror, their shining leather becoming rubies running with fragrant juice, cherries that burst into flames, singing blood. I walked a few paces in them, but I already knew they were perfect.

"I can come back for them. You don't need to spend your money on me, Dash. You *shouldn't*. And Dad would probably get them for me if I asked." I sat back down next to Dash on the bench and reached to untie them, but he caught hold of my hand and stopped me.

"Dad is absolutely not permitted to buy these boots for you. He can go ahead and get you all the things you don't actually care about. But these, these smite your heart with bright desire. I can see it. And that means that *I* will be the one to give them to you." He smiled, kissed my forehead, and handed the salesgirl a wad of cash without even looking at her. "Ruby slippers for you, my sweet Ruby-Ru. My precious baby sister. You'll be wearing them home, now. And you'll be thinking of me."

That was my older brother, and when he gave me that kiss he only had three days left to live. That was the person my dad says never should have been born. The son he wishes he'd had the foresight to murder while he was still a baby. And I'll never love anybody that much again.

All at once I'm positive I know the truth. I know now what *really* happened to Dashiell. How could I have been so blind?

Everett is in my room. I hear him behind me but I don't turn around. He came in without knocking, and he shouldn't think he has a right to do that, but I don't actually mind. "Ruby."

"Don't call me that," I say. "Either call me by my *real* name or shut up."

He hesitates and then puts a hand on my shoulder. "Hey, Ruby Slippers. Are you okay?"

"No, Never-Ever, I am not. But at least things make more sense now. You know how Dash had been completely clean for six months when he died? He'd been passing the drug tests and he had that new job and a girlfriend and he was making plans for new video projects and everything? That last day he came here he was happier than I'd ever seen him. So it—it was not *logical* that he would go and shoot up again, right?"

Everett doesn't answer so I twist on my chair to stare up at him. He's silent, brows drawn. Doing his very best not to understand what I'm telling him. "But Dad explained that! Remember? He said when junkies get clean for a while they lose their tolerance, so when they screw up and go back on the drugs they think they can handle the same dose they used before, but they can't, because their bodies are suddenly way more sensitive. He said that's when a lot of overdoses happen, and it's a really dangerous time. Remember, Ruby?"

"That's what he wants us to think," I say. "That's the cover story. But better late than never, right?"

Everett gapes at me like I just slammed him in the guts. His pale face takes on an eerie green glass glow like the sky during a tornado watch. Then he grabs me by the shoulders.

"Ruby. Ruby, that did not happen. What you are thinking— it did *not* happen. Never. Never. If you think that way you are going to go literally insane and get locked up, okay? Dad was just saying—what he said—to get through to you." He's wheezing and he turns away from me to take a pull on his inhaler, still gripping me with his free hand. "Take it back."

Maybe I went too far, not by thinking it but by saying it out loud, even to Everett. "I didn't say Dad did it. Not personally. But I bet he knew about it. Dashiell—you know he made a lot of people really upset. Like that insane bitch who got him fired a year ago? She was definitely rich enough to hire someone, right? That's the thing, somebody just had to make it *look* like an accidental overdose, and they'd know that nobody would suspect anything. Like, *Oh well, looks like he messed up. That's just how it goes with those people!*"

Everett's holding his head at a strange angle, tipped down and away from me, but he's still shaking it hard even as he tries to catch his breath.

"Dash was sleeping with that woman. She was giving him money. She just got mad when he disappeared on her and freaked out at Hugo, and Hugo didn't want to offend a big client like her." Hugo is a famous video artist and Dashiell worked as his assistant. For a while.

"So how does that prove she wouldn't want to murder him? Maybe just getting him fired wasn't enough revenge for her."

"No, Ruby." Everett is getting more of a grip on himself now. "Stop it right now. Don't think this ever again."

"I do think it!" I'm starting to yell. Out of everybody in the world, I thought Everett was the one person I could trust to open up his mind and really *hear* me. "Dashiell was clean. So he died of an overdose, sure, but that doesn't mean he did it to himself! He was clean. He was getting better. He told me he'd finally realized that he really *wanted* to live. But no one is ever going to prove it if we don't!"

I'm thinking of what our dad said—that Dash was killed by the darkness inside him. Like he was just some self-destructive loser. *No.* I won't accept that, and I won't let the world believe it, either. There's another truth, a different truth, if I could only find it.

Everett's still shaking his head. He has big, gray, heavy-lashed eyes, just like Dashiell's—they're the only thing about him that anyone could call beautiful. Mine are greener.

"Ruby. Ruby, you were the only one who believed that. I mean that Dash was going to stay clean. I *hoped* and everything, but I never really thought it was going to last."

I stand up. "You're saying you didn't have any faith in him."

Everett sighs. "It wasn't like that. But I understood what the heroin meant to him. Philosophically."

All I can think is *You too, you too.* All I can think is how I'm so alone now that it's like I've been buried alive. But at least it's finally clear: I'm the only one who will fight for Dash, now that he can't defend himself.

I push past Everett—he doesn't try to stop me or anything—and head straight for the front door.

Now do you believe I love you, Dashiell? But actually I know perfectly well that he wouldn't. This wouldn't be nearly enough to convince him. *I'll show you, Dash. I will.*

EVERETT

✳ ✳ ✳ ✳

Something catches my right wrist as Ruby walks by and gives me a little tug. Then the feeling disappears. I turn and look at her, surprised that she would touch me when she's in such a foul mood. Her arms are hugging her chest, though. It couldn't have been her.

And then she's gone, her footsteps snapping down the hallway. I hear the front door swing open and then closed. I hear her key turn. *Fine,* I tell myself. *Let her go. Let her be like that. I don't need her and her drama.* But I'm still remembering the sensation on my wrist. I thought for a second that it was a hand, but now I think about it there was no warmth and no texture like skin. It was more like empty energy in the shape of a hand. A slight prickling and pressure with no matter behind it. Force, even a little bit of force like that tug I felt, is matter times velocity. So what I felt is physically impossible. Therefore it did not happen and I am going as crazy as Ruby if I let myself believe in it.

Fine. Settled.

Except that I know what that pressure, that feeling with nothing behind it, was trying to tell me. It wants me to follow

Ruby. The sane thing to do is ignore it. So I try. I lock my muscles tight and stand as still as I can in the middle of her room, trying to feel nothing.

And then I give up and go after her. Because I know, somehow, that I'll be sorry if I don't. It's like I have to choose between acting insane now, or feeling so terrible later that insanity is actually the rational choice.

I stop to put on my jacket, and by the time I get down to the street she's one long block away, already crossing 5th Avenue and walking straight and hard like she knows exactly where she's going. I semi-run until there's only about half a block between us and then I just follow her, watching her shiny red boots flash back and forth. It's cold out, a disgusting gray November day, but she isn't wearing anything over her blue dress and her arms are bare and blotchy red. She's carrying a handbag but that's it. She turns on 3rd Avenue then again on Union, heading toward the Gowanus Canal. I shouldn't be doing this, I know. I should turn around and go home. I do not want to deal with her putting on some huge freak-out if she sees me.

When she gets to the bridge she stops and leans over the stinking water and for a moment I'm afraid of what she's going to do. Then I see that she's just taking those stupid butterflies out of her hair, one by one, and dropping them into the canal. She was wearing her hair looped up and it starts to fall over her face and shoulders in a big blondish mess. It looks like she hasn't brushed it in a week. She yanks the last butterfly out and throws it as far as she can. Spitefully. Even from here I can see that.

If she looked around she would spot me, but I'm not worried about that anymore. She's staring at the water too hard. It's obvious she's not seeing anything except the sick visions in her own head.

Then she's walking on, fast, up the low hill past the brick houses with their front yards full of dried-up brown flowers. At Smith Street she turns right, weaving between the people out shopping. From the way she moves it seems like she doesn't even realize they're people. They could be a telephone poles or parked cars. Wherever she's going, she's in a big hurry.

Until she's not. Suddenly she stops at a store window and just stands there, which means that I have to stop, too, and find things to pretend to look at. Bad timing since I'm in front of a restaurant and it looks like I'm stalking the women who are in there eating brunch. They glance up and smirk and I can see them thinking, *Oh look! An insignificant nerd-boy, giving us the creep-eye due to our unspeakable hotness.* I hurry backward and stare in the window of a dry cleaners instead. Anything can be fascinating if you look at it the right way, if you imagine you're an alien seeing those shapes and colors for the first time. For a few minutes I manage to keep myself in that state of mind, where the clothes on their hangers become weird abstract entities. But Ruby won't move. People start to veer out around her as they go by like they can sense that there's something wrong with her, looking back over their shoulders as they pass. And at last a salesgirl comes out of the store and says something. Ruby jerks back like she's been electrocuted, shakes her head, and flings herself up the street again.

When I catch up to where she was I peer in to see what the deal was. But it's nothing special. Just shoes.

Next stop is a Rite Aid. I'm afraid I'm going to get stuck forever again but this time she's back in less than a minute, ripping open some sealed plastic pack with her teeth. She pulls out scissors. Then she walks to the nearest garbage can ten paces away, chucks the packaging, flips her head upside down, and starts hacking at her hair.

Now people are *really* giving her room. Tan hair scribbles the sidewalk; pieces worm their way down the wind. And Ruby keeps chopping, running the fingers of her free hand through it to feel how short it's getting. When she finally straightens up I can see that it's asymmetric, bristling out around her ear on the right side, but angling in a long ragged waterfall on the left. It spills over her eye, drags down one shoulder. She shakes herself and stops to look at her reflection in a rearview mirror on a van, and takes one more snip at her new slanting bangs. Smiles.

Even from here I can tell it's not a good smile.

I can barely imagine the shitstorm this is going to start when Dad sees her, or when she walks into school on Monday. Should I try to stop her before she does anything worse? We walk two more blocks and she swings into another store.

This time it takes longer. After a while I go sit down in a bus shelter across the street and wait. I can see from here that it's a vintage clothing store. Maybe she's finally calmed down enough to notice how cold it is and decided to buy a sweater.

No. When Ruby comes out her ugly blue dress is wadded in her hands and she's wearing a black velvet one instead. Tight as far as the waist but then spreading out into a wide skirt. And, Christ, fishnet stockings. The only thing about her that's the same as when she left our house is those shiny red boots. They look even brighter with all the black. Flashing like some kind of signal lights.

I don't want to see it. She's my sister, after all. But suddenly she looks chubby in a way that's actually sexy, all big curves, and her butchered hair comes across as more dangerous than stupid, and she's walking with a long, hard stride like no one had better mess with her. I'm not so sure now that she'll be getting flack in school. As she walks she's snipping chunks off her old dress with the scissors and letting the scraps fall to the pavement, so there's a trail of blue dots behind her. *Slash-Dot-Dot. Dash-Dot-Dot.* Ruby isn't normally someone who would litter, either. She excels at being the girl whom adults regard with approval.

I think of calling our dad and then decide not to. He's probably digging holes in someone's brain right now. And what would I say? That I can tell Ruby is losing her mind because she's shopping on Smith Street? What else are girls supposed to do on the weekend?

Put it that way and I feel disgusted with myself.

If it wasn't for the thing that snatched at my wrist, I'd just walk away and leave Ruby to her oh-so-fabulous makeover. Because that's all it is, right? And anyway nothing grabbed my wrist, because grabbing is an action that requires an animate being with a body and willpower to do it, and there wasn't one there.

Ruby turns left onto Atlantic. That should be the end of it. She'll come home when she gets too cold and tired to keep on acting for some imaginary audience. Drama Queen Productions, except no one cares and no one is looking—except me. I stop at the corner and watch her walk off, still oblivious to me, smacking down her steps in a way that tells everyone to leave her the hell alone.

Then I go after her again, and I don't even know why.

We start turning more often, zigzagging through Brooklyn Heights, so I have to keep closer to her. She pauses once to look in the window of a bar and then zooms off again. Another ten minutes and we're crossing the big roads that surround Dumbo and then heading in the direction of the East River. Dumbo is what it always is, warehouses that have been turned into fancy loft buildings and fancy people in extreme outfits pushing strollers but still being semi-arty about it. You probably couldn't find people anywhere who have bigger ideas of how important and glamorous and outstanding they are, like they think their lives are nonstop advertisements for something but no one really knows what.

Ruby's walking downhill. It's just a few blocks until we're in the park, a wide stretch of green reaching down to the water. She pauses just long enough to throw out her ruined blue dress and the scissors, too. Fog sits over Manhattan and makes the skyscrapers fuzzy and gray. It's not quite drizzling but water is mixed in with the air until the wind feels like a wet dog, and my jeans are starting to stick to my legs. The few people who are here are mostly leaving because it's just getting colder and nastier out, and who wants to deal?

Right at the edge of the water there's a bank of broken rocks, some big enough to sit on but most of them smaller. I watch while Ruby bends to pick up a grapefruit-sized chunk and then just stands there, cradling it in both hands.

Then she slings her handbag so the strap angles across her torso, opens up the bag, and stuffs the rock in. At first I can't understand why she would want something like that, but I do know on some weird blurred level that this is the answer. This is the secret reason why I've been following her, the thing that I knew all along without knowing I knew it. She edges closer to the river until it's licking the toes of her boots and stoops down for another rock. Crams that in her bag, too. Another step forward and the water spits up to her ankles. She's leaning weirdly against the weight pulling on her. Another step, the river around her calves now, and she wobbles like she's losing her balance.

Then something in me snaps and I'm running over the grass and then the stones even before I consciously understand. I crash into her sidelong and we both stagger, water squelching in my socks, and I'm yanking the strap of her bag over her head and throwing it back onto the shore. It lands with a hard whack, rock on rock. She probably thinks she's being mugged and she gets her arm back to punch me before she sees my face.

"Fuck you," I tell her, and it's only as I say it that I really understand why blood is pounding up through my head and making it echo inside. My face is burning and slicked with tears and snot, because something inside me just broke completely. Those stones were meant to drag her under, pull her deep below the river's surface and guarantee she wouldn't ever make it out. "Fuck you, Ruby. And don't tell me to call you *Slippers* because I never will again. You don't deserve that name. You can't handle it. Dad was right!"

I expect Ruby to blow a fuse. Start screaming at me about how it's her life and her decision. Tell me what a creeper I am for following her. But she doesn't. She looks at me with wide, confused eyes and then flings her arms around my neck, and for a second I think she's going to try to pull me in too, and drown both of us. But no, she presses her face against my shoulder and I can feel shivers running down her body in waves.

"Everett," she says, and her voice is quiet and crumpled. "Everett. How did you know?"

"Fuck you, Ruby," I say again, but it comes out weak and whining. "Did you even think about me and Dad? Did you think about *anything* except being as stupid as possible? Like hey, that maybe we love you, and we've already lost Dashiell, and this would completely destroy us?" Wind is driving the river in thin splashes over our feet, so I drag Ruby back across the rocks and then pull her down next to me. We're sitting in a tangle on the grass and she's shaking from more than the cold. She keeps hugging me the whole time and I'm holding her too, though I feel more like stomping her face in.

"But that's the thing," Ruby says. "Dad hates me. He doesn't realize he hates me, but if Dashiell shouldn't have been born then I shouldn't either. Because Dash is a huge part of me, and he *has* to be a huge part of me, because there's nowhere *else* he can be now!"

"You mean, like, Dash lives on in our hearts?" That seems like way too clichéd of an idea for Ruby, but I'm not sure what else she could mean. "I loved him too, Ruby. A *lot* a lot. But acting insane isn't going to make him any less dead. Okay? Tell me you get that now."

Ruby barely seems like she hears me, though. "I started thinking—that dream I had—I started thinking you were right and it was a message—like his death and my death were all one thing and I'm already partly dead and that's how it's *supposed* to be. Like he was telling me what he needed from me. But I don't know, Ever, I might have it all wrong."

Has she forgotten that I don't know anything about her

dream, except that Dashiell was in it? "I was being an idiot," I tell her. "Your dreams are just dreams, Ruby. There is no message. I didn't want to believe that Dashiell's gone so I was fooling myself into this idea that he's actually been visiting you. But that's not rational. It was a weak wish-fulfillment thing, because I want to see him again so much. I'm sorry. I loved him too."

"*Past* tense, you loved him? That's all wrong, Ever. Dashiell needs us to love him *now*. He needs us now so that he can be somewhere."

She sounds a little hysterical still. It seems like a bad idea to point out that dead people aren't capable of needing anything, because I'm not sure she can deal with hearing that at the moment.

"Yeah, well, he can live on in your heart a lot better if *you* live. Right? Is that what you're saying?"

Ruby finally lifts her face off my chest, so I can see it for the first time since I tackled her. She's been crying—no surprise there—and her new slashed hair tumbles down in this wild triangle over her streaky cheeks. She stares off at the river like there's something she can't figure out.

"I think—I feel like it's more than that? I feel like, the way Dash needs us—it's a lot more serious than what people mean when they say that stuff."

"Ruby? What are you talking about?"

She purses her lips in frustration and then shakes her head hard. "I don't know. It's just an idea that keeps coming to me. That Dashiell needs us now way more than he did when he was alive. We have to be ready to fight for him, Ever, and if *you* won't then I'll do it by myself!" She glances over at me long enough to give me a confused frown and then goes back to gazing at the river, and her eyes look so far away that something blurs inside them.

Then she looks at me again, but this time the sadness is gone and her expression is teasing and confident.

"Never-Ever," Ruby says, but the voice is not her voice. It's dropped by at least an octave and she's doing such a perfect imitation of Dashiell's sly sassing tone that my flesh crawls like massed worms. "Our little Miss Slippers was in such a distraught state that I probably couldn't have held her back on my own. And to think that you nearly ignored me. What would have happened to our sweet girl then?"

"What the hell?" I sputter. "Ruby, Jesus, *don't*—"

"You said you wanted to see me, Never-Ever," Ruby says. She really sounds exactly like him and there's something distracting and shifty in her eyes even though she's staring straight into mine. "So why don't you welcome me home?"

That does it. I aim a hard smack at her cheek, and another, and she sort of tumbles over onto her side but she doesn't even put up her arms to defend herself. She doesn't cry out. I slap her again but she doesn't react at all, just slumps on the grass looking vague, and I can't understand what's going on. I start to wonder if she's having some kind of seizure, but then her mouth opens and she looks at me like she can see me. My hand is hanging in midair above her face, poised to strike.

"Everett, stop!" Her voice is back to normal. Squeaky and girlish.

"Ruby, that was *the* most, the absolutely most messed-up, emotionally disturbed thing you have *ever* done! I don't care what you're going through. That was—" I can't even speak. Anger is so thick in me that it's making my mouth feel swollen and my tongue trip.

Ruby pulls herself back up to sitting. A little away from me, now. "I know I was being selfish, Ever. I really, truly appreciate that you came after me and stopped me. I do. I guess I already should have thanked you, but you don't need to hit me!"

It takes me a long moment to understand that we're not talking about the same thing. "I don't even *mean* that! I mean—that thing you were just pretending."

From Ruby's expression I could almost swear that she's genuinely stunned and bewildered and innocent. That she has no idea what I'm talking about. But she's just proved what an incredible actor she is, so that only infuriates me more.

"Pretending? I didn't even know you were following me! Who do you think I was pretending for?" She looks around. We're almost completely alone in the park and the mist is condensing into something more like drool, but there is someone hidden under a big umbrella walking near us. Ruby drops her voice. "Maybe I wouldn't have gone through with it. I don't *know*. I just know—it felt like I was dragging around a dead copy of myself, and I couldn't stand it." She hesitates. "Please don't tell Dad, okay? He'd probably send me to a mental hospital for real if he knew."

I stare at her. All that awful faked confidence is gone from her eyes, and they're green and scared and full of racing reflections off the clouds. "Ruby, you *know* that is not what I'm talking about!"

But she doesn't know. I can see that now. She's shaking hard, her face is shiny with rain, and she stares at me like every word

I'm saying is coming to her in a nightmare where nothing makes sense anymore.

"Everett? Can we go home? I'm freezing."

I stand up and go get her handbag from where I threw it and toss the rocks back on the bank. She's up, too, and waiting awkwardly, holding herself tight. I hesitate, because she doesn't deserve it, but then I take off my jacket and hand it to her.

"Come on. Do you have money for a cab? Because I don't."

"Probably. You can check in my bag." The jacket sticks to her wet dress and she has to wriggle to get it on. "Everett? What were you *talking* about? What do you think I did?"

I don't answer that. Because if what I think just happened, happened—if Ruby really misses Dashiell so much that she's going into fugue states where she pretends to be him and she's not conscious she's doing it at all—then that is definite clinical insanity. It's way worse, even, than the fact that she was about to attempt suicide. That is denial he's dead to such an extreme that it crosses every line I can think of, straight out of reality and into some horrible zone beyond.

And that means I need to think about what to do, before I do anything.

ALOYSIUS

* * * * *

Not yet a hundred years dead, and how many lives have I sucked down and savored and taken for my own? Seven, if memory serves, though some have been on the mayfly side and might slip my mind. If a body is not one's own, not one's personal gut and sinew—well, it does tend to alter one's attitude as to how best to make use of it. Having already died, and violently at that, the terror has quite leached from death, and all that remains for me is death's unspeakable boredom. I grasp, as none of the living can, how very ephemeral the pleasures of the flesh must be. So why be overly fussy about preserving the flesh in hand? There's more where that came from. Why, new lives squeeze forth on the daily, plump and squalling, and why should I not make lavish use of that supply?

Over the years, I've come to see all of them, bakers and barbers and courtesans, rakes and ingenues, in the just same light: as potentially *mine*. Mine, if only I can seize them.

When I can, though of late it's proved disagreeably tricky to snap up mortal husks. But that, ah, that should be about to change.

Life is wasted on the living, I always say.

I pace in the gray, waiting for news of the efforts to locate
our bitty truant Mabel—there's nothing to see here, and there
never is, except in those choice intervals when we happen to
entertain a beating heart as our guest—and while I wait I slip
into a reverie. A nostalgic accounting of those I've owned before, until such time as I'd gulped down the juice they had to
offer, and cast the rinds aside.

Ah, once upon a time the soft-skinned and blue-eyed
Martin Rhodes was mine; he was a luxurious fleshling, prettily
muscled and slim, with a face that let me exploit without
mercy all the dumb and dewy damsels who flocked to him. The
boy was strong enough to come in handy for dirtier tasks as well,
until one night I shattered him with an unfortunate combination
of excellent Scotch, a cliff, and a sports car. Call me profligate,
if you like, but I was in no mood to save my pennies. And it was
all worth it, wasn't it, in the final accounting? Why, I hadn't drunk
Scotch that fine in twenty years!

There was somebody's twelve-year-old sister, can't put a name
to her, only a decade after my murder; such a squealing, doughy
little lambkin that not a one of my old enemies felt the slightest
apprehension when she showed up peddling flowers. I'd even let
them knock her around a while, just for old time's sake, before I
used her hand to slice their guts. Betwixt hits I'd have her work
the streets—opium and good steaks don't come cheap—and
when she came down with a troubling case of syphilis I plopped
her naked in a snowbank. That took care of that, and I began to
think of making a more secure provision for my future sojourns
amongst the living.

My own mother, though, was my first; she was the easiest to
come by, after all. She waddled straight up to me, here in my

vaporous domain, and gawped at me with fondly rheumy eyes. A quick snap, a moment of senile mewling, and the acquisition was made.

I suppose I entertained a certain naïve optimism as to her usefulness. I found to my chagrin that her arthritis made her hardly worth my while—I might as well have put on a rusted-out bicycle, creaking and lurching every inch of the way—and soon enough she tripped and fell. As it happened, she was standing on the roof of her tenement, rather near the edge. And then, well, she wasn't.

She'd had her nerve, I thought, outliving me.

"Aloysius," Charlie says to me as he lurches grayly into my ken. He's speaking in a voice that I might characterize as breathless; that is, if any of us had such a thing as breath, or voices for that matter. It's evident that he dreads the consequences of coughing up some tidbit, but fears still more what I might do to him if he withholds his information. His quailing is only proper, of course. "Aloysius, I . . . we've searched everywhere, we didn't want to believe it at first, but he . . . gone, I mean. Gone!"

"Slap a name on this *he*, Charlie. Pronto. I'm about to lose patience."

A spasm convulses the gray smudge that I know to be Charlie; the best approximation one of us can give of a pathetic cringe. "Dashiell Bohnacker."

"You don't say." Charlie would never dare impart such unwelcome news if he hadn't made very, very sure of the facts beforehand. He knows as well as I do how this development will stymie my plans—and coming right on the heels of Mabel's escape, well, it's the sort of insolence that the other dead might find a sliver too *inspiring*. "Quite a few of you must have been slack indeed, then, in the performance of your duties. Worthless nitwits, the lot of you. And I suppose you were dawdling about and paying no mind, while that impudent lout worked up the brass to *defy* me?"

Charlie tries to speak, or perhaps to sputter, or most likely to whine for mercy. I quell him with a look; not that I have eyes to look with, naturally, but he can sense my stare nonetheless.

Charlie's panic when he came to me? Why, it was quite the thing.

RUBY

* * * *

Manhattan receded into fog, the towers so gray and diffuse that they seemed to be falling to the opposite side of the earth, and the river seemed to widen until it became a new and undiscovered sea. I thought then that my dream was more than a dream, and that I was carrying my own dead body in my arms to put it to rest in the waves. I thought there was more than one person inside me, that I was filled with Ruby and Dashiell and all the hatred and envy and resentment people had ever felt for Dashiell, but none of the love, and that I couldn't keep going on like that.

I wanted the truth of what had happened to Dash, and I thought I could see it shining in the river's depths—as if I could catch hold of him there, and dream all his dreams. We'd be together again, and we'd know each other *perfectly*.

It was some kind of wild trance, though, because when Everett grabbed me all those thoughts vanished in an instant. Then I was sick at the realization of how close I'd really come to doing it. Now I'm soaking in a hot bath, trying to get the deep chill out of my body, and the last thing I want to do is go under the water. Just watching the lights wobbling on the surface is pretty disquieting. I already drowned in my dream and now I never want to feel those sensations again, my lungs choked and glutted.

If I don't want to die—if I *know* I don't want to die—then why did I almost kill myself today? Why did I make Everett save my life?

"Ruby?" he calls through the door. He went from spitting with anger to over-the-top nice, and now his voice bends and flows like he's trying to wrap it around me. I really scared him and I know it wasn't fair. "Ruby? Pizza and watch *Cosmos*? Sound good?"

"That sounds great, Ever. Thank you." I'm being too nice too, uncomfortably nice, as if that could possibly make up for everything I put him through. "I'll be there in five minutes." He must be worrying that I'll try something again because I don't hear him walking away from the door. He's waiting there listening. Just in case.

So I get out, splashing loudly, and open the drain, and wrap myself in towels. I don't really know what I was thinking, chopping my hair off like that, and I'll need to get someone to fix it up a little, but when I look in the mirror it could be worse. It's almost stylish. But that black dress is ridiculous, at least for someone like me. What kind of vampire princess trip was I on? I stare at the velvet wadded up with the crimson toes of my boots sticking out beneath it and I can barely remember why buying it seemed like such a wonderful idea, or how I thought I'd be fooling anybody.

I change into fluffy pink pajamas and a red robe with cartoon animals on it. Everett's finally gone to the kitchen, and when he sees me walk in I can tell he's relieved that I'm back to more or less normal. "Are you better now?"

"Way better," I say, but Everett is still looking at me warily and I know he must be wondering if he should tell our dad what happened. He'll feel obliged to tell, to protect me from myself, unless I can persuade him that my behavior today was really just a passing aberration; I couldn't even blame him if he did. "That fight with Dad made me crazy, Everett. I couldn't believe he said those things and they completely spun me out. But I'm over it now. I promise I won't do anything like that again."

The timer rings and Everett gets pot holders and pulls the pizza from the oven, frowning down at it as if it presented some unsolvable problem. "I am still concerned. About that thing you said this morning. That you think Dash was murdered."

"That was a bonkers thing to say. I was just really upset, Ever." Am I lying now? I picture Dashiell the way I heard they found him, naked in his girlfriend's bed in the East Village with his head hanging over the edge and the needle still in his arm. Eyes wide and gray in the silvery morning light. I try to feel the truth behind the image: did someone else's hand slide in that syringe and press down the plunger? It seems unthinkable that Dash did it to himself, and the idea that it was murder shines like a bright bauble, like a secret trying to be revealed.

No one will ever believe that, though. Not unless I can prove it.

"I'm worried—that maybe you feel irrationally guilty about what happened to him? Because people do have emotions that aren't connected to reality sometimes. So you're psyching your-self into these fantasies where it's absolutely one hundred percent that it's not your fault. To make yourself feel better." The pizza is sitting on a cutting board now but Everett is still staring at it.

"Fantasies," I say. "Is that what you think they are?"

"Like that somebody else murdered him." Everett gets out a knife, never looking at me, and starts dragging it through the cheese. I can see his knuckles going white as he squeezes the handle. "Or maybe that he's actually still alive somehow."

I don't know why that hurts so much. "Everett, I know Dashiell is dead. If I was possibly at all confused about that at first, then seeing him in his coffin really cleared things up for me."

"You kept talking about him *needing* us today. About fighting for him. One thing I know for a fact is that people have to be alive to *need* anything."

Why is it so sharp in my heart, the conviction that Everett is wrong about that? All the desperate, swirling feelings and thoughts that took over today have quieted down now, but one idea is still just as overwhelming as ever: that dead or not, Dashiell needs us to be there for him. There's something we have to do. Is it finding his killer?

That's what I thought before—that's even what I thought half a minute ago—but now it's like the truth keeps pulling away from me, leading me deeper in.

It's a bit more complex than that, Ruby-Ru, Dash's voice whispers in my mind. *Unfortunately even the dead can be murdered, again and again.*

But Everett will definitely think I need medication, at the very least, if I breathe a word of this.

"You'd just stopped me from walking into the East River," I say. "I didn't know what I was saying. I probably said all kinds of crazy things that I don't even remember now!"

Everett finally turns to me with a slab of pizza draping over his hand; he takes a bite and chews for a while, thinking.

"You *really* don't remember." That should be a question, but it's not. "But I do, Ruby. That's kind of the problem."

And something flares up in my mind like a dream with the wind behind it, making it billow and spread: a memory from today of talking with Everett in the park, and then all at once there was a dark hole where I was supposed to be. A moment later I was lying on the grass with Everett's palm hovering over me like he was about to slap me, and I had no idea why he was so angry.

But my cheek was stinging. He'd smacked me already, more than once.

My twin had hit me in the face and I'd had no awareness of it.

That happened, and then he was yelling about what I'd done, and the argument picked me up and carried me away from a moment that had no explanation, that seemed like it couldn't truly have occurred at all.

"What did I do today, Everett?"

"Let's go watch *Cosmos*. I'll get the pizza if you bring our drinks."

"Right before you hit me. What did I do to make you suddenly flip out like that?"

Everett flashes me a wild look and his mouth goes round. Then I watch him close his lips. I watch his face settle into the lie. "I think a *suicide attempt* is more than enough to justify me kicking your ass all the way to Coney Island. I'm prepared to defend any actions I took to smack some sense into you."

We stare into each other's eyes, and we both know we've been lying to each other. It's not normal for Everett and me, doing that; we might deceive other people but honesty has always been a deep part of our twin-ness, something that formed when we were gurgling together in the same amniotic soup.

But I can read his expression, at least enough to know that he's lying because the truth scares him. Whatever I did in those obliterated moments, it was frightening enough that Everett can't bring himself to name it out loud.

And that scares *me* enough that I stop bugging him about it. I go sit with him in the living room, and eat my pizza, and sail away through an inconceivable luxuriance of space and stars. Even if it's only on TV.

EVERETT

Ruby launches into flawless calm-and-together mode for the rest of the afternoon, chatting and smiling and texting with her friend Liv—neither of us are exactly popularity central, but to be honest Ruby does better than I do, at least with other teacher's-pet types—and then in the evening she decides to bake cookies. I know it's an act but I start to fall for it anyway, because falling for it is the easy and obvious thing to do. It's not as if I *want* to tell our dad, and start a catastrophic fight, and then deal with the fallout for weeks to come. I don't want to get Ruby locked up in a psych ward, not unless I'm completely morally obliged to and there's no other choice. And if she's okay enough to fake being okay this persuasively, then maybe that's okay enough for me to play along, if that makes sense.

All this sounds pretty all right to me. I get a good flow of rationalization going and I coast with it. Our dad texts to say he's having dinner out and won't be home until late, and Ruby and I hang out and watch movies until after one in the morning. We're careful to stay away from awkward subjects like dead junkies and murder and early-onset schizophrenia, and I know all of that stuff is just drama anyway. Those are the kinds of noises people make to convince themselves that their lives are intense and important. But suffering is ultimately just as boring and trivial as expensive cars and fancy outfits. None of it matters. I should have kept that in mind today and not let myself get so worked up.

It gets late, and our dad texts again to say we shouldn't wait up for him, so he's probably with some girlfriend. It starts to feel like Ruby and I are waiting for something—not Dad, that's for sure—but whatever it is doesn't happen and eventually we give up and go to bed.

And I wake to find a shadow bending over me, someone's weight mashing down the side of my mattress, and more warmth than there should be in my bedroom at who-knows-what a.m. There's enough light from the street that I can make out the slanting hair and I know it must be Ruby, freakishly invading my privacy and sitting on my bed in the darkness. Watching me sleep.

Except that the posture is wrong for Ruby. Too sultry and arrogant. The whole atmosphere of personality around that gray shape is wrong for Ruby. I sit up so fast my shoulder blades crack and throw myself back against the wall. My breathing is so loud it sounds like I'm trying to say something, just with huffing air instead of words. I scramble for my inhaler—it's right there on the nightstand—and suck in hard.

"Well hi, Never-Ever," the not-Ruby says—and of course I recognize that voice, even though it isn't hers. The tone is slow and teasing. "I'm curious. Who would you say is talking to you now?"

I can't think *Ruby* or *she* anymore, but *he* would be even worse. *It* tips back a little and contemplates me with a sliver of smile, barely visible in the dimness. "You can't be Dashiell," I say.

I shouldn't have said even that much. I should have left that name out of it completely. I'm still a little bit asleep and my guard is down.

"I can't be Dashiell? What a shame that is, Never-Ever, considering that I've always sucked at being anyone else." It grins. *He* grins. "And to think that you accuse our lovely Miss Slippers of being in denial. Oh, the hypocrisy!"

"You are my twin sister, Ruby, and you have completely lost your mind," I say. I'm trying to make it sound firm and calm, but I realize that I don't entirely believe any of what I'm saying now. My blood is throbbing so hard it smacks against my eardrums. "You've gone insane from grief over Dashiell, but you are not him no matter how intensely you pretend to be. Because once someone is dead they are *gone*, and that's it."

Dashiell's harsh laugh burbles up through Ruby's throat. My eyes have adjusted enough to make out her round cheeks and snubby nose wrapped in this burned-tinfoil light.

"Ruby Slippers has been taking it hard indeed, poor sweet girl. Hard enough to make this ludicrously easy, but she's definitely not insane. Just very confused and out of her depth. Now *you* would have hung back on the riverbank, Never-Ever. You would have made self-preservation your top priority and told me to scamper off to hell. Not so my Ruby-Ru. She was ready to go to the most extravagant lengths to bring me safely home."

I don't understand any of this. The light from the window looks grubby and it can't quite reach around the room. But I don't like the mention of the riverbank, I know that, and I don't like the phrase *out of her depth*.

"Was that *you* today? You were going to make Ruby walk into the river and *drown*, just so you don't have to be dead all alone—"

I stop, because everything I'm saying implies that I've started to believe that this is actually Dashiell sitting on my bed and watching me with Ruby's eyes, smiling slyly with her mouth. And I am not the type of person who would believe something that is so clearly impossible.

Therefore I don't believe it. In fact, I *know* that this is Ruby. Ruby having some kind of sick breakdown. I have to keep a tight grip on that thought: *It's not him.*

"I have never been less alone than I am now. What a grave misunderstanding of my circumstances, Never. There is no fine and private place out there, I promise you. And I brought you along today precisely so that you would stop Miss Slippers from doing anything that we would all regret. It took a *terrific* effort, by the way, summoning sufficient oomph to make you feel me touch your wrist. I wouldn't go to all that trouble lightly."

"Then you knew! You knew she was going to try it!"

Ugh. I just did it again. I'm talking to this blob, this psychotic nothing controlling Ruby's body, just as if it was truly and in genuine fact my dead brother, and I cannot stop myself. The voice, tone, and gestures are all so *Dashiell* that I feel slashed every time he moves.

He, he, he. Even though it can't be.

"I knew there was a risk," the not-Ruby concedes. "I knew the initial adjustment would be difficult for her. What might be described as an *identity crisis*, if it helps you to think of it that way, a jostling and discomfort at having too many minds in the pot. I'd heard that the experience can drive people to extremes, especially before they've had time to get used to it. But I was looking after my darling baby sister through it all, even if I had to solicit your help with the physical aspects, yanking her back from the brink and all that. And aren't you glad you tagged along on our walk with us?"

Us.

I don't know why that makes me believe it, or *almost* believe it. But it does.

"Is Ruby even going to remember this?" I ask. And then I try it out. "Dash-Dot-Dot." *If it's really you, then what are you doing here?*

Now he grins for real. A very Dashiell grin, impish and conspiratorial. He leans closer. "Well, Never-Ever, I could choose to let her remember. I could choose to let her listen in on our conversation right now. Do you think I should?"

The idea makes me nauseous with panic and I'm shaking my head frantically before I can find the words to stop him. "Dash, don't! Do *not* do that! There's no way she'll be able to handle it."

"Maybe I'll let her remember just a taste of it. A few fragments, hazy, like something out of a dream. Ruby-Ru loves nothing more than dreaming about me, does she?"

"She said those dreams were horrible."

Ruby's mouth twists mockingly. Ruby's face is being used to make fun of Ruby, and she doesn't even know it. Ruby's hand lifts up and pats me on the shoulder, and I flinch.

"Dashiell," I say, though I still don't know how I can say that. "You shouldn't be doing this. You should go back to wherever you're supposed to be. Just because Ruby loves you doesn't mean you get to *use* her!"

"Oh, pah. And do you think Ruby would say that? 'Dashiell, get out of here! Dashiell, just go back to being dead!'" Ruby's throat and tongue mimic Ruby's squeaky voice and it is the most disgusting thing I've ever heard. Chill patters down my spine and my guts roll over. "Is that what she would do, Never-Ever?"

I can't say anything. Because we both know beyond all doubt that Ruby would never tell Dashiell, dead or not, to go away.

We both know that she'd do anything at all to keep him alive. Or even half alive. Or whatever the hell he is now. Just as long as he stayed with her.

Ruby's mouth curls in an ironic smile. And then Ruby-Dashiell presses in and hugs me tight. I sit rigid with my arms tucked in, too freaked to move, but something fires in my memory. "She said you need her."

"Ah, well, she's starting to understand. I do need her."

"She said you need both of us."

He-she lets me go and angles back enough to look at me. "And my Ruby Slippers is right about that too." A hand that should belong to Ruby and doesn't lifts my chin—a totally Dashiell thing to do, to make you look at him even when you don't want to. "You still haven't welcomed me home, Never-Ever."

DASHIELL

* * * * *

How soft the night is, with Ruby-Ru's dreams wrapped around me. Everett has crashed back into what may be a none-too-restful sleep and I've slipped into my old room—though it's been reduced to a state of revolting blandness, all my old possessions ruthlessly purged, and while I was still alive at that. How determined our father was to erase every trace of me, and yet here I am, cross-legged on the bed in indigo darkness. He sees me as a blotch on the family, a stain on all their hearts, and just look at that stain now.

I refuse to come out.

Even dead. Even dead. I'd like to scream it in his face, but I suppose that might not be my most inspired idea. He called me a monster and I listened, here in my dear sister's skull, clenching teeth that aren't technically mine. And to think how over-joyed I'd been to see him again, when Ru-Ru first carried me into the kitchen!

I'd like to call our mother in London as well, whisper her own words back to her: *You're the only one who can make the decision to live, Dashiell. If you're determined to kill yourself in slow motion, you can stop waiting for me to interfere. I respect your choices, even when I don't like them, and I'm afraid it's up to you.* Whisper them again and again, until she can't help but recognize my voice. And when she hangs up in terror, I'll call her back, and repeat it all into her voice mail. Haunting could turn out to be much more fun than I'd imagined, back when I was first hatching my plans in the gray blur of nothingness.

But I have to prioritize. Tormenting my parents isn't my primary reason for being here, after all. I have more pressing concerns.

Death is a bit like an unending childhood, the ghosts milling about with no real responsibilities, nothing in particular to do. No sources of amusement but the suffering we can inflict on one another. People like to talk about the cruelty of children, ah, but it's nothing compared to the cruelty the dead get up to, in our dreary, everlasting after-school.

Aloysius will find it challenging to pursue me here. I don't doubt he'll try, though, if only on principle. I suppose he isn't worried, *yet*, about what I might do with the benefit of breath, since he'd never expect that anyone would have the nerve to challenge him; he'll only see that I've conned him out of a prize he feels entitled to. He's much too spoiled to let that slide, and vindictive enough that he'll most likely strive to destroy whatever he can't claim for himself. But Aloysius isn't the only one who might feel strongly about territorial issues.

What am I, then, now that I've made it this far? The twists in his maze, the wraith that will shriek from his shadow. Ah, he was so sure he had me crushed, helpless and submissive to all his orders. But now? I'd like to see him try to take me down.

My sister stirs faintly, her drowsy consciousness rustling

against mine for a moment before she subsides. *Back to sleep, now. Don't be afraid, sweet Ru.* I lift Ruby Slippers's sleeping hand to her own lips, kiss the back of it.

It couldn't be you, I say into her dreams. *No, simply. No.* Never *you, my own Ruby-Ru.*

RUBY

✳ ✳ ✳ ✳ ✳

I wake up to soft golden light that rambles through my room, folding on sheets and fluttering through curtains. It's crazy late, already way after noon, and I stretch and wallow for a while before I realize what I'm feeling. I'm happy in a way that I haven't been for a long time, and I actually feel rested. Brooklyn today will be a marvelous place, full of birds and windows that flicker and beckon, and subtly enchanted garbage cans, and graffiti painted by rebel angels.

There's no good reason for it. It's just the way it is. Even doing research for my history paper sounds like an exciting adventure. I take my time getting up, letting my soles explore the wood floor for a while, then walking with a lot of slow pivots and twirls to the bathroom, just to thoroughly enjoy being a girl in a body in a house in Brooklyn. I don't care how silly that would sound to anyone else. I shower in the same lazy way and then let my toes squirm slowly down the fuzzy tunnels of my socks, pretending my feet are two badgers digging their way to China.

As soon as I'm dressed there's a knock on my door. "Ruby?"

I jump up and fling it open. "Never-Ever-Everett. Whaz-zup?"

The look on his face is so urgent and tense that it nearly punches a hole straight through my fabulous mood, but then he just stands there awkwardly staring at me with his big soft mouth opening and closing. "Can I come in?"

"Since when do you ask?" I say and spin back from the door, then sit on my bed and start bouncing. I can see that Everett is still flipping out, and I know I gave him plenty of reason to be on edge, but I'm just not ready to feel like crap yet. "Everett, you don't have to be worried about me anymore, okay? I'm sorry I stressed you out so bad, but I am truly fine now."

"You seem fine." He says it almost like that's the problem, though. "Um, Ruby? Did you have any dreams?"

That wallops me with surprise, I admit, because it hadn't even crossed my mind. "Oh! I didn't dream at all. I mean, now that you mention it . . ." I search through what little memory I have of last night, and all I come up with is an impression of profound, velvety, purplish warmth. Complete serenity. "God, no *wonder* I feel so much better! After two straight months of nightmares—no, nothing." I smile at Everett where he stands watching me from under his sloppy brown hair. "I guess Dashiell decided to give me a break, already."

I meant it as a joke, but I can tell that Everett's not taking it that way. At first he sort of recoils and then he forces an incredibly tortured smile onto his face. "I guess so."

"Why?" I ask after a moment—because it's getting harder not to notice that something's really wrong with him. "Did you?"

Everett hesitates. "I guess I had your nightmare instead."

"About him?"

"Yeah. Him."

I must be so happy from pure relief at the burden of those dreams being lifted, because now I can see the same heaviness dragging Everett toward the floor. It would be too cruel to say, *Well, you said you wanted to dream about him.* "What happened? It wasn't—" *You didn't dream that he murdered you, did you?*

"It wasn't like your dreams. I mean, I knew he wasn't alive again. It was a dream about his ghost."

"Okay," I say, but Everett is still staring at me like he's waiting for a bigger reaction—and in fact my heart is speeding up. Some delicate, alien tremor seems to lift through my chest and flood the back of my head. "Like, you dreamed he was haunting us?"

"I dreamed his ghost was looking for someone to possess."

There's a quickening flourish somewhere inside me. I get a bizarre impression of emotions streaming through my mind without actually belonging to me: a thick seethe of amusement and irritation. It makes me feel a little sick, and a little cloudy. I lean back against the wall and look out at the trees: boughs arching like the arms of swimmers in a sea of infinite vibrations.

"Ruby!" Everett says. He lunges across my bed and starts shaking me, hard. "Ruby, don't!"

"Don't what? Everett, you know you can stop attacking me all the time, right?"

"You were phasing out." He's gone bone white and his lower lip is shaking. "I could tell."

Phasing out, not *spacing* out? There's something off and awful about the phrase.

"I was just thinking about what you'd said." Is that true? It felt deeper, more engulfing, than regular thinking, somehow. "About Dashiell possessing people. He kind of did that even when he was alive, right? He had such a vivid personality that being around him—it could feel like he was taking over your mind. Do you know what I mean?"

Everett gawks at me and bites his lower lip. I think he's about to cry.

"So that's probably why you had that dream, Ever," I say. I'm trying to be reassuring but I don't think it's doing much good. "Dash's ghost possessing people—it was probably a metaphor your brain came up with. A metaphor for the *kind* of person he was. It's okay."

"Ruby. It wasn't a *metaphor.*"

It seems out of character for Everett to be so grim, especially about a dream, and I'm about to ask what he means by that when we both hear the doorbell and then our dad's steps going to answer it. My bedroom is on our bottom floor along with the kitchen and living room, so we're close enough to hear right away that it isn't anything like a delivery; that our dad is first chilly, then exasperated, and that the person who's out there is a girl, pleading with him. I'm instantly up and sliding out of my room as quietly as I can with Everett close behind me, so we both see her at the same time. She's standing very near our dad just inside the front door, leaning in like she's trying to insinu-ate her way deeper into the house.

Long, sleek black hair with heavy bangs around a pale face so beautiful it looks almost iridescent. Crimson lipstick. A ragged, antique lace dress, skintight down to her hips; the lace is dyed in pink and blue blotches. Little black granny boots. I've never seen her before but I know right away who she must be, and I can tell Everett does too, without even glancing at him. She's too stunning to have belonged to anyone but Dashiell.

Her belly is a tiny bit too round for how thin she is.

"I should have known the instant his name was mentioned," our dad snaps, "that a request for money was in the offing. I'm sure you must realize that I'm not legally responsible for anything Dashiell did. I have my surviving children to consider."

"But you won't consider your *grandchild* at all? Dr. Bohnacker?" Tears form two shining rivulets down her cheeks. "I was planning to get an abortion, but there was no way I could do that once Dash was dead, when I knew that this was all that was left of him. You can—you *have* to understand that!" Her voice is satin smooth and she reaches out to grab his arm; he shakes her off. Somehow I know he'd be gentler with her if she weren't so outrageously beautiful. If she wasn't gazing at him with that palpitating sweetness.

"I don't believe giving you money would be in that child's best interest. If that is in fact my grandchild, then I have all the more reason to refuse." At first I don't understand what he's driving at, but then it all falls into place: he suspects she's on drugs the way Dashiell used to be. He thinks her silky eagerness and wide eyes are all about suckering him into feeding her addiction even while she's pregnant, and he despises her for it. She's so pearl-skinned and flawless that I never would have thought of anything like that—Dashiell looked kind of tattered whenever he was using—but maybe Dad is right? "Perhaps you should reconsider while you still have the chance. That, I would be prepared to help you with. How many weeks are you exactly?"

She looks a little shocked, and then she notices me standing fifteen feet away from her in the hallway's crooked shadows. "You must be Ruby. Ruby Slippers. Do you want me to kill your brother's baby?"

"No," I say, but I can feel myself starting to hate her too. Syrupy-sweet vampire princess. She's talking like she loved Dash so much, but I sure didn't see her at his funeral. I know somehow that she usually wears baby-blue lipstick and that she put on the red today because she thought our dad would like it better; I know it the way you know things in dreams, with the crystalline certainty of having seen it all before, over and over again. "I want you to give the baby to us. We'll do a better job raising it than you will."

Our dad's eyebrows shoot up—partly at what I've said and maybe also because he's just registered my hair—and Everett jabs me in the back.

For being rude to her. Of *course.*

Our dad sighs. "I will pay your rent *once.* Once only. How much is it?"

She softens her gaze and I get the feeling she needs to use all her willpower not to stick her hand out right away. "Almost four thousand. Dr. Bohnacker, I am so, so grateful. . . ."

He snorts at the number; she does live in Manhattan but that's still a lot of money. "How much *exactly?*"

A pause. "Three thousand, seven hundred. And then I have to pay the electric."

He nods. "I'll mail the check directly to your landlord, then, Miss Kittering, if you'll be so good as to send me a copy of the invoice. Now please go. My children have been through enough without having to listen to this."

She's a lot less grateful now than she was a moment ago. Her brows draw together and her mouth tweaks. "So it's worth almost four thousand dollars to you just to stop me from talking to your little Ruby?"

He actually smiles: at seeing her drop her angel-kitten pose, at her cynicism finally coming out to play. "You understand me perfectly."

"What are you afraid I'll say to her? Do you think I know something about the way Dashiell died that she's not *mature* enough to hear?" Her smile tightens now like she's slurping down bitter juice. Our dad doesn't even deign to answer, just opens the door and stands there holding it and sort of crushing her personal space, though without touching her, like he can drive her out by increasing the air pressure.

She keeps looking at me for as long as she can get away with it. Everett is tucked partly into my doorway, so maybe she can't get such a straight shot at him. I'm not trying to look friendly, though, and after a long moment she gives up and turns her back on us. Her dress swishes behind her as she goes, blue and pink like a captive sunset. When our dad slams the door his face is crimped with distaste.

Dashiell exhibited truly crappy judgment sometimes, but there is no *way* he could have been serious about her.

"I didn't even get to ask her name!" Everett says, coming out into the hall. "I couldn't say anything."

Our dad gazes at him. "Paige Kittering. Not that she calls herself that, of course. Galadriel or something equally inane."

Everett scowls. "*Not* Galadriel. No chance."

"Probably not," Dad agrees vaguely, but I can tell he's thinking about something else.

"Probably Vampire Barbie," I say, and he cracks up laughing while Everett glares.

"A very astute guess!" our dad says. Then he looks sharply my way. "Ruby?"

Do you still hate me? he means. *Are you speaking to me again?*

I barely know what I'm doing when I run up and hug him. He's squeezing me and stroking my hair as I start to think about what Paige said: that my dad was paying her off so she wouldn't spill some terrible secret about the *way Dashiell died.* That was one gorgeously timed comment, coming at the perfect moment to send all my dark suspicions flaring up again, leaping and spinning.

I know she did it on purpose. I know she was poisoning my mind as part of some evil game, probably just crude stupid blackmail. Is she trying to make me suspect my dad? Well, if that's what she wants, then it's a pretty good sign that I should look in any direction but his.

I still don't know what Dash needs from me, but I've got to start somewhere.

EVERETT

Ruby is Ruby. Most of the time. She does homework and goes out to a salon to get her hacked-up hair trimmed and layered until it looks almost like something a reasonable person might do on purpose. It's not like an epileptic fit interpreted in hair anymore, at least. She cooks everyone dinner, and tells big dramatic stories about the Peloponnesian War with her hands waving. I know it's mostly an act: to convince me she's okay enough that I won't mention anything about rocks and the East River, to convince herself that whatever weirdness is going on in her head isn't a big deal. I know she has to feel something happening to her, even if she doesn't understand what it is. She's almost overdoing acting like herself. *An identity crisis,* Dashiell called it, and now it's like she's overcompensating for that by playing *Ruby* on a million imaginary TVs.

Because she isn't Ruby *all* the time. There are moments where she phases right out of herself, slips into some hole behind her brain, and then she's just gone. I keep watching her whenever we're in the same room together and I'm learning to spot the signs. It always starts with her looking really spaced out and a scattery shimmer breaking up her stare. Her rounded shoulders roll back, square off and tilt, her back stretches sexily, and this knowing smirk takes over her mouth. Then Dashiell looks out of her eyes, and every single time he turns her head until he's staring straight at me with her chin lifted, daring me to recognize him. He never says anything, and it never lasts for more than a few seconds, but I must catch him *controlling* her that way half a dozen times.

Once when our dad is with us in the kitchen Dashiell rolls Ruby's eyes in his direction, grins, and lifts one finger up to her lips. *Hush hush, Never-Ever. Don't say a word to anyone. There's a good little nerdling.* God, and for a few hours there I'd almost managed to convince myself it's not him, that I'd just had a dream or even a hallucination; whatever it takes so I could tell myself it isn't freaking Dashiell. But it is. It *has* to be. Each time I see it happen, the reek of his whole way of being just gets stronger.

It is the slowest and most sickening Sunday I've ever lived through, and whenever I'm not watching Ruby for her next outbreak of dead brother I'm picturing *her*, Paige-who-calls-herself-something-else. Paige, who ground me into nothingness by just glancing in my general direction; one look from her and I knew I was a meaningless assemblage of atoms, something that might cause minor eye irritation until you managed to flush it out. I'm picturing what Dashiell must have done to her every night, her black hair whipping the pillows and his hands squeezing her hips. She was probably so hopelessly in love with him that she'd do anything he asked and then kiss him all over his chest afterward.

Dashiell always got everything he wanted, and what do you know? He still does. Even now that he's rotting in the ground and I've flung shovelfuls of dirt on his damned ass he goes on smugly sitting in my sister's brain, winking at me, knowing I won't tell Ruby anything—because after yesterday I know she's way too close to cracking up already.

Me and Dashiell, we're both waiting for the night.

I pretend to go to bed to keep our dad happy, but I'm not about to lie there like a lump until Dashiell sneaks in on me. At around one I get up and walk quietly downstairs, then sit on the bottom step. I have a good view of Ruby's door from here. After that there's nothing to do but wait. Cars go by in the street outside and throw light through the living room windows. Every time that happens, the shadow of the stairs' railings spins on the wall beside me like a carousel. It's kind of hypnotic and my head starts to tip over, then jerk up again.

I check my phone. Two thirty-eight a.m. The bastard's probably keeping me waiting on purpose.

On my left I can see the dark blocks of living room furniture and the TV like some creepy square black pool. On the right there's the hallway with its vine wallpaper and a row of low bookcases and Ruby's door with no sounds behind it. The longer I look at it the less it seems like a door and the more like an abstract pale trapezoid hanging in space. I'm slipping again.

Then my head jerks up. The angle of the door is different now.

Dashiell comes swaggering out, wearing Ruby's body like he's annoyed that it doesn't fit right. He spots me on the step and smiles. "Never-Ever. Are you experiencing difficulty sleeping, and on a school night at that? You know, if anything is troubling you, you can always unburden yourself to me."

I stare for a while, trying just *one more time* to persuade my-self that it isn't him, and he leans there and lets me look him over. Ruby's body is as chubby and curvy as ever in floppy plaid pajama bottoms and this stupid T-shirt with a cow on it, and it's all totally unlike him. But Dashiell-ness blasts through anyway, in the way her head tips back and her gaze sort of slants across her cheekbones, in the ironic pucker of her mouth. And then there's the voice. Now that I've had time to think about it, you can still tell it's coming through Ruby's vocal cords. It sounds like a girl's voice pitched way down. But every little shift in the tone is just too perfectly *Dashiell* to be an imitation. It's impos-sible that he's here and talking, but anyone *acting* this well? That would be double or triple impossible. So logic insists that it's him, him all over again. Great job on the goddamn dying, Dash.

"Let's go have a seat in the living room," Dash says. "We wouldn't want to wake anyone."

So I get up and follow him in there and sit on our big red sofa. I need to know what he wants if I'm going to have any chance of getting rid of him. I'm sorry he's dead, I really am, but once you're dead you have a serious moral obligation to stay that way and let everybody else recover from what a crazy jerk you were.

He turns on a side lamp and settles in too close to me. It isn't much light and there are still big piles of shadow everywhere.

"Why do you wait until Ruby's asleep?" I ask. "There were times today when you could have talked to me, if you've got something you need to say."

Dashiell shrugs. "Well, it's simpler this way, isn't it, Never-Ever? When Miss Slippers is out cold there isn't the hassle of some competing consciousness elbowing for position. And then if I displace her too often when she's awake she'll start to notice the lacunae: blackout confetti scattered around where her mind should be. I don't want to cause my baby sister any more distress than strictly necessary."

"You don't have to be here at all," I say. "It's seriously creepy that you're doing this at all." *Just rot already,* I think, but how can you say that to your own brother?

"Why, this is my home too, Never-Ever," he says, and there's a weird flash where I'm not sure if he's talking about the house, or about Ruby. "It surely belongs to me as much as it does to you. And I've already put you and Ruby at an advantage as far as inheritance goes. You heard our father today, fretting over keeping every nickel for his *surviving* children. How ecstatic do you think he must be, that I've spared him the unpleasantness of writing me out of his will by kicking off in the first bloom of my youth?"

I'm pretty sure he's just bringing up that conversation so I'll know that he's always there, watching us and listening to everything we say, even when it seems like Ruby is completely in control of herself. Does *he* ever sleep?

"Whatever," I say. "That doesn't make up for what you're doing at *all*."

"And there's poor Paige, lurching around in her delicate condition and begging for scraps," Dash says. He tips Ruby's head so her slashed hair falls across her left eye. "Ruby Slippers didn't seem like she was overly taken with Paige, did she?" He smiles. "But you were."

"Shut up," I tell him. But there was no shutting Dashiell up when he was alive and I know there won't be now.

"Ah, but you must feel immense sympathy for her. On her

own like that, just nineteen years old, with the father of her child abruptly deceased? She's in desperate need of help, and you could be the face of that help when it comes to her. Her hero. Not much to look at, maybe, but with a nobility of character that commands attention. Doesn't that sound like something you might enjoy?"

I open my mouth to tell him to go to hell, but then I close it again and sit there trying to breathe while he waits. By the time I can speak I've changed my mind. "What are you getting at, Dash-Dot-Dot?"

Because maybe this is it. In the stories ghosts usually just need you to do one thing for them before they can go into the light or wherever. Maybe Dashiell came back because he needs to make sure his girlfriend and his baby are going to be okay, and then he'll be at peace and get out of Ruby's head and leave us all alone.

"Paige won't have the faintest idea that it's me coming to call on her," Dash explains, and I sit there confused, wishing I hadn't left my inhaler upstairs. "She'll see you bring her the money, and then I'll get out of the way and you can have the full benefit of her gratitude."

I'm not sure what to ask first: *What money?* or, *Full benefit?* or, *Are you talking about freaking* possessing *me too? You are, aren't you?*

Instead I say, "What about Ruby? If you're—riding around— in my head instead?"

Dashiell actually laughs at that. He thinks that is very, very goddamn funny and he laughs for a while. "And here we come to another consideration that might motivate you, Never-Ever! I can't be in more than one place at a time. Ergo, if you take me on for the duration of this mission, then I'll be clearing out of our sweet Miss Slippers. Simple." He tips Ruby's head and considers me for a while. "I wouldn't think that you'd be so anxious to protect her from me, Never. Ruby-Ru has our father for that, after all, always champing to shelter her from the unsavory influences. And you've seen how well *that* works." He grins in a way that says it all: our dad can't protect Ruby for dirt. Not even from the dead guy. "You should know I have her best interests at heart."

"I want to be conscious," I say. "That's my price. Like you said you could let Ruby *listen in* on our conversation if you felt like it? Whatever you're doing with my body, I want to know about it."

Dashiell shakes his head, or actually Ruby's head. "I can't agree to that, Never. It wouldn't be safe for you."

"But it's my *body* we're talking about!"

"I know where there's a stash, at least twenty grand. Thirty. It's in the mailbox of an abandoned house in Queens. But the men that money belongs to—these are not perfect gentlemen we're talking about. Not people I'd care to see developing an *interest* in you and Miss Slippers, Never. The less you know, the better."

"But—"

"Absolutely not. It wouldn't be responsible for me to involve you in this."

The amazing thing is that Dashiell says it like he means it— like he thinks joyriding around in my body wouldn't count as *involving* me. And then something else weird occurs to me. Why are we negotiating at all?

"Why are you even *asking* me? It's not like you went and got

Ruby's permission before you freaking hijacked her. Why don't you just—bulldoze your way into me—like you did with her?"

He looks at me for a while. It's getting to the point where I can half-forget that those are Ruby's green eyes rotating to home in on me. She's fast asleep somewhere inside her own body, totally clueless and seeing nothing through her own wide pupils. But I'm starting to lose track of that.

I'm starting to see just Dashiell, even with Ruby's dark blond hair slopping over his stealthy smile. Dashiell staring at me in a dim room.

"Well, Never-Ever, because I can't just *bulldoze* in. I require your kind cooperation."

"But Ruby didn't cooperate!" I say and then stop, with everything I don't know balled up in my mouth. There's too much. I could choke on it.

"Ah, but she did. I called Miss Slippers and she came to me, Never, on an impulse of the purest faith and devotion. But I knew all along that you'd be a tougher nut to crack. Your instincts would flare up and warn you to keep the hell away from me. I'd cry out, 'Never-Ever, come get me!' and you'd just back off, gawking at me like you thought I was going to murder you."

I can't follow any of this. "What are you *talking* about?"

Dashiell smiles. "It will be a mere insubstantial dream, Never. Gossamer and smoke. Nothing that happens to you there will be *real* in the conventional sense. But the dream, and what you choose to do in it, will have real consequences. It will be a *real* rite of passage."

"Those dreams Ruby's been having—*that's* what you mean? She did something when she was dreaming about you, and that's how this happened?"

Dashiell doesn't answer that, just nestles back into the cushions and watches me patiently.

"She went to you in a dream, and somehow that let you possess her," I say. I'm starting to sort it out, at least a little. "She dreamed about you and I didn't, because you figured she'd be easier to take advantage of."

I can see that Dashiell's not thrilled with my putting it that way—he's never been much good at taking criticism.

"I wouldn't call that a fair characterization at *all*, Never. Ruby Slippers acted out of love, and then she's incomparably more courageous than you are. There's not a lot of inhibition in my sweet girl, at least where her emotions are concerned. You're a hundred times more cautious by nature. Now you, when you're looking at me across whatever landscape we wind up in—you'll have to make a deliberate effort to override your fear. You'll need to be prepared, and Ru-Ru didn't."

"But she didn't know! I mean, she didn't realize—what would happen afterward?"

"I didn't exactly have an opportunity to explain the details to her beforehand, Never. So you're right, our Miss Slippers is still safe from understanding the situation. All she knows is that she's been feeling unsettled. Nothing specific about the reasons for it."

I think about that. I hope to God it's true. "But then—once I let you—you'll leave Ruby alone. You'll let her have her body back?"

"I already mentioned that I'll be obliged to vacate the premises. Before you and I can go adventuring together."

"And then, once Paige has all that money and you know she's going to be fine—you'll be at peace?"

"Well naturally, Never-Ever. I'll be far less concerned about her situation. Paige isn't much good at looking after herself, and you wouldn't want me to leave her without any means of support. Not exactly chivalrous."

Paige's rent is so high that even thirty thousand dollars won't last her very long, but I guess if that doesn't bother Dashiell it shouldn't bother me.

"Okay," I say. And then I wonder what's wrong with me. But that's the thing, if this works then maybe I can get rid of him and Ruby will never have to know what happened to her. Maybe she'll be able to recover and get over him—and I know I'm always saying that nothing matters, but actually Ruby's sanity matters a lot to me, it turns out. "So this means I'll be dreaming about you soon?"

Dashiell barely smiles. "Soon enough."

"And then I just have to go to wherever you are? That's it?"

"Just come when you're called. Ruby Slippers had to swim to reach me. I can't predict what the experience will be like for you." He grins, but with the light behind Ruby's head the teeth look gray and jagged. "It will be a surprise for both of us."

RUBY

✳ ✳ ✳ ✳ ✳

I'm awake and I don't know why. I'm a girl with a drumming heart in a bedroom at night, and the darkness creases into complicated origami against my walls. The same darkness unfolds into pulsing wings beyond my window, and the wings' beat smacks my thoughts and sets them spinning. I'm almost positive there were voices talking quietly, just outside a room much smaller than this one: as small as my own skull.

I heard my two brothers, one dead and one living, murmuring together, but I couldn't catch what they were saying.

That is something that could only happen in a dream, so I really ought to feel like I was dreaming. But I have a strange deep sense that I was wide awake, just awake in a way where I couldn't open my eyes or move the smallest muscle or even feel my own skin. And I was afraid.

Specifically, I was afraid that something terrible was going to happen to Everett, but I couldn't make any sound to warn him. I could feel that something, or someone, was shadowing him: a ghostly, predatory darkness. The feeling of it sharpens in my chest until I'm getting out of bed without thinking it through. It would be too crazy to go bang on his door at this hour, when the red glow of my clock says it's just after four and there's no hint of gray yet in the sky. But maybe I'll feel better if I just go upstairs and listen near his door for a while.

As soon as I slip from my bedroom I can see coral-colored light rushing out of the living room. I stop with my chest rattling—though really, why should a lamp left on by accident seem so frightening? Because that's probably all it is; nothing unusual about it. I should do the right thing and go switch it off, and then I should forget all my paranoid ideas and go back to bed. Why should I let myself give in to a delusion that there's someone in the house with us?

And even worse: I have a whirling impression of forces gathering just outside, tapping at the glass and probing for weak spots. I try to push the feeling away.

When I draw close I see it at once: a head of brown hair, a blue shoulder, sitting absolutely still on the red sofa. I fall back so suddenly that my elbow smacks the doorframe: a whispery thud, but loud enough that there's no way the stranger won't hear. The person on the sofa jerks as if the soft sound was a gunshot, spins around, and then jumps again when he sees me.

It's only Everett. How dumb can I be? But he's gaping at me like I'm the enemy, like he has to watch intently for my next move.

"Everett?" I say. "Are you okay?"

His posture loosens and he spills back into the cushions. So he's just been sitting here alone, not playing video games or anything? *Ruby.* Hey."

"Who did you think I was?" I ask. If Everett's awake, of course, then there might be an explanation for that conversation I thought I heard. Maybe he was on the phone, and the only part I made up was that I could hear Dashiell with him. "Were you talking to someone?"

He tenses and the guarded expression seizes his face again. "What makes you say that?"

"I thought I heard voices," I tell him, and then Everett's stare reminds me that he's already worrying about my mental health. He even accused me of being in denial that Dashiell is dead, and nothing could possibly make his concerns go through the roof more quickly and efficiently than my saying, *I thought you were talking to Dashiell, and it scared me. It's crazy, I know, but I was afraid—that somehow Dash had escaped from my nightmares and come to us, with evil trailing after him.* "But maybe it was just some people out in the street."

Everett relaxes as soon as I say it. "Probably. That, or you were dreaming."

I hesitate to ask because the last thing I want to do is upset him again, but as the moments keep beating away through the darkness the question starts to feel completely necessary.

"Ever? Did *you* have another dream? Is that why you're awake?"

He jumps again. I said the wrong thing.

"Oh—no," Everett tells me at last. "No dreams. I can't sleep at all. But, Ruby? I wanted to ask you something?"

"Okay," I say, though I don't really feel okay about any of it. I'm still too rattled by the memory of Dashiell's voice purring through the corners of my head, and by the intimation I had of something else, something savage and ravenous and much too close to us. I'd like to believe it was all imaginary—but Ever's face is too taut, like he feels it, too.

"I need to ask about the last time you did. Dreamed about

Dash, I mean. Right before you got so agitated, with the hair and . . . I guess it was Saturday morning? It feels like that was so *long* ago."

"Saturday morning," I repeat, and then my mind jerks back to the oily wobble of that water closing over my head and Dashiell's hands driving me under with a thrust that was almost casual, as if he was just going through the motions. Like he barely cared at all. "What I was dreaming then? Before you heard me yell?"

"Yeah," Everett says, and his face is strained like it's trying to stretch across the gap between us. "Ruby, I really need to know."

"I can't talk about that," I say and take a step back toward the hallway. My chest and head are throbbing violently, a warning code banged out inside my body. It's not just because that dream was too painful to tell anyone, either. I have this icy nagging sense that talking about it is somehow off-limits, not *allowed*: a violation of something inside me so powerful and private and raw that touching it would drop me to my knees. "Don't ask me, Ever."

"You said it was horrible. Listen, Ruby, I wouldn't ask if I didn't *really* need—"

"Don't ask me!" My panicked voice shoots from my mouth, shrill and out of control, and Everett fires a glance at the stairs, obviously worried that I might wake our dad. "You *don't* need to know! It's cruel to try and make me tell. Don't!"

Everett is off the sofa now, reaching out for me. I shy back. His face driving through the shadows looks too gray, too big and glassy. "Ruby, calm down. It's okay. Ruby, I'm sorry. I just want—"

"No!"

"But it was bad, right? Whatever happened in that dream. Can I just ask you that?"

"It was bad," I agree, and close my eyes. I'm leaning against the wall, my whole body pulsing with feverish heat and slippery cold, and I feel like everything is sliding. "It was the worst thing possible. Ever, I really, *really* can't tell you anything else."

Everett is stroking my hair and it's like we're not twins at all. It's like I'm suddenly way younger and he's looking after me. *I'm* supposed to be the mature one, though, right?

"It's okay. I think I understand why you can't. I understand. Ruby, it's going to be okay."

"No, it's *not*," I tell him, but I can't begin to justify feeling so disturbed. And really, why should I have such a frantic reaction at the thought of telling Everett my dream, when I know that's all it was? *Just a bad dream. As in, it was not real.* My heart is finally slowing a little but I won't open my eyes. Instead I stare into watery darkness streaked with bubbles of shining red. "None of it is okay, and it's never going to be!"

"It is," Everett insists. "It is, Ruby. Because I'm going to take care of it."

"I'm worried about you," I tell him. "I know you're worried about me but I'm afraid for you too. When I woke up just now I was sure . . . I don't know, that you were in trouble." *Stay away from him,* I almost say, but then I think of how insane that would sound.

And who do I mean by *him*? Dashiell?

Don't you dare dream about Dashiell, I want to say. These awful, senseless thoughts keep intruding on my mind, and I can't stop them. Maybe Everett is right, and madness like a snapping fox is chasing me through my own brain. *But not just about Dash. Don't dream about anyone. Please.*

Stay away from—God, what's wrong with me?—*from all the dead.*

Everett would just point out that it's pretty easy to stay away from people who are buried; there's a lot of dirt in the way, after all. And how could I possibly tell Everett to stay away from our brother, even if there was any choice? That's obviously wrong, when Dashiell needs—

One thing I know for a fact is that people have to be alive to need *anything.*

Right. I open my eyes and suddenly everything seems a little calmer.

"I'm fine," Everett says. "Everything's going to be fine, okay, Ruby? Are you going back to bed?" He kisses me on the forehead, sweetly, the way Dashiell used to do, but maybe Ever doesn't remember that.

"Okay," I say. "You too? We have to get up in like two hours."

He's already turning away from me, heading up the stairs, when he mutters something under his breath. *I'm not that big of a coward*, it almost sounds like. But what sense would that make?

"What? Everett . . ."

When he pivots back to me I can't help seeing how much he's changed in the last two days. His big sloppy mouth is sort of held together more and he has an expression I never would have imagined he *could* have, hounded and ironic and wise at the same time. And I can promise that nobody has ever flashed on the word *wise* in connection with Everett before this moment, not once.

It's my fault. It has to be. He never looked this way before he had to drag me out of the East River.

"Nothing, Ruby," he says, and smiles wearily down from the third step. "It's nothing. I just need to sleep."

No, I almost say. *You can't.* But then something shining catches at the edge of my vision, and my head jerks toward the window. There are two winking, greenish dots on the fire escape, but I can't process what I'm seeing until a soft paw bats at the pane.

I'm so on edge that even a cat can send my heart leaping into my throat.

ALOYSIUS

* * * * *

And if young Mr. Bohnacker believes that he has given us all the slip, whose fault is that?

If he thinks he's tossed the world like a coin and righted himself again on the other side, where we have no sway—if he thinks he can proceed unsupervised and unobserved, cosseted in the bodies of innocents—well, put that down to a lack of experience. He's a callow boy, recently slotted under the humus, the grass above not yet grown thick enough to tuck him in properly at night. An inconvenience, that, when it's night all the time.

Two months dead, and he's enough of a child to think he can outsmart his betters. It might occur to him that we are vastly more knowledgeable in these affairs. It might occur to him that we have ways of checking up on the business of the living, and ways as well of sniffing out the stowaways in their pretty heads. Though as it happens, he could hardly have picked a more obvious vessel. Naturally, I would never *think* to peek inside his noisy and sentimental younger sister! How clever of him.

Roughly as clever as a toddler hiding under a bed.

Ah, but since he lacks our dear Mabel's talents, he was hardly likely to come up with anything better, now was he?

The girl steps out her door in the morning's consumptive pallor, vulgarly attired in painful colors and more than slightly the worse for wear. She's puffy-eyed and unsteady on her feet. Dashiell Bohnacker isn't easy on his clothes, it seems. Ludicrous hair, this girl has, and excess flesh. What has become of women as I once knew them? Sylphs in silk with marcel waves. Refined, intoxicating creatures, so long as they kept their mouths shut.

The boy with her, though, looks wretched. He hasn't slept a wink, I'd swear it. Could young Mr. Bohnacker be fool enough to reveal his current place of residence to a beating heart, family or no? The question presents itself vividly in this youth's unprepossessing face—looking, as it does, like he'd seen a ghost, or at least listened to one prattling on through the small hours of the night.

The girl bounces down the steps with a high-strung mockery of cheer and doesn't observe me, but the boy crouches on the sidewalk close by and reaches out his fingers, crooning. I turn away from him and lick my fur. It seems to be the thing to do.

Why, cats can dream as well, Mr. Bohnacker. They can dream of a very nice man with a can of tuna in his outstretched hand.

EVERETT

School. I know I went there. I know I sat in classes listening to white noise that was probably teachers trying really hard to explain essential concepts. I know I looked up at people, but they all seemed so gray. Jell-O on legs, tottering and shouting. Or was that me?

I guess I'm not doing very well. It's Tuesday—only Tuesday?—and I haven't slept for one second in the last two nights. But I'm really trying to. I absolutely intend to fall into a deep sleep, let my eyes start rolling fast under their lids, and dream whatever horrible things I have to dream to save my sister. But it's not working, so maybe Dashiell is right about me. Maybe my whole problem is that I'm not brave enough to be a valuable and complete person. *She's incomparably more courageous than you are,* he said. Like I don't hear enough about Ruby's all-purpose superiority, how smart and creative and dynamic and all the other crap. Though people don't usually say the *more than you* part out loud.

Doesn't matter. I can still hear it. I can hear it with every step that smacks into the sidewalk. Going home? That's right, I'm going home and I'm going to fall—

I'm waiting for the light to change so I can cross 6th Avenue. Almost to our house. I start to nod off standing right there on the corner, and all at once adrenaline stabs through me. My head flies upright and my arms spasm out like I'm trying to push something away. My heart goes berserk and I start wheezing and the hair prickles on my neck. I'd either puke or piss from terror if I could just make up my mind which one would be more humiliating.

And then I'm wide awake all over again, feeling my chest hammering as if it's going to split. The orange trees wave like they think I'm being totally entertaining.

The same thing happened at breakfast, it happened in chemistry, it happened in the locker room. And about fifty times last night. I start to fall, the world starts to fade. And then bam! A knife of pure, electric, horrified alertness guts me again.

Stab and twist. That's how you do the most damage.

Because I'm too afraid of what I don't know, obviously. I'm terrified of what Dashiell's going to do as soon as he catches me dreaming. *Coward.* But I keep remembering how hard Ruby freaked when I asked. *The worst thing possible.* That was it. That was all she'd say.

See that little glowing green guy? That means you're supposed to cross the street. Keep walking. Almost there. Kids in striped mittens. It's that cold. Women with yoga mats hanging down their backs.

Anyway, for Ruby probably the worst thing possible would be if she had to hurt someone else. If she had to hurt *him.* So maybe I'm going to dream that I have to blow Dashiell's brains out, and at this point that might be okay with me.

If he shows up again I'll tell him that. But he hasn't. I've kept waiting, staring at Ruby—staring so much there's no way she won't notice. But nothing. Not a glimpse of him since Sunday night. It's all Ruby, all the time. And she's acting like none of the craziness ever happened. I'm actually relieved that she's gone off to the library with Liv today, so I can stop *wondering* for a few hours—

Maybe he's lying low and waiting for me.

Or maybe I'm the one who's losing my mind, not Ruby, and I invented the entire thing. Maybe on those nights when I thought Dashiell was jerking Ruby's body around she was actually fast asleep in bed, and my brain was projecting complete garbage and I was sitting there jabbering to an empty room.

But if I really believed that it was all hallucinations, I wouldn't have any problem going to sleep. I can't sleep because I know for a sick, sure fact that Ruby's possessed, and soon I will be too. *Ergo,* as Dash would say.

Er-freaking-*go,* the bastard will show up anytime, just as soon as my brain gives in to exhaustion and I collapse. And it will be a dream—*gossamer and smoke*—but one with the power to drag reality around after it.

That snotty-ass gray tabby is hanging out on our stoop again, giving me the once-over. I usually love cats but this one is asking for a kick in the face. Like, I could swear it's smirking at me, and it dodges at my heels as I open the door like it's trying to sneak inside. Like hell. I shove it back hard with the door and it yowls at me.

I manage to make a sandwich. I can still spread mayonnaise just fine, and put slabs of leftover chicken on the mayo, and bread on top of that. Maybe that's not enough to qualify me as incredibly high-functioning but it's good enough for now. The kitchen is blurring in front of me. I sit down at the table and try to eat, but the bread seems too thick and dry.

Something moves in the corner of my right eye. A shadow just behind my shoulder. I jerk around in time to catch a dim imprint of a tall human shape blinking out.

Sleep deprivation does bring on hallucinations, though. That's absolutely a known thing.

I keep turning farther in my chair, scanning the whole room. Just in case. I guess it's a nice kitchen, all steel appliances and ash-black polished wood. Walls a soft honey color. Copper pots hanging and Ruby's framed collages on the wall. People with fox and owl heads and streams of disconnected words on banners spilling from their mouths. A purple-haired girl hiding her face behind a swan wing.

But through it all I keep getting little pops of colors that don't belong here, always at the edge of my right eye. Harsh electric green. Dark red. And I keep turning, chasing whatever it is I'm seeing. Somehow I've stood up.

It's getting too dark in here, like maybe clouds have suddenly covered the sun. Maybe I never turned on the light. But those bright, gnashing colors just get stronger. I could be in a maze of green pipes that won't stop moving, shoving at me and herding me along.

Okay, I tell myself, this is obviously not our kitchen anymore. Our kitchen isn't made of weird shuffling clockwork, gears shining blood red in the darkness. Its floor doesn't twitch and jolt sideways. Therefore this is not real. It's a hallucination.

But actually I know it's something worse than that.

It's a dream.

I stumble forward and I'm sure now that I'm not alone in

here. I can't see anybody but I *feel* a whole crowd hidden in random angles of the darkness. Or maybe it's that I'm blinded by the colors flashing at me; some kind of huge engine, scaffolding . . .

"Hey, Never-Ever!"

My heart lurches at my throat; it doesn't help that I've been expecting this all along. My mouth is dry and pasty. I'm still trying to chew that stupid sandwich and I can't make myself swallow. The bread is buzzing in my mouth.

"Never-Ever! I'm up here!" Dashiell laughs. "You've been playing far too many video games, apparently, Never. Look at this place!"

There's something moving high up in the scaffolding. The metal grid is horribly, violently yellow. Eye-scalding brightness, so the most I can make out is a shadow clambering around.

It's him, though. I know the smell of who he is. I don't like to put it like this, but I know the way his freaking *soul* moves, and I can recognize it now. Graceful, okay, but with this monkey stealth that creeps me the hell out. I can't talk so I turn my head and spit up the mouthful of pulped sandwich. That helps. I feel a little clearer.

"Never? Are you coming? Can you see where you're going at all?"

"Not really," I call back. "Where *are* we?"

"Oh, Land of the Dead," Dash says casually. "Where did you think? With the material details, of course, generously provided for us by your subconscious mind. Sorry, but it looks like you're going to have to climb. Are you still scared of heights?"

That's not what I'm scared of. At least it's not the main thing. Dash was right when he talked about my instincts telling me to get away from him. Every nerve in my body is jumping with the urge to turn around and *run*—

I grab on to the bottom of the scaffolding but it's hard to really feel it. I make myself hold it anyway. The rung feels like hot static, slipping through my palm and getting lost inside my flesh. Somehow I'm going up, though. "What are you going to do to me? When I get up there?"

When I look down I can see my feet lifting and planting themselves on the metal beams, pushing me higher. But I can't *feel* anything except a dark suction on my back and heels. The dark is trying to pry me off and send me plummeting.

"You're making progress," Dashiell calls down. I can see his shadow-shape leaning over some edge high above, a reddish stroke of his lit-up hair. "I have to say, Never-Ever, you're exceeding my expectations. You've been keeping it together under some fairly trying circumstances."

"Ruby wouldn't tell me what happened in her dream," I say. "Because you wouldn't let her, right? So what are you going to *do*, Dash-Dot-Dot?"

"Are you backing out? Because neither of us wants me relying on Ruby to get the job done."

"I'm not backing out," I say. "I just want to know. Whatever I'm doing, I want it to be, like, *conscious*."

"You're dreaming, Never-Ever," Dashiell says, and now he sounds gentle and maybe sorrowful. Almost like he genuinely feels bad about something. "Not conscious by definition, then. None of it will be real. Try to remember that."

Suddenly I'm almost there and he's leaning out over me, though it's still hard to get much of a sense of his face. It's a jumble, a web of reflected reds and golds, all shifting and flaring. He stretches a hand to grab me but I'm still just an inch out of reach.

And then I get a flash of another color in the dimness. Silver. A bright-edged point in Dashiell's hand.

All at once I know what it has to be. I know what Ruby wouldn't tell me and my arms fly up to fight him off.

Which means that I've let go of the rungs.

The slip, the drop. My stomach slamming up and bile spitting from my mouth.

I hear the wind whistling past my ears and the darkness shooting up as I fall. Ripping space and then the impact.

I'm still screaming and gasping. I'm clutching our kitchen floor, my sandwich a foot away on the blue glass shards of what was my plate.

The lights have been on the whole time. And hey, it looks like I've cut my thumb. A little spatter of red is soaking the margin of the zebra-stripe rug. *The bastard did that to Ruby. She went to him because she loves him, and he hurt her.* I'm staring at the rug and I know I should get my face off the floor and go get a bandage, but I can't. All I can do is keep holding tight to something that sure isn't going to hold me back. Everything is spinning. *No wonder she couldn't say it. She wouldn't want to tell me anything that would make Dashiell sound—*

But that's not the worst part, and I know it. The worst part is that I panicked. Just like a goddamn weak coward. I didn't go *through* with it.

Neither of us wants me relying on Ruby to get the job done, he said. I don't know about him but *I* don't want that is right! He can't have her. I've really, truly made up my mind about that. And it turns out that making up my mind, and being a determined person, is something I can in fact do. No matter how vague and waffling other people maybe think I am.

So I guess I'll have to go back and deal with the whole thing again. All the way to the end, whatever that end turns out to be, whether it's real or not. And God, who could face that?

RUBY

* * * * *

The East Village is a good place to be if you don't want to know where you are anymore, or if you want to *pretend* you don't know. It could be an alternate world, with the trapeze sweeping of the golden branches overhead and the shop windows full of fairy dresses with tulle ruffles and the gorgeous college girls wearing crowns of silk flowers with their vintage tweed coats. And I need to be lost and stumbling into another world, because I need to find a place where impossible things can be true.

I can't shake the feeling of him, is the problem. I can't forget that must-have-been-dream, the sound of Dashiell's voice coming to me through mazy walls, and Everett's voice *answering* him. I can't purge the impression that Dash is right here some-where, just behind me or beside me, a voice always waiting to whisper in my ear but never saying anything, a hand constantly about to brush my cheek but never quite touching down.

So maybe Everett is right, and I'm in denial about the fact that Dashiell is dead. Even loopier is that I've been in denial about the denial, my mind spinning to escape the truth like dead leaves whisked in a rising helix—

Or else—and this is where my thoughts really get out of control—maybe it's *true*. Maybe Dash is back in some way I can't understand. Maybe if I could just find him I could throw my arms around him and cry on his chest, and this time he wouldn't tell me I'm being too emotional.

Because Dashiell loves me, too. He still does. I can feel it. That's what matters, and what was *really* crazy was that hour in the dead of night when I was afraid he might put Everett at risk somehow.

The night got into me, that's all. Now that I'm out in the shimmery afternoon, everything feels so much clearer. If Dash needs me, then I'm ready, and if there *is* danger involved I'll be the one to take it on, because the risk is trivial compared to what we feel for each other.

I take the paper out of my pocket again and double-check the address, though I know that this is the place. A six-story red-brick building on East 7th Street. I ring the intercom for her apartment; somehow I'm sure she'll be home.

"Yes?"

"It's me," I say—though why would she know who *me* is? "Ruby Bohnacker."

"Fifth floor," Paige says and cuts off, just like she's been expecting me. The door vibrates and I step through. It's a pretty lobby, black art deco tiles and sconces with sculpted glass flames. In the elevator I watch the red numbers winking higher. Dashiell must have watched them the same way the day he died, and once they got to *five*—that was as high as he was ever going to go.

When I get out she's waiting for me, hanging languidly out of her door in a silver silk robe with white embroidery. Shining black hair and luminous skin. She's beautiful to the point where it's almost grotesque; looking at her is like biting into something so sweet it shatters your teeth.

"Ruby *Bohnacker*," she says, and her voice is as syrupy as ever. "Not Ruby Slippers?"

"Not to you," I say. "Only people I love get to call me that."

Paige smiles the same tight, acrid smile I saw when she was on our doorstep. "Didn't stop you from coming. Did you find me the way I think you did?"

The invoice was slipped under our door this morning before Everett was up. No stamp; someone hand delivered it. I brought it to my dad while he was drinking his coffee.

"He was so mad he threw your invoice on the floor," I say. "So I copied down the address while he was in the bathroom."

Paige barks with laughter. The invoice was for three months' rent, not one, but on the other hand it was a lot less per month than she'd said it was, twenty-five hundred instead of thirty-seven. "But he'll pay it?"

"He already mailed the check. I don't think he'll do it again, though. He got super burned out on stuff like that with Dashiell."

"And so we come to the reason for your visit, Miss Slippers," Paige says. It takes me a moment to realize that she's mimicking Dashiell's way of talking, just a little bit. My breathing gets faster. "Why don't you come in and have some tea? You know I know why you don't like me, anyway."

I follow her into her living room and drop my coat and bag on the floor; the kitchen is on one wall behind a marble counter. Victorian sofas upholstered in pearl gray brocade and a black glass chandelier. A pink pony-skin ottoman. Candy-goth, the kind of tasteful that makes me a little queasy, like being in an expensive lingerie store.

"That's not the reason."

"Believe me, I got completely sick of hearing him talk about *you*. Dashiell knew how to make it into a race to the finish, didn't he? He told me over and over that you were the only person in the world who truly loved him. *Really* and truly." She kind of simpers the last part. She's turned away from me to put the kettle on, but I can hear the sharpness in her voice. White knives, blades whickering in midair.

Then what she said sinks in, and I have to catch hold of her counter. "That's not what he told me."

"Oh, no? 'My Ruby loves me through to her bones. My precious Ruby-Ru, she'd be there for me no matter the extremity, no matter the darkness I found myself in. And she loves me without harboring any desperate denial about who I really am. She's seen into the depths and she hasn't turned away.' That was how the song went, Ruby. Oh, but of course not to you. Then you wouldn't have kept trying so hard, would you?"

I can't let myself break down sobbing in front of her, I can't let myself fall.

You haven't lived long enough yet to demonstrate *love. We'll just have to wait and find out.* But he knew the whole time; of course he knew. I could scream and howl from the wild relief of it—at least he believed in me before he died. So even if he *did* shoot up again, it wasn't because—

I hear a clink and look up. Paige is putting tea bags into two cups, watching me hard across the counter.

"I would have tried anyway," I tell her. I pull myself up straight. "Always. Dash could have told me the truth."

"Have a *seat*, Ruby," Paige says in a tone just snide enough to let me know she can see how faint I'm feeling. She nods toward the sofas. "Go on. It's probably not easy for you to be in this apartment, is it?" *Where he died,* she means.

I'm just settling onto one of her gray sofas when it hits me. I'm thinking of Paige saying *that was how the song went* and suddenly I'm remembering watching her from a bench in a park. I can see her swishing along in a different lace dress, this one white with red roses embroidered at the hem; she's wearing baby-blue lipstick and crescents of blood red are painted above the crease of her lids. And Dashiell's voice is there, singing so close to me that it's almost like his voice is spilling from my chest: *"Her eyes are red and her lips are blue; she must have drowned in a cold, cold sky. And oh, how she must have cried, to see herself going down. . . ."*

Paige has walked on a few yards but now she glances back to see the singer—where *is* he? And then she turns and examines him more deliberately, and her mouth curls into a slow smile.

I remember that happening so clearly, and I'm positive it was the first time they met. But I definitely wasn't there and I never even heard it as a story, I *know* that. I know Dash never told me.

"Ruby? Don't pass out on me, please." She sets down the mugs on a tiny silver table; green tea with ginger, I think. She perches on the ottoman across from me and tips her head. "I won't be calling an ambulance for another inert Bohnacker. Go out in the street if you have to do that."

"I'm *fine*," I say, but my face is suddenly blazing at what she said and my nails are digging into my palms. "I'm fine! I just need—I came because—"

"Like I don't know that, Ruby?" Paige is smirking, holding her tea against the slight roundness of her belly. "You want me to tell you everything I know. About your dear brother's last days. *No detail is too small*, is it?"

That's what the police say; just like I thought before, she wants me to think that this is like an investigation, but anything she says will just lead me away from the truth. I take a deep breath because this is the part I've been practicing in my mind all day. This is the part I have to get right.

"No," I say. "I don't want you to tell me anything. Because I'd never know how much of what you said was lies, or if *any* of it was true, and I'd never be able to stop wondering, and that would just make it all so much worse."

"And why would I lie to you?" There's a dark flash in Paige's eyes.

"To get at my dad," I tell her. "You pretty much said that when you were at our house. I'm not going to let you use me as a way to mess with him."

I leave out the *other* reason why she might lie. If Dash were murdered, she'd be the obvious suspect.

Paige gives another hard laugh. "Why, what good thinking, Ruby! Dashiell said you were a bright girl."

"I just need to see where it happened." The words come out like a slow, hard wind, driving up from someplace deep inside me. But I know it's right; I know I'll see more of the truth on my own than I could ever learn by listening to Paige tell it her way.

"You mean my *bed*?" Paige asks and arches her brows. Her tone says, *That's not the only thing that happened there, Miss Slippers.*

"Yes," I say. "Then I'll go. You won't need to call an *ambulance* for me."

For a while we just stare at each other. She has deep brown irises; somehow I'd thought they were blue. "Fine," Paige says at last. "Don't think you'll be welcome here again, though. This was your one chance."

Paige stands and I get up and follow her. It's a Manhattan apartment so all the rooms are small; her bedroom barely fits a big wrought-iron bed that was maybe made from an old cemetery fence, a gilt mirror on one wall, and a dresser. Lots of embroidered pillows are piled on the bed and a matching coverlet lies wadded in a heap. Something looks wrong to me, though.

"I guess the sheets are different."

"I didn't keep the *sheets* Dashiell died on, Ruby-Ru."

I'm staring and I can almost see the line of Dashiell's arm hanging over the side of the bed. "They were blue that night," I say without thinking. "Like, the palest possible blue. Silk broadcloth." Beautiful sheets; they must have cost a fortune.

I wasn't looking at Paige but she jerks in the corner of my eye. "Did the police show you a picture?"

How *did* I know that? "No." I hesitate. "Maybe somebody told me? I don't remember." *No one told me, and no one showed me anything. I can see for myself.* I kneel down to touch the edge of the mattress, exactly where his head fell back; I know Paige is staring but I don't care what she thinks. "And you weren't here."

"We'd had a fight," Paige says coolly; of course, she must have had to repeat the story over and over; it must taste stale and crumbling in her mouth. "I went out and I didn't come home until after eleven the next morning. He was already cold."

God, how I see it all, and feel it: that night two months ago glancing through the daylight, this room doubling back on it-self. I remember to look around the memory for Dash's mur-derer, but I don't see anyone.

"He was alone," I say, and press my forehead to his; even though he's long gone I can *feel* it, like a memory made flesh. "You didn't come back and Dash died all alone."

"That's what happened," Paige agrees irritably. "Ruby, I've had enough of this."

"He'll never be alone again," I say.

She *really* jumps at that. I don't know why I said it, but it felt like the truth. "Most people would say the opposite. Now could you please leave?"

But I can sense him, and he's right here. Maybe even if it's too late to save him I can at least make it easier. I can hold him so he knows he wasn't abandoned at the end.

Paige bends down, grabs my elbow, and yanks me stumbling onto my feet. "Out! Out, out, out. My God, you're a creepy little thing, Ruby. Get out of my home."

She didn't want to call an ambulance, but she's ready to call the police if I don't go. I don't want to be forced to explain to my dad or Everett what I was doing here.

"I'm going. You don't have to freak out." I pull away and stalk out across her living room without waiting for her—neither of us drank our tea—and grab my coat and bag. I think she's watching me from the bedroom doorway but I don't turn around to check, and I don't say goodbye. I leave. I shut her front door behind me and make it as far as the elevator before I start shaking so hard I can barely press the button.

I needed to find a place where impossible things could be true. And I stepped through her door, and then I knew things I *couldn't* know. Dashiell's memories should have vanished when he died, but instead they woke up in my mind and their eyes flashed wide open and shining. They looked at me.

Maybe Dash is dead, but he's close enough that I can catch the edge of his dreams.

EVERETT

✳ ✳ ✳ ✳ ✳

Just keep shooting. Keep dodging. If something is moving, it is by definition something that should get the living crap blown out of it. If it's something tall and pretty—some goddamn golden-haired elf lord—then that's even better. That is just begging to get mowed down and then have a whole barrage of extra lightning slammed into its twitching corpse. I've learned that there are certain people who can never be dead enough.

Because he did something horrible to her, even if it was in a dream. And maybe she *let* him do it. And because she still defends him anyway. She tried to say hello to me an hour ago and I couldn't stand to look at her. I just grunted and after a few minutes she went away pissed.

But now she comes back with two bowls of pasta, with the rest of the leftover chicken and spinach mixed into some gooey cheese sauce—Ruby is a pretty awesome cook—and plonks one in front of me. "Dinnertime." Then she curls up at the far end of the sofa and starts reading, with her bowl on her lap and her posture strongly expressing that I have hurt and offended her, and that I'm an asshole, but that hey, she's not going to let me starve just because I'm throwing some incomprehensible tantrum. And I am hungry, I guess.

"Thanks." I still don't want to look at her. Food provides a decent excuse not to, though. I pause my game and start mauling, eyes lowered. For a while we ignore each other, or pretend to, but then the food starts to run out and it's like I'm exposed to a new kind of enemy fire, blasts made out of awareness of my sister sitting near me. And awareness of that brother-thing still probably inside her, watching me and whistling *coward* down deep in her brain stem where I can't hear it. Laughing at the way I freaked out.

"So. How's the war?" Ruby's a little closer to me now and she puts her book down.

"Sucks. There's not nearly enough stuff to kill."

Ruby laughs. "Everett the Destroyer, wading through the blood of his enemies but still unsatisfied! Let them breed captive elves by the thousands, solely to slake the thirst of his blade."

"Now you're talking *sense*." I want to keep hating her, but it's hard. Especially when I can hear the strained sound of her voice, like she's putting on an act again, which probably means that she has something to hide. And once I start wondering what that might be it basically scares the hell out of me.

"You hurt yourself?" Ruby nods toward my bandaged thumb and I don't answer. "Ever?"

I stare at the smears on my plate, and after a moment Ruby reaches out and takes my cut hand and starts gently stroking my thumb with hers. I can see from the corner of my eyes that she's looking at me with this weird, hungry attention, and all at once I realize why.

"You couldn't wait until she's asleep?" I say. "Like, her brain is blipping out now for no reason. You think she won't notice that?"

"I can't always stop Ru-Ru from noticing more than I'd like," Dashiell says. "But I didn't think this discussion could wait, Never. Not after what happened today."

And I finally look up: Dashiell's stare, so concerned and tender that you could swear he *means* it, lances straight out of Ruby's face. He's still pawing at my thumb.

"You were going to freaking *stab* me," I tell him. "So what the hell did you do to her?"

Dash doesn't answer right away, just turns my hand and inspects it. "You know, you dropped at least thirty feet when you threw yourself off that scaffolding. Quite the nasty fall that was, Never. So are you injured now? Anything broken?"

I pull my hand away. "Just my thumb got hurt. I fell on the kitchen floor and smashed a plate."

"So the only harm that came to you was from what you did in *reaction* to your dream. Not from what happened in the dream itself. Isn't that right, Never-Ever?"

I know what he's getting at. "I don't *care* if it was a dream. What did you do to her?"

"Ruby Slippers bounced out of bed on Saturday morning, full of life and perfectly healthy. The only danger lay in an impulse toward reenactment that came over her *after* she woke up, a drifting back toward the scene. But you know, Never, I took measures to keep her from coming to the slightest harm while she was still feeling overcome. She didn't even catch a cold."

Reenactment. Drifting back. Ruby on the river's brink with waves sloshing at her ankles, ready to keep walking forward. And now I remember: Dash said she swam to reach him. "Did you *drown* her?"

"In a way Ru-Ru and I got lucky with the scenario that presented itself," Dash says, answering the question without answering it. "I think you have a harder row to hoe than she did, Never. I wanted to tell you that I'm sorry for that, but it's not something I have any control over; you're the one whose mind dictates the details, unfortunately. But the salient thing is that it's just a ritual, a rite of passage. It will be hard to get through it, but then on the other side you'll be perfectly fine. We'll continue with our plans and you'll feel as strong as ever."

That's why he's here. "I'm *not* backing out, Dash. I wouldn't have—tried to get away today—if you had just told me the truth already. About what was going to happen."

He tips Ruby's head and smiles, examining me. "You still want to go ahead, then. With our adventure."

"I still want you to get the hell out of Ruby. She isn't *yours*, Dash-Dot-Dot."

Weirdly, Ruby's blondish lashes start to flutter halfway closed and the smile on her face gets wider, more blissed out. For half a second I'm not sure which of them I'm looking at.

"Oh, I hate to disillusion you, Never. But that wasn't at all how it seemed to me today, and you know I have a remarkably privileged view of the situation. My Ruby-Ru showed me her colors, and they were the truest of blues."

I want to ignore him, but I can't. My heart starts this achy thudding and my breath feels thick. "What are you talking about?"

"Miss Slippers told you she was off to the library," Dashiell says—and the quirk of his smile tells me that Ruby was lying to me, and that he thinks it's freaking hysterical that I was dumb enough to fall for it. "Didn't she?"

"So where was she?" But I shouldn't ask. I shouldn't let him taunt me into wondering what he knows that I don't.

"She went to visit Paige. Not so long after you took your tumble, Never, Ruby Slippers went strolling up my old block in the East Village. It was nice to see the place again."

It takes me a moment to process all that—so he can only see the East Village by hitching a ride on somebody? He can't just waft over there disembodied anytime he feels like it?—but then it hits me how crazy it is.

"What did she want with *Paige*? Ruby—did she go to ask—" Ugh. I already know. Ruby said she'd forget her paranoid ideas about murder, but she was lying about that, too. Of *course*.

Dashiell shakes Ruby's head, her hacked hair swinging. "That was what Paige seemed to expect, but as it transpired Ruby didn't choose to ask her anything. She went looking for me, in a sense. She gravitated toward the scene of my death, as surely as if she'd done the deed herself. And she found a bit more than I'd intended."

I could keep repeating myself, saying *What are you talking about, Dash?* over and over like some idiot automaton. But I'm suddenly sick of him jerking me around and I glare at him instead. He'll tell me anyway, because he's dying to tell me—to rub it in that he has Ruby by the balls, or by whatever counts as balls for a girl.

"She's starting to overhear me, a little," Dash keeps on after a moment. See, I *knew* he would. He can't stop himself. "There's some bleeding of consciousness, back and forth, and I can't entirely prevent it. I know how much you want to preserve Ru-Ru's innocence, Ever, as far as my proximity is concerned, but the

longer I'm in residence—we both know she's a sensitive girl."
There he goes tightening the screws, even though he doesn't
need to. "But I was very touched by her response to *what* she
sensed, to my memories seeping into her awareness. It was a
beautiful demonstration of loyalty." He grins. "I don't think Paige
enjoyed it much, though."

"So Ruby still loves you," I snarl. "Even after you freaking
murdered her. That doesn't make her *yours*, Dashiell. You can't
have her."

The arch of his eyebrows—or actually of *Ruby's* eyebrows,
because it's really important to remember that—says, *Oh, can't I?*
But what he says out loud is, "But I can have you instead? That's
the deal you want to propose, Never-Ever? A fair trade?"

Wasn't he the one who proposed it? "You can use me. For
a while. Until you do what you have to do. Get the money and
whatever, like you said." I stare at him, because I can't shake
the feeling that there's a catch somewhere. "Do what you need
to, and then get out."

"I wish I could make it easier for you," Dashiell says softly. "I
can't. There's no alternative method that I know of. We're both
obliged to see things through to the end."

Like it's totally equivalent, me getting slashed to death and him
obliged to swing the knife at me. "Whatever. And anyway I'm not
obliged. I'm doing it on purpose."

"You're doing it for your sister's sake," Dashiell agrees. "I understand that. It's what a *man* would do, Never-Ever. And I truly
appreciate it."

And then he's gone. Ruby's eyes roll back and her head pitches
around—and then she's launching herself off the sofa and staggering fast toward the bathroom under the stairs. She slams the

door and I can hear her throwing up, coughing and sobbing. I've followed her by reflex and I'm leaning on the wall outside. "Ruby? Ruby, are you okay?"

"Oh, Jesus Christ," Ruby moans. "What is *happening* to me? What is—"

What did it do to her, when she started *overhearing* Dashiell? How could anyone deal with that, some dead guy's memories oozing up in their brain like toxic sludge? And he pretty much just came out and said it will get worse; he's probably doing it on purpose, just to keep the pressure on me. It's totally working.

I've got to get him out, that's all there is to it. He's killing her.

DASHIELL

*   *   *   *   *

There's always an eye to be kept on the darkness that loosed me—an eye for movement, an ear tuned to the chance of footsteps or breath. Distractions abound in my current environs: at the moment fingers are lathering her hair and bubbles skid down her wrists. On her pale thigh liquid fireworks burst, fantastically brilliant after my long stretch of sensory deprivation. I could forget to pay attention to what's back there, drugged by the sensual intricacy of being so alive in my dear sister's skin. Warmth, saliva, drumming blood.

And then there's the thrill when she feels me: my thoughts sliding over her thoughts, mind whispering on her mind. The living have their lovers, their children, but they never have anyone the way I have her now. She stops washing her hair; she leans against the tiles and closes her eyes.

"Dashiell?" A long hesitation. "Are you *there*?"

Soon enough, Ruby-Ru. Soon enough I'll answer the question. Be patient for now, sweet one.

Because out there in the shadowy places someone is coming. I can feel the vibrations of someone still alive, straying on the margin where death overlaps dreams. Where do they come from,

I used to wonder, those strangers we glimpse in the deepest alleys of our sleep? Now I know.

But out there now it's your twin brother's footsteps, Miss Slippers. He's already storming toward the same scaffold where he fell before, stomping as he goes, refusing to let himself so much as glance to the side. Coming to save you, he tells himself, but the truth is that he's raging with jealousy that you will never love him as you love me. Coming to save you from *me*, when you are so utterly mine that the idea of extricating you is beyond absurdity.

"Dashiell? You died, I *know* you died. So why do I keep feeling—"

Hush, Ruby-Ru, Ruby-Ru. Don't cry.

There's something I have to attend to now. But I'll be back with you very soon.

EVERETT

* * * *

I didn't notice when I fell asleep, but I obviously am. I know this place. Even that sick feeling of people watching me feels way too familiar already. There's an intense vibe of invisible eyes in the corners, but like that's a completely normal thing here.

So ignore it, then. This won't get any easier if I hang back. I still have to climb that goddamn scaffold, and I still have to just sit there and *take* it when Dashiell shoves that knife into my guts. Fine. I won't let him see me chicken out a second time. I don't see him lurking up there at first, but by the time I've got a grip on those shining yellow rungs he's hanging over me.

"Never-Ever," he calls down, "you've come back so promptly! No shirking of your duty whatsoever. Attaboy."

"Shut up, Dash," I say. "It's enough that you're getting everything your way *again*. Right? You don't have to gloat about it."

"You might be getting more things your way soon enough," Dashiell observes. He's still pretty far up and the climb seems harder this time, like maybe there's more gravity now. My legs drag with every step. "I truly appreciate what you're doing, Never-Ever. I think some positive reinforcement will be in order, just as soon as I can arrange for it."

You can't bribe *me, you bastard.* "I don't want it. Your positive reinforcement. You can shove it, Dash. Okay?"

He laughs. Of course. "Still mad, Never? I thought we'd worked through our differences."

I'm still pulling myself up and suddenly the climb is going faster, so fast that I'm getting dizzy, like I can't control it.

"We'll have worked it out once you leave my family alone. You're supposed to be dead, Dash. Like, rest the hell in peace? Did you not get the *memo?*"

And now I can see him. Clearly this time. His bare feet dangle over the edge, kicking in frayed jeans. There's just enough yellow glow that I can see his obnoxiously chiseled male-model face, and his gray eyes, and his wavy pinkish-gold hair. And all at once I'm remembering Ruby—maybe we were eight?—spreading strawberry jam on top of a scone and then running around the table to Dashiell, holding the scone up next to his head. Then getting a knife and wiping some of the jam off, because she was trying to match the color of his hair *exactly.* And every time she went near him he'd grab her and tickle her, and she'd squeal and try to get away.

Except not really.

He ended up with jam all over one ear and they were falling over each other laughing. If we were eight then, he must have been fourteen, or fifteen at most. Was he already turning into the person he is now? Was there a specific moment when Dashiell cracked? For a whole three years after our mom left he was too pissed to talk to her. He'd storm out of the room if anyone mentioned her at all. I was pretty little then, but you don't forget something like that, your big brother red-faced and weeping with rage.

He was so damned used to being adored that it must have blown his mind that anyone would *leave* him. And I guess once our mom was out of the picture, he started focusing more on squeezing adoration out of Ruby. Like, as a substitute.

"*Our* family," Dash corrects me. "You don't break those connections simply by dying, Never. The dead have every right to demand their due. Recognition, basically. Of all the ways we're still with you."

And then I'm up there, hoisting myself onto the wide plank where Dash is sitting—he's already got hold of my shoulder—and dream or no dream I'm gasping for breath and I don't have my inhaler.

Not that it's going to matter. His left hand is sort of cradling the back of my neck and his right hand is holding the knife. If it wasn't for the psycho-killer accessory, he could be posing in an ad for jeans—since that's what he's wearing. And nothing else.

"So what'll it be, Never?" Dash asks. "The throat is foolproof, but a bit ugly. Going for your heart would be more dignified, for both of us, but then there's the risk I'll miss on the first try. You'll suffer. So the question is, is dignity worth it?"

"I don't care," I tell him; it comes out broken-up and wheezing. Even though I know it's just a dream, my heart is trying to spit itself out of my throat. "I don't care about any of it."

"Oh, pah. You care immensely. Or you wouldn't be here."

Red and green lights spin through the distance, but I can't decipher much of where we are. "You know we aren't alone here, right, Dash? There are definitely people out there. I mean, we're being watched."

For a flash his eyes go wide and he stares around; I could almost swear he's afraid. Something in his face sharpens, and it makes me think he's looking for somebody in particular. Leave it to Dash to make enemies wherever he goes. "Random passersby, maybe. Anyone could stumble in here. This is a slippery place."

They're not passing by, and he knows it, but it's not worth arguing about. "Dashiell? I want you to admit something first, that's all. Admit I'm not a coward."

"No," he agrees, and again there's that eerie tenderness that could totally pass for sincere if I didn't know better. I see the flash of his rising knife and a spasm runs through me. "No, Never-Ever, you're proving to be remarkably brave, in fact. And I've given you the opportunity to learn that about yourself, haven't I?"

And then there's a moment when I'm launched out of myself—because hey, that happens in dreams—and I'm watching the whole thing from above: the golden-haired jeans model cradling the fat loser. The silver streak of his knife sailing up. I'm kind of proud of my expression, though. I'm absolutely giving him attitude, and I look way more defiant than scared.

Out of my body or not, I still feel it when he slits my throat.

RUBY SLIPPERS

The hush of the night. Our house crowned in darkness. And I'm awake again, my breath fast, almost sure that I heard something moving. A soft step near my door.

Everett's been having trouble sleeping and maybe it's him, just heading to the kitchen for something to eat. I roll over, trying to make it sound like the unconscious way I'd roll in my sleep, and check to see if there's any light fanning under my door. Because wouldn't Everett turn on a light to eat?

Nothing, just blackness. And the sound comes again, slow and stealthy: definitely someone trying not to be heard. Last time I got freaked like this it turned out that I was being paranoid and it was only Everett staring into space, not a stranger in the house at all, but my heart is still racing whispery-quick and I reach out silently for my phone on the nightstand. Just in case.

My doorknob starts turning. A tiny rattle in the latch. I punch in 911, my thumb ready to hit *send,* and then the door swings open and I see a vague dark lump standing in the gap.

"Ever?" It's shaped like him, more or less, only maybe a little straighter and with a more assertive line to the shoulders. But there's no answer and my voice shoots higher. "Everett? Is that—"

"Softly now, Ruby Slippers," says a voice—and it is not Everett's. "Hush, my sweet Ru. There's nothing here for you to be afraid of."

And then I've dropped the phone with a *crack* and I'm half-leaping and half-stumbling across the room. Because I walked across the threshold of Paige's prissy, pretentious apartment this afternoon, and somehow by doing that I slipped out of ordinary reality and into a zone where anything could be true. Because I've known he was so *close,* just on the inside of each breath that curled out of me, or helping to cast my shadow from underneath the street, with a buried sun behind him. Because I've heard him, murmuring in the darkness.

"Dashiell!"

And he's already squeezing me tight, both arms locked around me and his hands wandering in my hair.

But everything is wrong. The body I'm holding is too plump, not roped in taut muscles the way Dashiell's was, not tall enough—

Not him.

He feels me trying to pull away and clamps down. "It's truly me, Ruby-Ru. One difficulty with dying is that I don't have the use of my proper body anymore, so I've had to take out a loan. It was the only way I could see you." He reaches to turn on a nearby lamp, and after a moment—*I can't think, I can't breathe*—I stop trying to break free.

Because it's Everett after all. Except that it's not. It's Everett if you pulled him through some dream-liquid made of Dashiell and brought him up dripping, if Dashiell was darting inside him like a thousand sparks. Whatever it is, it's tugging me closer again and brushing kisses all over the side of my face.

"Everett?" I try.

The arms let me go. "Oh, pah. I'm gone for two months, only *two*, and has my sweet Ru dumped out the last dregs of her imagination since then? Truly, Miss Slippers? You can mistake me for *Everett* now? A lady of slipping and sliding should understand that other people can sometimes do it too, whatever appearance might meet her eyes." He sounds annoyed—whoever he is—but then he smiles. Everett's soft mouth, but the curl of it is ironic and sweet and insolent all at once.

And God, how deeply I know that smile. "Dash-Dot-Dot. Excuse me. I know you. I knew—I was sure you were close. You—" It's one of those things that's almost impossible to say, but we've established tonight that impossibility is something to flick aside like a fly. "You're borrowing Everett's body. But it's you."

I sensed him close by, but that he might be *inside* Everett—that never would have occurred to me. He grins so impishly, though, that I have to believe it, believe and believe all over again.

"And are you happy to see me, Ruby-Ru? Even if it's not the face you were used to? I'm sorry to say that face is long gone—it suited me admirably—but you can see that *I'm* not."

And then I hug him again, because Dashiell has to know—he has to *feel*—how desperately we all want him home. "It felt like half the world was gone, Dash. Without you. And I've dreamed and dreamed about you." He's stroking my hair again, very softly. "But Everett—I mean—does he know that you—"

I don't know how to finish the question. We're closed together in this tiny bubble of light and the night outside just keeps getting bigger. And I can't get used to seeing Everett's face this way, *stretched* somehow; it's still his but also transformed, tense and confident.

"Everett knows perfectly," Dashiell says. "I'm slinging this carcass around with his full consent and approval. That said, though, he would be very upset if he found out I was using it to talk to you, Miss Slippers. So don't tell him, please. He doesn't want you to know I'm here at all."

"But why not?" I'm still trying to understand—though maybe this explains a lot about how strangely Everett's been acting. "Why shouldn't I know? This is the most important thing that's happened *ever*. Oh, I heard you talking to Everett the other night! I *heard* you. I couldn't make out what you were saying, though. And then he said he hadn't been talking to anyone. He said I'd dreamed it."

"Hush, Ru-Ru," Dash says. "Softly. Everything is fine. I'm here with you. And Never-Ever is striving to protect you. After recent events, he's understandably concerned about your state of mind. He thinks that knowing I'm here—when any reasonable person would expect me to have been snuffed out like a candle—Never's convinced that the knowledge would overwhelm you. He thinks you'd be permanently unhinged by the discovery."

"So *he* can handle knowing, and I can't?" The question comes out like a whip and Dashiell runs a finger over my cheek, soothing me. "Since when does Ever get to decide what I'm capable of dealing with? He's *twelve minutes* older than me!"

"Ru-Ru. You *know* why. Everett is acting out of love for you. Try to respect that."

Dashiell's been back with me for just a few moments and he's already reproaching me, and he's already taking Everett's side. I feel like breaking down sobbing. Then it hits me.

"I know why? Dash—I mean—did Everett *tell* you?" *The river wrapping my feet in running silver, Manhattan fading into gray, and my bag dragging me sideways with the weight of those stones.*

"He didn't need to tell me anything, Miss Slippers. I was there. I was watching you through it all. Unfortunately there wasn't much I could do to stop things from getting out of hand—and you would have found it so deeply unsettling if I *had* stepped in that it likely would have made the situation even worse. I certainly would have tried my best, though, if Never-Ever hadn't been there to look after you."

"You were there?" I say. Dashiell was never the guardian angel type, but maybe death changes you in unpredictable ways. "Dash—*watching* me? Where were you?" I don't want him to see it, but I've started crying.

"Shh, Miss Slippers. I was with you. That's what matters."

"And, Dash? Do you believe I love you now? I can say it, and you won't tell me I'm being mawkish or maudlin, or I've had too much hot fudge?"

That makes him laugh—*his* laugh. Even out of death and oblivion and infinite unraveling space, it's his and no one else's. "It's a school night, sweet Ru. Go to sleep. I'll be upstairs, and in the morning Everett will be back. Just don't mention that you saw me. It will only make him worry about you."

I usually can't stand people telling me what to do. But this is Dashiell, or his spirit anyway, returned to me by a piercing, glorious miracle. It's like my dreams, but so much better and sweeter. He can boss me around if he wants to.

"I won't tell him," I say. "But Dash? You do believe me?" I

almost say, *Paige said you always knew,* but I don't want to remind him of her. Not tonight. Maybe not ever.

"I believe you, Ruby-Ru." He smiles and kisses me gently on the forehead, just the way he always did. "Dying has proved to be an illuminating experience, Ru. It's enhanced my understanding of quite a few things. And of you, most especially."

NEVER-EVER

* * * *

Well, there's one thing Dash wasn't lying about. He said I'd feel as strong as ever, and I do. I get out of bed and shower, feeling almost too energized and quick and *definite* to fit in an ordinary human body. I'm walking differently without trying—bigger strides. A little swing to them. Then I get it: I'm *swaggering* and it doesn't feel phony or pathetic at all. I stare at myself in the mirror. I look taller and firmer, and my head tips back just a touch without me telling it to, and my shoulders have this slinky lean to them. All my normal clothes seem too schlubby, and I reach into a box on the floor of my closet and pull out this black cashmere thermal sweater that he left here one time—gaping moth holes around the neck, but that just makes it look cooler. I tug it on, and for about ten seconds I feel completely awesome about it, like I'm this smoking-hot badass dragon-slaying *machine.* And then I realize what I'm doing.

To hell with his clothes. I'm sure he'd love for me to wear his sweater, but I won't do it. In fact, I'll wear the sloppiest, dorkiest T-shirt I own: one that's way too big. With an anthropomorphic hot dog. *Screw you, Dashiell.*

If somebody slits your throat at night, you are under no obligation whatsoever to be nice about it in the morning.

I can't shake him that easily, though. I gallop down the stairs like my body has a spanking-new, gorgeously oiled robot inside it. And when I get to the kitchen both my dad and Ruby stare.

"Growth spurt," Dad decides after a moment. "You might get my side of the family's height after all, Everett." He's still looking me over, confused. I can see him decide not to say, *You're starting to look like your brother.* The whole thing is way too awkward, so I make myself cereal. It gives me an excuse to turn my back on him.

"You look good, Ever," Ruby says behind me. It sounds a little condescending and I don't answer. In fact, I basically feel like ignoring her completely.

And at school the magic continues: girls who have always treated me like a rock—like I momentarily count if they happen to stub their toes on me—are suddenly gazing at me with perplexed expressions, as if they're at a total loss to understand how I could seem interesting. Kids smarter than me ask my opinion. My English teacher says I'm insightful. Maybe I shouldn't like it—I'm not so clueless that I can't figure out this must be the *positive reinforcement* Dashiell was talking about—but I really do. I can talk to anyone without feeling like I'm a glob of amorphous slime, intruding on their field of vision. And when I make a joke, Elena Shawn—who is punkishly cool and beautiful, both, with bright blue highlights—cracks up and leans against me while she laughs. Then she lifts her head and whispers in my ear.

"It's a good look for you, Everett. I mean, *talking* to me." She gives me the sweetest smile before she walks off.

It's enough to make me get flustered and quiet again, though not for too long. I mean, the only reason I *don't* have a raging crush on Elena is that it would be so stupidly hopeless if I did. I try not to be more of an idiot than I can help.

But if Dashiell kept on possessing me, maybe liking her wouldn't be so pathetic. I wouldn't still be a virgin when I hit twenty-five. My grades would go up. Maybe I'd still be a fat loser, but people would perceive that as a fabulous thing to be in my very special case.

He isn't taking me over outright, but it's like he's *leaking,* seeping through me. I'm me, but people can smell the him-ish-ness and they just eat it up. It's like when Ruby bought that sexy velvet dress, probably, but I get the feeling Dash is deliberately going a little heavier with me. He's letting me have the benefit of being more like he was.

I catch Ruby looking at me funny. But so's everybody else. I'm just sorry I didn't wear the sweater.

I told him he couldn't bribe me—didn't I? But possibly that's not entirely true. *Every man has his price, Never-Ever.* I don't know if it's me thinking in Dashiell's voice, or Dash oozing the words at me from wherever he's hiding. By the end of the day I've been invited to a party on Friday by kids who would maybe say hi to Ruby, but never glance at me: they're all *achievement-oriented* but also glamorous rebel types, destined to mouth off at their professors at Yale. And to know more than their professors do, too. They'll be human rights lawyers and curate art museums and marry analogues of each other, and everything they do will be so inevitable that it's almost like they've got no choice at all.

It's that kind of school, the kind that costs more than most colleges. Ruby and I are maybe overprivileged—I know we are, actually—but we pale by freaking comparison with a lot of the kids here. I could almost understand why Dashiell did the things he did, looking at them. He made bad choices, no one is arguing about that part. But choices are what they were.

It was the fact that his behavior was so utterly, hopelessly bad that *proved* he was choosing. If that makes any sense.

He lets me enjoy it until school lets out. Then it's like, *Playtime's over, Never-Ever*—though I still don't know if it's me or him thinking the words—and another mind kind of up and *shoves* my mind out of the way. There's a nauseating sideways lurch inside my skull and the trees in front of me lean like a ship going under. But instead of leaning into ocean waves, they're falling from the onslaught of headachey darkness.

And then that's all I see, darkness. Or maybe I don't see it. I'm just lost in this not-place.

I panic—because it's disturbing as hell—and I try to shove back, to see, to claw my way to a surface I can barely sense. *This isn't the moment for that, Never,* and this time it's him for real. *Just relax while I take care of things, and you'll be back in the saddle soon enough.* And for an instant my vision comes back like a strobe, I guess like how he said he could *choose* to let Ruby be conscious if he felt like it. I can feel my body, in this abrupt flickering way, enough to register my legs walking briskly. And I can see enough of the world to understand that we're angling fast toward the 7th Avenue subway.

That's it for a while. I try not to fight, to just bob around in my black Jell-O galaxy. Because, I mean, I *told* him he could. We have a deal and this is my end of it. I can still think, but in a drowsy way where the processing goes at about half the normal speed. But I do get that this is why he usually waited until Ruby was asleep to take over her body; he didn't want her struggling. He didn't want to spend the effort to keep stuffing her down. Dashiell's always hated competition.

I don't know how much time passes, but after a while he starts giving me little two-second windows onto where we are, maybe just for kicks. An ancient man in ragged blue stands in front of us in a subway car, swaying and singing to himself with his eyes closed. Some strange language; high, throbbing notes. Later there's an ugly street with run-down salons and a live-chicken-slaughtering place venting a stink of blood and rotting feathers. A man walks by with a flailing bird stuffed under his arm. It's definitely not a part of New York I've ever seen before, because I guess I've mostly seen the fancy parts. Then an African-American girl about my age, with corkscrew hair and a pink satin jacket, dancing down the sidewalk—I think just because Dashiell thinks she's pretty.

And then nothing, nothing, nothing, until the darkness has a beat.

I hear something outside the isolation chamber where Dashiell's got me stuffed. I'm not even sure I hear it because he wants me to; it might just be so loud that he can't completely keep it out. There was that time Ruby overheard us talking, so maybe his censorship isn't always a hundred percent? A grinding noise. Then I get a quick glimpse: Dashiell's hand—or technically that would be *my* hand—holding some buzzing, growling tool I don't recognize. Did he shoplift it in my body? My hand vibrates and the tool chews away at a rusty chain. I try to look around and I just manage to see a boarded-up, rat-packed, fire-singed house a few feet away—this must be the place. Then Dashiell gets irritated; I'm grabbing for control, after all. He practically slams my consciousness back down into nowhere.

But I find myself pushing back. Not even on purpose. I just want to see what's happening, and it turns out that Dashiell can't completely stop me, though I can feel he's trying hard. It's like my mind crests to the surface—and I see a busted-open mailbox shuffling with age-crisped Chinese takeout menus and crumbling leaves. The rusty chain, popped and dangling. Then Dash shoves me under. Then I'm up again, gulping at external reality—his hand, or that would be *my* hand, digging under all the crap. No wonder he prefers to do this with somebody who's asleep, all weak and passive. Under again. If these were our bodies struggling and not our minds, Dashiell would be sitting on my head. In a completely nonmaterial way, I mean, that's kind of what it feels like.

I'm in the darkness and he slams me down hard: I'm knocked someplace where I can't do anything but fall. All at once I'm sliding deeper, through these jagged icebergs of detritus that I can barely make out. After a while I feel myself tap down in whirls of reddish blur.

Then maybe I'm adjusting to being here, because it's starting to look like I'm in some kind of factory made out of shadows. I'm able to see shapes that resemble machinery: cylinders and gears lit in smoky neon green and flashing scarlet. In fact, whatever this place is, it's looking pretty familiar.

And I hear footsteps. Soft and stealthy, but whispering closer. Definitely more than one person; maybe three or four?

The crazy thing is that the steps aren't coming from the outside world, where Dashiell's controlling the show again.

They're coming from the darkness behind me. *Land of the Dead,* Dash called it. And I know he hears them too, because I can feel his terror blasting through me.

RUBY SLIPPERS

Liv wants to hang out after school, and I'm glad to go back to her house since I need anything in the world that can distract me from the memory of what I saw last night: Everett speaking with Dashiell's voice, Everett animated by Dashiell's will. I would drive myself insane wondering if there was any way that could be untrue—because possibly, possibly Everett dreamed he was Dashiell and sleepwalked to my door. Possibly he was dreaming so hard that the dream took him over, filled him completely like helium swelling a balloon, and he talked to me and hugged me convinced he was our big brother. Alive again, warm and breathing.

But I can't take that idea seriously, because I promised Dash I believed in him. And besides, I saw how Ever was acting today, colored all over by Dashiell's way of being. I *know* the truth.

I have trouble focusing on what Liv is talking about, though—boys and clothes and teachers and clothes and more boys. It's not that I think those things don't matter, because I do, and I want Liv to get everything that's important to her, Aidan Clarke and that rhinestone-speckled sweater and a rain of flowers whenever she's sad. But it's hard to care about those things as much as I used to, because all of them are within the realm of possibility: even Aidan, even if Liv doesn't think so.

My heart now belongs to the impossible, to everything that is luminous and ascendant and free of everyday tedium. Whatever cannot, absolutely *cannot* be is the new center of the universe for me, and everything that used to matter is far away, orbiting so slowly and dimly that I can barely remember what it looked like. I know I won't miss my old world, either.

How could I not feel this way, when my brother who died has come back to me?

It's November; the light gives up early. In Liv's window the sky is first that incredible violet-blue: a blue that's so beautifully close to impossible that I can really *see* it. Then plain, dull, starless black—and Liv's house is up past Court Street, so it means a long walk over the Gowanus Canal and then through the industrial areas near it, which can feel a little spooky after dark. "I should go."

"You can wait for my mom if you want. She'll drive you. She might not be home until later, though."

I don't want to wait, not for anything. The night outside looks vast and wild enough to encompass anything, no matter how extraordinary. It looks big enough to hold *me*. "That's okay. I feel like walking."

Liv looks kind of worried; she's always nervous about muggers and perverts and creatures spun out of candy wrappers and air. But she doesn't say anything, because she doesn't want me to make fun of her. There're a few more minutes of chitchat to get through, but then I'm outside and in my new world where the crazier something seems, the truer it has to be.

And since I am a walking miracle myself, I believe I'll be perfectly at home here.

As I step through her front door I completely lose track of myself for a long, drowsy moment. My mind disappears inside a black velvet kiss; that's been happening to me recently, and I'm learning to accept it.

Then I'm back on Liv's stoop, conscious again, holding tight to her railing and staring down at a potted rosebush by the gate. One wilted apricot flower still clings there, its petals shuddering.

At first I don't want to go straight home. The night is so fresh and cool that it crystallizes in my hair, bright and flashing. I wander down Smith Street, and in the store windows the dresses waft on invisible gusts and wave to me. For a while I sit in a café sipping cocoa and just absorbing how beautiful everything is, every last shadow on the sidewalk outside.

But then it occurs to me that Dashiell might be waiting for me back at our house, Dashiell in Everett's body. I've known for days now Dash needs us, that we have to be ready, and maybe I'm finally about to learn why; I can't just leave him hanging! I jump up and run out into the street again. A few more blocks and I've reached the Union Street Bridge. The Gowanus has its usual rank, yellowish smell but I stop for a moment anyway to catch my breath and watch the rippling reflections: brilliance suspended on the dark.

"Ruby," someone calls. The voice is a little girl's—nine years old, maybe? The freakiest part is that it sounds like it's coming from *under* the bridge, where nobody should be, especially not a child. The Gowanus is incredibly polluted and you should be careful to stay away from the water. "Ruby! Down here."

I'm already bending over the railing, searching for the girl who's calling me; I mean, apart from the fact that she recognizes me from *somewhere,* she probably needs help. There's some kind of platform made of squared-off logs sticking out under the walkway, I can see it now, with a ladder leading down to it. I can make out a mass of darkness that might be a person, but it's way too big to be a child.

"Ruby!" the dark shape calls. "Ruby, come down to me! Please!"

Shivers dart through me and my heart lurches. "No!"

"Ruby Bohnacker," the figure calls, wheedling now, "*please* come." And then it bursts into peals of childish laughter.

And it steps out to where a beam of light projects from a building on shore, showing itself to me.

It's a man, probably in his late fifties, gray and thick-bodied and bearded. He's still laughing hysterically in his fourth-grade voice—though now I can hear how forced it is, an awful piercing falsetto.

"See," he says once he catches his breath—if I should even call this person *he,* because the high, sassy tone and the fluttering hands and the giggling are all so baby-girlish, even prissy, that it's repulsive to see. My back is prickling. "See, it's too hard with a stranger! They won't come. It's easier for me because I can look so innocent sometimes, but I still have to try and try, over and over and *over.* . . ."

Innocent? The guy looks halfway between an old hippie and

a serial killer. I should run, I know it—but on the other hand if he moves for that ladder I'll see right away, and I'll have a decent head start. "Who are you?"

The man shrugs. "You can call me Mabel, if you'd like to. I don't mind if you do or you don't."

I can't get used to that birdlike voice warbling out of that oversized, hairy face, with its watery blue eyes turned up to look at me. "Mabel," I say; it's definitely a name for the voice, not for the hulking body. "Mabel. How do you know about me?"

"From Dashiell," Mabel says, like that was an idiotic question. "He told me. He showed me. He said it was nice being with me, because it was almost like having his little sister back again."

That does it, I'm shivering and the prickling on my back and neck needles me like ice. "How—" I start. "I mean, *when* did you meet Dashiell?" I can barely choke the words out. "Was it recently?"

Mabel shrugs again, but now *she's* smiling. Because it's unavoidable now: whatever this person looks like, it's a *she*. It's a horrible smile, the smile of a sadistic child crushing a puppy's foot.

"Do you want to know what I did?" she asks. She waves both hands up and down her thick man's body. "I blew a big hole through him. With a gun. *He* was the one who put the gun there, but he was still so surprised that his eyes popped out! And then they rolled away."

My legs are wavering under me, but as far as I can see the man is fine. There's no blood on his clothes or anything, so probably what Mabel is telling me is just some kind of eerie make-believe.

"Do you mean—are you saying you shot the man you're inside right *now*?"

A gray tabby cat comes stalking along the bridge's railing and Mabel glances at it nervously; it's still fifteen feet away, but heading in our direction in a weirdly determined manner. Then another cat follows, a puffy, swaying marmalade; I've never seen *cats* on this bridge before. Another, just behind: a slim tuxedo.

"I don't care to speak to you any longer," Mabel mutters, not looking at me. "You should go away."

"Mabel, I need to understand what you've been telling me! When you met Dashiell—"

"Be quiet! And anyway I'm not the only one who knows about you!"

The gray cat leading the procession rubs against my elbow. Then it pounces, a smoky blur plunging straight for Mabel's big bearded face.

She, or he, screams. And leaps into the canal, splashing through water so toxic that I've been warned all my life to never even *touch* it.

The gray cat lands heavily on the wooden platform, back bristling, and bursts into a long yowl. The others—and there are more of them now, a lot more, like they've whispered in from nowhere—thump down after him, twisting together in a knot of fur inches from the water. All of them are screaming and spitting after Mabel, now swimming fast for a barge near the shore. Except for a single, curious glance from the fat orange one, none of the cats seem much interested in me.

But that doesn't stop me from running, charging frantically off the bridge and up the street, my stomach and throat full of something that feels like bubbling lead and my heart banging at my ribs. I know I just saw something very important, but I can't guess what it means.

Should I have known? Just because impossible things are true in this world, that doesn't mean all of them are miracles. And it doesn't mean they won't try to hurt me.

NEVER-EVER

* * * *

I'm alone, in this vague, green-spangled space vibrating with the steps of people I can't see. Adrenaline hits the air like a shock wave; I don't know who's out there or what they want, but I know they're coming after me. I want to run, but for a long moment—too long—it's like I can't remember how to control my own legs, or where they are under me. I can feel Dashiell's anxiety raining down from somewhere far away, saying, *Move, Never, move, Never, move!* The shiver of those steps is closing in on three sides of me, now; they've almost got me surrounded.

Then my feet solidify out of the dream-mush and instantly explode into motion. What I see is so jumbled, though, all flashing golden tubes and red-rimmed pits. I'm weaving from side to side, trying to guess which slab of darkness is a way through and which is just a wall. The people behind me are running too, and the pulses from their steps surge up my legs and drive my fear higher and tighter in my chest. I crash into some kind of blockage I can't even see, roll off sideways, and purely by luck slide into a green-lit gap that wasn't there an instant before.

I'm not going to make it, though. This is their territory, they must know every bend in the place, and they can just herd me into a dead end. *Dash, I can't get out of here. Dash, please help.* I'm thinking it but I know it's useless. He's not about to risk himself for me; I'm on my own.

My foot hits something like greased space and I go into a swooping slide, teeter, and catch myself at an angle on some kind of tank. The footsteps are pounding so close that I can't stop myself from gawking back at the people chasing me.

I mean, if they are people. From what I see that's not really the right word to use. Their heads are humanesque but huge, bobbing things a yard tall, and they look like the machinery does, made of glowing red and yellow lines that shine out of pitch blackness. They loom over me, like their sharp-edged lights are about to carve me to pieces.

"Everett Bohnacker," someone says—a thin, creaking voice—and laughs. "Everett, you enjoyed meeting your brother here, didn't you? Why would we be any worse?"

But now Dash is next to me, out of nowhere; he's looking exactly like he did when he murdered me, barefoot and shirtless. Before I can understand it—how can he be simultaneously in charge of my body and down *here*?—he's got me by my elbow, because it appears that I have one at the moment. And he's pulling hard. He must know his way around here pretty well, because he yanks me through this slippery patch of night that looks too small to put a hand through.

He drags me to my feet and we're running again, his hand crushing mine. It might make me feel better having Dash with me if I didn't hear how his breath was whistling, if I couldn't feel the terror popping in his muscles as he pauses to insinuate me straight through what looks like a wall. We emerge into some kind of narrow corridor and all the blinking random colors are gone. For a moment we balance against each other in dead blackness.

Then a green-streaked haze washes in at our feet, throwing our knife-thin shadows up the passage. They're after us again and we plunge on. At a bend I glance back. Those blob-headed guys are maybe thirty feet behind, glowing scarlet, shining green— and *that's* what it is, they almost look like old neon signs, except of course they're three-dimensional. I can see their light pulsing into the corners of my eyes when they're gaining on us, dimming a little, surging brighter again.

And then I start wheezing. I'm gasping and doubling up as I run, and I still can't get enough air. That's right: even in this insane place, I still have my damned asthma.

Even though it's not a real place, not in the normal sense. It's probably not real air. Whatever, I'm sucking at it as hard as I can with my lungs aching, and my legs are starting to buckle beneath me. "Never," Dash says, dragging at me. "Never, there's no time for this!"

Like I can help it. I'm almost on the floor. And its glossy cement is swarming with reflected red and yellow lights.

Dashiell is going to abandon me here, that's what he's going to do. He's going to leave me as a gasping, broken sacrifice for those not-human things and save his own ass. Obviously. Because treachery is the essence of who my brother really is, at least when you know him the way I do. Realizing that is just making me wheeze harder, and tears start up in my eyes because I'm so desperate to finally just finally please *breathe*.

Then Dash throws himself on top of me, knocking me flat. And drives both of us straight through the pavement.

I guess he's counting on me to break his fall, because it's a long way down.

Except that I don't land anywhere. All at once I'm sitting on piss-reeking cement with my head tipped against a steel security gate. My breath is coming in, hard and rapid. I stagger to my feet, so dizzy that I can barely get a grip on myself, and look around. It looks like the loading dock of a warehouse. Dash must have parked my body here before he came plunging after me, and it's probably just luck that no one got around to robbing or killing me while my brain was out of commission. I'm in the middle of some horrible part of what must be Queens, all caved-in buildings and psychotic drunks gabbling and fighting with imaginary demons. The sky is getting dusky, and I am completely and hopelessly lost.

But it's still a huge improvement over what I just left.

Get us to the subway, Never, Dash says in my thoughts. *Head for Manhattan. I'll be back soon.*

So he didn't abandon me, exactly. He shot me back to the surface, back to driving my own body around, while he stayed down below with those glow-headed freaks.

As in, did Dashiell just *save* me? Save me by endangering himself? It's hard to believe, but I can't logically see my way to a different conclusion, at least not right at the moment. I have to move, though, not stop and think about this. There's a guy in the middle of the street staggering and stabbing at the air with his fingers; his eyes are starting to home in on me and he's heading my way.

I walk at first, trying to act casual, but I can't maintain it. There's still too much fear slamming around in me and I start to get the twitchy feeling that the homeless guy's head is inflating, flashing, twisting with red and green beams. I burst into a run, telling myself at every step that I need to calm down, that I'll only attract attention and that's a really bad idea here.

I round a corner with a seedy bodega on it and make myself wheel to a stop. I peer back up the street I just left, pressing up against the faded ads for beer. My face is full of greenish-beige tits in a vaguely gold bikini and my breath surges through my lungs again and again, just like it never ditched out on me.

There's no one and nothing back there. Okay. I'm getting a grip, now. The subway. "So where would I find the freaking subway around here, Dash?"

No answer. I guess that's fair. He's busy.

There's a weirdly heavy bundle stuffed against my guts; I'm wearing a bomber jacket with elastic at the bottom so whatever it is doesn't fall out. It makes a muffled clacking sound as I walk, so there must be more in it than just the money. I'm not crazy about walking around a neighborhood like this with thousands and thousands of dollars on me, though I guess I don't look like the type who would have much of anything valuable. But I sure don't look like I belong here, either.

In the distance I can see an intersection that seems brighter and busier than the rest of this mess of sort-of-city. Lots of cars zipping along, maybe stores. That's probably a good place to start looking.

It takes me at least half an hour of wandering around, and the dark is really settling in. But at last I see a lit-up green globe in the distance, the kind that marks a station entrance. It turns out that we're at the very end of the line.

This part I know how to do. I stop at a newsstand and buy a candy bar before I go in, because I'm getting famished. Head down the stairs, blip my way through the turnstile, head down some more.

It's all so everyday, so *normal*, that I feel kind of disappointed. Hey world, I'm just your average, generic nobody after all. The adrenaline has totally washed out of me and I just feel drab and tired. I know I was in terrible danger, but now that I'm out it's hard not to feel sort of nostalgic about it; I was scared, sure, but also bright and vital in a way that I usually only get to imagine.

The train comes, and I sit through station after station that I've never even heard of before. The whole time I'm thinking mean things, like how stupid that woman's dress is, and how the guy spreading his legs three feet apart isn't fooling anybody into thinking that it's because his dick is so big. *Sorry, dude.* Seriously, I hate everyone.

I guess I shouldn't have worried. We're just cruising through the tunnel into Manhattan when Dash comes back. And then I can't hate the people on the train very effectively anymore, because I can't even see them. I'm not in the glowing factory this time. Just in the darkness.

I don't fight him, and he doesn't bother giving me little glimpses of the world now. I get the feeling he might be pretty pissed off with me. For all I can tell, I stay in the darkness for hours on end.

The next thing I know, we're walking down a nice-looking street full of fancy boutiques and restaurants—where? It looks like the East Village, probably pretty late at night, since all the bars are packed and clamoring. Dash is still controlling my body, but I guess he's decided to let me be conscious for a while. We head up to one of the apartment buildings, and Dash presses a buzzer on the intercom.

"Yes?"

"It's Everett Bohnacker," Dashiell says, and he really manages to sound almost exactly like me, though I guess using my vocal cords makes that a lot easier. "Dashiell's brother. I need to speak to you privately."

A sharp bark of laughter comes through the speaker, and the door buzzes open.

We head inside the lobby—lots of black stone—and walk straight to the elevator. I must be slow on the uptake, but it's just sinking in now that we're going to see *her*—I guess I somehow thought Dash would wait a day or two? I'm starting to kick and spasm and it must annoy him, because my awareness starts kind of strobing again. Thin slices of blackout alternate with moments where I can see our surroundings. So I'm not conscious when we get on the elevator, but I get a flash of the numbers going up. And for a moment I feel my hand fumbling in that package inside my jacket, and pulling out an object I can't identify. Whatever it is, it gets stuffed into the back pocket of my jeans.

I don't see us step out on Paige's floor, or walk into her apartment.

I do hear my own voice talking—but way, way more confidently than I usually would. Dash is still pretending to be me, just a new and improved version. And she's there, inches away from me, looking skeptical and wearing this silvery robe that clings to her body. Every time I inhale I smell the perfume in her black hair. And then my hand pulls the package out of my jacket and flings it on this tiny silver table. It's wrapped in layers and layers of half-rotten newspapers, and when it hits the table the paper splits wide.

Jesus. We didn't bring Paige a pile of hundred-dollar bills. No wonder that package was so heavy.

Gold coins roll chiming over the table and shudder on the floor. Light flashes and spins, and Paige is staring in shock from the gold, to me, to the gold. And then I'm walking toward her with that swaggering stride, pushing her back against a wall. I can't understand why she doesn't just punch me in the face. Seriously, if I could stop my body from acting this way I would do it, but Dashiell's got a good hold on me now and he lifts my hand and runs a single finger around the side of her jaw and down her neck.

And under the edge of her robe.

Everything goes back to black, and when I know where I am again all my clothes are off. And so are Paige's.

I guess Dashiell is messing with me, because he doesn't let me feel what's happening for very long. Just long enough to drive me completely insane: her skin sliding under mine, her mouth moaning against my neck. It's all Dashiell, and I'm just along for the ride, but of course she's got no way of knowing that. Why would she let this happen?

But maybe I can guess: she doesn't have to consciously know he's here to pick up on something, like she probably thinks I just *remind* her of the guy she loved. I'm feeling almost sorry for her when my awareness blips out again, though God knows I try to get back to the surface.

She was so *soft*. So soft all over. A blur of shining black hair and satiny arms and wet lips; so, so many times over the most beautiful girl I've ever seen.

And then I'm lying next to her, gasping a little, and she's up on her elbow looking down at me. "We both miss Dashiell," she says, kind of coldly. "And you're more like your brother than anyone would think at first glance, aren't you, Everett? It's natural that we would try to comfort each other. It's nothing to be ashamed of."

I guess ashamed is how I must look. Seems reasonable.

Dashiell is nowhere that I can feel right now, though I try to sense him in this frantic, lurching way. I'm on my own and I'm completely out of my depth. I'm so afraid of making an ass of myself that I can't say anything.

Paige stares at me for a moment, then gets up and starts getting dressed—and her body is so far beyond anything I could have imagined, and she's pulling on the most amazing lace underwear. Then she turns, and there in my face is the last thing in the world I want to think about: it's pretty subtle, really, but her stomach is just a little too round. Dashiell's freaking baby.

"I have to get to work. Did Dashiell tell you? I get paid to go to parties." She laughs, maybe bitterly. "That's my life, Everett. Standing there being seen. I'm wallpaper."

I know I should say something—something about how her heart is even more beautiful than her face, maybe? But even thinking it makes me feel like a dork, and anyway it's probably not true.

Pretend to be Dashiell. Okay. *Do what he would do.*

I get up without saying anything and kiss her gently, first on the forehead, then on the cheek. Then, though I really have to work up my nerve to do it, on the mouth.

She just had sex with me, or with what she *thought* was me. So maybe she won't mind.

Now that I think about it, we just had sex on the same bed where Dashiell died.

"I should get going, too," I make myself say—or maybe *he* helps me say it. "You have a wonderful evening, sweet thing."

Ugh—that *definitely* wasn't me. Not by myself.

I need to get my clothes on and get the hell out of here, before it can get any worse. But Dashiell doesn't let me get dressed fast. Nope, we have to take our freaking time. Even worse, I've been wearing that moronic hot dog T-shirt all day, and Paige *sees* me in it.

When I pull my jeans on, I feel something strange stuck in my back pocket: a hard, ragged lump shaped like a horseshoe.

At least I get a little longer to watch Paige shimmying into a skintight shiny blue skirt and a metallic leather bustier. Baby-blue lipstick. Smears of weird colors on her eyes. The whole time she's watching me in a funny way; does she suspect there's something weird going on? "Everett? I hope you covered your tracks. No one knows where to look for that gold you *found*, do they?"

"It's fine, love," Dash says with my voice. "I've taken care of everything. There's nothing for you to worry about."

Then I'm finally free to move, and I'm walking past that pile of gold coins and out the door and pushing the elevator button.

And wondering the whole way if what we just did to Paige was some kind of bizarre rape. I mean, she absolutely has a right to know who's in bed with her, doesn't she? Like, she can't agree to sleeping with Dash when she has no idea he's here, so it was sort of like we tricked her. I hope that doesn't make it completely wrong, though, because even if I didn't have much to do with it, I can't say it wasn't the greatest thing that's ever happened to me.

Or that I'm not dying to do it again. I could swear I feel

Dashiell grinning. *And how did you enjoy your positive reinforcement, Never-Ever?*

I'm not sure which I want more: to stab myself to death right now, for being such an asshole.

Or to go on being Dashiell's puppet for as long as I possibly can.

RUBY SLIPPERS

When I get home it's already nine, and the awful thing is that I open our front door onto darkness and emptiness. And even once I've locked the door behind me and checked the lock over and over again, and turned on every light in the whole house, the aching emptiness filling the rooms doesn't go away at all. I can feel the darkness clawing at the back of every brilliantly lit surface, waiting to seize me again. Our dad isn't home, that's normal enough, but Everett isn't either, which is a lot more unusual. And he doesn't answer his phone, though I must call him five times in a row. I guess Dashiell is with him and maybe that should make me less worried, but it doesn't; not now that I've talked to Mabel. Not now that I've seen what's moving through the Brooklyn night.

Mabel's babyish voice, so discordant and so out of place in her hulking body—it was too much like the way I heard another voice recently, talking out of someone to whom it definitely didn't belong.

Then something occurs to me, and I start searching under the furniture and inside all the closets—just in case one of those cats got in here somehow. I don't find anything except some balls of dust and a dozen lost socks under Ever's bed upstairs, but that doesn't make me feel any better and I keep pacing through all the rooms and charging up and down the staircase. I would turn on music to bury the awful quiet, if I weren't so afraid of what else it might drown out. I'm listening so hard that the silence starts to whine in my ears: the music of nothingness, the shrill complaint of the void.

And what about the windows? They're closed in this weather, of course they must be, but possibly not all of them are locked. So I start my patrol all over again: first upstairs through Dad's bedroom and his tiny study, Everett's room, the bathroom, and then the room that used to be Dashiell's but got converted into a guest room. With every one of Dash's belongings cleared out of it, and all new furniture, the room feels lonely and barren and nobody ever goes in there. The windows are all fine, locked tight, and my breathing starts to flow just a little more smoothly. I gallop downstairs again and survey my own bedroom, then head to the kitchen, tugging back the striped drapes to check the latch. I can see our stoop from here, and the flowerpots that edge the brick steps. Lamplight gilds the tree just outside the window, making its meshed branches into a golden cage. A few dry leaves fidget in the wind.

And in that tree, something is gleaming. Just like on the night when I first heard Dashiell and Everett talking, two sequin-bright dots hover above a bare branch. Animal eyes: their twinned-moon shine. Oh, so they've been watching us for days now, circling our house. That sense I've had of horror tracking us, closing in: it's here. That's what Mabel was telling me.

There's a smear of gray as the cat jumps down onto the railing and then out of sight, but I see enough to recognize it, and I would have known anyway—because I'm forced to know a thousand times more than I can understand, and to feel more than I can begin to arrange into meaning. All there is around me now is possibility, possibility with no underlying sense it can cling to.

Possibility, and a gray tabby cat that can only be the same cat I saw leaping off the bridge earlier tonight with its claws outstretched, frantic to sink them into Mabel's bearded face, eager to rip flesh. Someone else might say that it has to be a different cat—because why would some random animal have followed me home? But I have no choice except to know.

I'm not the only one who knows about you. That's the last thing Mabel said before she plunged into the canal. The only one of what?

But really, don't I know that too?

Mabel never did tell me when she met Dashiell, or when Dash told her all about me. She didn't happen to mention if he was still breathing at the time.

I go back to calling and texting Everett, and at last around 10:45 I get a message in return. But Ever isn't the one who wrote it. *Don't fret anymore, Ru. We're all perfectly safe. Delete this.*

And I do. I do what Dashiell tells me. Even though the part about how we're safe is so very, very untrue. Just in time, because a key is turning in the lock and I shove my phone into my pocket with anxiety buzzing through my hands. Dad walks in and sees me standing in the kitchen doorway, and he must notice something wrong with my expression because he looks at me for a long time.

"Ruby. Everett texted me to say that he was playing video

games at a friend's house. He wasn't any more specific than that. Do you know what friend that might be?"

"Not really," I say—and for half a moment I want to say, *Everett is with someone, all right, but I wouldn't call him a friend, exactly.* "But maybe Noah? Noah Somethingberg? They've been hanging out recently."

Dad nods but he doesn't stop staring at me. Trying to see into my mind. "As long as he's home by eleven. Didn't the two of you have homework?"

"Not too much," I say. "Ever probably got it done this afternoon." And then it takes all my strength not to break out laughing, not to choke and cry with laughter, because to even be talking about something like homework is so empty and absurd. The world we're in now is one where ordinary words like that can't stick to the things we're talking about. No matter how hard those words try to keep on going in the way they're used to, they can't *mean* anything anymore.

He kisses me and tells me it's bedtime, but I can see he's worried—that I'm lying, and maybe that Ever is taking drugs. It's always been his worst fear, that one of us might end up like Dashiell. And I feel sorry for him, I do, but there's nothing I can say that would make things any better. There isn't even a language I could use.

I go to bed and watch the night creeping across my ceiling. It's way after midnight when Everett finally comes home. And I wait, listening to Ever climb the stairs, listening to the water humming in the pipes, because Dashiell *has* to come to me; I have to tell him everything that happened and ask him what it means. Until he explains what I saw tonight, I won't know if I can so much as walk across the floor without slipping through.

But Dash doesn't show. I wait for him, but sleep starts rising up. It's swallowing me.

And in it there are dreams.

I know where I am at once, because it's the last place I ever wanted to see again—that sluggish river, the muddy bank, the rows of leaning shacks behind me. I'm walking so close to the edge that my feet sink into the muck and the prints I leave brim with water, black as pupils, all of them looking at me. Because that's the biggest difference: when I drowned in this river the whole landscape felt deserted, just Dashiell and me and endless loneliness. Now everything is watchful, and those broken houses swell with unseen eyes.

It's just a dream, I tell myself. *It is very, very not real.* But after everything I've been through the distinction doesn't feel as compelling as it used to. Just the fact that I'm back here makes it feel way too much like this is an actual place, and if that's true then maybe the things that happened here before might be just a little bit real too. I can't help staring at the water, dreading the possibility that Dashiell might be out there once again, white arms arching lazily from the current.

The river stays vacant and slippery under coils of light reflected from nowhere. But something pale shifts in the corner of my eye, right beside me, and I jerk toward it just as he slips his arm around my shoulder.

"You can dream any dream but this one," Dash says. "This isn't a good place for you, my sweet Ruby-Ru. It's not ideal for me, either, truthfully. Come with me now."

The water sheeting his arm drenches my dress where he's

touching me. He must have emerged from the river moments ago, and my back stiffens even as he pulls me closer. "Dashiell . . ." I know there are questions that I need to ask him, that something awful and urgent happened earlier, but now I can't remember what it was. "Dashiell, how can we be here?"

"You're dreaming, Miss Slippers. But you've slipped too deep in your dreams tonight. I'll show you the way out of here." His voice is soft but there's a hint of tension inside it, and even though I'm a little afraid of him—since we're back in the worst dream of my life, how can I know what he'll do?—I let him guide me along the bank. Last time I saw him here he was naked, but now he's wearing blue jeans so sopping that the wet denim scrapes at my hip. Droplets weep down my thigh. Ahead of us the shore is vague and so jumbled with detritus that it looks like brownish fog.

"So are you dreaming, too?" For some reason it seems like an important question.

"*I'll sleep when I'm dead*, you mean, Ru? *Perchance to dream?* It's not like that. I can only experience other people's dreams now. Not even many of those."

Bitterness edges his tone and I can't keep on distrusting him, not when he's lost so much, and so young. I stop where we are and bury my face against his damp chest. He sighs, maybe impatiently, but he still wraps me tight in his arms and kisses my hair.

"Dashiell?" I can't bring myself to ask him if he murdered me, not even if he did it here, in this place where the usual rules don't count. But I have to ask *something*. "Dash, I mean, if this is a dream—then reality doesn't apply here? Whatever happens— it means something completely different than it would if it happened when I'm awake?"

Dashiell leans back to look at me. "Nothing here is real, but that doesn't mean this isn't a dangerous place for you. Unreality can follow you out of here by circuitous routes, Ruby-Ru, and dreams can have consequences years after you think they're long gone. That's why you need to do exactly what I tell you, sweetness. Come along now."

He pulls me but I hold still, just a moment longer. "But Dash . . ." I'm not sure how to say this; every way I can think of to formulate it seems absurd. "*Love* still must apply here, even if reality doesn't. Isn't that right?"

Dash looks hard at me, and maybe he understands. Maybe he knows what I'm really asking him: *Please, Dashiell, tell me it's not true. Tell me that dream was only a figment, something invented by the ugliest parts of my mind, and you had nothing to do with it. The you that's here now holding me can't be the same as the Dashiell that drowned me.*

"Always, my Ru. Love always applies. No matter what happens, you need to remember how absolutely true that is. All right?"

"Okay," I tell him. "Okay. I'll come now, wherever you tell me to. I'm sorry, Dash-Dot-Dot, I'm sorry. I *had* to ask."

Dashiell just smiles in response, maybe ruefully, and hustles me faster along the bank. The faintest possible vibration shivers in the mud. Is someone following us? On our right the river squirms with strange colors now, chartreuse and saffron gold and scarlet; there's nothing here in this dim haphazard mess that could possibly project shades so brilliant. And on the left a long, muddy lump lies splayed as if it had toppled from the doorway of the shack just behind.

I twist back against Dashiell's arm as we hurry along, staring at whatever that shape is, because I halfway know already. There's a sense of nagging recognition and I have to resolve the shadows roiling in my mind into *something*.

It's a man, tall and thickset and bearded. His skin is gray and there's a huge round hole where most of his chest should be: a dark passage, a way through to a deeper nowhere. His eyes are wide open and the sockets are empty. Pinkish animals scramble from the hollow in his ribs; at first I think crabs must be devouring him, and I gasp. Dashiell hears me and turns to see what I'm seeing, then jerks me away and slaps his hand over my eyes.

But not before I see enough to know that it's Mabel, or the body she was wearing anyway. Not before I've realized that those creatures eating the corpse have tiny human hands, as dainty as the hands of dolls. "Mabel!" I yell. "Dash, that's what I need to tell you! She—I saw her tonight—and she was talking about you."

Dashiell's squeezing me from behind, his palm still blinding my eyes, the weight of his body bending me toward the ground. It feels almost like he's squeezing me *through* something, maybe a snarl of roots? There's a rapid twist and he lets me go, then shoves me headlong into darkness.

MABEL

* * * * *

It is the silliest person who sees it happen and still doesn't know anything. I can drop Old Body in the park, and when he wakes up on the grass with his clothes all wet and sticky he won't know how he got there. He won't know it was me. But he saw me with the gun. He saw his blood fly out at me. He heard his feet drum on the wood floor, stagger, stomp, bumble backward from the blast that opened him like a doughnut. Because he didn't believe it was happening, he didn't know to die for a while. I waited. He died and made room for me. Then I sat in his head while he rocked back and forth, and I listened to him whimper *justadream justadream.*

Now he's been me every night for a whole week. But he doesn't know anything. He only knows it doesn't help to sleep, because he wakes up tired and sick-feeling. He only knows that he hears my voice in his head at night; *notgoingcrazy notgoingcrazy* he says, and nobody hears him but me.

Sure you are, I tell him, and he still doesn't know who's inside him, the very same little dollgirl in the white lace who called to him, oh help me sir please, and he said *poorlittlething* and he came and bang! *You sure are going crazy. Crazier than a monkey!* So stupid he deserves anything I do with him. I won't ever say I'm sorry, not even while he's sick all over himself from the stinking water.

But the Ruby-girl is even sillier. Because she saw her big brother drown her, and she knows he's not with the other dead people like he's supposed to be. And oh, whoops, I even *told* her what I did to the old body on me. But she still won't understand how he's sneaking inside her, because *ohDashiell Dashiell-wouldn'thurtme*. And so oh well, I shouldn't have bothered to warn her. Why warn somebody who won't listen to what you're saying? Too stubborn or too stupid or too *loveme loveme*?

Except *they* don't want her to understand anything. That's what I don't know: why? Why don't they want her to understand about Dashiell? They know all about her. They know where he's hiding. So why don't the cats come and rip her open so he can't stay in her, instead of chasing me for just a little bit of talking to Ruby? I was curious to meet her, after all the Dashiell whispering. I knew he was out of her, far away, and so he couldn't do anything to stop me.

But if they don't want her to know, then I *do* want her to know! Whatever they want to *neverever* happen I want to make it happen and tell them ha! I am not a servant girl, I am from a very good family, everybody always told me. Ninety-eight years they think they can order me here and there, and what to do, but I'm out now and I'm too fast for them and I say ha!

Unless he dies too, my old body, and then I won't have a home here anymore. That's what happened to the last one, she died and spilled me back again, and then everything I remembered about my sisters got snatched to punish me for running away from them. But can *they* kill Old Body and send me back? I don't know.

NEVER-EVER

✳ ✳ ✳ ✳ ✳

I'm so exhausted that I'm completely out of my mind and it takes everything I've got just to make it home, get upstairs, and get to bed. I don't feel Dashiell at all; no consciousness but mine in here, so there's no way I can try to ask him what happened. He already must be gone, then, into the light or into the better world people like to talk about. It's just like him, to come smashing through my skull, take whatever he wants, and leave me hollowed out and aching. It's like him to abandon us all over again, forever this time, and not bother even saying goodbye.

Whatever. I've got to sleep and in the morning I'll probably be in the biggest trouble of my life. The insanity will all be over, and I'll have to get used to being a nobody again. I guess I should be relieved—Dash is gone, just the way I wanted, and Ruby is safe, and no matter how huge and ridiculous the world is I'm small and singular inside it. Again. I don't have to worry anymore that my life will be exciting or adventurous or anything like that. And even if I miss him way more than I should, I swear I'll get over it soon.

I'm so tired I can't make myself wake up, not even when I hear someone rustling around in my room. Maybe I'm dreaming—and just a normal dream, not the extra-special kind where I get bled out like a pig—and so I don't have to deal with it.

Except that the noise keeps on going, and my brain starts to drag itself out of the sleep-swamp like some slobbering beast in an old horror movie. *Get back in there, brain!* But it won't, not when I feel a hand gently shaking my shoulder.

"Never-Ever."

It *can't* be. Can it?

"Never, I'm sorry to disturb your rest. But there are matters that we need to discuss, and I'd prefer not to keep our sweet Miss Slippers out of bed any longer than necessary."

Okay. This can't be happening. That I even *think* this is happening is just totally unacceptable.

I force my eyes open, and there it is, the horrible truth. Ruby is crouched over me, her chopped hair dragging on my face. "Dashiell . . ." I'm struggling to sit up. "Dashiell, what the hell are you thinking? Ruby . . . we agreed! You said you were going to keep out of her!"

Dashiell uses Ruby's face to grin at me, then perches on the side of my bed and sort of swags against the wall. There's enough scorched light from the window that I can see Ruby's mouth take on this smug pout.

"Jealous, Never? Don't concern yourself. We'll be spending more time together soon."

"You *know* that is not what I'm saying!" The reality is sinking in now and I'm stammering from pure frustration. "Dash, you promised! You said you'd leave Ruby out of this."

"You were the only one who said anything of the kind, Never. What I told you was that I could only be in one place at a time, and that was perfectly true."

"Get out of her! Dash, now! I'm not kidding. You can use me, you don't *need* to . . ." And then I'm half-wheezing and half-sobbing, and I have to grab my inhaler. Did I imagine that I *missed* him? It's possible to feel that way, as long as you totally obliterate all your memories of what he's actually like.

"Pah. It's too difficult for us to have a conversation like that, with me parked inside you. You can't reliably tell the difference between what I've said and what you're merely imagining, Never. Can you? And truthfully, I missed my sweet Ru today. There's no harm in my looking after my baby sister while she's dreaming, is there?"

God. What is Ruby dreaming now? "You've *looked after* her enough!"

Dashiell shrugs. I'm cracking up and he's just brushing me off. "She needed me more than you can possibly guess tonight. And in any case the connection is solidly established now, Never. With both of you. I'm free to move between you whenever I consider it appropriate. Why not accept that?"

"You're saying you'll do whatever the hell you want with us, and I can't *stop* you?" Does this mean the whole into-the-light thing is off the table, and I let him murder me for nothing?

Another shrug, and he stretches out a hand and casually ruffles my hair. I wish I could throttle him without Ruby's throat getting in the way. "Aren't there other matters that interest you, Never, besides the fact that Ruby Slippers is up and about in the night? I expected that you'd have any number of questions for me."

I'm holding myself in a tight ball, arms around my knees, but I still can't stop my legs from shaking. I'm damned if I'm playing. "Like what?"

"Oh, like, *How did you ever get away, Dash?* Like, *Who were those terrible men?*" He tips Ruby's head to rest on my wall and looks at me sidelong, and then her lips peel up in that obnoxiously confident grin. "Or maybe like, *Oh, Dash, when can we see Paige again?*"

"Yeah, well, maybe you've noticed that I'm not asking you anything." But I can't help it, my heart jumps when he says her name.

Dash ignores that. Of course he does. "I'm sorry to say that I can't get Paige for you again. Or, well, maybe I could, once or twice, but it won't be an ongoing thing, Never-Ever. I thought I should let you know that it's time to start looking elsewhere."

I can't let Dash get to me, I know it, but hearing that I need to forget about her still sends pain smacking through my chest. "Because—even with you controlling me—it was still that repulsive for her? I mean, she just hated having to touch me?" My voice is breaking up; I don't want him to hear it, but of course, of *course* I should have known how she must feel about me.

Dashiell freaking laughs at me, now, right when it's got to hurt the most. "Oh, Paige had a wonderful time. I made sure of that much, Never."

"But then—"

"Why can't you simply jump in and take over for me? Become her new boyfriend? Well, apart from the question of your age and your status more generally, Paige is certain to feel that you treated her like a prostitute. You can imagine, Never-Ever, she gets that a lot—my old dealer offered her an absolute *fortune* once, as if that would make her fall in love with him. It's become something of a sensitive issue."

All those gold coins. I'm an idiot. "But the money wouldn't have anything to do with—with what Paige would do!"

"It's not such a simple question, Never, is it? Why anyone makes the choices that they do? There might be any number of factors involved."

"And if anybody treated her like a prostitute it was you! I didn't—I never would have done anything to make her feel that way! Dash, I mean, you *know* that's true. I wouldn't have touched her at all."

"I'm sure you wouldn't, Never. You would have backed out of her apartment sputtering if she so much as glanced at you. That's why I thought you could use my help—*getting over the hump,* if I can express it that way."

It takes me a second to get what he's saying. What makes it even more obscene is that it's coming out of Ruby's mouth, and it's Ruby's lips quirking that sick smile at me, and her green eyes casting that sly look. In my window the sky is getting lighter: depressing faded gray. "Screw you, Dash."

"You know, Never-Ever, I've come to realize that I haven't been a very good brother to you. There's so much you don't know, simply, and I should have taken it on myself to show you how things are done while I was still living. Luckily, though, we've been presented with a fresh opportunity. I'm ideally positioned to help you."

"You're the one who asked for *my* help. I didn't ask you for anything."

"Your little friend Elena. I thought she was charming."

God, I'm slow. Because my brain goes *thud, thud, thud* in response, and then: *Elena? You mean Elena Shawn, from school?* And it's only after that whole sequence that I start to get mad.

"Don't you *dare* touch her."

Ruby's eyebrows shoot up. "I think she'd be a far more appropriate cynosure for your attention. Don't you? And I believe she'll be at that party on Friday, quite possibly hoping to see you."

He can do it, too. I know that. All I have to do is tell him to go ahead and he'll have Elena's dress on the floor this Friday by midnight. He'll use me to use her, and she won't have any idea; he's that good at faking my voice. She'll even wait for me to text her afterward.

"Do not freaking *breathe* on Elena. Dash, if you do, I swear I'll never stop fighting you. Okay? I'll shove back as hard as I can whenever you're in me. You won't get to do *anything*. You—"

"Oh, I'm well aware that you can complicate my situation, Never-Ever. God knows you did enough of that today."

Even if I didn't already know for sure that this is Dashiell, I would recognize him by his incredible knack for spinning the subject around on me so that he always has the upper hand. I know when he's doing it but I've never figured out how to stop him while it's happening. "You were the one who was doing almost everything."

"I *should* have been doing everything, you mean. We had an arrangement." No mention of the fact that he's blown whatever *arrangement* we had sky-high, and I guess that was always his plan. No mention of him playing me for a sucker. "Really, Never, you picked a remarkably ill-considered moment to start thrashing around on me. I needed my concentration. And in the course of doing what was necessary to maintain control, I knocked you down—deeper than I'd meant to. You nearly did immense harm to us both."

"Harm?" And I give up trying to resist; I just plain collapse and start asking him the questions he's been waiting for all along. "You mean those things chasing us? What were they, Dash?"

"I told you what that place is, Never. Didn't I?"

"You said it's the Land of the Dead."

"Specifically, it's the borderlands. A margin where the Land of the Dead overlaps the deepest reaches of the unconscious mind. So the only place, really, where the living and the dead are likely to come into contact."

"So those were dead guys."

"Dead guys. Precisely. The very same dead guys I'd already warned you against."

The men that money belongs to—these are not perfect gentlemen we're talking about. That must have been them. I'd just *assumed* he meant people who were still alive, but if this whole possession thing is a regular racket for ghosts, then I guess having gold stashed would be a smart thing for them.

"They didn't look like guys. Dead or not dead. They really didn't look like you could call them human."

Dashiell rolls his head—or that would be *Ruby's* head—in exasperation. "And are you really going to make me get pedantic on your ass, Never-Ever? Can't you sort through any of this on your own?"

I don't say anything, just glare at him—because how am I supposed to make sense of this mess without help? And it's not like Dash ever really minds an excuse to keep spouting off, anyway.

"We're dead, Never. Our bodies, the faces we used to have—those things simply aren't in effect anymore. So what you see

while you're there might incorporate a certain amount of suggestion on our side—some of us are better at nudging the im-
agery than others—but for the most part it's supplied by your
own mind."

"*You* look like yourself there. You look exactly how you
used to."

"Because you know what I'm supposed to look like. I have
my old appearance courtesy of your memories. Strangers who
are meeting you postmortem won't have that luxury."

Okay. "So they looked like scary freaks because I thought
they were scary freaks. That's what you're saying? But they were
really just ex-people?" Everything Dash has been telling me is
still sinking in and fear is just starting to kick inside me. "So
would they have killed me?"

Dash sort of lolls back, and in the dawn light I can see his
expression enough to know that there's something going on that
he doesn't understand, either. "There would be no percentage
for them in that. Killing you in the dreamspace without your
active participation. To forge the kind of connection that you
and I have, your host has to approach you voluntarily. You can't
simply hunt them down. The ritual aspect is essential." Ruby's
lips purse as he thinks about it. "But they could try to keep you
there, Never. Prevent you from waking up again."

That sounds bad. "Why would they bother?"

"To cause trouble for me, probably," Dash says. "They know
I'd do anything for you and Miss Slippers." But Ruby's mouth is
still drawn tight and her green eyes have gone shadowy. Dashiell's worried and there's something he's not telling me. As usual,
I guess.

And then a harsh buzz starts blasting from the end of the

hallway: Dad's alarm going off. Dash's expression seizes up and mine must too; I'm wondering how we can get Ruby back downstairs without Dad noticing. And wondering if he might have heard a voice that really, really shouldn't be talking in his house in the sludgy November dawn.

RUBY SLIPPERS

* * * * *

I feel my head pitching rapidly forward, and there's a loud crack as my brow collides—with what? The pain chiming through my skull brings me up blinking. I have a confused feeling that I've been falling in a dark space for a long, long time, but now I'm in a room lit by hazy yellow-gray glow and I've just slammed my head hard against what appears to be a bedpost. Someone catches me by my shoulders and pulls me upright. "Dashiell?"

A choked laugh breaks out at my back. "Not exactly, Ruby-Ru."

I turn and it's Everett in a sloppy T-shirt and a tangle of blankets. Right, this is his room with its silver metallic walls, and that glow in the sky is probably dawn, and I have no possible reason for being slouched on his bed at this hour. There are footsteps out in the hallway and a brisk knock on the door before the knob starts turning.

"What is going *on* in here?"

Dad. He's in the doorway, and I can't think my way to the tips of my own fingers, much less through to what I should say. My head is throbbing and sparks flash in my eyes.

"I think Ruby must have been sleepwalking?" Everett says, looking up at him. "She just hit her head pretty hard, and I can't tell if she's okay or not."

That was the best excuse anyone could have possibly come up with, and now that I think about it, it might even be true. Because how else did I get up here? Dad has already made the transition from peeved to concerned, and he's tipping me back to inspect my forehead. I flinch when his cool hands probe the swelling. "She'll have an impressive bump, that's certain. Ruby, *sleepwalking*? Is that how this happened?"

"I don't know," I say. "I just woke up now, I think? I mean, the last thing I knew—there was this dead body with these pink things crawling out of it? That *must* have been a nightmare, though." And Dashiell was there, dripping wet and golden in the darkness; Dash said it was a dangerous place for me and somehow he dragged me away, but I don't mention any of that.

Everett starts. "Whose body was it? Could you tell?"

"Everett, please. Your sister is disoriented. There might be a mild concussion." Dad is staring at me, looking older than he ever has before. "Ruby? Tell me today's date."

And then I see his face shift; he's sorry he asked that particular question, because it's the anniversary of something he wishes never happened at all. I'm still foggy enough that I might have had trouble remembering if I didn't see the grim pinch of his mouth.

"November nineteenth," I say. "It's Dashiell's twenty-third birthday."

"You're right," he says, a little curtly. "Maybe that's why."

"Why what?" It's Everett again and our dad glances at him, not trying to hide how annoyed he's getting.

"Does it matter? Help me get your sister downstairs, please. Ruby, you don't look well at all. You'll be staying home today."

I pull away and stand up. "I'm fine. I'm totally fine." But my vision bobs with firefly lights and I'm swaying on my feet when somebody catches me.

"I think you've proved my point, Ruby. Everett?" And then they're both holding me by my arms and maneuvering me out into the hallway and down the staircase. Once we get as far as my room I break free from them and stumble to my bed.

"Why what?" Everett asks again. "Why does it matter that it's Dash's birthday?"

A sharp glance from our dad, from Everett to me and back. "Ruby isn't the only one who was troubled by disturbing dreams, that's all. I must have had an unconscious response to the date. Ruby? Can I bring you something for breakfast?"

"I think I just need to sleep," I say. I don't know why, but I'm exhausted and everything I see looks blurred, like the dream-fog is flowing after me.

"I'll call you every few hours today. It's important that you don't sleep too deeply," Dad says. Everett is a smoky silhouette in my doorway, but I can still see him flinch.

"Dad? What did you dream?" Everett can't let it go, and I'm just starting to understand that he must have a reason. "Did you dream about Dashiell?"

"Everett, I hope you're aware that the two of us have more serious issues to address than an entirely predictable nightmare? My firstborn son died in appalling circumstances two months ago, after a life spent wreaking havoc on anyone foolish enough to care about him. Today would have been his birthday. If he had lived, maybe he would have condescended to let his family take him out for dinner tonight. Ruby would be planning his cake. Of course I dreamed about him." Dad is pulling blankets over me as he says this, but his eyes are fixed on the wall above my head; he doesn't want me to see the tears swelling on his lashes. "So, what time did you come home last night? Everett, I'm not used to that kind of behavior from you."

Then the tears break loose and he swings his face away from me; it's the first time I've seen him cry for Dashiell. Even at the funeral he was locked down, cold and rigid and blank, but maybe it just took him this long to really feel it.

"Dad?" I'm struggling to sit up and hug him but he's already walking toward my door, snapping his steps down and holding his head too straight. Because if he didn't he would crumple, I can *see* it.

"I got home around one," Everett says. "You can go ahead and punish me, I don't care. Just tell me what you dreamed." And now our dad is standing inches away from Everett, obviously wanting to escape and go sob someplace where we won't see him, but Ever won't move. He's holding both sides of the doorframe and his feet are planted so that you'd have to shove him viciously to get past. "I really need to know."

Isn't that exactly what Everett said to me, when he was asking what *I'd* dreamed about Dash?

"I truly don't think it's any of your business, Everett. And I don't appreciate your obstructing me."

"It's—" And Ever stops dead, staring into space, almost like he's listening for something. "It's *family* business. Just tell me and I'll stop bugging you."

Dad sighs and shoots a worried look my way. "I want to hear, too," I say, but only because it's normal for me to back up Everett when he needs me.

Though maybe I *don't* want to hear it. Maybe there are things it would be better not to know.

"All right, then. I dreamed that Dashiell was back in our house. I could hear his voice incessantly, coming through the walls and out of the vents and from around corners. I kept searching for him, for what felt like hours, but I couldn't find him anywhere. Now are you satisfied, Everett? Can I proceed where I like in my own home? And I suppose you're grounded, not that I'm here enough to enforce that effectively. It will have to be on the honor system."

Everett folds himself out of the way, stepping deeper into my room, and our dad stalks through. His words stay behind him, though, like curls of paper whispering on the floor: *I dreamed that Dashiell was back.*

So Dad senses it on some level, too, even if his mind can't come to terms with what it almost knows. Dashiell *is* all over this house: the walls are made of his laughter, he permeates our skin, and the breath inside my lungs has the same wave as his hair. So why can't any of us say it?

Everett is staring at me, layers of gray sliding in his eyes. He bites his lower lip and steps closer, and from the angle of his head I know he's seen something in my face.

"Ruby. You *know*, don't you? You do!"

I promised Dashiell I wouldn't say anything, though. "Know what?"

"You've been lying to me. Ruby, we never lie to each other! That is not what we do."

Everett is almost sputtering, he's so upset, and I feel heat flushing my cheeks, because he's right. No matter how badly Ever and I argue sometimes, we've always been basically loyal to each other no matter what else we do.

"Well, then you've been lying to me, too."

And there it is: everything we haven't said is seeping like cold wind between our words. "I *had* to. It didn't work, but I was trying—God, Ruby, has he *talked* to you? Just in your dreams, or—" Everett's eyes go wide for a moment, then squeeze closed, and he breaks out in shocked, gasping laughter. "Oho, that bastard. That bastard. I never even thought—Ruby, you didn't *tell* me that? You just sat there watching him use me, and you didn't say anything? Really?"

"He told me not to." The words sound thin, little scratches on the air. "He said you wanted to protect me from knowing the truth, and it would just make you worried about me."

Everett snorts. "It's my *body*, Ruby. So maybe I have a right to know what the hell he's doing with it?" He gives me a disbelieving glare. "But I guess you're completely on his side now, not mine. You don't care what he does, and you'll just tell whatever lies he wants you to?"

"He's our brother," I say. "We should all be on the same side."

"*Should,*" Everett says contemptuously. "Do you have any idea how he's been playing with *you*?" And he spins away and slams my door behind him.

I told you Dashiell needs us, I think. *I told you we had to be ready to fight for him. How could you expect me to ignore him, when he asked me to keep quiet?*

Ready to fight. Yes, those are the words that have been

whispering in my mind, ever since that day when I walked into the river. A sense of something awful, closing in on all of us.

When I turn to my window, I already know what I'll see: a dozen yellow eyes, waiting to meet mine.

NEVER-EVER

* * * *

Where is he now? That's the worst of it, he can knock back and forth between me and Ruby and I can't guess where he's hiding until the moment when he happens to feel like letting me know. He can bash Ruby's head into my freaking bedpost—and I *know* he did that on purpose, I know he wanted our dad to hear, even if I have no clue why—and then hunker down under somebody's brain and laugh at how he's had us both so duped.

I'm on my own with this mess, because I can't trust my twin sister to tell me the truth anymore. Everything I did to protect her backfired straight into my face. And I definitely won't get any information out of Dashiell unless it's convenient for him to tell me, and half of what he says is probably lies anyway. I'm so pissed I'm shaking as I get dressed, yanking up my jeans and pulling on my sweater so hard that I rip its holes even wider.

Oh. It's not my sweater at all but Dashiell's black cashmere one, and I didn't even notice that I'd reached for it. *Hi, Dash. Nice job looking after Ruby. Is that your idea of a fun way to spend your birthday, giving her a concussion?*

No response except for maybe a vague hint that I don't know what I'm talking about and that I'm being an unreasonable douche. I nearly tear the sweater off, but the problem is that all my own clothes really do look like ass, and with Dashiell hanging around in me I might get to talk with Elena again. I'm not going to let him mess with her, I swear it, but this is probably the only chance I'll ever have to get to know her for real.

Or maybe he's tricking me into thinking this way. Maybe I'm only half myself, and the other half is like some dead insect that's crawling just because Dashiell is zapping it. *I thought she was charming.* Yeah, absolutely, Dash. That's what she is, and cool and funny and smart as hell. And there's no reason on earth why she'd ever bother with someone like me.

When I head downstairs I'm still wearing the sweater, though, and I don't remember deciding to keep it on.

Dad is in the kitchen, making scrambled eggs, which is not a thing he would ever normally do. Takeout is pretty much his limit, or maybe toast at a stretch. Of course; the eggs must be for poor, hurt, oh-so-special Ruby. He takes one look at me and winces.

"Everett, that sweater is full of holes. Can't you put on something decent before you walk out in public?" Then he shakes his head and jabs a sharper look at me. "Why do I keep getting the impression that you've changed somehow? Is there something you should tell me?"

"I'm just in a horrible mood," I say. "It's the Dashiell thing." And hey, that would be a totally factual statement, but one that still manages to hide the truth; basically it's the same way Dash talks. I can't tell who I am anymore, and right now I'm not sure if I'll ever know again.

"Of course. It's a difficult anniversary for all of us." Dad turns off the burner and stares down into the pan. "Eat something.

Have some eggs. Nothing anyone did could save your brother, but at least—his death can serve as a reminder that we can still take care of one another. We can cherish what's left."

It's so far out of character for him to talk this way that I don't even know how to answer. "Aren't those for Ruby?"

"They're for both of you." He's holding on to the side of the stove like he's trying not to fall and his head is sagging. *Defeated.* That's the word for how he looks. Dashiell fought him and messed with him and stole from him for years, but he couldn't actually beat our dad.

Except by dying. I didn't understand until right now, but now I get it: that was Dashiell's one definitive victory, in a way.

I go up to him and hug him, and I don't remember deciding to do that, either.

When it's time to go I don't even say goodbye to Ruby. It's been, what, six days since Dash came back? So that's all the time it took for her to betray me, and I bet she'd do it again in a heartbeat. Why was I in such a big hurry to save her, when what she actually wants more than anything in the world is to be Dashiell's bitch?

I can't concentrate at all in school. Because I can only guess at how things went down between Dash and Ruby. I don't remember any of it—probably Dash hauled me out of bed and waltzed me all over the place while I was asleep, the way he likes to do with her—but I can't rule out the possibility that my unconscious recorded the whole thing. Maybe the memory is knocking around in my head, just someplace where I can't get at it—but if I really, really concentrate I'll be able to track it down.

People are still looking at me a lot at lunch, trying to get my attention, but I'm in such a foul mood I don't care. Oh, like I'm a fabulous man of mystery and I can afford to blow off my fans? I guess that is how I'm acting, and I guess it makes me a jerk. But I'm too busy digging around in my brain, and I can't tell if I'm remembering fragments of what happened or just plain inventing them: my silent footsteps in the dark hallway, my hand brushing Ruby's knob, and then my mouth opening and saying—what?

"Everett?" It's Elena, right on cue; her neon blue highlights do this waterfall tumble as she leans forward. The reality, though, is that she's not here for me, and I need to keep that in mind. The reality is that talking to her at all just gives Dashiell an opportunity to start reeling her in, and I'm the scum of the earth if I let him do that. "You look upset. Are you okay?"

I should be as rude to her as possible. I should do my best to make her run like hell, just so Dash can't get at her. But, I mean, her eyes are wide and concerned, and she's already sitting down close to me and curling a hand on my arm. Hurting her on purpose is more than I can stand.

"Not really." I have a good excuse: Dashiell's practically a legend at our school. "You know about my brother?"

"I know." Her voice is instantly soft. "I never actually met him, but my sister did, and she still talks about him a lot. Everett, I'm so sorry—about what you went through. I can barely imagine how that must hurt."

"Thanks. So today is his birthday, and I feel like complete shit." I'd like to tell her everything. I'd like to say, *Look, you've got no reason to be this sweet to me. Really the person you're trying to be sweet to is him.* But I can't do that. "Elena, you should probably leave me alone. Okay?"

There. I did it, and I can feel kind of a burp of annoyance from Dashiell. Of course, he knows exactly what I'm up to; it's not like he's ever had any trouble seeing through me, because I'm just that crude and obvious. Especially compared to him.

"If you want me to, I will," Elena says, not looking at me anymore, and gets up faster than she needs to. It's not like I don't want her to stay. If it was me she liked and not some sneaky ghost bastard, I'd call after her and apologize, but really she's just another sucker for Dash and his creepy magnetism.

Just like Ruby. In which case, I guess, to hell with both of them.

DASHIELL

* * * *

No sooner are we out the door of that dreary school than I catch a glimpse of the face Ruby-Ru brought to my attention last night. Then it was a hirsute mess above a chest hollowed out by a shotgun blast at close range; now it's upright and looks minimally healthier. The blue marble eyes have returned to their usual location. People should know better than to provide artillery for the figments that populate their dreams. Even a slip of a girl can take out a grown man if you put a gun within easy reach. Now that I know the appearance in question, it's simple enough to detect the essence hidden behind it: a mismatch between the carcass and the spirit putting it through its paces. If Never had any plans for his afternoon, they'll have to wait for me to finish my business with her. Ah, now she's spotted me too, and she's spinning her pet corpus on its heels and shuffling away up the ochre-leafed street.

Once I shunt Never out of my way—without any trouble, since his consciousness is already slack and wandering—I fall into step beside her. She's walking fast, which suits me admirably; soon enough we shake free of the slop of teenagers loosed by the same bell that freed me. All the usual accoutrements of bourgeois Brooklyn parade past: the prim brownstones with nests of ivy ruffling in their gardens, the babies in design-conscious strollers; it's all vile, really, but I'll admit I missed the place. Mabel's new body is a poor fit for her, much too large to be wieldy, and she conducts it gracelessly, sometimes tangling its feet and nearly falling.

"Were you looking for someone?" I say. "Maybe hoping for another chance to converse with Miss Slippers? I've arranged to keep her out of your reach for now, so there isn't much point in your waiting around here."

Mabel's head switches as if to dispel a nagging swarm of flies; presumably her host is offering the usual feeble resistance. Never proved himself to be vastly stronger than I ever would have anticipated. The boy can put up a genuinely troubling fight.

"Are you angry with me? You can't be angry with me!"

"I can't be angry that you went out of your way to interfere with me? To plant disturbing ideas in my dear sister's mind? Of course I can't. Tell me, Mabel, what did you say to her?"

She pouts defiantly; it's comical, that child's mope on her aging drunkard's face. There are hideous blots of rash on the neck and hands, with pustules red and weeping. "I told her they know about her! And it's true! They can chop up *both* your bodies and make you go back, and then what will you do?"

"Chop up Never and Ru? Won't they need hands to swing the axe?" They do know where I am; I've been perfectly aware of that since they came chasing after Never. Clearly enough they were lying in wait, but it's telling that they were obliged to lurk on the other side. On this side they appeared to have no one in their arsenal whatsoever; there wasn't a single guard at the old squat in Queens. It tended to confirm the rumors I've heard, that they've been suffering from a dearth of hosts in recent years. Ah, how that must rankle Aloysius, to find himself fresh out of flesh, unable to lift a living finger against me. "They don't have bodies that I know of, Mabel. And they won't get hold of anyone easily. That's the major difficulty with having kicked off decades ago, isn't it? You don't know anyone alive who might have enough emotional investment in you to come close and stick out their neck. Or have you heard anything different?"

Mabel looks around skittishly and tries to shrink down between her overgrown shoulders. Cold wind buffets our cheeks. "I shouldn't tell you! They came jumping after me already, claws all over, just for talking a tiny *bit* to your Ruby."

"Claws?" I can't stop laughing. Mabel apparently hasn't registered the advantages of sporting a body six-foot-two in steel-toed boots. Plant one of those with force on an animal's neck, and it wouldn't be pestering her further. "*Cats*, Miss Mabel? Are you telling me they've collected a posse of fearsome kitties, and I should be on the lookout in case my sweet sister gets a scratch?"

Mabel scowls. "A *lot* of cats."

It's the funniest thing I've heard since I died. "I'll set out a saucer of cream for Aloysius, then." Now that I think of it, there has been a gray tabby skulking around the house; I didn't pay it much attention, but next time it comes slithering by I'll be sure to get a better look. "Cats aren't much for *chopping people up*, Mabel. Their poor little paws can't get a grip on the hatchet."

"They can try," Mabel insists. "They can do *something*. And if they see me talking to you, they'll do it to Old Body, too."

"And what else did you tell Miss Slippers? I imagine she was observant enough to realize that body isn't your native habitat.

You'd have done better to pick out a girl, Mabel. The voice is a tad dissonant."

Mabel is still sulking, glancing around as if the next turn might offer her a chance to run away. "I wanted a girl! It took me years and years to get *anyone*. And he was the first one *ever* who dreamed up a gun for me. Pow!"

"And did you mention that to my sister—how thoughtfully your staggering wreck there provided the gun you used to send his heart flying clear across the room?"

Mabel isn't a stupid girl; she's aware of why I'd like to know this, and she looks understandably worried. "No-oo," she says, and the lie scrapes like a nail.

It won't be long until Ruby Slippers parses the significance of our personal history, then: she'll connect Mabel's story with that nighttime swim we took together. I'll need to be ready. "Thank you for your honesty."

"You should let me have her," Mabel says suddenly. "Ruby. I need a girl. And I'll trade you Old Body."

That makes me laugh again; only a child would think up something so preposterous. "And why would either of them cooperate with such a thing, Miss Mabel? I expect they've both learned their lesson. Your Old Body won't be lured by a stranger again, and I'm confident that Ru-Ru would have the sense to avoid *you*."

"You could *ask* her to do it," Mabel coos hopefully. "I bet she'd do it for you."

It might be entertaining to let the idea play out for a while, if I didn't find myself resenting it so much. "Ruby-Ru is mine," I say. "She's my darling sister. I couldn't trust you to take decent care of her. I don't imagine you'd even brush her teeth at night."

"You have your brother, anyway, so you don't even need her! And you could *do* things with Old Body that you wouldn't want to do with her," Mabel adds with a sudden flurry of enthusiasm. "That thing you liked to do!" I know what she means, of course, but she feels the need to elaborate. "With the needle."

That would be one advantage—the only one, really, to swapping a healthy sixteen-year-old for that poxy wretch she's wearing. A more precious commodity than access to my sweet Ru, or even to Never, simply doesn't exist; Aloysius and his crew would bargain everything they have for either one of them. Treat them reasonably well and they could be good for another seventy years or more, invaluable years of light and breath and sensation, of music and flavors and the sheer exuberance of commanding a physical self—though Aloysius does have a reputation for squandering the lives of his hosts at remarkable speed.

"You can't have Ruby Slippers. Don't let me hear you mention this again. And if you come after her at all, I'll chop up your Old Body myself, Mabel. Please keep that in mind."

I hear a light scrape on the pavement behind us, just a bit too close. I spin—if one of them does get his hands on a living human, then that could present real difficulties. Ah, but it's only Never's pretty friend Elena, her blue hair flicking like dragonflies.

A moment is all it takes to sort what must have happened: a glimpse of Everett talking to an old freak like Mabel was enough to pique Elena's curiosity, and what she heard when she drew closer sent her into spasms of worry. She likes him far more than he's capable of understanding, and I'd wager that she's nurtured a quiet interest in him for years. So she followed us to eavesdrop, and no doubt she noticed that the voice wasn't the one she's used to hearing. That might be awkward for Never when he sees her in school tomorrow, but for me it doesn't make much difference.

There's no point in pretending that she hasn't heard what she's heard, so I don't bother mimicking him. Instead I smile at her, and she skips back as if the smile was a knife.

Mabel takes advantage of my distraction, galloping to the best of her limited ability around the corner. It's a subpar effort and I could catch her easily, but why bother? I've learned enough for now.

"What are you?" Elena asks, cowering back but not running herself. Ah, so she knows she's not talking to Everett; she'd rather credit something far out of her experience, than believe in him putting on such an elaborate act. I'm pleased to see that she's been so attentive to his character.

"That's a valid question," I tell her. "You're a wonderfully engaging girl, so I'm sorry that I can't oblige you by answering it." I take a step closer and she almost shies away, then changes her mind and stays where she is. "I'm myself, Elena, and I'm here. Isn't that what matters?"

RUBY SLIPPERS

＊　＊　＊　＊

I'm trying to read—*Lord Jim*, since we have an essay on it due next week—but all the things Ever said to me this morning keep slipping in between the words on the page: *there is to my mind a sort of profound and terrifying logic in it* skids into *do you have any idea how he's been playing with* you?

I shake Everett's voice out again—he was being so completely unfair. If he agreed to let Dashiell use his body, how could he think for one second that Dash wouldn't come talk to me? So I make myself focus on the book: *as if it were our imagination alone that could set loose upon us the might of an overwhelming destiny.* Is it really imagination that creates our destiny? I longed for Dashiell and he came back to us. Does that prove Joseph Conrad was right? But if I'm responsible for Dash returning, then how did he wind up inside Everett? Does that mean they're *both* trying to protect me, and keep me out of whatever is happening?

I won't let them.

Whatever it is that's come after Dash, whatever is using those cats to spy on us, this is my battle, too. I keep the blinds drawn now, in every room, but I can still hear them out there: a soft cheek nudging at my windowpane. A thin whine.

Ruby, you didn't tell *me that?* And it's Everett again, his shocked voice colliding with the voice in the story, sending it whipping off on some strange trajectory. I've covered five pages but I feel as if I've been reading for hours. *This astounding adventure, of which the most astounding part is that it is true, comes on as an unavoidable consequence.* I can only sustain my attention for that single sentence, though. *I guess you're completely on his side now, not mine.* It's a relief when the phone rings: I'll take any voice but Everett's, battering through my memory.

My dad, I think, though for some reason I have trouble deciphering the screen. He's called four times today already, checking on me and making sure I don't fall too deeply asleep. It's maybe overkill but still sweet. "Hey. I'm feeling way better now."

"I have a proposition for you, Ruby Bohnacker." The voice is low and croaking, breaking up with eggshell fissures: definitely no one I know. "Come on down." And then my phone starts squirming in my hand. It feels warm and pliant, like a living muscle ripped from someone's arm and still flexing. I can't tell if I've thrown it in disgust or if it escaped on its own, but when I spot it again it's on my floor, slipping toward a wide gutter in the pounding rain. An eddy picks the phone up and spins it back, and it rubs eel-like against a dropped shoe. I lunge after it, droplets bursting on my skin. As soon as my fingers close around it the gutter seems to spread itself wider, and I'm going down.

I can't go too deep, I try to object. *Dashiell said so. My dad said so. I might have a concussion. It's not safe.* But it doesn't matter what I say, because the darkness dilates to take me in and then squeezes closed behind me. An infinite series of jet wings clap above my head.

When I land it's as light as wind. A cat spools past my feet, halfway transparent, like smoke at the instant you blow out a candle. I'm not surprised at all this time to see the black gelatinous river lapping near my feet, the shacks, the glow that doesn't need a moon to fall from. I must have known all along where I was going. In my hand my warm eel of a phone goes limp—and I know I need to get out of here, as fast as I possibly can.

But Dash isn't here this time. He can't show me the way out. I start walking along the bank, trying to move casually as if I belonged here. I don't know exactly how Dash got me out before, but I'm pretty sure the exit was somewhere in this direction.

Right near that corpse with the blasted chest. There's no other landmark I would recognize. The thought of looking into those gaping sockets again curdles my stomach, but I pick up my pace anyway—and nearly bash into a tall chain-link fence that wasn't here before. It spreads in both directions so far that I can't see its limit, pushing between the shanties on my left and cleaving the river to my right. It's at least twenty feet tall and topped in hoops of razor wire.

"There you are, dearest Ruby. You're looking captivating today. Won't you come up and talk to me?"

It's the same crackled voice that I heard on the phone, but no matter how I turn I can't spot anyone else on the shore.

"Above you, Ruby Bohnacker. You know, I only glimpsed you in the distance during your last visit here, but now that I get a better look at you I can't help noticing that you're far too good for that brother of yours. He's nothing but heartache to you, isn't he? You need a man who can appreciate you as a blossoming woman. Not see you as his little brat of a sister."

When I look up I can see the soles of shoes above my head, legs foreshortened into blobs, something dim and boxy higher up. I scuttle ten feet back, both to get away and also to see who's speaking to me. At first I think the man up there is clinging to the fence, but then I realize that's not it at all. The wires of the fence pierce straight into his body and hold him transfixed, but there's no blood.

It looks more like his flesh, his back and legs, grew *around* the wires the way trees sometimes do. There are ridges of swelling where the fence is embedded in his naked chest. Only his arms are free, curling to beckon me. He's tall and broad-shouldered, wearing shiny black shoes and what looks like a pair of tuxedo pants ripped off above the knee; he's slim and muscular and it would be an incredibly beautiful body, if only it weren't so horrifying.

There's something squarish and dark covering his head, I think. Then I start to wonder if maybe it *is* his head. A beam of yellow light drifts in from nowhere and settles on him, and for a moment I can see the boxy shape clearly. It's a dollhouse: a toy-sized version of a Brooklyn brownstone, with black shutters and leaf shadows stirring on its walls even though there are no trees nearby. Then I catch a glimpse of my bird-print curtains in a second floor window and my breath catches in my throat. *Our* house. I can see his neck growing into the foundation.

"Yes, Ruby, this is how I look to you here. But take it from me, in reality I'm an exceptionally handsome man. And you can set me free. Imagine how deeply grateful I'll be, and what I'll do to show it. Climb up, and we'll discuss our future together." The dollhouse door bangs open and closed as he speaks; if I could draw a breath I might scream.

The beam flurries away from him, and the lights turn on all at once in his windows. He's shining at me and my legs go so cold and fluid that I don't think I can move without falling.

"Ruby? Don't you have anything to say to me? You know, I was a movie director once, though you're probably too young to have heard of me. I took ordinary girls—girls far more ordinary than you could ever be—and I made them into magic. You see, you need me more than I need you. Come to me, child."

See, it's too hard with a stranger! They won't come. That's what Mabel told me. The memory of her words sends a spurt of energy through my legs, and I'm finally able to take a few steps: away from the dollhouse man, away from the river. Then my legs start to buckle at the knees and I can't keep going.

But if I can't get through the fence, I'll never find the exit, will I?

"Ruby, my dear! Your brother doesn't deserve you. You and I, we can embark on a splendid partnership. I'll be Business, and you'll be Pleasure, and we'll mix delightfully." He laughs and his door clacks against its frame. "Really, Dashiell Bohnacker is too much of a hothead for you, and also much too greedy. Why on earth did he need to stake a claim to both you and his brother?"

"I won't listen to you insult Dashiell," I say. Oh, of course everyone here knows him, just the way Mabel knew him. "And I don't know what you're talking about." There, I finally managed to say something, and I think it was even true.

"*Don't* you? Climb up to me and I'll be happy to explain. Don't make me angry, Ruby. Let's get this off to a good start, shall we?"

His hands twist around a column of air. Then he seems to catch himself doing it, and he stuffs both hands deep into his pants pockets. The links rattle every time he moves.

"I don't want your explanation." I take another step, rock a little, and catch myself again. "And we're not starting anything!" My heart is pounding so hard that I can feel my throat shuddering in time. But why? The man can't chase me, not with a fence growing through him.

Then I realize. I'm afraid of understanding what he's saying, and what Mabel said, because I know their messages are connected somehow. I'm afraid of the moment when it's all going to become clear to me. That's the fear that courses through me in electric jags and finally frees me to run headlong, weaving and stumbling among the dark shacks lining the shore.

I can hear him howling after me as if dark, ravening animals, somewhere between bears and wolves, were pouring from the dollhouse's windows and baying in midair. *He was crazy*, I tell myself, *he was just crazy. A beast. Nothing he said had any meaning. It was pure babble.* The air around my ears jostles with tiny yapping animals; I can smell their rank fur. The dollhouse man sent them in pursuit, I know it. I would dive into one of the yawning doorways around me if I weren't so afraid of what might be in there. Needle-sharp teeth nip and goad me, and I slap with my hands as I run, trying to drive them off. The shacks fall away and I'm running through a thin, scrubby forest, but the wind thickens with those flying miniscule wolf-creatures: motes of living torment, biting me everywhere.

And then I see the cliff ahead. A dense scaffolding of vines grows over it, all the vines shining with toxic yellow light. I'll climb up and the beasts won't follow me; I don't know how I know that, but I do.

I go up, grappling with arm-thick vines that snap at my shoulders and sometimes lick playfully around an ankle before they let me go again. I've never been comfortable climbing anything.

The vine I'm gripping swings loose and my heart lurches. Queasiness floods me like cold grease and my foot slips. For a long, horrible moment both my legs flail in midair and my arms strain to hold me.

Then my right foot finds a purchase again. My left. I keep going up. Maybe, just maybe, the clifftop will lead me around that fence, and I'll find my way home.

Another step. This time I have to heave my leg painfully high before I can reach a toehold. My arms scrape against the rough tendrils and they writhe at my touch. I keep hauling myself up; I must be high above the ground by now. Emptiness echoes at my feet and I know I can't look down. The earth might have vanished completely. But, thank God, I think I might be getting close.

Something pale and cold brushes at my forehead; it's definitely not the same texture as the vines. I can't think about what it might be, not until I'm safe. I give a huge pull and lever my chest onto a hard shelf of rock. Another heave and my legs come slapping after me. For a few moments I just clutch the rock and gasp. I can barely believe I'm still alive.

Something dark and lumpy is lying near me: so near that it blocks my vision completely. I lift myself on my elbows—the barrier isn't very high—and I realize that the thing in my way is a leg in blue sweatpants.

My first thought is that it's the man Mabel shot, that I've found some impossible route back to him, and I sit up fast. Ugh—the thing that brushed my face before was a dead hand projecting over the cliff's edge. I see a bare arm, gray and milky, and a T-shirt drenched in a long bib of crimson blood. It doesn't look like the same man and for what feels like minutes I just stare, straining to make out the face. I don't know why I can't see it clearly. There's a dark V-shaped ditch cutting across the throat, a severed ring of windpipe—that much I can take in. A long knife leans against a stone, the blade flashing silver and scarlet.

Then I do see the face, as suddenly as a camera coming into focus. And I'm up on my feet and screaming.

Everett, it's Everett, his throat gashed wide open. And suddenly I understand everything.

I knew I had to warn him—oh, in my heart I even knew who I had to warn him *against*—and I didn't do it. And now it's too late, and Dashiell's murdered him just like he murdered me. Mabel is living in the man she killed here, just the way Dashiell . . . How *could* he, though? And why would he choose the two people who love him most in the world to hurt that way?

See, it's too hard with a stranger! They won't come.

And even worse, there's what he told me himself, what I made myself pretend I'd forgotten: *I did it because there's no place like home.*

That's why. He knew we'd come to him even if nobody else would, because we missed him and trusted him so much. Did I understand all along? Oh, and there were Dashiell's memories whispering into my thoughts, and that feeling I had that he was too close to see, too close to find. Everett, what have I done to you? I was first. I was the one who let him in—and then he must have used me as a way to get to you.

I betrayed you, and that's how Dash was able to betray us both.

I'm still screaming, my voice coming in short blasts, so it takes me a while to notice that there's another sound. It's my phone and it won't stop ringing. Voice mail isn't picking up?

I pull in my breath and answer it. "Hello?"

"Ruby, it's me! Listen, you have to wake up."

"Ever! Ever, oh God, it's all my fault! There's blood all over you, and your *throat*—"

"I don't care about that! You have to wake up now! Dash says if he comes after you he might not reach you in time. He didn't notice fast enough that you were there. Wake UP!" Now Everett is the one screaming into my ear, even while I stare at his dead face: a lump of tallow among stones. His hair cascades back and his gray eyes stare up into nothing. "Wake up, wake up, wake up!"

And I do. It feels like being pulled through a thousand layers of death and sorrow piled above me in the form of black membranes. Then I'm out, lying in my own bed again, and fingers are slipping through my hair. Someone is bending over me.

At first I think it's Everett.

And then I know it's not.

NEVER-EVER

* * * *

That's what I get for spacing out and daydreaming about Paige and Elena, or about some messed-up combination of the two of them: a dark-haired girl twisting in my arms, but lit up by flashes of blue. I can't afford to let down my guard like that, because I'm so out of my head and so oblivious to everything around me that I don't even notice at first that Dash has bopped me under the surface again. And when I *do* realize what's happening, he has me completely squashed. I kick a little; it doesn't seem to do much, but maybe I'm not actually trying that hard. Maybe I'm too tired and bummed to really fight.

Have fun out there, Dash. You like this crappy world so much, you can have it. Personally I'm done caring what happens. I tried caring for a while and it turned out to be a huge mistake.

All at once I'm remembering something, so intensely that it's like the memory has swelled up around me: I'm back in Paige's bedroom. I'm sitting cross-legged on her bed staring down at my left hand cradling a phone—when did *that* happen?—feeling so totally miserable it seems like too much work to even breathe. My right hand keeps stroking the sheets: they're very light blue with a little bit of sheen. And I'm thinking of Ruby. I was about to send a text message to someone—who?—but for half a minute that's enough to stop me: the thought of how disappointed Ruby will be if she hears I've started using again.

Using what, though? If this is my memory shouldn't it make some kind of sense, maybe even be about something that actually happened to me? Then I look up and see my reflection in the mirror: wavy pinkish gold hair and a face that always looks like it's trying to sell you something, and probably not just cologne.

Okay. This is a memory, all right, but it's definitely not mine. There's an atmosphere of emotion in here so sick and brutal that I realize all at once where I must be: I'm remembering the night Dash died. He said something, didn't he, about his memories leaking into Ruby's mind while he was possessing her? It's pretty unbearable, but I should probably try to stay with it, to find out once and for all exactly what happened to him. I haven't forgotten about Ruby's crazy suspicions, and even though I'm sure she's wrong it would be good to really, definitively know.

I should go ahead and break Ruby's heart. Get it over with. She's old enough to learn that she can't count on anyone but herself. She's old enough to ditch her supremely irritating innocence, her glowing expectations. I mean, I don't hear those words exactly, but that's a rough translation of the feelings sliding through my mind. There's even this weird idea that Ruby's innocence is a kind of parasite, and that it's feeding on me. Sometimes I enjoy it, but tonight it's just making me resentful. I feel like she's linked to me—the light that makes me a shadow, maybe? And I'm sick to death of it. It's all mixed in with rage at Dad for rejecting me, and at our mom for ditching us, and at Paige, for some reason I can't identify.

Dad won't even let me in the house. It's like I'm not even part of the family. That's one emotion that repeats like a drumroll: *I'm not allowed in my own home. I'm too much of a* problem *to be allowed in my own home.* The bitterness of it sets my teeth on edge—and I get a flash of barreling Ruby back from the front door and shoving into our hallway, just to prove I could.

There's a spasmodic urge to steal Ruby from our dad, to coax her into running away with me to nowhere at all. And then a sharp recoil of shame at the thought. Actual shame; like, who knew Dash had it in him?

I can see my left thumb—or that would be *Dashiell's* thumb—hit *send* on the phone. And then I instantly regret it and start crying uncontrollably.

Jesus, Dash, I try to say—but it's just a memory, a dead moment, boxed up and buried in time, so how could he hear me? *You don't have to do this. You can still change your mind.* He can't, though. His last chance slipped away months ago. *Dash-Dot-Dot, you know it's not just Ruby's heart you're going to break, right? Did you see Dad's face* this morning?

And then I hear something. At first I think it's a huge moth flapping at the window, but once I focus I can make out a voice. It seems like it's coming into Paige's bedroom from every side, smacking at the walls and ceiling. It's Dashiell; I must be over-hearing him talking to someone in the world outside, just like that time Ruby heard him talking to me and I had to tell her she'd dreamed it. What I thought were wingbeats are actually words.

He's not pretending to be me, though. I can't catch what he's saying, but he's definitely using his own voice. And somebody is answering him. Who, though? I'm concentrating as hard as I can, trying to hear the tone over the slurring of cars on the street, the twittering birds.

"*What* you are is even more important to me, actually. And another thing that matters to me is what you've done with Everett. Is he even *in* there? Because I know him, and I know that he would never, *ever* mess with me this way. Not if he had any choice!"

Oh hell. It's Elena, and I can tell from her voice how she's scared and working hard to sound brave. He's talking to *Elena* out of my freaking face and she's going to think I'm a complete lunatic. I forget all about not caring and start smashing at him as hard as I can. The memory around me jolts. Another shove and Paige's bedroom cracks from top to bottom.

Dash doesn't even try to hold me down, though. He just kind of steps aside, if you can describe a mind as *stepping* anywhere, and lets me go shooting straight back to the surface. The world punches up like a fist in my teeth and my arms fly out instinctively, like I need to protect myself from falling leaves and daylight. Elena barely gets out of the way in time.

"Sorry," I sputter, and then I realize how far beyond idiotic that must sound.

"Everett! You're back?" Her eyes are so wide and bright that I feel burned just looking at them. She's hugging herself and her knuckles shine against her fuzzy blue jacket.

"Yeah," I tell her. "But listen, Elena, you can't trust it when you *think* it's me, okay? He's so good at pretending that you won't know the difference. Seriously. That's why I told you to leave me alone. I mean, if it *was* me I wouldn't say it." I'm babbling. Dashiell's listening and I can tell that he thinks it's incredibly amusing.

"Who's good at pretending?" She's trying to stay calm but it's not going so well. "You know what that was, Everett? What was it? Who was just *talking* to me? I know that wasn't you!" She's edging up on a complete breakdown, actually.

"I can't talk about it. It's personal. It's about as personal as anything can be."

Her eyes flare up at that. I almost think she might hit me. "Oh, in *that* case I'll act like none of this happened. I won't bother worrying about you anymore!" Her tone is mixed-up fury and sarcasm. "What, do you have multiple personality disorder? So usually you're a hopeless geek who won't talk to anyone, but for special occasions you transform into a raving psycho and start babbling about cats?"

Normally I'd be crushed by that—I'd be hurt that she's *trying* to hurt me, and right when I'm doing my best to warn her. But I'm not feeling like my usual self now, and I actually laugh.

"Sure," I tell her, and God, do I sound like him. "Go with that. That explains *everything*."

I turn my back on her and start walking, even though that means I'm heading in the wrong direction.

"Do you even know what that—whatever—is *doing* while you're out to lunch?" Elena calls after me. "He was talking about Ruby. Your alter ego, I mean. Did you hear that?"

And I freeze in midstride, but at first I don't turn around to look at her. Because I'm supposed to be done caring about anything, but *especially* about Ruby, after how she screwed me over. I can hear Elena's steps coming up behind me.

"Did you know?" she asks again, but this time her voice is way gentler.

Here's one more item for the list of what's wrong with me: I'm obviously incapable of learning from my mistakes.

"You mean to you?" I ask. "Did he talk about Ruby to you?"

The tough, swaggering Dashiell-ness is completely gone, and I'm raw and alone. Even the wind feels colder, like my ribs have cracked open and my guts are all wet and exposed. Light pulses off the storefronts: 6th Avenue is one big, vacant heart.

I guess Elena can hear the difference in me because she rests her hand on my shoulder. She's actually too nice of a person to keep up the aggro act for long. "Not to me. To this old, scruffy guy with an extremely creepy voice, like a little girl's. Do you know who that was?"

How can things keep getting worse? "No idea." I finally turn to face her. "Elena, listen, I really need to know what they were saying. Just the fact that it was about Ruby . . ."

"How can you not *know*? You were really that far gone?" She doesn't expect an answer, though. "I only heard part of it. And most of what I did hear didn't make much sense. But the old guy said something like, *You should give me Ruby.* Something about a trade? And your alter ego got pissed off. I think threatened to kill him, even."

Dashiell's planning to use my body to go around committing murders? That sounds like a fantastic idea. And would *giving* somebody Ruby mean what I think it means?

"Everett, listen . . ." Elena pulls me closer. I can feel her breath on my cheek. "Will you please just tell me what's happening to you? Because there's no way I can believe you aren't in trouble, not when I've just heard some alter-ego thing talking *through* you."

"He's not my alter ego," I say. "But I shouldn't even tell you that much." I guess I am in trouble, but it's not like there's anything she could do to help, even though it's sweet that she wants to. I'd rather die than let her get tangled up in this, anyway.

"He's just, like, hanging out." That makes me laugh again, but sort of hysterically.

"He *has* to be. Part of you, I mean. He kept saying that Ruby is his sister. His *darling* sister, even. So what else could he be?"

I don't answer that—and Elena is seriously too smart for silence to throw her off. I'd have to actively lie my ass off to stop her from doing the math, and I can see it in her face: her eyes go wide when she gets it, then narrow again as she shoves the idea away. Too crazy.

"So, my—whatever he is—he definitely told the old guy no? He said, *You can't have Ruby?*"

"Those were his exact words, as it happens. How did you guess?" Okay, that would be more sarcasm. She's looking for a less insane hypothesis than the true one, I can see it, and all the alternatives involve me being either psychotic or a massive liar. It's funny that she was just talking about cats, because there's one rubbing at my ankles right now—nosing me pretty hard, like it would enjoy watching me trip and break my head open.

"I know him really well, is how," I tell her, and the hysterical laugh is back. I can't stop it. "We're close." I hold up crossed fingers. "I mean, like *that*. We're the absolute closest." *So close that I share his memories. So close that I was about to experience his death from the inside, and I would have gone through with it if I wasn't worried about you.*

"Good*bye*, Everett," Elena singsongs, parodying the kind of chirpy girl that she definitely isn't. "See you and your whatever *around*!" I watch her stomping away from me, her blue-streaked hair fluttering, her blue fuzzy jacket reflecting in the plate glass on the stores. I've never seen Elena this angry before, and we've been in the same classes off and on since kindergarten. But, really, the more she hates me the better. Dashiell's about a million times too interested in her, I can feel it. What the hell was he thinking, coming out and showing himself to someone I have to deal with every day? And if she tells everybody—

She won't, though. I realize why I didn't ask her to keep her mouth shut: it's because I knew I didn't have to. Asking her to keep it a secret would have basically been an insult.

Realizing that kind of makes me love her a tiny bit. But not too much. Because that would be a terrible idea. As terrible as Dashiell *trading* Ruby, though for what? When he was a kid he liked action figures, but now?

I'm just heading up the steps of our house—right, I'm supposed to be grounded—when I feel Dashiell tense inside me like he's just noticed something that bothers him. *You'll have to stand down for a while, Never-Ever. I'm afraid it's important. Don't go kicking up a fuss.*

And our brownstone topples into blackness in front of my eyes. Fine. I can't deal with being myself anymore, anyway. The last thing I feel is one hand digging out my keys in a hurry while the other grabs my phone, and then I'm under. Nobody in particular, floating peacefully along in the slime of nothingness.

Maybe it would be the perfect solution to this mess if I just stayed here. At least it's nice and dark.

RUBY SLIPPERS

It's Everett; Ever with Dashiell streaming through him again. His fingers twirl my hair and then give a little tug, and his face is so near mine that I have to squirm away before I can sit up. My head is throbbing; the painkillers must have worn off.

"Ah, Miss Slippers, didn't I ask you to kindly stick to alternative dreams—to *any* dream but that one, in fact? Doesn't that leave you enough options? You could have dreamed about a meadow full of towering rabbits, a ship caught in a storm, a little hut on chicken legs, but no. You had to go and put yourself in danger again. I can't always be on hand to extract you."

"Where's *Everett*?" I ask. My voice comes out in shrill bursts and I can't control it. The shadows in Dash's eyes sway like branches at Everett's name, and I know he knows exactly what I just saw. "Everett just *called* me."

"Where do you think he is?" Dashiell smiles at me; Everett's mouth is bending in a strange wind. "He's still a bit depressed over his tiff with you this morning, but he's perfectly safe, Ruby-Ru. Just like you'll stay safe, if you'll only listen to me and keep away from zones that I've warned you are unhealthy for both of us. Never is exhausted. He's taking a much-needed rest."

"Dash, I saw what happened to him! You know I did. There was blood all over him, his shirt was soaked, and his throat . . . I can't understand how you could *do* that." He's sitting on my bed and I'm squeezed against the wall, as far from him as I can get. He reaches out and catches my hand in his, then drags my fingers from the bottom of Everett's chin down to his collar: warm skin shaken by a pulse like footsteps wandering through an endless corridor.

"Never-Ever made a choice, my Ru, and he was entirely aware of what he was doing. He joined forces with me of his own free will, and I made the process as easy for him as I possibly could. You can feel for yourself that his throat didn't suffer any lasting damage from the episode. Did it? Hasn't he been blasting away at his video games and bickering with you, as physically intact as ever?"

Maybe all of that is true, but it doesn't make me feel any calmer.

"But he *felt* it when you did that to him! He must have been scared out of his mind, and he went through as much pain as he would have if—if that happened in real life." My voice drags out of me in a thread of sound, stitching into silence so that I can barely get out the words. Dash still has a grip on my hand.

"And how do you know that, Miss Slippers? You almost sound as if you were speaking from personal experience."

I can't believe he can say this to me, not when we both *know*. . . . All I can do is gape at him, breathing hard and trying to stop the heat flooding my face and eyes. Dashiell stares back, then sighs and yanks my wrist so hard that I topple forward.

Straight into his arms. I'm struggling but he keeps me clamped tight against him, with his cheek pressed to mine and his breath rushing in my ear.

"Dash, let me go!"

"It was only a dream, my sweet Ruby Slippers. A bone of vision, buried deep beneath the earth. But even so, even knowing that you wouldn't be harmed in the slightest, drowning you was still the hardest thing I've ever had to do. There. We've come to the crux of what's troubling you, haven't we?"

There's nothing left inside me but formless aching. How can I make that into words? I've stopped fighting and my forehead falls onto his shoulder. I could almost forget that this shoulder has been Everett's for sixteen years, because even the blood thrumming in my ear sounds like Dashiell: a tone deeper than a voice.

"This is all happening because of me, Dash? I'm the one who let you come home?"

"You *brought* me home, Ruby-Ru. You passed through a terrible ordeal for my sake, but that was the only way you could get me out of that place. And you have no idea what you saved me from, sweetness. Are you sorry that you did?"

The river enclosing me in its cold body, the water reaching deep into my lungs. Somehow I hadn't thought about the possibility that Dash might have done that to me out of desperation—that the pain and terror I went through might have been trivial in comparison to everything he'd been suffering. Maybe he didn't have any choice.

"Dash? What happened to you? That place—is that where *everybody* ends up when they die?"

"Not everyone, no. A very small percentage, as far as I can

make out. There are certain conditions that make some of us more susceptible to getting trapped in the borderlands. There's what you might describe as a fickle quality to our deaths, as if we'd been caught sporting with our own mortality, so maybe getting stuck is our punishment for indecisiveness? And then there are some among the dead in that place—the cruelest ones— who choose to take advantage of the fact that not everyone can get across. Do you understand, Ruby-Ru?"

"A little," I tell him. *Take advantage?* I want to ask what they were doing to him but the words halt in my throat. If Dash isn't telling me the details, it's probably because he knows I couldn't stand to hear them. Just thinking of Dashiell being trapped is enough to make me want to claw and thrash at the limits of my own skin.

"The people in control there were vicious when they were alive, the worst kind of gangsters and sadists, and they're vicious now. And my only hope of escape was through you. My lady of slipping and sliding would be the keyhole where I could effect my own slipping away. But for that I had to hurt you, Ru." I've been pressed against him for so long that when he tips me back flaming hoops wobble in my vision. He holds my face in both hands. "So are you sorry now that you swam out to me? If there had been enough time for me to explain, would you have refused and abandoned me there?"

His thumbs brush the tears from my cheeks. I hadn't known I was crying.

"No," I tell him, and I know it's true. Even if the consequences of what I did are brutal and terrifying, I never could have left him alone in that nightmare. "I would have come for you, Dash. No matter what I had to go through." I'm still figuring it all out.

"But then—if I'd already brought you home, weren't you living in me? The way you're in Everett now?"

"Exactly so. That's how I was able to discuss the situation with him."

"Then why did you have to hurt him, too? Dash, if you were safe, you didn't need to—to do what you did to him!"

Because it would be one thing if it was just me. That would be so, so much easier for me to accept than the thought of Ever suffering.

Dash's face tightens, and I almost think he's angry with me for challenging him.

"Ru. I did need to. Because it wasn't easy for you, carrying me on your own. Never and I were both there that day by the East River, remember. We agreed that the strain was too much for you, and Never chose to step in." A pained smile twists his mouth. "He wanted to *protect* you from me, if you can imagine that, Ruby-Ru. As if there was anyone, living or dead, who cares about you more than I do. I've done my best not to take offense, but it's been a real struggle."

I'm listening to Dash, watching him billow inside Everett's face like wind throbbing in a sail, here in my ordinary robin's-egg blue room on what should be an ordinary autumn afternoon. A skateboard rattles along the street outside and leaf shadows crest on the curtains. And at the same time I'm still picturing Everett, his face waxy and bloodless above the crimson trench opening his throat, and Dashiell with his head lolling back and the needle in his arm. Did I wound one brother to save the other? Could I have done anything else?

"Dash? Were you murdered?"

Bizarrely he laughs at that, though his brows are still drawn and his smile is more like a grimace. "Ah, Miss Slippers, I've been wondering when you'd ask me that. It's not a simple question."

"How can that not be *simple*? Either somebody else did that to you, or . . ."

He shakes his head. "It isn't a binary choice, Ru. Not in the least. Let's just say that my death had a number of components, and murder might have been one of them."

"That doesn't make any sense, though!"

"In any case I believe that you're the one who owes *me* an explanation. Didn't I explicitly warn you against returning to that dream again? I thought I'd shut down the routes you'd be likely to follow there, too. So how did you wind up there?"

I'm lost again. Dashiell's words carry my thoughts down dizzying channels and I can barely understand. "It was my phone."

"I could tell that you had your phone with you. Very unusual, carrying an object from this side into the dreamspace that way. How did that come about?"

"Someone called me. I guess I was already asleep, and I didn't know it? And then my phone pulled me down a storm drain."

His forehead is furrowed. "Was it Mabel? She wouldn't be likely to think of using a telephone as bait, though."

"Someone else. He tried to get me to climb a fence to him." Everything that happened before I saw Everett's corpse seems faded, uncertain, and I'm straining to remember. "His head was a dollhouse."

"His appearance is no help to me. Can you recall anything else? This could be important, Ru-Ru."

"He said he'd been a movie director."

Dashiell cracks up laughing so hard that tears come to his eyes; he almost sounds relieved. "Oh. *That* idiot. They've taken so much from him that he can't remember his own name, but it hasn't made him any less vile, has it? If he'd only asked me, I could have told him he'd be wasting his time making a play for you. It would be beyond his comprehension, though, that a girl your age could be so much smarter than he is."

"He wanted—the same thing you did? To get out?"

Dash stops laughing. "If only that were all, Miss Slippers. I'm afraid the fact that you've taken me on—it will make the others regard you as a hot prospect, to express it crudely. *Easy,* if you'll excuse the term. And ditching their bodies hasn't made them lose their old desires; it's only made it impossible for them to scratch all their nasty little itches. What they'd do with a sixteen-year-old girl in their possession doesn't bear thinking of. You can't let yourself slip into that dream again, but if you do you need to stay far away from *everyone*. No matter what they try to use to coax you closer. Do you understand me?"

I understand enough that nausea rolls in the pit of my stomach. "I think so." But I can't stop picturing Ever. The gash in his throat seems to run across the blue wall in front of me; the plaster peels back and blood gurgles through staring arteries. "Dash, I mean, when Everett came to you—in that dream, and you say he was making a choice—"

Dash looks bored now; I can't help seeing it. He's been playing with my hair all this time, but now he lets me go and tips against the wall. "Yes, Ru-Ru?"

"Did he know *what* you were going to do?"

"Never-Ever knew precisely what would happen. We'd discussed it. And he accepted that pain out of love for you. His attitude grated on me, I admit, but I had to admire the nobility of the impulse."

"If he did that for me, then isn't it my fault?"

"How could someone else's choice be your fault? It was a difficult experience for him, but Never will be a better and a stronger man because of it. If anything, Ru, you gave him a chance that he needed desperately, if he was ever going to appreciate his own worth. Never proved his mettle, and he did it for your sake. No one can take that from him." Dashiell tips his head and considers me for a long time, and I'm sorry I ever doubted him. "But you're the one who did it for me, sweetest Ru. You're the only one who would. And I won't forget that."

He leans in and kisses me on the mouth. So softly and slowly that it's almost like Everett isn't still here between us.

ALOYSIUS

Charlie comes knocking catside to inform me of matters that need my attention. He intrudes just as I'm getting into the spirit of the thing, disemboweling a plump rat behind some garbage cans. One must take one's little pleasures as they come. But, well, if Charlie's report is accurate—if my temporary removal from the scene has led to such an act of insolence—then ceding the froth of blood on my jowls is a sad necessity.

Seven decades of death haven't sufficed to teach the sad fool anything, it seems. He might have recalled the punishments he's endured in the past. He might have deduced that we can strip him of all he has left. Do you try to snatch so fine a rat as she is—all of sixteen, pink and beaming—from the cat's jaws and still escape a maiming? Not if I'm the tom in question.

No beating heart is presently on hand to provide us with their mental frills and furbelows, palaces or lilies or spinning wheels as the case may be. When no one living happens to be visiting us, we enjoy a scenic view of gray haze. An equally gray river. In the haze, the ruins of a man await, pinned in place for my convenience.

"I believe you were aware that I'd taken an interest in Miss Bohnacker?"

He lacks anything that might be termed a personal appearance, as do I, but it's no trouble for us to recognize one another. "Aloysius! I was only teasing her. A little harmless flirtation as she happened to be strolling by. I thought it would warm her up to the idea. Make her more welcoming to you, when the time comes."

"You called me Aloysius." He doesn't respond. "Can you recall other names? The names of your three wives, perhaps? Your four children?"

"Four? There were four?" He yanks at his bonds. Tantalus's tongue uncoils to lap the sweet juice of information. "Aloysius, were they fine boys? Are they still alive?"

He baited his oldest son for me some sixty-eight years ago, the toady. The delicious young Martin Rhodes, not that his father here has the slightest recollection of the name. The boy didn't live to be particularly old after that. "You can't remember. That's the price you've paid for your past indiscretions. What shall I take from you now, I wonder, for soliciting a young lady whose favors I'd reserved for myself?" No reply beyond a pitiable writhing. "I'd planned to keep Miss Bohnacker blissfully ignorant, in the hope that she'd come gamboling up to me for some small incentive; to rescue one of her brothers, perhaps. Friendly as a kitten. Now, thanks to you and Mabel, I'm afraid she's cottoned on."

"She doesn't know! She doesn't know anything! Aloysius, I was able to find that out for you. The little bitch is a blank slate. Just waiting to be *inscribed*." One thing I can say with assurance about death: it's never made anyone cleverer. A vulgar fool will remain one no matter how deep you dig his grave.

"As she hurried to remove herself from the pleasure of your company, she happened to meet her twin brother. Or, to be clearer, his butchered corpse. Are you still sure that she knows nothing?"

One of the peculiarities of our climate is that such shadow-bodies don't decay. Everett Bohnacker's sliced meat will stay as fresh as a daisy; his blood remains fragrant and moist. Miss Bohnacker would be similarly well-preserved, should we succeed in fishing her from the river before her older brother manages it. My informants have spotted him swimming here despite the risk, clearly in the hope of retrieving her corpse. In order to hide it from me, naturally, lest I find some delightful use for it. Having secured safe haven in that pretty pair of mortal frames, he's green enough to think that he can prance back here and elude capture. And he has so far, I'll admit, but it's only a matter of time before he slips.

"She doesn't know! Aloysius, take it from me, she's nothing but a senseless chit. Easy pickings." If there were such a thing as easy pickings, not one of us would be here. He knows that, naturally. Even the most witless of the beating hearts will tend to spook badly at our advances. Ah, that's why I had such high hopes, when he first came, that Dashiell Bohnacker would see his way to helping us befriend his dainty younger siblings, rather than snatching all the biscuits for himself. We'll see who ends up eating them, though.

"That chit of Dashiell's is now alert to the possibilities, and it's only fair that I credit you with enlightening her. Tell me, what do you have left? Your name? Or—let me see—I removed that last time you annoyed us. But you do still remember that you once directed motion pictures, don't you?" He twitches, as might be expected. Ah, the coup de grâce. His fine boy was a pittance compared to his bloated and boorish vanity. "It's a paltry enough memory as payment for your gaffe. But I'll make do."

"Aloysius, wait! I'll make it up to you! Let me down and I'll find a way to bring her straight to you. I swear it!"

"She's a silly chit, as you say. And now she'll be too skittish to be worth pursuing. I've reconsidered my interest in her. Perhaps I'd prefer someone else."

I step close. If the others resent the fact that certain unpleasant entities have chosen me to be their delegate in this place, well, they might try to learn from my example. Powers have been vested in me sufficient to pop the cork on any ghost here and drain the contents. *Why him,* my compatriots in loss and decay are always grumbling. *Why Aloysius? He's only a ghost like us. Formerly a living man, tapped for promotion by a dozen bullets fired one foggy night in 1929. What did* he *do to enjoy such privileges?*

Dear friends, I have these powers, and you do not, for a very sound reason. It's because I can be trusted to make good use of them.

NEVER-EVER

* * * *

When I come to again I'm lying on the living room sofa. The windows are pitch dark, so it must be at least six o'clock. And I can hear Ruby banging around in the kitchen. Getting rid of Dashiell seems like it's not so much of an option, but neither is disappearing forever into the darkness and letting him run my damn body if he wants it so bad. Right, Dash only wants it for the fun parts. He'll leave all the hassle of consciousness to me whenever everything sucks.

For a while I sprawl there, wishing the nothingness would take me over again so I could just forget everything that's happened. No dice, though. I have to get up and go through the motions, and pretend I'm Everett and not some mutant blend of myself and the dead guy, and worry all the time about what messed-up thing he'll try next. He could kill somebody and I'm the one who'd go to prison for it. He can talk out of my mouth and persuade my twin sister to turn on me until I can't trust anything she says anymore. He freaked Elena out and he made Paige think that I'm a complete asshole. I wish he was dead—a whole lot deader than this, I mean.

I kind of feel like I never want to see Ruby again, but realistically that's another not-option. I'm starving and she's got the kitchen covered, like she's some occupying army keeping me away from the food. The house reeks of baking chocolate. So fine, whatever, just because I'm in the same room with her doesn't mean I have to speak. It doesn't mean I have to look at her. If she wants to have a conversation with my freaking face, she can wait until somebody else is running its mouth.

So I get up and go down the hall and she's wearing her shiny red boots again, like I should have known she would be. It's not like it's a secret anymore where her allegiance is. There are mixing bowls heaped in the sink and two round pans of chocolate cake cooling on the counter; there's also a fat bruise where Dashiell bashed her head this morning. I wasn't going to say anything, but there's something about the combination of Ruby sitting there mixing up lavender frosting, and that lump on her forehead, and her expression as she glances up at me— shamefaced? but still stubborn?—that gets under my skin like a pile of seething worms.

"You're making him a *cake*."

"It's his birthday. You know that." Ruby sounds pissy, like she has any right to be—like she isn't the one who owes me the biggest apology of her life. She isn't even looking at me.

"So who do you think is going to eat it? The bastard doesn't have a *mouth* of his own anymore. Are you going to take that to the graveyard and dig him up so he can stuff his dead face?" I guess I'm trying to make her mad—and not just her, honestly. I can feel Dash sort of tense up inside me and I wish to God he'd just whack me out of the way. I could use some serious, long-term oblivion. Ruby just kind of flicks this irritable half-second stare at me and goes back to swirling her frosting. Around and around.

"You like cake, Never. It's *chocolate*."

It takes me a moment to process that—what she just called me. "I'm not eating that, Miss *Slippers*. He's been using me for too much crap already, without me feeding him cake. Did Dash tell you about how he went and had sex with Paige in my body, and she didn't even know it was him? And now he's after Elena?"

That gets to her, I can see it, and I have this sudden, queasy realization: Ruby loves him, all right, but maybe not in the way anyone should love their own brother. Her mouth is sort of scrunched up and her cheeks are flaming red, because she knows that both Paige and Elena are a million times prettier than she'll ever be—and that's the only part that really bothers her. She doesn't care that Dash used me and Paige both for his cheap thrills without asking our permission. I'd laugh at her if it wasn't so horrible. "He *drowned* you, Ruby. He slit my freaking throat. What would he have to do to make you finally tell him to drop dead?"

"Dash did what he had to do. He didn't hurt us in real life. Anyway, you told me you didn't care about that." Maybe she's decided that her frosting is mixed enough because she gets up fast, her chair squealing across the floor, and stomps over to the counter.

Then it sinks in. "I told you *what*? When did I say that?"

"Today. When you called me. To get me out of that dream." She bites her lip, and—about time—there's something in her expression like she actually gives a damn about me. "Ever, I mean, I know you agreed—but *seeing* you that way, and all the blood, and your eyes that empty. I've never seen anything that awful, is all. And now I can't stop thinking about it."

I guess this means she found my dead body, in that place Dash calls the borderlands. "Not awful enough to stop you from baking the bastard a birthday cake. I mean, *apparently*, Ruby? And I didn't call you."

"Yeah, you did! You said I had to wake up right away, because Dash wouldn't reach me in time. You said—"

"That wasn't me. Don't you get it? He's in my body, he can imitate my voice when he wants to. Paige can't tell the difference, either. He's fooling both of you." Okay, so I brought up Paige again to bug her. It works really well. "This could be Dashiell talking to you right now. Telling you what a sucker you are for keeping up your stupid devotion to him." I can feel Dash sort of fidgeting inside me, like he's almost mad enough to come slamming back to the surface. Then I get a better idea. "You're the one who wants him, not me. So why doesn't he just go camp out in you and jerk *your* body around and leave me the hell alone? I guess it might be harder for him to screw random girls that way. But maybe he could still pull it off. Do you think he's that good?"

Now Ruby's face is working like crazy. She might be about to cry and I don't even care. "Since when are you this mean, Never?"

Since you lied to me just because he told you to. Since I had to watch you making a cake for someone who murdered me, dream or no dream.

"Since you started *calling* me that. You're just like him. Dash? I know you can hear me. Go possess Ruby, okay? I don't want you. I'm done."

"He's been trying to help you. Like, to be more confident? It's not like you weren't basically in love with Paige as soon as you saw her, just because of what she *looks* like. So why do you hate him so much?"

I don't hate him, actually. Or at least, if I didn't still love him, then I wouldn't have to hate him this much. That's kind of the problem. "Because it makes me sick. The way he's using everyone. Dash, get *out!*" I guess I'm cracking up, a little bit. Because I've always been the one who thinks drama is for idiots, but that doesn't stop me from dropping down on my knees and slamming my head into the floor, over and over. "Get out, get out, get out!"

Ruby stares in total shock, because this is not the me she's used to, then runs over and starts trying to haul me up by my shoulders. Her bowl of frosting clangs down and rolls across the floorboards.

"Dashiell, please?" Oh great. She's talking in my direction, but *through* me. "You have to leave Ne—Everett. He's not okay."

And then it's over. The drama drains out of me so suddenly that I slump. Ruby's crying; I'm wheezing and halfway laughing at the same time, just from relief at knowing he's gone and I can talk and think again without having him smeared all over me. I fumble around in my pockets and find my inhaler, suck in.

"Better. Okay. I'm better now." I get to my feet while Ruby kind of flops, her hair sticking to her tear-streaked face and one hand reaching vaguely toward me. "I'm going out. You have an awesome time with Dashiell. Eat some cake."

"You're supposed to be grounded. Remember?"

"Whatever. If Dad actually cared what we do maybe he'd be home more." I know Dashiell is out of me now—I'm sure I felt him go—but God, do I sound like him. "Tell Dad whatever you want. You don't have to lie for *me*." I turn away from her and it's satisfying as hell.

"Never-Ever." I guess I knew this was coming. I'm not even through the kitchen door and Ruby's already been displaced by her favorite ghoul. It takes a lot more than rotting to shut some people up. A thousand years could go by, New York could be under the ocean and wasted by nuclear bombs and cratered by a meteor, and Dashiell would still be jabbering on from some splintered TV in the ruins. "Never, listen to me. It could be dangerous for you out there, especially on your own. You and Miss Slippers have attracted a bit too much interest. Why do you think I took steps to keep her home from school today?"

I haven't looked back but I can feel him right behind me. I can *smell* who he is. "So you admit it. That you bashed her head on purpose."

"I haven't claimed anything else, Never-Ever. Miss Slippers mentioned an unexpected meeting with someone I know. It was cause for concern, simply. So I made sure she wouldn't be leaving the house before I could investigate."

I've stopped dead, because something is fluttering at the edge of my brain. A memory: my mouth with his voice talking out of it. Ruby's eyes so close to me that they blur a little, greenish smudges on her plaintive face. *You're the one who did it for me, sweetest Ru.* When did that happen? *I won't forget that.* And then . . .

Jesus. "You *kissed* her. Ruby. On the lips."

I still have my back to him. I don't have to see the bastard to know the way he's shrugging. "Why wouldn't I kiss her? She's my precious girl."

I've started trembling so hard I'm afraid my legs might collapse. "If I remember that, Dash," I say—and now I'm finally turning, half-leaning against the doorframe—"what *don't* I remember?"

There he is in front of me: Ruby's face, but wrenched out of shape by that sulky, arrogant look Dash always got when somebody had the balls to confront him. There's a pause, like maybe he thinks it's beneath him to even respond, but then he does.

"I didn't *molest* my baby sister, Never. If that's what you're implying."

Blood pounds in my head until I can barely see. "You've lied about everything else. And what you're doing right *now* is basically molesting her, anyway. You know how she feels about you!"

Another pause. "Ruby Slippers isn't much of one for concealing her emotions, is she? Of course I know. I know how you feel about me, too, Never-Ever."

That does it. I turn and head for the front door. In the hallway mirror I see my face working through these horrible contortions.

"Never. It isn't safe for you out there. Not without me."

"That's awesome," I snap. "Maybe somebody will stab me for real this time."

"Stay with me and Miss Slippers. I'm truly sorry our situation is so painful for you, Never. I'm working to find a resolution."

I don't bother answering that, I just flip back the lock. Talking to Dash means letting him shove your brain in circles until he's got you exactly where he wants you.

"If you come weaseling around in me again, I'll throw myself off a bridge, Dash. Okay?"

"I'm doing my best to look after you, Never. Try to understand that." The door is hanging open in front of me. A filthy, rust-colored sky above rows of shining windows across the street; the stink of pulped leaves.

"The name is Everett, actually," I tell him. "*You* try to understand, for once." And I storm off into the Brooklyn night.

RUBY SLIPPERS

* * * * *

A second skin of darkness sucks in, tight but elastic, stretching as I struggle against it. It squeezes me again; even my eyelids are bandaged by slick black. *Dash,* I try to call, *Dash, please let me out!* Can't he hear me? Stomping shakes up from below—is he running up the stairs? Is he crashing through the hallways, slamming open a door? Has he forgotten I'm here?

"*Yes, Dashiell, you're correct. There are indeed conditions on my love for you. I don't see those conditions as particularly onerous, however. Or unreasonable. Basic human decency, that would be more than enough. I would be only too glad to love you again, if you would give me the opportunity.*" It's Dad's voice, but where is he? Why can I hear him so clearly in the swerving dark, almost as if he was murmuring in my ear? His voice drowns out the noise of something smashing in the distance. Then the same smash comes back like an echo, gradually breaking into static. "*Don't think you can take advantage of Ruby again to come in this house. I've impressed on her how serious this is. Really, Dashiell, duping your fourteen-year-old sister into acting as an accessory to your thefts? Coaching her to lie to me? And even after you've gone that far, you can talk to me as if you were somehow the* victim *in all this?*"

Why is Dad going on about something that happened more than two years ago, though? He must be talking about the time when Dash told me he had to pick up some things he'd left in his room, and copied our dad's credit card information down instead while I cooked dinner. Dad's voice rumbles in my head until I want to scream. But how can he look at me and know that Dashiell is the mind inside me?

Unless this isn't happening, or not now. It must be a memory like an earthquake, quivering every joint of the dark. I can barely hear what I think might be footsteps charging down the steps, banging sounds, footsteps again. No matter how quickly Dash races through the house, our dad's voice keeps on chasing him: *"No one has injured you except yourself. This is not an injustice. Acknowledge that much, and it will at least allow me to regain some respect for you. Can you do that? Dashiell?"*

Waves of pain beat through my thoughts, but I know, I can feel, that the pain isn't mine. *Dash? Are you okay? It's me, Ruby-Ru. Please just say something.* If he can hear me, he isn't answering; how long will he leave me adrift in this rocking void?

I am the night's unborn child, and that means I should not be alone at all. But somehow I've lost my twin.

"Did you take pleasure in involving her? Tell me, was corrupting Ruby incidental to your purpose? Or is that actually your goal? I'd forbid her to see you if I weren't concerned that she would go behind my back. I've decided it's better if I know. This is what we've come to, though: that I'm genuinely afraid to let my daughter spend time with the brother she adores. Think about that."

How could Dad say that to him? I remember how bad the fights got that summer, but I know I never heard Dad tell him anything quite this awful. If I'd been there I would have run out and screamed in Dashiell's defense, said anything I could to prove how crazy Dad's ideas were, so this must have happened when I wasn't around to stop it. Maybe when Ever and I went to Paris for two weeks that August, to see our mom? She dragged us to every tourist attraction and department store she could think of, like if we all stayed busy enough she wouldn't have to really look in our faces. She thinks, if she goes through the motions every few years, then Ever and I won't have any excuse to resent her.

I feel a cold blast brushing over me. For half an instant it's as if I owned my skin again. As if I was running up a street in chill shadow, my face floating on scrolls of wind. Have we gone out somewhere?

Then I'm completely gone, into the darkness. I can't guess for how long.

Once I smell upturned earth. Once I think my hands might be buried in dank soil. I almost panic, but then the dark comes back and soothes me.

Hot petals tumble down—or no, I'm in the shower, suds sheeting down my arms. A crimson fluid spirals toward the drain and my hand instinctively jerks to my throat. But I'm not hurt, or anyway not seriously. My calf is stinging and I look to see deep parallel scratches running down my shin, and I have no idea how they got there. Four thin ridges of dried blood. But they're just *scratches*. Dash would never let anything bad happen to me, not truly.

It's a long time, though, before I feel calm enough to turn off the water, and then I sit wrapped in a towel on my bed with my clothes heaped at my feet. Oh, so Dashiell must have undressed me, but if we're sharing the same body how can he avoid it? The darkness that squeezed me before is still close. I can feel how it's shrunk to limn the inside of my skin, rustling when I move: an internal shadow, barely caged. My clock says it's after eleven, but the house is submerged in such deep silence that I'm almost positive no one else is home.

When I finally get pajamas on and wander to the kitchen I see Dashiell's cake. I remember dropping the bowl of frosting when I was fighting with Everett, but now the layers are stacked together and the frosting is perfectly swirled over them. Twenty-three candles bristle from one side, their wicks blackened; he must have used every stubby burned-down birthday candle he could find, clumps of them in different colors. A big piece is missing, and a frosting-streaked plate and fork are in the sink with the mixing bowls.

I know what made him flip out: it was Everett, and how harsh he was with both of us. Dashiell might act like he doesn't care sometimes, but he's actually way too sensitive to cope with someone he loves being so cruel to him. I know Dash finished making the cake and then started eating it as a kind of message. "Dash?" I whisper. "Are you okay now?"

He doesn't answer me, not exactly, but I can tell that he isn't feeling much better. Grief still reverberates from shore to shore: endless ripples on a black river.

EVERETT

* * * *

So yeah, that would be someone following me. That would be someone not even trying to hide it, really. Big, flat, flapping footsteps have stayed ten feet back around the last three turns, and I guess it proves Dashiell's point about how I shouldn't be wandering around out here, and that pisses me off more than anything. Who's this asshole making it seem like Dash is *right*? The air is damp and sludgy, with a hard wind smacking the hell out of everything so that everybody walks with their heads squashed down between their shoulders. Not a lot of people are out, even though I've turned on to 7th Avenue so that I'll be able to duck into a restaurant if I have to.

But even on 7th Avenue the stores don't go on forever, or not the stores that stay open late anyway, and I'm starting to edge up on the blocks where darkness eats at the houses and only crumbs come through in the lit-up spots. It doesn't seem like a great idea to keep going and I stop and stare in a toy store's window, just in case I'm wrong and whoever it is behind me totally coincidentally has been following my exact route. A little model carousel goes around and around, purple horses bobbing, and twinkly lights beaming everywhere. I try to let go of myself and just be what I'm seeing: one tiny horse galloping slowly above meadows of plastic crap. Maybe that person tracking me—who's actually standing like three feet to my left, now, and who is obviously big enough to beat in my face without even breaking a sweat—will get bored and move on. I'm trying not to look but his eyes are glued to my reflection. Bulky guy. Older, hairy. Looks like ass, not to pull punches or anything. Some kind of sick rash. Awesome.

"Um, hello Everett! I hope you're having a pleasant evening. We *all* hope so."

The voice comes from pretty high up but I still look down, because it seems like this dude must have a kid with him and I just didn't notice her. But no, there's no little girl next to him, so apparently that horrible chirping voice is his. It should make me collapse on the sidewalk from sheer creep-out, but at this point I'm so angry—at everything being weird, and diseased, and distorted, at death needing a serious tune-up and ghosts crawling like roaches through my guts—that I barely care.

"Right. Do I know you?"

"You don't need to know me. I'm a friend of the family! That's what they told me to say." I'm looking at him this time, checking to make sure that that voice is really coming out of his ugly face. Yup. Ah, so I guess this must be the guy Elena was talking about, the one she saw talking to Dashiell?

The one who wanted him to *trade* Ruby. "You know my brother, you mean. That doesn't make you anyone's friend."

"I don't want to be Dashiell's friend anymore!" he squeals; getting excited makes him seem even more like a little girl. His hands fly up to shoulder height and do this baby-bird spazz. I might be not quite as worried now about him beating me up.

"He isn't very polite. He says nasty things to me and he gets angry for no reason! I don't *care* if I do—things he wouldn't like. As long as he can't catch me after."

It's not like I think anything good about this person, but I still can't help grinning at that. A hard, twisted grin, all gritted teeth, like I could bite through someone's neck for kicks.

"I'm not his biggest fan, either."

"That's what they thought? They thought maybe you're getting mad at him? And so maybe you would—let them help you?"

"That's really a lot of *theys*," I say. I have kind of a queasy feeling that I might have met *them* before, too.

"There are a lot," he agrees. Nervously, which isn't super encouraging. "And they have a lot of cats."

I laugh, and I sound just like Dash all over again. Maybe when he clears out of me he leaves a thick slime of him-ness behind, sticking all over my heart and entrails, and I'll never be completely purged of him. "Are you another ghost, then?" Not a lot of other options, now that I think of it.

"I don't like that word. It's very rude to call somebody names like that. I'm *Mabel*."

Okay. I guess it's not just that he sounds like a girl, then. "And they told you to talk to me about how intensely they want to help me out? What are you getting out of it?"

Mabel's eyes slide sideways. "Um, they were mad at me for running away? So they promised not to be mad anymore. If I would talk to you. Because they just have cats right now, so they can't talk to anybody up here?"

Right; Elena said she heard them *babbling about cats*, but that's not all she told me. "Yeah? And what about Ruby?"

It's hard to describe the look on Mabel's face: almost like his, or her, eyes are staring straight into the middle of her brain. Bullets of concentration shooting right for the hippocampus. It goes on for a while. We haven't moved away from the toy shop window, and the lights from that miniature merry-go-round spark in Mabel's big glassy eyes.

"They say they can't help Ruby," Mabel finally reports. "Not yet. Because they're missing something important? It got lost? They can help you but Ruby is just too bad."

That wasn't what I meant, but it still makes me curious. "What kind of *help* are we talking about?"

Mabel's head swings to stare at me and her big bearded jaw drops in surprise. "Push him out! And shut the door on him, bang! Don't you want that? No more Dashiell in you? Out, out, out!"

Until right now I was just kind of playing along for the hell of it. That, and to figure out more about what the deal is. But this is the one thing Mabel could have said to yank my attention into one big tight bundle—because why, yes, I *do* want that.

"Why would they care what I want? It's got nothing to do with them." My mouth has gone dry. Eagerness has a taste, it turns out. Sour and crinkly, like aluminum.

Mabel's listening again. She could be trying to wad up her crusty ears and stuff them into her head, to hear what's going on in there. "Highly displeased? They say I should say that Dashiell stole something from them. Something valuable. And that he cheated them out of their rights. They say to tell you that they are *highly displeased* with him, and that closing you up would be a suitable punishment? It will teach him that his disrespect won't be tolerated. Those are the words they are telling me to say."

He stole something is right, with my hands doing the swiping. What happened to that weird object he stuffed in my pocket? My brain's been so overloaded that I haven't thought about it since that night at Paige's apartment, but I know I've worn the same jeans again and it definitely wasn't in there anymore.

"A whole lot of people have tried to teach Dash that. Hasn't worked yet."

Mabel gives me a coy smile that makes the hair around her lips stick out in spikes. "Um, they say they feel confident in their ability to do a better job instructing him. And they think you'd appreciate that?"

Okay. *They* know way too much about me, considering that the only time we met I was running like hell and not stopping to have long conversations about my feelings. I know I'm not subtle or anything, but there is still something really wrong going on here. I should tell Mabel and her invisible friends to go play in traffic. That's obvious.

Except that they're my only chance to maybe own my brain and body for real again. Dash is out for right now, but I'm not kidding myself that it's going to stay this way. He'll give me enough of a break to calm down, but I already know he'll come slinking back when he thinks it's *appropriate,* and for the rest of my life that will keep happening. I'll be myself and not myself, and I won't be able to rely on really basic assumptions, like that my thoughts actually belong to me.

"Okay, I'm convinced. That sounds great. Go ahead and tell me how to shut Dash out. If there's really a way to do that."

They say it won't work for Ruby because *something got lost—* but if I'm in charge of my own brain again then maybe I could try to find whatever went missing? Because it suddenly hits me:

I've been so sticky and confused with Dashiell-ness that I've barely known what I was doing, and maybe it's the same for her and I'm in the wrong for not realizing that sooner. Like, she might not be entirely responsible for her actions, and I should cut her some slack? So if there's any way I can help her, I *still* have to do it.

"It's not something we can tell you, they say. But we can show you in person," Mabel says, and she's looking twitchy again. Every fidget on that big, coarse face is practically jangling a warning bell at me: *bad idea, Everett; ding-dong, bad, bad idea.* If I could think of any alternative I'd totally pay attention. But what do you do, when the only people who can help you are monsters? You make a deal.

"Show me in person? Where?"

Mabel's face goes slack with relief, which is possibly the only thing more repulsive than seeing her tense and spastic. She doesn't wait to hear what *they* have to say this time.

"Like you don't know where!"

Right. I guess I do know. I also know that Dashiell said those not-perfect-gentlemen-things might try to stop me from ever waking up again, if they caught me there. Keep me as a kind of hostage. Maybe that's their whole plan. Or maybe it's *Dashiell's* plan, to make sure I'm so freaked out that I'll never let them give me any information. *They know I'd do anything for you and Miss Slippers.* Yeah, really, Dash? Would you go all Special Forces and try to rescue me, if I needed you?

"I'll think about it."

That's not what she wanted to hear. Her eyes bug and her huge scabby paws do that horrible flutter again. "But—this is *special*. We don't just help people normally! And if you make him wait he'll get angry and change his mind!"

Them has compacted down into *him* now, I notice. "Who's going to get angry, Mabel? Want to explain who you're talking about?"

"Aloysius." She says it in this dread-stricken whisper, so maybe she doesn't think he's an awesome gentleman any more than Dash does.

"Aloysius? He's the one who's been doing all the blabbing in there?"

"You should try to have nicer manners, Everett Bohnacker. Aloysius is in *charge*. And he knows you helped Dashiell steal from him. So you have to behave now. Do what you're told and no more talking back!"

Ah. A dead-guy authority figure. No wonder he and Dashiell can't stand each other. "I said I'll think about it. I've had enough of dead people telling me what to do. Okay?" God, though, how I wish I could talk to Dash about this. Ask his advice. The awful thing is that, if Dash wasn't my enemy, I'm pretty sure he'd know how to handle these people, or not-so-much-people. But I can't exactly ask him to explain the best way to betray him.

Mabel's attention has rolled into her head again. "Oh! He says okay."

"What?"

"He says, 'Tell young master Bohnacker to mull matters at his leisure. Not the slightest pressure. He isn't the one who owes respect here. Yet.' That's what he says. But Aloysius is *never* nice like that! He—"

There's a kind of wheeze-gag way down in her throat that

shuts her up. Suddenly I feel the size of the night again, like it's gobbling up way more of the world than it has any right to. And way more of me, too. Above the streetlights it's a gulping, sucking thing, and 7th Avenue really seems to go on forever now—but whichever direction I go, I'll end up in the same hole. All I can think is that I need to get away from Mabel, now, even if I have to dig my way out through the darkness.

"Great. Nice meeting you. I'm leaving."

Mabel isn't talking yet but she gives this panicky jerk and grabs for me. Fingers drag at my jacket and I jump away just in time. I'm too scared to turn my back on her so I do this ridiculous hobbling hop-step backward until I'm out of range if she lunges for me.

"Everett!" She spits it out, and all at once I get how completely pitiful she is, kind of slurping at the air like she can pull me back that way. I mean, is she actually a little kid, stuck on her own in that blob of a body? Shouldn't she have parents taking care of her? "Can't I come with you?"

Ugh. I'm sorry for her, but not that sorry. "No, actually. I want to be alone."

"Then do something for me? Tell Ruby I like her? A *lot*. I don't care how silly she is. Tell her I want to be good friends."

That won't be happening. Mabel's looking more and more like the huge, sluggish tongue of whatever is trying to swallow me. All I want are the rules back; I don't mean anything fancy, just dead-is-dead and I-am-me. If something grabs me, it should be made out of molecules. Laws of physics. Standard shit.

"Ruby doesn't want friends. She just wants Dashiell. Sorry if that bums you out, but it's the truth."

Mabel looks at me like I just killed her puppy. But she really shouldn't take it so personally.

Ruby doesn't even want me anymore. Maybe she doesn't want herself, either.

MABEL

* * * *

Wait right here, Aloysius said. Wait here where there's gray and no skin and nothing to touch, and never any food, and no warmth or sleep or blankets. There's air like paste, and there's the river, and even when we talk to each other we do it without sound. *Wait right here, and the boy will be along in good time. Put on your prettiest appearance for him when he arrives, there's a pet.* Because almost nobody here can look like anything but horrors, but I can hint *littlegirl, sweetdollgirl* at living people, and most of the time that's what they see: pretty thing, curly hair, even though none of it is there. Aloysius knows that's special about me, I hint so much better than he can. I can make them see me almost like I used to be.

So I wait in the gray, and it isn't even dust, and I'm not even a twist of yarn here. I can feel Old Body far away, so scared and empty that he keeps glass after glass of stinking spirits dumping down his face. He's sitting on the dirty bed in his room: a cold, ugly room with a sink on the wall, where he eats greasy food out of bags. *Don't you miss me?* I want to say, but I'm too far away for him to hear me. He can hear me only when I'm whispering right there in his head, and even then he gets confused. *Don't you miss your Mabel, who makes you forget half your life?*

If I go back to him the body will be so sick and spinning that I won't be able to lift it out of bed, but I'd rather be sick inside him than gray here, with no face or eyes or moving blood. But Aloysius said *stay,* and if I trip away into Old Body even for a few little moments and miss the boy when he comes then Aloysius will be angry all over again, and then he'll never do what he promised. And I need him to help me. Because Old Body is getting crazier every day, and I don't know how much longer I can keep him.

I don't like being here. It isn't good for me to be away from him. I know he's standing up and staring in the mirror over the sink, whining to himself, tra-la-la. *The evil,* he calls me, because he's so stupid. *The evil is out for now, but it will come back, I know it will come back.* It scares me when he thinks that way. It scares me, what he might do, when I have to stay here with the dead people and then maybe Old Body will do something bad too fast for me to stop him.

I'll be nicer, I tell him, even though he doesn't hear. *I'll be nicer to you from now on, and comb your hair, and you'll wake up in your soft warm bed every morning and not out on the wet ground anymore. Don't do anything silly!* He's leaving his room now, number 218, and walking down the hallway with his arm smearing on the wall. I don't like it at all, and I almost jump back into him, but Aloysius has too many spies and if I leave here even for one second they might tell him.

Wearing Old Body feels so filthy, though. He's reeking and dingy and full of holes, like a rag dress a beggar child would wear. If I can get someone else then I won't care and he can do what he wants. Ruby is so fresh, like stockings drying on the line and clean new wool. But I don't have her yet and Aloysius might try to sneak out on his promises, and now Old Body is banging on a door, big paw swinging hard into wood like he thinks it's empty air, and he's hollering, and someone is saying *goddamnyouNick, don'tyouknowwhattime.* And Old Body says, *I'vegotthemoney, lookhere, I'vegotit.*

Then I have to turn away from the living world, because the gray here flashes red-green-red and the mush starts to think it has shapes and I can suddenly see myself: lace dress and shiny shoes and doll-pink ankles. Is it Everett, almost here, showing us what he sees? Can I politely escort him now like Aloysius told me? I have to forget whatever Old Body is doing because I need to be properly attentive like they said I should. I am looking like a dollgirl, but it's not quite right: dozens of little hand-crabs are crawling all over my dress, grabbing everywhere, and I can't let Everett see me like this or he'll scream and run away and then Aloysius will punish me. I have to use my whole strength to hint better, to push out a nicer shape for myself that the living boy will see: little girl, poorlittlegirl, lost and alone in this bad place. I can't look like a horror. Even when I look my prettiest, living people feel afraid of me.

But no, whoever was coming here slides away and leaves us with gray and no-shape and sad old nothingness again. I hate it. I hate being dead worse than anything; I'd rather be Old Body so drunk he pees in his bed than be here. Everett Bohnacker is very wrong to make me wait and wait so long, so he deserves whatever happens to him, and I won't feel guilty that I helped. I will sleep in Ruby and I will wear her hair in beautiful curls and dress her up in floating dresses, and I'll make Everett sorry he told me to go away.

That's what I'm thinking when I feel Old Body holding the gun tight in both hands, and then I don't care anymore what Aloysius does to me and I rush back in a blast to that room where the paint peels in long sores. I stream back into his brain and we wrestle together—Jacob wrestled with the angel, and Old Body is wrong, I'm his angel and not his evil! He's so upset that it makes him strong, too strong; I'm wrestling but I can't take him over like I'm trying, and the gun rocks up and down, black hole at his chest, his eye, the sky, and back down.

Stop it please, I'll be nicer to you from now on, I'm your angel here to save you, I chatter into his thoughts, and I know he hears me but he doesn't listen to what I say, and then bang!

RUBY DASHIELL SLIPPERS

✳ ✳ ✳ ✳

I am remembering, and I am not myself.

I remember being a cloud below a caved-in ceiling. In a brick house charred, its silence scratched by rats. But I didn't care, because I was rain suspended and sustained in a velvet atmosphere so richly pillowing that my fall was too slow to be seen by the naked eye. Falling. I was not alone in this room, but I might as well have been, because what were these people to me? No one would bother us. This was a house left well alone, and not just because it might collapse at any moment. Everyone said it was haunted.

The raindrops must have been silver, because they rang out on the floor. I turned my head to see my phone's glowing screen saying, *Dashiell, it's been over a month. I'm worried. Please just say you're okay. Your Ruby-Ru.* A blood-daubed rag beside it. I looked away, then slid the phone into my jeans.

Ruby had kept my last visit a secret, just as I'd asked, but our father found out in due course and barred me from the house of my childhood, cut me off, gutted my bedroom, and replaced my belongings with smug new trash from Pottery Barn. But what did it matter? I was rain and I washed everything away, even my father, even my sister.

Someone pawed at my shoulder and I looked again, unwilling to see. "You don't know what I am," a man named Harper Wills said; he'd bellied his way to me across the floor and he twined serpentine among the rags and dropped needles, his face craning up at me. "You don't know. I've been dead since '77 and this was my *home*. My home, where I lived with my wife. I've come back to haunt you all!"

"You've done an excellent job on the putrefaction," I said—but I was dreaming, I was the fall of the sky, and the words were distant chimes. Harper Wills couldn't have been born yet in '77, that was obvious; he was barely older than me. "Such advanced decay in four short decades? I'm impressed."

He floundered for a long moment, trying to parse what I'd said, his greenish face pitching in the shadows like a storm-tossed boat. Then the meaning beached on his brain.

"Not this body. This isn't what died."

And I laughed at him, but sleepily, the laugh rolling over vast unsteady distances. It seemed to provoke him.

"They gave me a *job* to do," he said. "An assignment. You don't know anything about it, but the way you're going you'll learn soon enough!"

"Of course," I said, still laughing. "Lolling high on the floor of a squat in Queens? That's a mission of the greatest importance. No wonder they entrusted it to a man of your caliber."

"Pretentious little *shit*," Harper snarled, but I noticed he was clutching something inside his shirt and his eyes were suddenly shifty and afraid—afraid he'd said too much. Afraid I would notice his crackling anxiety. Ah, so someone *had* given him a task to do, perhaps involving hiding or delivering a package of some value, and it seemed worth paying attention. I started to nod into my bundled jacket—feigning, because I was actually returning to prosaic wakefulness.

I am remembering, and I am Ruby Slippers once again.

The winter when I was fourteen and then fifteen Dashiell disappeared completely, and I called and texted him again and again with no reply. Now that I know the things our dad said to him, maybe I can understand a little better why he wouldn't speak to me. I know all the way through my chest how hurt Dash must have been. *Dash-Dot-Dot, I know you were angry, but you didn't need to take it out on me!* Dashiell doesn't answer but I can feel him buried inside me, listening to every thought flashing through my mind. And I remember:

How afraid I was for him that winter. How wherever I walked in the city I would try to feel if he had walked there, too. I would imagine that I was slipping my footsteps into his, feeling out the grooves he'd left on the air, and in that way I would find him. My dad and Everett would talk to me and I wouldn't hear them, because I was listening for my older brother: for the imperceptible disturbance that his coat might have stirred into the wind a week before.

And then I started sneaking into Manhattan alone, and going up to strangers in Tompkins Square Park. To people on the benches who were beautiful but frightening, pockmarked and too thin, like him. To people who looked at me with contempt, and who made me feel even pinker and younger and dumber than I was. I'd say, *I'm looking for my brother. Dashiell Bohnacker. Do you know him?* They usually laughed at me, or scowled, or said, *Sure, honey, I can take you to him right now,* in a way that I knew meant something much worse.

All through our fifteenth birthday I kept listening for the phone or the doorbell, listening so hard that the air sang like a finger on wet glass, because no matter what happened Dash had never missed our birthday before. The silence was so absolute and shrill and terrible that it started to sound like death, and I didn't know if it was Dash's death I was hearing or my own.

Maybe a week later I overheard a senior at my school talking about a bar at the south end of the Williamsburg waterfront; he'd gone in with a fake ID, but it was so creepy in there he and his friends left right away. Full of junkies, he said, and so after school I took the train there and then walked up and down the block out front, waiting for someone I could ask about Dashiell. Striations of wet snow sliced the sky into huge angled pieces, and smokestacks without smoke loomed across the street. So much snow kept blurring down that the gray scribble of the Williamsburg Bridge was half-erased.

There was a big plate-glass window and I peered in, but it was too dark to see anything besides the empty front counter and a few swags of Christmas lights way in the back. A few people wandered by, but no one came out of the bar, and after an hour I gave up and started walking back in the direction of the subway. I remember that my corduroys were soaking wet, caked in white from the knees down, and how even in my thick coat I was shivering. I remember the whining scrape of my pants as I walked and the slush plopping off my boots, and how utterly miserable I was. It was the first time I felt absolutely sure that he was gone, and gone forever.

I'd walked a block when I heard footsteps hissing in the snow behind me. It was still late gray afternoon and at first the noise was just another element in the desolation, like those steps didn't have any identity apart from me and how awful I felt. Then they started to come a little quicker and closer, snapping at my awareness so that I knew I had to pay attention. Each footstep sent a tiny vibrating current through my body, and I was looking around for strangers I could yell to, just in case.

I was passing the open mouth of an alley when the steps burst into a run, and before I could turn around I was slamming into the alley's shadows, then driven face-first against the brick. Tense hands gripped my wrists and pinned them to the wall above my head, then one shifted down to seize my mouth, and I was sure I was about to be raped, or worse. The man holding me there was tall and thin, and a sweet, feverish stench glutted my throat while I strained to pull free. He pressed in, grinding my right cheek against the wall.

"This is only a test, Ruby-Ru," a voice said. "The Emergency Broadcast System is here to inform you that your broken corpse will be found in an alley much like this one, if you don't desist from what you're doing immediately. My social milieu is not at all a suitable place for you to put yourself into circulation. You will not come looking for me again."

Dashiell! I tried to say. *I had to see you. I had to know you were alive. How could I worry about whether or not it was dangerous?* But he still wouldn't let go of my mouth and all that came out was a muffled groan. My saliva slicked his palm and my body felt watery, buckling and sliding away from me even as Dash pinned me there.

"Whose decision is it, Ru? When and in what manner and condition you see me?" It was his voice but also wrong, wild, rasping. "What right do you have to treat me as some beast, to hunt me down and snap your precious mental pictures of me against my will? If I don't call, if you don't see me, you should know that it's because I've decided that's in your best interests. You won't be seeing me now, either. I'm a wraith. I'm the dusk come to devour you. Nod if you understand me."

I didn't understand, not really, but I nodded. Because I was afraid in a way I'd never been before, the world slitting through me in shards of ice. Because Dash seemed so crazed that I would have done anything to calm him. The hand clutching my wrists relaxed but he still held me squeezed against the bricks, his body crushing my back, shoulders, thighs.

"You have a task in front of you, Ruby Slippers, if you want me ever to forgive you for this extraordinary violation. You will walk away. You will not speak one word or turn or try to look at me. You do not have my permission to see me like this. You do not have my permission to remember what happened here today. You will return to your life as a good little girl, and you will keep your image of me as bright and clean and blazing as a supernova. Nod."

I nodded. Dusk mingled with the snow. I still couldn't completely take it in, though: that this was really him and not just in my head; that he truly would force me to leave, after months apart, without ever holding him or gazing at his face. The cuff of his leather jacket rubbed my neck as he pulled his hand from my mouth. For a long moment we stayed like that, our feet sunk in slush and dirty water crying into our faces, both of us breathing hard. Maybe Dash was checking to see if I would break his rules and speak, but I didn't. I was too stunned, even if I'd wanted to.

"I think you're ready to go now, Miss Slippers. I think you can emerge from this detour into foulness with your heart still pure. Remember not to look at me. Look now, and I swear you'll never see me again." He leaned sideways and kissed me: a slow kiss on the edge of my cheekbone, so that a single scroll of his filthy hair wavered in the corner of my eye.

Then he let me go, stepping deeper into the alley, and I made myself walk away from him. His presence exerted an overwhelming gravity all over my nape and skull, and I stumbled from the longing to run back to him, but I knew I couldn't give in. He'd meant what he said and I had to fight the weight of his closeness, to grab hold of the nearest corner and pull myself around it and back onto the street. I walked for the next half block with my eyes closed and my fingertips trailing along the wall, to stop myself from glancing around. It was only when I nearly tripped on a crack that I let myself see again.

The air was full of indigo dust and a thousand moons were falling.

I must have reached the subway, made it home somehow, but this is where the memory breaks. I didn't say a word to anyone, not even to Everett, because I didn't know how to whisper about that encounter in my own mind, much less describe it to anyone else. I said I'd slipped on the ice to explain the scrapes on my face.

A week later Dash called our dad and we all went out for brunch together. Dashiell was too pale and thin, his eyes too glassy, but you could tell he'd made an effort to look as scrubbed and beautiful as he could. And he was so sweet and playful with

me that I was almost convinced he didn't remember what had
happened at all. I started to wonder if that bizarre afternoon
had been real, or something I'd imagined—except that he was
better about keeping in touch with us after that.

Dashiell remembers. He always did, and his memory of that
day and mine twine around each other. I know now why he acted
the way he did. I know that if our dad hadn't said those brutal
things, hadn't accused Dash of trying to corrupt me, then when
he saw me through the bar's wide window he might have chosen very differently. He couldn't stand to let our father be right,
so his pride stopped him from coming outside and hugging me
and taking me someplace. I can't tell where.

I am remembering, and I am Dashiell Bohnacker. I am of two
minds, and my memory navigates among my sister's thoughts. I
know she hears me, and I choose to let her hear without restric-
tion. Living as we are at such close quarters, webbed into the
same synapses and veins, I might as well allow her to know me
better.

I let her see it, projected high and glowering: that burned-out
house in Queens on a lightless day late last February; that is, almost precisely one year after our chance meeting in Williamsburg.
Five days after she and Never turned sixteen and I took them
both to the movies with borrowed money, our father watching
out the window in a hysterical flutter for the moment I'd deliver
them safely home again.

Remember, then, Ruby-Ru, as if it's all happening again,
afresh, this very moment; consider it my gift.

I went back to the squat in Queens, having stolen a glimpse

of what Harper Wills secreted on the property; idiots, whoever they were, to entrust a hapless junkie like him with a pile
of gold coins, along with an odder item whose significance I
wholly failed to grasp until much later. The fact that Harper had
followed through on their instructions at all—that he'd hidden the
package, however ineptly, rather than simply vanishing with the
contents—suggested that they must be exceptionally dangerous
idiots. He'd clearly been cringing in terror of his employers; that
observation had kept me too wary to mess with their belongings until now, when I found myself with no other means of
support at hand, and some overdue bills to pay.

I hadn't been back here in a year. The place was dark and silent.
I'd heard rumors to the effect that even the most desperate squat-
ters had abandoned the house some time before, since anyone
who slept in it was visited by dismaying dreams. Saw dreadful
apparitions mingling with the grime. For my purposes privacy
was all to the good, of course. I was sure that the money was in
here somewhere, since Harper had spent too much time skulking in odd corners for it to signify anything other than a hunt
for a hiding spot. But I was anticipating a long search, probably
involving torn-up floorboards and avalanches of dead rats. I had
a battery-powered lantern with me and a crowbar, and I thought
those simple tools should be sufficient to my task.

As usual, the front door appeared to be boarded up, but it was
all a sham: the boards weren't attached to the door itself and
I merely had to turn the knob and then duck below the planks
into unrelieved must and gloom. I'd enjoyed the abandonment
of staying somewhere so unapologetically degrading during my
time here. I'd enjoyed traveling from this vile hovel into Chel-
sea, showering at Hugo's studio and changing into the clothes

I stored with him, then after work going off with my grotesquely spoiled and much older girlfriend Alexis, if girlfriend was the proper term, to a dinner that cost more than Hugo paid me in a week and from there to her extravagant bed. I liked constructing my life out of the most extreme contrasts available.

By the February day when I returned here both Alexis and Hugo were behind me, and their disapprobation was a matter of complete indifference. Even the resulting inconvenience of being so utterly broke could be amended, so I thought, with a few hours in this stinking darkness.

I was only a few steps inside the door when the stench—of feces rat and human, of desiccated mice, stale sweat, and charred wood—seemed to rise up in an animate miasma. It assumed a roughly humanoid form just behind my left shoulder, regarding me. For another few steps I was able to dismiss the impression as absurd. The house was groaning all around me and the suggestion of a looming, hazy figure at my shoulder was getting ever more insistent. I finally spun to confront it, with the confused idea that I could dissolve the thing with the pure force of my disdain. I couldn't see much in the dimness, just a blur of motion, and then something collided with my head. Hard enough to drop me, whatever it was; possibly a loose board.

That's all there was for a while, Miss Slippers. Stay with me and remember the darkness. We are here together in this memory, lying half-conscious and immobile in the dense filth on that floor, my skin impregnated with bottle caps and broken glass. I hope you find the experience educational.

Then I began to see a landscape that you've come to know quite well—though since I was still alive on this occasion, I could bring my own imagination to bear on the place. For me it wasn't dim but blindingly bright, all dazzling blues and greens, with a levitating river of neon aquamarine and trees sprouting poisonous suns.

"Young Mr. Bohnacker," someone said—again, just behind my left shoulder. I turned to see a man chartreuse and scaled like a snake, dressed in a business suit. It was my introduction to Aloysius, though I didn't know anything about him at the time. I was nonplussed and didn't immediately reply, and he gave me a smile that pleated his whole face. "Young Mr. Bohnacker, I have every reason to believe you'll be on painfully intimate terms with us quite soon. You will discover then that it's much, much more pleasant here if you haven't done anything to annoy us in the meantime. You will find yourself anxious to be on the best possible footing with me in particular. I wouldn't advise touching anything in this house that doesn't belong to you. Keep your thievish dope-fiend's mitts to yourself, there's a good lad, and we'll get along splendidly."

I'd have liked to respond with something snappy and dismissive, but my body and even the garish world around me crystallized into a solid block of terror. Bright, icy, faceted, winking in the impossible sun. The snake-man was gone and for a long time I couldn't move, my heart frozen in a violent contraction.

Darkness again. After some indeterminate time, the floor again, a thin stripe of light slicing in around the door. I was still paralyzed, unable to raise a hand as the cold claws of rats scrabbled across my neck. Hours of it, Ru-Ru, though I'll spare you from remembering them in detail. Hours of dried shit and glass and rubbery tails flicking my lips. Only my heart kept palpitating in the most abject horror.

At dawn my limbs started banging around in wild convulsions, and the moment I regained an inkling of self-control I was on my feet and out the door. As I ran I noticed the chain binding the mailbox—how had I missed it yesterday? Ugh, and to think I could have spared myself from entering the house at all! But knowing where the stash was didn't inspire me to try for it, not after that appalling night.

Withdrawal was starting to seem remarkably appealing, in view of my adventures.

There you go, Ru-Ru. That's what happened. And as you may deduce, this was the occasion that moved me to go cold turkey, in the hope that I would never endure anything of the kind again. It worked for six long months, until an especially bad night shook my resolve.

So now here I am, the worm in your sweet apple. I can't honestly say I don't enjoy it, this opportunity to batten on your freshness. I can't say I don't enjoy living on your innocence, sharing your soft breath when you toss in your sleep. Ah, but could I possibly corrupt you more profoundly than I do by letting you be me?

I hold my pillow and listen to my dad yelling at Everett just outside my room. Ever didn't deserve Dash, that's all. Now that Dashiell and I are living in one body, one brain, aren't we becoming a single person, a compound mind?

I am Ruby Dashiell Slippers. I am an endless message, dots and dashes spelled out in fire.

EVERETT

* ∗ ∗ ∗ ∗

Okay. To my dad it's absolutely a serious thing that he grounded me, and here I am straggling in at one in the morning, right in his face, like I don't give a damn what he thinks. It's frightening for him, because he worries all the time about me and Ruby going off the deep end and dragging him through a repeat of Dashiell. I get that. I even empathize. If my underperforming nerd son suddenly started acting the way I've been doing, I'd be concerned, too.

"Isn't seeing what happened to your brother enough to make you think twice about imitating his behavior? Everett? Should I take this defiance as a bid for my attention, or are we already at the point where I have to resort to urine tests to stop you from destroying yourself? What have you been *doing*?"

He's yelling, and the interesting thing is that what I pick up on now isn't so much that he's mad at me, but that he's scared shitless. And I guess it's because of some leftover trace of Dashiell in me that his fear makes me tempted to go on the attack. Like he's prey. Like he's already weakened by what Dash did to him, and it wouldn't be so hard to—what? Finish him off? I have to deliberately squelch an impulse to say something cruel.

"I had a fight with Ruby," I say—Dash's old trick of using the truth to lie, basically. "I just needed to get out for a walk."

His fear is so ludicrous, though. That's what's getting under my skin—that he's afraid of all the wrong things, and also not nearly afraid enough. I can't say I understand what's happening, but it's obvious that it's going to be the most dangerous decision of my life: if I should trust a pack of strange ghosts, just because they're my only hope of ever getting free of Dashiell. Now Dad is skeptically pinching his mouth at me, and he has no clue what the real risks are. He doesn't even know what's already living in his house. It's hard not to look down on him for it—though really, how is he supposed to know? *Dad, see, Ruby and I are both possessed by our dead brother, and it's been super stressful.*

Yeah, I won't be saying that.

"I thought we had a strong relationship," he says. At least he's not yelling now, but he's looking at me way too hard. Leaning on the wall with his silver hair gleaming. "I thought you trusted me, Everett. But there is clearly something very wrong here, and it's affecting both you and Ruby, and I need to know what it is. Tell me the truth. Please."

"I'm not on drugs. I don't even smoke pot. Watching Dash left me completely skeeved out about that stuff."

"Maybe so. But then what *is* this?" He stares. Bright gray eyes, totally focused on me. He's not a dumb guy at all, and he's not weak; it's good to be reminded of that. "Did you know that Ruby baked what appears to be a *birthday* cake? I found it in the kitchen. It might not be so disturbing if she hadn't gone to the extent of putting candles on it and blowing them out. Twenty-three of them. I counted. Or did you do that?"

"I had nothing to do with it." We're still in the front hallway, sandwiched between Ruby's room and the kitchen, and I'm suddenly so exhausted I feel nauseous—or maybe the nausea comes from thinking about that cake again.

"But you'd agree that it seems like a strange thing to do? Baking a cake for a dead man, even one she loved intensely? Engaging in this pretense that he can *get older*?"

"That's why we were fighting," I say. I'm swaying on my feet, dying to get away from him and collapse upstairs, but really this is my chance to push his anxiety off me. I can deflect it onto Ruby. *Simple*, as Dash would say. "That's what upset me so much I had to get out of the house." Dad starts opening his mouth, obviously to ask me why I didn't just go to my room if I needed space. "That cake started giving me this weird feeling like maybe the house is haunted, like in your dream? I know that's not rational but it still tripped me out."

And now he's nodding like that explains everything. "Delayed reaction. I'm afraid I've seriously underestimated how deeply traumatized you both are. You're still grounded—don't think I won't respond much more severely if you ignore that again—but I'm afraid this is my fault, Everett. I should have cut back on my hours much sooner. I should have anticipated that the two of you would need much more from me, in the wake of . . . of the absolute catastrophe our family has endured. You have my apology for that."

He turns his back on me decisively, like *that settles that*, and marches into the kitchen. He's moving in this hard, snapping way, but some of the defeated sag I saw this morning is back in his shoulders. I follow him in, still processing what he just said, and watch while he picks up the cake, stomps over to the garbage, levers up the lid, and tips it in. It skids sluggishly off the plate and splats down in a mess.

"There. No more delusions. We've lost him and we all have to accept that, no matter how painful it is. Tomorrow I'll start making enquiries. A good therapist. Someone who specializes in grieving. Works well with teenagers. It's been entirely too much."

My brain's not working so well, because it's taken me this long to figure out we have a problem. "You're cutting back on your hours?" If he's around the house more, it'll be a lot harder to hide from him just how messed up and insane everything is now. We're doing a lousy job of hiding it as it is, obviously. What was Ruby thinking, leaving that cake out for him to find?

Before I felt like hurting him, sick as that urge was, but now I'm completely pissed at Ruby for not realizing that we need to protect him. Like, maybe we're still kids, but when it comes to Dashiell haunting us, it's our dad who's the innocent. He thinks a *therapist* is going to fix this?

"I am. The hospital offered me a part-time schedule last spring. I declined; I'm well aware that there are still your college expenses and Ruby's to get through. But I think if I go back to them now and explain . . . even if it's only temporary . . ."

His foot is still on the lever of the garbage can. He's still standing over it, staring down at the heap of lavender frosting and crumbs and tipped birthday candles. The garbage is full enough that I can see the candles from halfway across the room. Jagged and mismatched, twisty little fingers trying to claw their way out of the ground.

I wonder if that's what he's seeing, too: smashed brown

cake like upturned earth, and something in it struggling to get free.

Brushing my teeth and getting ready for bed have never felt like such a big deal before. It's like some kind of elaborate purification ritual before I go off to battle. Because even if Mabel and her friends told me I could take my time deciding, I'm pretty sure they're not going to be all that patient in practice. I've given up, for now, on trying to figure out what I should do until I'm actually there, and maybe then I'll get a better idea by observing how they act.

When I finally lie down and start to drift off I hear something scratching and pounding at the floorboards beneath my bed. Over and over the noise wakes me up, but every time I open my eyes onto my dark room it's instantly totally silent. My bedroom is right above our kitchen, and finally I get up and sneak downstairs to see what's going on, shadows rumpling around me and weird sparks floating in my eyes. I half-expect to find Ruby in there, in full-on Dashiell mode, doing something perverse like digging the rest of his cake out of the garbage with both hands and stuffing it in her face. But no: the room is empty. Streetlamp glow kites across the ceiling and the curtains shift a little in a draft. There's no light under Ruby's door, either. So I go back to bed, but as soon as my thoughts start to slither around in that pre-sleep way the noise jars me again.

It's not until maybe the fourth or fifth time that I get it: there isn't anything clawing at the floor of my room.

They're attacking the floor of my *sleep*. The ghosts are down on some deeper level and the way between us is blocked or barricaded somehow. It's not hard to guess who must have done that, and I know it should piss me off; I have to get down there, after all, if I'm ever going to learn the secret to being Dashiell-proof. But it's actually kind of reassuring, because honestly I'm not ready to make such a huge decision. And maybe the scratching means I'm safe for now. It finally quiets down like they've given up for the night, and I'm able to relax in a way that I haven't since this whole mess started; Christ, less than a week ago.

I'm finally able to fall into serious sleep. Nice and dark and soft, just like none of this ever happened. When my alarm starts screaming at me in the morning, I smack it dead and roll over.

And keep rolling. My eyes start to jumble with shaken-kaleidoscope flashes. I'm standing on the bank of a river. The light looks predawn gray, but the river is shining in a million twisted colors, red and lime and blue-violet.

And a little girl is standing right next to me. Thick, dark brown curls, pink cheeks, a fluffy white dress with a black sash. You can tell she's been crying for a long time, because her eyes are red and her face is bloated and streaky. If I had only heard Mabel's voice without seeing her lumbering old-dude body, this is pretty much exactly how I would have pictured her.

"Don't worry," she says, and she's Mabel all right. "I can't do anything to you, Everett Bohnacker. You didn't do—what you'd have to do. And even if I could, I'd get in too much trouble!" Then she gets this self-conscious expression and swats something off her dress. I don't get a good look at whatever it is, but it crawls away at a good clip.

"I'm not worried," I say—and in the same moment I realize that hey, I really should be. "Why were you crying?" It's easier to be nice to her now that her body isn't so eerily out of whack with her voice; I guess it's superficial to judge on stuff like that, but it's hard to fight that kind of visceral creep-out.

"Somebody got *hurt*," Mabel whispers. "He might even die. So I was crying about him, and then Aloysius got angry at me again! Even though I *had* to go! How could I stay here when he was pointing a gun around?"

"A gun?" I say. "Aloysius has a gun?" I'm starting to wish my alarm would go off again, but I already know that time might not work the same way in this place. The snooze button on my clock is set for eight minutes of silence between noise-bursts.

Eight minutes in the real world might get translated down here into all the time they need.

She shakes her head. "I don't mean him. That's not what he has." The whole statement is way too vague to be comforting. "So can I take you now? Where we're supposed to go?"

Bad idea, Everett. I know I have to think fast, and clearly, but the truth is that I don't have enough information to make a good choice. So Aloysius is pretty clearly evil, but is he really any worse than my fabulously dead, throat-slitting older brother? That's probably the essential question, but there's no realistic way that I can get an answer. *Ding-dong, bad idea.*

"Where do you have in mind?"

"Oh!" Mabel says, and wipes her face with the back of one hand. Like she's surprised that it isn't obvious. "Just, um, back where you were before? When you came here? If you want to close yourself up so Dashiell can't get in anymore, then we have to go there together. Okay?" Her tone has shifted into this sickly sweet coo, like she's coaxing a rabbit.

"I'll go take a look," I tell her. I still have no idea what I'm doing, but maybe this way I can learn more. It's also a chance to stall for time—because there's always the possibility that my alarm will blast through here and save me from deciding. Nuke me out of this place. "I'm not making any promises about what I'll do when we get there, though."

She gives me this little, nervous smirk. It's taken me this long to notice that the light on her looks too bright for the dimness around us, like she has an overcast afternoon all to herself.

"I know you don't trust me, Everett," she trills. "But we really can, *really* can help you. There *is* a secret way to shut him out! We don't tell it to anybody alive, not ever, but we're going to tell you. You'll see. And then you'll like me better, won't you? And you'll tell Ruby how nice I was?"

"Ruby and I aren't talking much right now," I say, but Mabel's got this faraway, drifty look on her face and she just holds out one sticky little hand for me.

And I take it. Dashiell's always telling me how cautious and self-protective I am, and it seems like a fun change of pace to try being as reckless and chaotic as he is. He always gets away with it—he even got away with *dying*. So why shouldn't I?

Really, I already know the answer to that question. I'm just not interested in knowing it.

Up on the bank there's a gigantic, slabbish building made of corrugated steel, maybe some kind of warehouse. Mabel drags me up to it and opens a door in the side, and then we're back in the same old hell-zone where I met Dashiell, half naked and languid and dangling his feet while he waited to butcher me. We're walking through the same maze of phosphorescent scarlet gears taller than my head, and shuffling floors, and creaking green engines, and everything shifts in confusion but Mabel still has her fluffy daylight clarity. She's bouncing with excitement now, urging me to go faster.

"How did you die so young, anyway?"

Her happy little face collapses and she shoots me a reproachful look over her shoulder. I guess it was insensitive of me to bring it up. "Scarlet fever. My favorite cousin was quarantined. I snuck in to see her, and then *she* got better! *She* was just fine, and she grew up and lived in a beautiful mansion with big chandeliers. But I had to come here."

"That sucks," I say, partly because it's true and partly to make up for upsetting her. She's just a little kid who had horrible luck and it's totally understandable that she resents never getting to have a regular life. "I'm really sorry."

"She was *much* prettier than Ruby," Mabel says primly, like she's correcting me. "But Ruby seems so nice."

That's not the word I would use, but I don't feel like arguing. We've come within sight of that glowing yellow scaffolding; it sears my eyes and makes it hard to focus on anything else, but I can just make out some pale slug shape dangling off the edge of the platform high above. I can't tell what it is, but something about it makes me flinch back in revulsion.

Mabel flicks me a worried look and yanks my hand. "You might not like it very much. But you have to go up there!"

"What the hell *is* that?" I say, and she just wrinkles her nose at me. We're close enough now that I can see wormish protuberances at the pale thing's end, maybe suckers or eyestalks or something. "What if I decide I'm not interested?" We're almost at the scaffold's base and I start glancing around without knowing what I'm looking for.

Then I realize. I'm waiting for Dashiell to come waltzing in here. Grab me by the scruff of the neck and tell Mabel that he's sorry but we've got some cake to eat. I'm waiting for him to stop me.

"That would be really bad, Everett. If you said you didn't want to. Because Aloysius is counting on you to help teach Dashiell a *lesson*." Her nails are squeezing into my palm and I look down at her. Her gaze is darting around like she's afraid to look at me, and then as I watch her eyes come unmoored in her face, one driving sideways toward her hairline and the other pushing at a downward slant through her cheek. Like two boats drifting through pinkish water, shoving up ripples as they go. I shriek and twitch my hand away and she's turning, shaking her curls over her face to hide what's happening. "Go up! Climb up the way you did before! Don't be so silly that you're scared of your own body!"

My body. All of Mabel is going wriggly and deformed now: her neck isn't in quite the right place and one shoulder hunches out above her heart. I look from her to that horrible pale thing sticking out overhead, and maybe it is an arm with dribbling fingers. Maybe it even used to be mine. I'm still not sure what to do except get away from Mabel as quickly as possible. That means my choices are to either start climbing, or run like a maniac away from here. Run into the random, slippery complexities of this place, hoping like hell that something happens to save me before Aloysius and his goons track me down and express their *displeasure* with me for messing up their plans. Maybe by holding me captive and using me to try to lure Dashiell here. Or maybe they'd think up something even worse.

This is their territory. Whatever I do, the reality is that they've got a huge advantage.

"It's your fault I look like this, Everett! You made me too nervous! I was a lovely little girl!"

I grab the highest yellow rung I can reach and haul myself up. *A good therapist. Someone who specializes in grieving.* That sounds fantastic, Dad. That's exactly what I need right now. Another three rungs, feet kicking for a second as I miss a step. Mabel is whimpering behind me, but when I glance down I can't see her. I can't see anything at all except wallowing dark. *You like cake, Never. It's chocolate.* That sounds delicious. Maybe there's an undigested chunk of it in the stomach of my corpse up there, and I can have a snack. *You know, Never-Ever, I've come to realize that I haven't been a very good brother to you.*

No kidding. Where are you now that I actually need you? And why do I always have to miss you, even when I know exactly what kind of a monster you are? All at once I realize I'm almost at the top, though it seems too soon.

I push myself up and swing a leg onto the planks. The climb was so much easier this time, like my body's been hollowed out and I barely weigh anything. I'm not even out of breath. There's a lumpy shape six feet to my left, but even letting it into the corner of my vision is so sickening that I can't bring myself to look at it directly. I know what it's like anyway: my podgy torso gone ice-cold and sticky with damp, my eyes vacant and stupid. Who could stand to see themselves like that? I can smell the rusty stink of my own blood, and vomit shoves through my throat and into my mouth. I gulp it down. My muscles feel like they're trying to crawl out of me.

Now that I'm up here I've got no clue what I'm supposed to do next. There's a wet wind blowing but no other sound at all, so I sit on the edge with my legs dangling and stare out over the

Land of the Dead. Except that it's gone. I can't see any of the strange revolving lights that used to be there; it's like a dark gray fog has poured in and devoured everything.

"Mabel?" I try. "Are you still there? I need instructions."

No reply.

"Dashiell? Can you hear me?"

Silence, so I guess there's nothing for me to do but wait. A white blob shape that I know must be the sole of my corpse's sneaker waits with me. It's almost like it's bumping on the corner of my eye, nosing at me to demand my attention.

Something moves. It only takes a split second for me to envision my cold, saggy corpse stumbling over and smearing its stale blood all over me, and I jerk in that direction so quickly that I almost slip off the planks.

A man, or something like a man, is standing with his feet apart, one on each side of my dead body's head. I see my ice-gray skin and flopped-open mouth and the sheet of crimson covering half my body, and I'm dying to turn away, but I can't stop staring at the stranger. His arms are folded tight across his chest, maybe because he's cold. He's wearing an obviously fancy, old-school pin-striped suit with a narrow collar, but he doesn't have a head. Not in the normal sense. A streaky beam of red and green light projects straight out of his neck and up into the sky. I scramble up and stand facing him, but I don't feel like getting any closer.

"Everett Bohnacker," the guy says. Fizzling, cool voice, kind of high-pitched for a man. "I'm pleased you saw fit to join us."

I didn't, exactly, but of course he has to know that. "You're Aloysius?"

"I am. I've come to assist you in taking steps that will be

beneficial to both of us. You can stop your brother from employing your body as the vehicle for his crimes, and I can deprive him of a beachhead among the living. A win for all concerned."

Well, a win for all except Dashiell. "Yeah, that's what Mabel said. So what do I do?"

"Come here to me, and reclaim this dead meat. I believe it properly belongs to you."

I don't like any part of that statement. My guts kick in protest and shivers cascade down my back. "Reclaim it?"

"Take it in a loving embrace. Never mind the spilled gore. You'll find it's eager to return to you."

Jesus. "I don't think so."

"Really? Consider the implications of your refusal, Master Bohnacker. It's the fact of this corpse being *here* that leaves room for your brother to be *there*. Unless I'm mistaken, you aren't under any illusions regarding his character. Or are you? He'll seize the first opportunity to ravish a certain young lady of your acquaintance, someone I believe you esteem greatly. Don't suppose for one instant that he won't. And if he uses your body for the act, why, you'll be just as guilty as he is. Won't you?"

God, I feel sick. My stomach is sliding around like wet soap. I don't think Dash would actually *rape* Elena, but he'd love to seduce her in some creepy way that would be almost as bad. And Aloysius is right, I'd be totally responsible for giving him the chance.

"Dash wouldn't do that," I say, without even meaning to— like the lie just spits out of me.

"Wouldn't he? Are you so certain of that that you're prepared to gamble with her happiness? He'll throw her down and take what he likes from her without mercy, and she won't be the last.

Ruined virtue and blighted affections will follow wherever he goes. Can you deny it? Why do you think that he was so concerned to procure a *male* body for his use? Why wasn't your sister enough for him?"

Right. My sister. "So would it work the same way for Ruby? I mean, if we could find her body, she could—reclaim it?" Then *maybe*, just maybe, we could be the way we were: heartbroken over Dashiell's death, sure. Bursting into tears at random moments, wondering what we could have done differently that might have saved him. Fine. But at least we'd be together, and we could start to move on. *We can cherish what's left.*

Though realistically, I know Ruby wouldn't see it that way. She'd never agree to force Dash out, no matter what happened.

"Dashiell Bohnacker drowned your sister in the river. The current has carried her body far away from here by now. I'm sorry to say that she's irretrievably lost."

"But the principle would be the same." I don't know why I'm so hung up on this, really. "It would work if we *could* find her?"

That column of light where his head should be flickers irritably. "Of course."

"Okay," I say, and I make myself really look at my dead body sprawled out on the planks. Dash slit my throat practically to the spine and my head has fallen back so that the gash has pulled wide open. And bizarrely my shirt is still sopping wet and bright crimson. Aloysius's not-head reflects in green smears where the blood has puddled by my side. The idea of getting anywhere near that thing, much less touching it with a single finger, is so appalling that I feel like throwing myself off the platform again.

Jumping wouldn't kill me, not in real life. I'll just wake up. A dream-suicide is totally my ticket out of here.

Except that Aloysius might have a point about Elena. As long as Dashiell can log onto my body whenever he wants I've got no way to predict what he'll do with it. Including to Elena. Including to Ruby.

Because that kiss he gave Ruby with *my* mouth was way too slow and sexy for me to convince myself it was anywhere near okay, even if he didn't go any further—and if he didn't, he might next time. It's pretty hard to feel calm about the possibility of Dash using my body to commit incest.

I take a step closer to my corpse. I've never been as disgusted with myself as I am right now, looking at that bled-out gray slug and knowing that it's me. I don't care that I'm not handsome the way Dash was; what I can't stand is that I look so *weak*.

Aloysius doesn't move at all. I take another step, the planks creaking beneath me. If I yield to my disgust, refuse to give that flabby thing a hug, then I really *am* a weakling. I owe it to Elena to be better that that. Maybe I even owe it to myself. But God, reaching out for that cold, pathetic sack of dead Everett feels a lot more horrible than it did volunteering to be murdered.

I'm close enough to bend down and touch my own ankle. It's just as revolting as I knew it would be, like a wet mattress.

When something's really bad it's easier to just jump in all at once. So I pull in a deep breath and brace myself. And fling myself belly-first on top of my own dead flesh.

There's no resistance. I burst right into it, like I've dropped into a pool of maggots. Cold, writhing masses drive into my body, and I gag and scream but I can't tip off the corpse or push it away—because it's me, it's who I really am, and it's determined to come back to me.

And then I'm thrashing around on the planks, beached and

feeble. And the dead version of me has vanished completely. I'm on my own, flat on my face and too drained to move. But it definitely worked. I can feel how I'm complete again: too stuffed with my own being to leave any space for Dashiell. The cuffs of Aloysius's trousers brush my head.

"You know, Everett," Aloysius says, "I intend to make an example of your brother. Hundreds of years from now the dead will tell tales of the revenge I took on him. No one will ever dare to do as he's done again."

I'm pissed off at Dash, all right, but not like that. "Then I'll stop you. I won't let anyone hurt him."

"So you can see that a Chinaman or a Brazilian is no use to me. I need someone who cuts close to home, so to speak."

It takes me one quick sliver of time to figure out what that means—God, I'm slow—and then I'm rolling toward the platform's edge just as the blade whistles past my ear and stabs the planks. He's yanking the knife out with one hand and grabbing for my hair with the other. My legs are wheeling at the emptiness and I'm trying to rip his hand off me, trying to fall. I have to kill myself before he can kill me, and I claw at him and fling myself from side to side, but he's too strong. Half my body is swinging into space but I can't break free of his grasp.

And then the knife pierces straight into my back. It skewers my chest and pins me to the wood, but he must have missed my heart because the pain goes on and on: a million winking red discs of hurt, twirling in my eyes. He gets one foot on my neck for leverage and yanks the blade out, and the feeling of the metal dragging out between my ribs sends my scream shooting into space. I hear the song of the knife scraping bone.

Suddenly I'm floating above the whole scene, watching the

knife arc up above my spine. It's the same knife Dash used, I recognize it, and I can't believe I was so stupid that I didn't wonder where it had gone.

The next stab drives home and sends my thoughts sailing into darkness just as my alarm goes off. I'm screaming so loudly that my throat feels torn. I've fallen halfway out of bed, and I'm still trying to keep falling forever. Please, please let me fall and die on my own, before it's too late.

Except I know his knife found my heart at the last moment. And that means it's too late already.

RUBY SLIPPERS

* * * *

I wake up with my hand spinning a pen through Dashiell's handwriting, slanting and elegant and totally distinctive. I'm sitting up in bed with a spiral notebook spread out on my lap, and as I pull myself into consciousness my hand starts to falter and sway and the line trails into a drowsy horizon. My glance falls onto the words, and before I'm fully awake I'm reading and I can't look away.

Dearest Ru, I'm afraid we have a significant problem on our hands. I've lost our Never and he's been taken over by an extravagantly vicious man, a dead old crook, one Aloysius. I'm very sorry to say that I realized too late what was underway; they staged a diversion, moving in on you, so that I was obliged to spend the night shoring up your defenses. And I'd received the distinct impression that you were their primary object of interest in any case. I didn't anticipate an attempt to invade Never, at least not so soon.

I'll be with you when I can, but dealing with Aloysius will require me to absent myself sometimes. Be extraordinarily careful. Guard yourself as never before. Sleep at a friend's house tonight, please. Never is no longer your brother, no matter how he appears to you. He will almost certainly try to kill you.

All my love,

— ˙˙

*They know you're my final sanctuary
in this world, Ruby-Ru.*

"Dash?" I say, but I feel a yawning ache in my chest and I know he's gone. I can hear water singing in the pipes, probably Everett in the shower upstairs, and someone clattering in the kitchen. I read Dashiell's letter over again, but no matter how many times the words play in my head I can't take them in. Maybe Everett is in trouble, maybe Dash is right about that, but then why would I go to a friend's house instead of staying close so I can help him? What sense does it make to say that Ever *isn't my brother*? Dash sounds so agitated that I almost doubt he knew what he was saying.

Taken Everett over. *Invaded* him. One Aloysius. I'm finally absorbing it, and I know it means that Ever has a new ghost living in him, one that doesn't belong here. It means an enemy has slipped into our house. Someone who might want to hurt me. But that doesn't mean I can just abandon my twin brother.

There's a brisk knock on my door. "Ruby? Are you dressed, sweetheart? Breakfast is ready."

It's our dad and everything about his voice is wrong, too high and cloying. And since when does he make breakfast?

"I'll be there in three minutes." I can smell it now, bacon and something else warm and cinnamony. I squirm into clothes without showering and barely brush my hair. I have to see Everett as soon as I can. I can already hear his footsteps in the hallway. Then they pause outside my door.

My phone chimes. I'm so distracted by waiting for Everett to knock, waiting for him to say something, that I barely understand the message at first: *Hey Ruby my mom says yes of course to you sleeping over! Abby and Louisa are coming too. Yay slumber party! Liv.* Dashiell texted Liv to make sure I stayed out of the house tonight.

A cold palpitation floods up my arm from the phone and hits my heart. I read what Dash told me, of course, but I didn't actually *feel* it until now. I couldn't let the horror in his words touch me, not when the horror is Everett. But Liv's text breaks through my resistance and now the chill of it moves like a tide through every part of me. Dashiell was deathly, utterly serious. I can't stay in the house with whatever is wearing Everett's face. With *Aloysius,* whoever he is.

Then what about our dad?

I take one more moment to grab the notebook with Dashiell's letter; the safest place to keep it is probably in my backpack so it's always with me. Something warns me that Dad is too on edge for me to wear my red boots, so I grab my rose-patterned shoes instead and bolt out into the hall. Ever isn't waiting there anymore.

He's sitting in the kitchen with a plate of French toast and bacon. Shadows pool under his eyes and he looks sick and nervous, but other than that nothing seems different about him. When Dashiell was in him it was obvious that something was going on.

"Hi, Ruby," he says; I'm listening hard and his voice *sounds* normal. It also sounds like we didn't have the worst fight of our lives last night. "Did you know Dad can cook French toast? Like, *delicious* French toast? 'Cause I'm in total shock."

Dad beams at him and goes to get me a plate, and while his back is turned Ever glances his way and then jabs a warning look at me: *for God's sake play normal. Do it for him.* So that's what it means that our dad is bustling around the kitchen, actually serving us hot food instead of just gulping coffee without even sitting down: it means he already knows too much, but he doesn't know what he knows. It means he's starting to crack up from the dreams in our walls and the voices coming through the vents. It means that, even if he isn't possessed like Ever and me, the ghosts are still getting to him.

"I thought we'd all go out for dinner and a movie this evening," Dad says. "Everett is grounded, of course, so he *shouldn't* be going anywhere else. But do you already have plans?"

"Liv just invited me to a sleepover," I say—and I can't help it, there's a tiny crackling in my voice. "Is that okay? Because I said yes, but I could tell her I forgot about going out with you."

"You should go to the sleepover, Ruby," Everett says before Dad can answer. "You know how hurt Liv gets when you bail on her." He says it too emphatically, like he has to force the words out. Like there's something inside him that doesn't want him to tell me any of that. "You should *really* go."

And now we're staring at each other across the kitchen table while Dad pours himself more coffee. Everett's eyes are wide and his brows are drawn tight; he's desperate and he wants to make sure I know it.

"But what about you and Dad?" I ask, and now I'm positive that Ever knows exactly what I mean by it.

"We *are* capable of having fun without you, Ruby," Dad says,

still in the artificially upbeat tone he's been using all morning.
"The three of us can go out together another time."

Everett was right, the French toast is delicious, but I can
barely choke it down. Everett gives my plate one of his new significant looks: *Eat your goddamn breakfast, Ruby. I don't care if
you puke as long as Dad sees you eat like you mean it.* So I keep
chewing and Everett gets up ostentatiously for seconds.

"This is seriously the best French toast *ever.* . . ." It's getting
to be overkill, the show he's putting on. "Dad's right, Ruby. We'll
be fine."

Once I've gulped down almost everything I get up to scrape
my plate—and then something happens. Dad tenses and starts
to stand up as he sees me head for the garbage, his face crinkling
with worry. I lever up the lid and see the cake I made, dark rifts
running through its lilac frosting and crumbs everywhere. I'd
forgotten all about it, but of course Dad must have found it the
same way I did.

With a piece missing. And twenty-three candles.

I finish clearing my plate and let the lid fall like nothing's
wrong. Dad starts to settle back down, obviously relieved that
I'm not throwing a fit, and then I feel something graze my back.
A hand made of static. For half an instant I can fool myself that
it's Everett—I'm standing near his chair—but when I jump around
he's still facing the table with a piece of bacon in one fist and his
fork in the other. And I can still feel that prickling, airy hand
traveling up my body. Exploring me.

It comes to rest softly curled around my neck.

"Ruby?" my dad is saying. "Sweetheart, are you all right?"

I know I can't let myself scream, not with him watching me.

My breath has stopped, dammed up and eddying inside my throat, and now Everett is twisting around to see what's happening. That hand isn't crushing my windpipe; it's gentle, a charged vapor, poised between caress and threat. I don't think it's even solid enough to choke me. But somehow I can't inhale and I stagger— still trying to play normal. Trying to set my plate down on the table before it slides from my hands and smashes on the floor.

Something in Everett's chair is smiling at me. And it is not Everett.

And then it passes. I'm gasping a little, fighting to stand up straight, just as my dad darts over and pulls me into his arms. "Ruby!"

"I'm fine," I say. "Really. I'm totally okay. I just felt dizzy for a second."

He still looks worried so I kiss him on the cheek, pull away, and walk as decisively as I can to the sink. Rinse my plate and fork and put them in the dishwasher. *Aloysius* can leer at my ass all he wants, but I'm going to make sure he knows that I'm truly Dashiell's sister and I can be just as fierce and defiant as my older brother. And that Dash and I will fight for Everett together. Won't we? Because this has to be it, the struggle that I've sensed was coming all along. I glance at Everett and I *think* he's himself again. His face is buried in his hands.

"I'm so sorry about the cake, Ruby," my dad says quietly behind me. "Seeing it, those candles—I hope you can understand—it was simply unbearable."

That's what he thinks is wrong with me. Our poor father.

And so I do what I have to do, even if it takes me a long moment to pull myself together. I go back and hug him and say of *course* I understand, and I'm sorry I upset him, and I don't know why I did that, baked that cake. I felt compelled and I can't explain it.

I say, *Something came over me.*

"Ever," I say. He's walking fast so that I have to trot to keep up with him. It's only a few blocks to our school and there's so much we have talk about first. "Ever, Dash told me."

"I could tell." It's the first time he doesn't sound quite like himself; the words are caged and snarling. "So why didn't he do anything, if he knew? Where the hell *was* he?"

"He said . . . he said they staged a diversion so he thought they were going after me. By the time he figured it out it was too late, Ever. Dash said—"

"Right. You're the one Dashiell would be worried about. Because he actually sort of gives a damn about you, in his sick way. I'd be the expendable one." His backpack is thudding on his shoulders and brown leaves sweep around us, each spiral and flurry like an extension of our arms. Making gestures we can't control.

"That's not true. Dashiell totally loves you. He loves us both." *Always, my Ru. Love always applies. No matter what happens, you need to remember how absolutely true that is.*

The look Everett flings over his shoulder snaps with pain. "So maybe one of us can go live with Mom in London? It has to be right away, though. I'll do it, if she'll even take me. Ruby, God, I was so *stupid*. They tricked me, but I really, really should have known. But I think—he has to know Dashiell *hates* our dad, right? Hurting Dad would basically be doing Dash a favor."

I'm about to protest, but then I understand: Everett's not saying this part for me, but for the ghost listening inside him.

"No one has to leave," I say. Living with our mom sounds miserable; she'd never let him forget that he was in the way of her *real* life. "Ever, Dash is already working on it. On helping you. I mean, that's why he's not here."

"It's not going to do any *good*," Everett spits. Every muscle in his body is tensed and thrumming, I can see it. "What, you think they're such morons that they'll leave my corpse lying around where we can just find it? They won't, Ruby. They're professionals. I've already figured it out, so Dashiell will too. And even if it bugs him a little, he'll just say he's doing what he *has* to do. To protect you, maybe. Whatever."

His words rattle out fast and crazily, but nothing he's saying makes sense. "What are you *talking* about?"

"Oh, and you should watch out for Mabel. She's completely obsessed with you. Even if the treacherous little bitch *looks* cute, you need to tell her to get lost. Okay?"

I can't manage to feel surprised that he's met her, too. We're half a block from school now and Ever stops, staying out of earshot of the kids shoving up the front steps. He grabs my arm and I almost yank it away, but then I can see by the frantic sadness in his big gray eyes that it's really, truly him.

"One thing Mabel isn't is *cute*."

"Ruby? I'm not going in there. School, I mean. So this might be the last time I see you? We have to stay away from each other, I think forever. So I'm sorry for all the times I was a jerk."

I can't even begin to take this in. I can't *let* it make sense, but my heart goes tight and my eyes flood anyway. "Dashiell said . . . that whatever is in you might want to hurt me. But, Everett, we just have to stay apart for a little while! He said—"

"Not *hurt* you, Ruby. What would be the point of that? Murder. *Murder* you. Then Dashiell won't have anybody left he can use to stay here. He'll be forced to go back to being totally dead. You really don't get it? So Dashiell will try to stop Aloysius from doing that, obviously. And you know how Dash can be, like, *practical*. When he's working to get things his way. I wouldn't even blame him, really, if the whole freaking mess wasn't his fault to start with!"

"Everett . . ." Suddenly his face contorts into a slow, rippling grimace and he lets me go. His arm flies up in warning. I'm remembering that staticky hand crawling over my throat and I jump back, sure that Ever is about to lunge for me. Then he relaxes again and shakes his head hard.

"Dash said he might not have been able to keep you from walking into the river that time, because you were too upset for him to just bump you out of the way? So as long as I'm this completely out of my mind I guess we're cool. But if I fall asleep anywhere near you, Ruby, I won't be able to stop him. Or even if I space out for one *second*. Just like you won't be able to stop Dashiell."

"You're going to be okay, Ever. We're going to fight for you. I *promise*."

Everett stares at me. Gray eyes lost in the thick fringe of his lashes. Then his mouth wrenches into a terrible smile.

"You mean, you and *Dashiell* will fight for me? Ruby, you still don't get it. I'm really, really sorry, but you don't." I want to argue but the look in his eyes cuts through me, severs my voice like a falling ribbon, and I can't make a sound. "See, Ruby, I'll— my body, anyway—I'll do my best to murder you. I won't have any choice. But you'll try to murder me, too."

DASHIELL

*   *   *   *

"Well hi there, Miss Mabel. How are you this lovely morning?" She's weeping violently, or at least engaging in the best simulation of weeping that she can manage as a lump of gray haze. It wasn't hard to find her. The shadow corpse of her Old Body is gone, simply vanished from the scene, so she's come to mourn in the very spot where she once blasted him full of holes. She's a sentimental creature, our Mabel. "Your sad, abused Old Body has passed on to regions of peace and light, I take it? I'm sorry for your loss. But don't think you'll be acquiring my sister as his replacement. Aloysius has made you promises he can't keep, Mabel, assuming he ever had the slightest intention of trying. I think you know that."

Mabel snuffles, or at least vents an emotion that approximates snuffling. "I know you're angry at me." I don't say anything and she studies me eyelessly. "It's Aloysius's fault! I never would have been away from Old Body if he didn't make me! And while I was here Old Body got a gun and now he's *dead*, his whole body is dead, and I don't have anywhere to go."

"And since it's Aloysius's fault, he owes you Ruby Slippers twice over? Once for betraying me and handing over my poor brother to be used up and destroyed, and the second time for inconveniencing you? Even if Aloysius sees it that way, Mabel, he still can't make good. How can he possibly dislodge me from her when they don't even have her body? You wouldn't like having to share."

"They *do* have it," Mabel snaps. "They found it before you could! So there!"

She's being wonderfully cooperative today. "Ah. So they've tucked her away with Everett in some warren?" But Mabel's on her guard now, no doubt realizing she already said too much. "How do you suppose they'll persuade my Ruby-Ru to make the transition, though? Close herself to me, then sit back and relax while you hack away at her? Everett wanted me out and that made him vulnerable to your games. But Ru-Ru's happy as things are." I can imagine a few ways they might go about convincing Miss Slippers, in fact, so Mabel likely can as well. Torturing me would do the trick, for example, assuming they ever catch me, or threatening to toss Never in front of an oncoming train. "Aloysius won't bother, Mabel. He'll murder Ruby as soon as he gets the chance, and you'll lose her forever; she's hardly a girl who will end up *here*. Aloysius is well aware that Ruby and I together represent a threat to him. He didn't mention that?"

Mabel goggles at the startling idea of anyone posing a *threat* to Aloysius. "You can't do what Aloysius can do! He's the only one! He's the one who gets to hurt *everybody*, and no one can stop him. You're just being silly."

"I can't do what he can do, no. Even I'm more particular about my friends than he is. But I can do something else. You see, Miss Mabel, I have something of his."

There's a long lull while she ponders this, and I take advantage of the silence to listen to the muffled lapping of the river.

There's no other discernible movement but I shouldn't put too much trust in that.

"You mean like what happened with Constance?" she whispers at last. "You can *do* that to him? But you're dead! You can't bring anything from outside in here!"

"Ah, but my Ruby Slippers can. She's already carried her phone here, once. A fine proof of concept. The real difficulty now is getting Aloysius back here at the same moment, and ideally taking him by surprise. You see, Mabel, he's frightened. You've given him an exit, made it possible for him to cower inside my brother where I can't get at him. And you've provided him with the hands he'll use to kill Ruby. You can see that *chopping her up* is the simplest option for him, can't you? It would solve all his problems at a blow."

I won't say more to her at the moment. She'll brood on the thoughts I've offered and draw her own conclusions soon enough. I've almost certainly been observed by now and I should be on my way. I was careful to leave the corner back into my Ruby Slippers near at hand, of course, but it's drifted a bit down the shore, as such turning points tend to do. This is a slippery place and things don't necessarily stay where you put them. If any of Aloysius's henchmen come, I'll have to race for it.

"Wait!" Mabel says as I start to go. "Did you hide it?"

"Of course I did. Would I leave something as precious as *that* out on the street?"

"Aloysius will find it if it's in your house. And if you put it outside the *cats* will. They're always spying on you!"

If I had a mouth I would smile. "Oh, pah. The cats try their little best, Miss Mabel. Naturally they do. But they're such fragile animals."

EVERETT

✶ ✶ ✶ ✶ ✶

I've never actually cut school before and it's going to be one more thing to freak out our dad, but then I've got the whole *deeply traumatized* angle working for me. I'll tell him I had a panic attack or something, couldn't face going in. I can pick up on just enough of Aloysius's consciousness, like the *tone* of his mind, to feel how malice crests through him, how it drives him. The utter evil of him is trickling through me, cold and metallic like spilled mercury, and I'm sick with self-loathing that I let this happen. He doesn't have it in for Elena specifically the way he does for Ruby, but I don't want him anywhere near either of them.

So I walk to the Gowanus Canal at 9th Street, ignoring the *shouldn't-you-be-in-school* looks spewing from every grown-up I pass. There's an empty parking lot right by the water with big, cracked logs along its sides. I sit down and get my phone out and stare for a moment, dreading what I have to do; our mom left when we were five and it's not like I even know her that well. We visit her every couple of years, and maybe she calls on Thanksgiving and our birthday. She's too busy with her awesome-ass career, producing events for big-name artists and falling in and out of love with half of them. Romping around the planet like she owns it. One thing I'm pretty sure of: when she told me she'd realized that she and our dad *just wanted different things,* we topped the list of what she didn't want anymore. She was thrilled to give him custody and she won't see any reason to mess with the arrangement now.

But I've got my story already rattling through my head: *Everything in New York reminds me of Dashiell, it's too hard, I can't concentrate in school; I feel like I'm having some kind of nervous breakdown. I need to come and stay with you, right away. Tomorrow.* If I have to, I'll threaten suicide. I'll say whatever it takes. So I pull in a breath and call.

She doesn't pick up. I was ready to argue, cry, beg, but somehow it never occurred to me that she wouldn't even answer. It's two in the afternoon in London and I swear I can feel her from here, glancing down at the name *Everett* flashing on her screen. And deciding not to bother. Suddenly my whole body flares up with this dark fever and I'm gritting my teeth. It's crazy, I know it, but the whole time I'm listening to her—*This is Laura Tierney, please leave a detailed message at the tone*—my rage is getting thicker and hotter and I wish I could rake out her throat for the way she *abandoned* us. "Mom," I start, "it's Everett. Listen, I need—"

But the voice is all wrong, guttural and burbling. Monstrous. And then I'm choking on my spit, smacking at the phone to hang up. When I catch my breath again it's racked and ugly, so I start fumbling through my pockets. Ugh; I forgot my inhaler. I sit tight, clenching myself and concentrating on opening my lungs and pulling in air. After a minute the attack eases off.

Aloysius finds the whole thing perfectly enchanting. And

then before I know what he's doing he's taken hold of my arm and it's arcing high above my head. My phone sails up, its screen winking with confused reflections as it spins, then plops straight into the slimy water.

That'll be enough of that, boy. It's time to let go of your old attachments, isn't it. Prepare for your new life, however long that life might happen to last.

He was just playing with me, before. When I thought he was trying to seize control of my body outside our school he was only *playing*, twitching inside me to watch me jump. I could do an okay job of fighting Dashiell, at least some of the time, but suddenly I realize that Aloysius is a lot stronger, and a lot older. For Dash it was all a new experience and maybe kind of awkward, but Aloysius knows what he's *doing*.

At least that's what I'm thinking, but maybe they aren't even really my thoughts. The ideas slopping in my brain might be propaganda straight from Aloysius, meant to persuade me that it's futile to resist. Like, why even try?

Because we're already up and I definitely didn't make the decision to stand. We're already walking back the way I came: toward Park Slope, and my school. And toward our house.

So I play dead. I go floppy and passive inside my own body and let him think I've collapsed in despair. Ruby should have the sense to stay out at least until tomorrow and our dad won't be home again until evening, but the situation is so much worse than I thought—and it's a freaking *concept* that it's even possible for things to be worse—that I know I have to do something drastic.

Aloysius is a complacent bastard, basically. He's used to being in control, I can feel it, and he hates Dashiell so much because my brother was the first person in ages who put up a serious fight. Dashiell's *still* giving him hell, in fact. But I don't think Aloysius is expecting much trouble from me; I mean, to look at me, it's fair to assume that I'd be pretty pathetic. He thinks I'm so weak that he doesn't even make the effort to flip me into unconsciousness; like, who cares if I see what he's doing?

So I'll use that. I'll act as limp and stupid as I can and see if he gives me an opening—though an opening to do what?

Maybe Dashiell's going to butcher me—in real life, this time—and devastate our dad all over again, and get Ruby busted for my murder. She'll spend her life in some asylum, muttering to the ghost in her head. Realistically that's probably about the best-case scenario that can go down, and Dash has destroyed our whole family by dragging us into this mess. He deserves for all of us to hate him forever.

But going up against Aloysius was an incredibly brave thing to do, I know that now. The spirit inside me is cold and shifty; it clanks at the bottom of my guts. Dashiell's the one who had the nerve to push back at that overpowering evil, and I'm so proud of him that it hurts.

I catch myself wanting to make Dash proud of me, too. I want to prove that I'm worthy of being his brother. And right now I don't care how crazy that sounds.

We're a block and a half from home when my head pivots sharply left and my legs stop scissoring along. I'm staring transfixed at a creamy orange smudge under a shrub by the curb, then walking over and levering up the lower branches with my foot.

It's a dead cat. A fat, spoiled-looking old marmalade, and it's lying in such a crooked mess that its spine must be broken in three places. I feel the slap of Aloysius's anger, the red rumble of vindictive impulses; he's not paying attention to me at all. I don't try to slam him under; instead I softly take my own right hand back, the same way he stole control of it from *me* when he chucked my phone. Casually slide the hand into my pocket like it's just an idle, unconscious gesture, and slip one finger through my key ring.

He hasn't noticed yet. Who knew I could do this? It's like I'm learning to be a ghost haunting my own body, a stirring in the rooms. I wait for a moment with Mabel's voice playing in my memory, saying, *Dashiell stole something from them. Something valuable,* and I know Aloysius is after that bony curved object Dash stuffed in my pocket. It must be somewhere in our house.

Aloysius lets out a disgusted snort and lets the branch drop, swinging around on my heel. As he spins I fling up my right hand and use his momentum to send the keys skittering toward a storm drain. They're dangling over the metal lip and I have just enough to time to register the hard shock of Aloysius's rage before he smacks me into blackness.

Did the keys fall? I can't tell; there's nothing to feel here, no light or sound. Please, please, did the keys drop away into dark, hit the wet depths of the sewer? It won't keep him out of our house forever but it'll slow him down, buy Dash time to do whatever he's doing. I'm so desperate to know what's happening that I crash up at Aloysius, reaching for air and gray autumn light and the smell of wet leaves. His consciousness is so *heavy,* though: an iron weight, a wall that never stops collapsing on top of me.

Then something gives; light ruptures the shadows and I see my hand snatching the keys out of the gutter.

I feel his astonishment that I was able to push past him, even for a split second. And I feel him trying to hide his surprise from me before the darkness crushes me again. He didn't think I was strong enough to resist him at all and he's beyond pissed to find out that I can.

It's satisfying but it doesn't change the fact that I failed. My keys are clacking in my right hand, even if I can't see them. My legs must be running up our front steps by now. I slam back at him so hard the darkness fractures into sharp-edged rubble, but he's got his full concentration pressing on me now and I can't get through.

Dashiell? I really tried.

It's not enough. So, great, I'm not as helpless as people assume, but I'm still not nearly strong *enough*.

So I catch myself hoping that Dashiell stops me, even if he has to use a knife to do it. I'm fine with whatever it takes now, truly, just as long as he gets to me before I hurt anyone.

At some point in the blur of nothing, Aloysius gives me another blink of reality. It's so dazzling after all the dark that it takes me a second, but then I get it: my dad's bathroom, white tiles shining. There's something in my mouth sliding down with a gulp of water. Something small and cylindrical and amber brown in my hand, and I'm leering down at it.

A bottle of sleeping pills.

Just to make sure I don't cause any more trouble.

RUBY SLIPPERS

✳ ✳ ✳ ✳

"Ruby? Where's Everett?"

Never-Ever-Everett? He's trapped at the bottom of a well built from his own eyes and skin. Teeth in the walls, bones crossing out the sky.

Never is no longer your brother, no matter how he appears to you.

"He couldn't come today," I say. *And anyway, Elena, what is it to you? This is our disaster and we have no room for strangers.* "He's sick." *Sick with someone else's death. Why do you ask? It's not as if you ever talk to us.*

I was doing my best to be alone, sitting back in the farthest corner of the library, and I stare down at my book again. What makes it even more obnoxious is that everyone else is in the auditorium now, so she must have followed me in here on purpose. If I could I would slice the world away from me, peel it back and see nothing but the darkness it hides.

Dashiell, tell me that Never's accusations are insane. Tell me that what you did in our dreams will stay there. Promise that my twin's blood will never escape from that dream and flow into the waking world. We'd rather die than hurt him. Both of us. We'd die together first.

Elena sits down at my table, hard, and tugs her chair forward until our knees touch. She leans in on me, hair chocolate and blue, and slaps *Lord Jim* shut.

"Oh, he's sick? Then I guess he won't be coming to Nathan's party tonight. Will he?"

She delivers the words in a stony tone that means anything but what she's saying.

"He couldn't have gone out anyway. He's grounded." I try to slide away from her but I'm cornered by bookcases. Even with my head against the shelves she's too close, her face rolling in like fog. *Did Dash tell you about how he went and had sex with Paige in my body, and she didn't even know it wasn't me? And now he's after Elena.* I'd like to smack her.

"Ruby? Do you care about what's happening to him? Because there's no way I'll believe you haven't seen *something*. There's something really bad going on and you're just sitting there talking total shit."

"I care a lot more than you do!" My thoughts are wheeling through everything she just said. If *she's* seen Everett acting strange, then how much does she know? Her skin is silvery blue in the cold light fraying through the windows: the color of a knife blade left among stones. *I'll do my best to murder you. But you'll try to murder me, too.* "You didn't even notice him until two days ago. You don't get to suddenly pretend you're his best friend!"

"I noticed him. He's never been easy to talk to." The aggression has washed from her voice and she tips out of my face a little bit. Finally. "I'm really, really worried about him. And I'm not asking your permission for what I *get* to feel. I feel it.

What I want you to do is let me help. Ruby, I mean—do you understand—have you seen him *change* like that?"

"You mean," I say carefully, "have I seen him acting like a different person? When did you see that?"

"Yesterday." She breathes it out. "He talked to me in a completely different voice. He *was* a different person. And then he snapped out of it and told me it was too personal to talk about, but he really seemed like he was cracking up. Do *you* know what that is?"

"Why would I tell you anything if Ever wants to keep it private? Why are you prying?" She reels back in her chair, wide-eyed and glimmering with hurt; maybe that would work on Everett but it definitely won't on me. I stand up and grab my books. I'll have to climb over her to get out of my corner, but I don't care. Really, she wants to *help*? What does she think she could do, crawl down Everett's throat and chase the ghosts out? *We are rain and we wash everything away. You and me, Ruby-Ru.* I start to lift my right leg over Elena's lap. "Excuse me."

"Was it Dashiell?"

The knee supporting me wavers and I have to pull my right foot back so I won't pitch over.

He's here right now. I don't know when Dash whispered back into me, but he's here and he's listening. He thinks she's being completely adorable. The library starts slurring in front of me, the windows restlessly ascending and something foggy and angelic beating in the corners of my eyes.

"That's a horrible thing to say, Elena."

"He *wasn't* Everett, whoever he was. But he said you were his darling sister. I thought about it all night, and *Dashiell* is the only solution that makes sense. I don't even believe in anything supernatural, but—if someone I care about is in trouble, then I have to be open to *all* the possibilities. Even the impossible ones. Right, Ruby?"

I open my mouth to snap at her; *none* of this is her business, none of it, and she should know better than to mention Dashiell to me. But what comes out isn't my voice, and they aren't my words.

"She *is* my darling sister, Elena. No one is dearer to me than my Ru. So try to be nice to her, please, even if she's being distinctly irritable with you. For no reason whatever that I can see. *I* thought your offer was very gracious."

I feel myself smiling, sweet and insolent, into Elena's shocked face. I'm grinning with one hand curled under my chin when I'd rather scream, spit, claw at her cheeks.

She's trying to speak. All that comes out is a thin whine.

"Ah, so you didn't need me to tell you *what* I am, did you, Elena? You've done an elegant job of deduction on your own. No wonder Everett is so hopelessly smitten with you. Of course, our boy couldn't make *anything* easy for you, could he? Not any more than he does for me."

Dash, stop it! Stop right now!

"Leave Everett *alone*." Oh, so she's finally choked out something, even if it's something dull and predictable. It's more than I can do.

Oh, pah, Miss Slippers. Here we are, swept up together in this magnificent if rather desperate quest to save poor Never from a hideous fate, and you're telling me to stop? Fun is an important part of the heroic process.

"But, Elena, if I were so heartless as to leave Never-Ever alone now, his doom would be assured—his doom, that is, along with quite a few other people's. He's in terrible trouble and he needs all the help I can give him. And I was very touched to hear that you want to help him, too."

EVERETT

I'm a mess. I'm lying in a sloppy, bruised heap on the floor, and my mind is just as trashed as the room. *Where am I* and *what happened* are just more garbage, more torn rags and thrown papers, and the chaos I'm seeing gluts my skull until it's about to split wide open. It's our living room, I get that now, and every last book has been yanked off the shelves. Stuffing dribbles from slits in the red sofa. And someone is shaking my shoulder. Frantically.

Dad. I'm on my back and his gray puddle of a face sloshes just above.

"Everett! Everett, my God! Can you speak? What have they done to you?"

Sleeping pills; Aloysius made me swallow sleeping pills and I don't know how many I took. I've never had a headache this bad.

"Hi," I say, and it sounds pretty reasonable, like a regular human voice making a regular word. "What have they done? Who?" His mouth is chewing with worry; the puddle wobbles with each twitch.

"Shh. I'll call an ambulance. Lie still. Don't try to say any-thing." But wasn't he just asking me questions? "We've been

robbed. The whole house is torn apart. And then—they must
have knocked you unconscious." Daylight floats above us; I think
of gray boats sailing through the middle air. What is he doing
home so early?

"I don't need an ambulance," I say. "I'm—it must have been
Aloysius? He was looking for whatever Dashiell hid in here.
He—oh, no, did he *find* it?"

I can't understand why my dad is making that new, awful
expression, goggle-eyed and twisting, but then I remember:
Dashiell. Dad doesn't know he's back and I'm not supposed to
talk about him like he's been around recently. But why not? It
doesn't make any sense to keep that a secret.

"Dashiell's back," I explain. "I mean, he's still dead, but he's
here anyway. He's probably with Ruby. But now it's even worse,
because somebody's after him. Somebody bad. It's all my fault."

"Shh. You'll be fine, Everett. Everything's going to be all
right." His hand goes reaching into his pocket and comes out
holding his phone. I can feel Aloysius flex; Dad making that
call is *not acceptable*.

Something strikes out, snake-quick, and the phone spins away
from him and cracks on the wall. It's only when I see the outraged
stare he turns on me that I realize *I* knocked it out of his hand.
Why is it taking me so long to put everything together?

"Dad, get out! Now! Run away *now!*"

Aloysius is trying to drag me upright. Adrenaline races in
my chest and I'm awake enough now to know that, whatever he
tries, I have to throw all my strength into countering him. He's
trying to bump me aside, tip my mind upside down, and I'm
fighting so intensely to stay on top that pain flashes in my eyes.
Green and red stars. I'm making my body as heavy as possible,

sagging toward the floor. The struggle sends my limbs heaving in random directions and my arm smacks into the coffee table's edge so hard the skin breaks.

"Everett? You—you've had a shock. You're not acting rationally. Please try to calm down until I can get you help. *Please.*" He's up on his feet, at least, gaping at me in dismay.

God—Aloysius is just too strong for me. The hard rolling mass of mind on mind rocks in my head and I know I can't keep him down much longer. "Get out of the house! Dad! Plea—"

"Dr. Bohnacker." I've lost my voice, and what comes out in its place is high and fizzling. He's got hold of my throat, my mouth; I have to let them go and concentrate on keeping the rest of my body from sliding completely under his control. "There is no grief I know so sharp as the grief of a wayward son for his father, once he knows it's too late to make amends. However young Dashiell behaved toward you, I'm certain his suffering will be boundless—as mine was once, after I murdered my own papa."

I'm clambering to my feet now and I can't stop it. My dad is just standing there, too shocked to move, and I'm stumbling toward him. The most I can manage is to hobble all of Aloysius's movements; make him slower, sloppier, so that we stagger instead of pouncing. And how much longer can I even do this much?

"Everett—my dearest, *dearest* boy. This is not you. You are not well. Please."

For God's sake, Dad, get away! I'm fighting as hard as I can.

My hands are lifting up, reaching for his throat, and he stares at me with gray glassy eyes and doesn't make the smallest move to defend himself or even back away. No: instead he reaches out and strokes my cheek. It's maybe the first time ever that I've really understood, on a visceral level, how much he actually loves me. Everything in me that Aloysius doesn't control wants to break down crying: just flop on the floor and sob, but I can't. All I can do is let out this pitiful wheeze, and now my hands are closing in on his throat.

And he *still* doesn't get it. He puts his hands on mine, but he's not trying to yank me off him. He's covering them in this tender way, *caressing* them, and looking at me with unbearable devotion. Aloysius is going to win, and strangle my dad while I watch, and there's nothing I can do. I'm prying back from the inside at my own thumbs as they start to really squeeze his windpipe, and all it's going to do is make his death that much slower.

My breath rasps in my throat. Aloysius is putting all his energy into driving my arms forward, tightening his grip on my dad's neck, but there's part of me he's forgotten.

My lungs. My damned asthma. And hey, I forgot to bring my inhaler today.

It's a weird sensation, drifting stealthily inside my own body. I skim my attention toward my lungs and concentrate on stifling them. Aloysius is so caught up in the excitement of murdering my dad that he ignores it—and finally, *finally* Dad is fighting back, trying to tug my hands away.

At first Aloysius's wheezing is just, like, irritated. The emotion I pick up on is impatience that my body's not working the way he expects. I wring the air flowing through my throat, make it rake and choke; I crush my own lungs until my breath sounds like someone trying to claw their way through a brick wall. And I guess Aloysius doesn't have much experience with asthma, because he *really* doesn't know what hit him.

My lungs start to get that dry, empty burn in them. Every rag of air that scrapes in is thin and scraggly, not *enough*, and finally Aloysius lets go of my dad's neck and reaches for mine. I brought on the attack on purpose, but now it's taken hold for real and it's the worst I've ever had in my life. My instincts kick in, raging for oxygen, and my body drops onto its knees. Black dots surge across the room, and now my dad is beside me slapping all my pockets for an inhaler. Aloysius has given up trying to control me—right, just like Dashiell, he's only in it for the fun parts, and suffocating isn't all that entertaining. So I'm able to lift my hand and point upstairs—the inhaler's probably on my bedside table—and after half a second my dad gets it and jumps up.

"Hold on, sweetheart. I'll be right back. Hold on!"

I hear him sprinting up the steps, but really, that was stupid of me. It'll be better for everyone if he doesn't find it in time. Better if I die right here; that way Ruby and Dashiell won't go through the trauma of putting me out of my misery, and Aloysius won't be able to hurt anyone I love. I curl up on my side, feeling my chest spasm and hearing the airless hack in my throat. My lungs feel like smoldering cotton. I try to tell myself it's okay, that I did the best I could in the end. I'm going out honorably and that's more than anybody would have expected me to do.

I hear footsteps, but they aren't on the stairs. Is somebody else in the house?

And then my dad is beside me again, pulling my head back and spraying the medicine into my mouth. The cold blast of it is in my throat, and I'm still wheezing, but enough oxygen is getting in now that relief blazes through my body. He gives me another hit and I suck it down gratefully—even though I shouldn't. Even though I know it's a lame, pathetic thing to do. If I were a courageous person I would just freaking die, already.

"Shh. There you go, Everett. You'll be fine soon." He doesn't sound like he believes it, though. He sounds shattered, and his voice is rough, and I see him gingerly touching his throat. I probably bruised him pretty badly.

The shitty thing is that, as soon as I've recovered enough to tell him how sorry I am, I'll be a menace again. Aloysius will come raging back as soon as my body's fully operational, I know it, so I better say whatever I can while I still have a chance.

"Dad . . ." I try.

"Shh. I'm glad you recognize me now. You must have been so confused that you mistook me for one of your attackers. It's all right." He pulls a gutted cushion off the sofa and lowers my head onto it, then goes after his phone. He's tapping at it in this panicky way like it won't turn on.

Someone is standing in the open doorway. Ruby, still in her coat and scarf. I thought *she* at least knew enough to keep the hell away from here.

Then I notice the slant of her head, the angry forward tilt of her body. Dashiell's looking down at me furiously from her green eyes, and it's actually a smart strategy: he's here to do what he has to do while I'm still weak. Fine. I do my best to smile at him. I want him to know I understand. That we're fighting on the same side now, even if I'm the casualty.

"Aloysius," Dashiell says—and even though our dad's right here he's not trying to disguise his voice at all. "Really, trying to murder my father? Such a cheap move, isn't it, coming from a man who prides himself on his class and *connections*? No imagination whatsoever. No style. It's what I might expect from some taw-dry little hood."

Dad sits down suddenly in a pile of torn books and I'm worried he might have a heart attack.

"Cheap but effective," Aloysius sneers through my lips. I didn't even know he was here, much less that he had control of my voice. "Young Mr. Bohnacker, I believe you'll discover soon that a flair for the *imaginative* gesture isn't worth much. Not when it results in the most excruciating failure, and in the death of all you love."

I'm struggling to sit up, or maybe Aloysius is; I can't even tell. Dash stalks over—Dash, in Ruby's body, her raspberry corduroys, her floppy plaid coat and furry scarf—and viciously kicks me in the chest. Something yields with a loud crack. I'm still dizzy and unbalanced and I thud back down. There's a sharp star of pain to the left of my heart, like he might have snapped a rib or two.

"Ruby!" Dad yells reproachfully. "Don't—how could you? He needs help!"

I guess it's all too much for him to take in; seeing me and Ruby both turning into other people has just plain maxed out his brain.

"Dad," Dashiell says, and his off-key tenderness is on full blast. "No one wants to help our poor Never more than I do. Truly. I'm sorry to say that helping him might involve breaking both his legs, possibly in several places. But you'd prefer that, wouldn't you, to losing another son?"

I can feel Aloysius registering that—Dashiell's not kidding and maybe he counted too much on Dash wanting not to hurt me. I can feel him noting that my breathing's gone ragged again from that kick and I'm not at my strongest. And he knows I can resist him, too: maybe not that well, but enough to put him at a disadvantage.

Dad is gaping at Ruby where Dashiell's spirit, the whole sense of him, kind of leans out of her green eyes—gaping like he's starting to see his dead son in her face.

"That writing," Dad says at last. "Upstairs. It's not possible."

Writing? What is he *talking* about? God, I keep missing so much.

"Of course not," Dashiell agrees gently. "I can't take advantage of Ruby again to come in this house. You told me so yourself. Ergo, I can't possibly have written anything here." He walks across the room to our dad and slides an arm around him—and that's his freaking arrogance at work. He's acting like he can turn his back on Aloysius and be totally blasé about it. "Let me help you get to bed. You should rest. I'll make sure you're safe."

My body goes tense—Aloysius, evaluating whether to attack—and pain jabs my chest. I wheeze piteously. I guess it convinces him that this isn't the ideal moment to try murdering anybody and we stay where we are, flat on the floor. I'm not in great shape right now, obviously, but I know the total stillness has to be partly a sham; Aloysius wants Dash to think my injuries are worse than they really are.

"Dashiell," Dad says vaguely. He's in such extreme shock that his eyes look like spilled glitter. "It's not possible." He's staggering to his feet now and Dash has both arms wrapped around him.

"Ah, but supposing it is? Purely hypothetically, suppose I'm Dashiell, and that I've come back. Imagine that I'm here to—among other things—offer you an apology. Wouldn't you like to hear it?"

Dad is staring into Ruby's pink face like it's a dirty window and he's urgently trying to see through it. Then he sighs and covers his own face with both hands.

"Of course I would."

"Then I'm sorry," Dashiell says softly. "For having been myself." He starts leading our dad toward the stairs—which means that they have to walk past me where I'm splatted on the floor with sofa stuffing leaking into my nose. Dad looks at me and shakes his head to clear it, then reaches toward me. Dash pulls him back. "Come with me. You need to rest. Everett is my dear brother and I'll do the best I can for him."

You're a very poor physical specimen, aren't you, boy? Hardly worth keeping alive, once I'm done with the task at hand.

He's going to wait until they're upstairs and then bolt out of here, before Dash has a chance to take me totally out of commission. And I suddenly have this appalling sense of where we might be going next.

RUBY SLIPPERS

"I don't expect he'll come back to the house," Dashiell says from my lips, "not now that he's suffered such a bitter disappointment here. But he's made other moves I failed to anticipate, so you should stay somewhere else tonight. Rest for half an hour, then I'll call you a cab."

Our dad is curled trembling on the guest room bed, his eyes closed, but he nods. Dashiell strokes his forehead with our shared fingertips. I can still feel the echoes of the front door slamming downstairs.

Around us the walls that were smooth pearl gray two days ago are filigreed all over with crimson script: Dashiell's beautiful, loping handwriting. A jar of paint and a small brush lie abandoned on the dresser, and there's a shattered lamp on the floor. Other than that, this room has the least damage of any room in the house. It's so bland and lifeless there wasn't much to rip apart; you just have to yank open the drawers to see they're empty.

This is not an injustice, the walls announce a hundred times over.

No one has injured you except yourself. Again and again. Delicate, slanting letters written with ruby paint. Like a rain of blood streaking windows in a storm.

I'm genuinely afraid to let my daughter spend time with the brother she adores.

This is what we've come to. This is what we've come to.

Yes, Dashiell, you're correct. There are indeed conditions on my love for you.

This was Dashiell's room once, and in those days the walls were black and collaged everywhere with photographs and song lyrics; he sprawled on a different bed. He was a rivulet of dawn-colored life then, always rippling; laughing and tussling with me whenever I came near him. So I understand why he came back here to mourn, both for himself and for us, in messages red on the walls.

Dad's eyes open long enough to drift over the writing again, and then close. "Leave Ruby with me. One of my children, safe with me. Please."

"Ah, but I can't do that. Ruby Slippers has her part to play, too, if we're going to have the faintest hope of saving Never. She'll be traipsing along to her slumber party soon. Just as we arranged."

Dad groans and his eyes roll open again, sliding over the world but not accepting it. *Dash, how can you think of leaving him alone like this?*

I can't speak, but I can inscribe the words on Dashiell's mind. I can spin myself hands out of dream and sink their imprints into his consciousness. He knows me as utterly as I know him now: thought on thought in slow-moving currents. He lets me see with him, feel with him. We sit on the side of the bed and gaze down together at our heartbroken father.

"Ruby-Ru will be in far greater danger in the long run if she stays with you tonight," Dash says softly, both to our father and to me. "Never barely prevented the ghost driving him from murdering you, and it's clear to me that he only succeeded because he came up with a tactic that Aloysius wasn't remotely prepared for. Using his own lungs as a weapon won't work a second time; Aloysius will be on high alert for anything of the kind. He won't stop looking for opportunities to kill Ruby, and he'll slaughter Never-Ever as well once he's used him to destroy his own sister. Our Never will be a bit too strong and resourceful for his liking, simply. He's assuredly proved himself to be more trouble than he's worth already, from Aloysius's point of view."

I don't know how much of this our dad understands; he's clutching himself and rocking slightly in a twist of white sheet.

"I expect these are the last words you'd ever choose to hear from me," Dash says, "but you'll have to trust me. I'm doing what I can to ensure that your *surviving* children stay that way. Both of them, ideally."

Dashiell? You have to promise me something. I'll do whatever you need me to do, but tell me something first. Promise we won't kill Everett, no matter what happens.

I know he hears me. There's a pause, a hitch in our breath. But he doesn't answer.

Instead he strokes our dad's cropped silver hair.

"Everett wouldn't answer his phone," Dad says, and coughs laughter. "He wouldn't answer his phone, and suddenly I felt terribly afraid for him. He's been acting so strangely. He's been—not himself. I rushed back here and found such destruction. I searched for Everett upstairs first. I saw this room. The writing."

"Ah, well. I'd meant for you to see it eventually." I can feel my mouth crimp into Dashiell's pained smile. "But truthfully, you knew I'd come home without seeing anything."

Dashiell, promise me! I have to know. We'd rather die than hurt him. It isn't fair, not when he was pulled into this because of me. I won't let Ever be the sacrifice. No matter how much I love you. I started this. I was the one who brought you back.

"You *haven't* come home," Dad snaps; his eyes are shut tight. "It isn't possible."

Dashiell's horribly disappointed by that, I can feel it. "Of course not. I can't possibly be here with you. I'm stone dead and probably comfortably ensconced in hell. There's quite a list of things you've called me already; why not tack on *hallucination?*"

"An auditory hallucination. It *has* to be. That I see Ruby, but hear you . . . I am so deeply grateful to be hallucinating you, though, Dashiell. My desperate, my lost, my always-beloved son."

ALOYSIUS

* * * *

Seven long years since I've had a bale of human flesh at my disposal, and now this one is in such pain that I'm tempted to gouge out its eyes and discard it to slowly bleed to death under a bush. Profiting from it even to the smallest degree—enjoying a mortadella sandwich bought at a delicatessen on Court Street, for example—is ruined by the piercing discomfort of broken ribs. And adding this pain to Dashiell Bohnacker's account is useless, since I already propose to extract from him the final particles of his being.

Well then, his dislikable sprat of a younger brother can be made to pay—if not with physical suffering, which I would be obliged to share, then at least with mental anguish.

Young Everett, I address him, *wouldn't you be interested to learn why the brother you betrayed was fleeing from me in the first place? Did you so much as trouble to ask yourself what might have moved Dashiell to go on the lam, before you accepted my invitation?*

The runt is exhausted from pain, from his brush with suffocation, from the effort he poured into his impudent resistance. He's been in a swoon since I pocketed a knife from his father's kitchen and stepped out for a stroll. Too much weakened to keep struggling. On hearing the questions I've posed, though, he snaps to attention. Good boy.

I was very *pleased to make Dashiell's acquaintance, you see. It didn't take long to size him up as an amoral brute with pretensions, not half as clever as he thought, but also with the sort of attractiveness that might give him a hold on those who had known him. A young man, in short, whose near and dear ones might very well come at his call, even if they felt some horror at the prospect. And he struck me as the type who might not be overly fastidious, if he had to surrender such dear ones to save his own skin. Wouldn't you agree?*

The nauseated tension gripping young Everett nearly compensates me for the lack of savor in my food.

So I gave him a choice. Lure you or your sister close—or else that whore of his, if he preferred, it was all the same to me—and then step aside while I gutted the mark for my own use. It was that, I told him, or face prolonged torture. I expected he would find his decision an easy one.

Well, for some time he played at agonized acceptance of my proposal. He's a plausible actor, as you know. He pretended to lie in wait for you and Miss Bohnacker, with me concealed beside him. He suggested that she'd make the easier target and dutifully undermined her dreams, to increase the likelihood of a visit from her. He went along to get along, as the saying goes. Naturally, I intended to increase my demands as soon as I obtained one of you—to then require Dashiell to bait whichever of you remained as a reward for one of my lieutenants.

Dashiell's cooperation proved to be sadly insincere.

Ah, the self-lacerating buzz from young Everett, as he anticipates the rest of my story! The stabbing guilt and shame! No doubt the boy attributed Dashiell's actions to the purest selfishness, but now it starts to dawn on him that his brother's motivations might have been a wee bit more complicated than he'd supposed. If he had use of his teeth he'd gnaw himself down to the bone.

I can't be everywhere, can I? I had other business to attend to. And no doubt Dashiell meant all along to double-cross me. To cheat me out of my rights. He waited for his chance and got your sister alone. Snatched her body for himself and bolted off to the living world. You see, Everett, he was fool enough to think he could shelter you and Miss Bohnacker from me and somehow evade the consequences. How he deluded himself into believing he might get away with it, though, I'll never know. Does anything occur to you?

Ah, and here it comes: a flicker of suppressed consciousness. A memory, rapidly stifled, of the sharp curve of my jawbone in his back pocket. I pay keen attention, hoping for some raveling thread of thought that might lead me to that item's present location. It was nowhere in the house, of that I'm now certain. But no. This useless boy is hardly bright enough to conceal what he knows from me. I'm sadly forced to suspect that he knows nothing. In case I'm mistaken, though, it's time to apply such pressure as I can.

I take a piece of paper from Everett's pocket, unfold it, and spread it out before his dismayed eyes. The stub from an invoice, with Paige Kittering's address at the top, found in Dr. Bohnacker's study. Dashiell Bohnacker is all too aware that I'd like to drop his sister into the nearest grave, but I don't suppose he's terribly concerned about his slut of an inamorata. It won't cross his mind that I know where to find her.

If you happen to know where your brother secreted a certain object belonging to me, Everett Bohnacker, now would be a fine time to confess. I'm sure you're aware that the gold he stole was the least of it.

Losing money salted away for those occasions when I might happen to possess a body is an inconvenience, certainly. But he also took something rather more valuable; an item that was only in that package because the flunky who stashed it was such an utter incompetent. That's what I'd like back.

You have a few hours to think it over, of course. I believe an approach to Dashiell's whore will be best made late tonight. I'm prepared now for your tricks, and I'll have my knife in her back before you can flinch. If you'd like to prevent that, then tell me. Where did he hide it?

Hearing me ask that affords young Everett some slight relief, mixed in with his distress at my intentions. He's thrilled to realize that I failed to find what I need in his house. It's regrettable to leaven his terror and grief this way, but it can't be avoided. I face the urgent necessity of turning every stone until I locate my missing remains.

If there's one thing all the dead remember, it's what happened to Constance Marclay when her dear mother visited the borderlands, and rushed headlong to embrace her lost child. By an unfortunate chance, her mother had a locket full of Constance's hair swinging from her neck at the time.

RUBY SLIPPERS

The sky falls through violet, layer on darkening layer. We hug our father for a long moment, then open the cab door. Dad slides onto the seat and stares up at us, entranced by the impossibility facing him: Dashiell and me slipped into one skin, our voices alternating in a rapid blur as we tell him to be safe, to stay hidden; as we promise to call soon. He must think he's caught in a waking dream, because he doesn't try to resist when we give the driver our aunt's address and kiss him on the forehead.

"You'll find Everett? You know where he might be, Da—"

He doesn't finish the name. He doesn't know what to call us anymore.

"We'll do our best to bring Everett safely home," Dashiell assures him, and a few notes of my voice mix into his. Dash and I are together now, a flux of stirred thought—so I can feel Dashiell's mingling hope and doubt as if they were my own. He won't offer any more than that we'll *try*; he still refuses to promise me that Everett won't die tonight. "Ruby and I will do everything we can for him."

Dash says that as much for my sake as for our father's, but I can feel the suspended presence of what he won't say, what he won't even let himself think in so many words, because he knows that if he does I'll hear them: *Only as a last resort, Ruby-Ru. Only if we can't find another way.*

We close the cab door and watch the taillights sinking into dusk. "I'll be leaving you now, my Ru-Ru," Dash whispers through my lips—making sure I know it's definitely him and not my own thoughts. "You know what you have to do."

I know what you told me to do. But Dashiell, before you go, tell me we won't hurt him!

"Hush, Ru. Elena will be waiting for you. If all goes well, Never will be ours again by morning."

If we can't get him back, Dash, what will you do?

But he won't answer, because he can't honestly tell me the only thing I could stand to hear. He's already gone and I'm alone in the street. I'm lost among a hundred shining windows where dislocated hands clink glasses of wine, where children tumble off sofas and their small feet wave in pink socks above the sills. I could be a ghost looking back at the world I've left behind. I could be the final spark of a girl still haunted by the living. Transfixed by the beams of my memories.

And then I pull myself away and start the walk to Liv's house. I could lose everything tonight, my family and my future. Every blue shadow spanning under the streetlamps seems too vivid, too graphic, as if all the terrible possibilities confronting me were drawn on the ground. How will I ever convince Liv that everything is normal?

When I called her earlier to ask if I could bring Elena along to her sleepover, she was so startled that she could barely be polite—and Liv is always carefully polite and kind to everyone no matter how she feels about them. *I'm just surprised that Elena would want to hang out with us, that's all.* As overwhelmed as I'm feeling now, it's almost funny to think of what Liv couldn't bring herself to say: that Elena's way too cool for us. That if I'm starting to be friendly with Elena, then I might decide I'm too cool for Liv soon, too.

I couldn't tell her not to worry—or not to worry about anything so ordinary, so threaded into the living world. I couldn't say, *Liv, there's something buried under the potted rosebush on your stoop. My hands buried it there, and I didn't even know I'd left my house.*

I couldn't say, *A legion of ghosts would crush me if they could, to stop me from touching it again.*

Or, *If we can't save Everett tonight, what possibilities will be left for me?*

Something Dashiell said to me when he was still alive keeps on reverberating in my mind: *You haven't turned against me yet, but who knows if you will one day?*

Don't make me turn against you, Dash, I say in my thoughts. I don't know where he is now, or whether he's listening. *Please don't force me to choose between harming Everett and betraying you. I love you more than the whole world, but I can't let you hurt him. If someone has to be the sacrifice, then please let it be me.*

To my right a cat pads along like tensed air. As horrible as it is, I know what I have to do. That cat can't be allowed to see where I'm going. It can't watch me reach into the soil below that rosebush.

When I pass below a streetlamp, I'm the only one casting my shadow.

PAIGE

* * * * *

"Miss Kittering," a voice calls as I step out of my building's front door. I've only heard that voice before when it was insulting me. It sounds much better now that it's begging. "Miss Kittering, please. You know something. Tell me what happened to my son."

"Dr. Bohnacker," I say, suppressing a gag, or maybe it's a laugh. Why can't I shake these people? I turn and he's right behind me on the sidewalk, swaying a little. The old man must be drunk off his gourd. I don't smell booze but that doesn't prove anything. Last time I saw him he was perfectly dressed, crisp and controlled. Now his jacket is sagging off one shoulder and his hair sticks up in tufts. There are reddish-purple blotches on his throat. "I'm afraid I'm much too busy to talk to you. I have to get to work."

If I'd known the way Dashiell's family would plague me, I would have slapped his face when we first met instead of taking him home. Even though, incredibly, that gold Everett said he *found* has turned out to be completely real, I'm still utterly sick of these people. They're all as exhausting as Dash was, but not nearly as much fun.

"I'll compensate you," Dr. Bohnacker rasps, one hand flapping vaguely in my direction. "Whatever you lose by missing work, I'll more than make it up to you. You know something you didn't tell the police, didn't tell anyone. I'm sure of it. Tell me now. Please. What happened to Dashiell?"

Passersby turn to stare. Who doesn't love a random spectacle on a dark street in New York? There are silver feathers glued around my eyes, and more feathers plastered in winglike strokes from the tops of my breasts to my collarbone. A ruff of brittle silver arabesques sticks out around my neck. And this silver-haired, broken-down ass is whining and pawing the air near my arm.

Why, of *course* I know things you don't know. Do you believe you have the slightest idea who Dashiell was?

"If I didn't tell anyone, Dr. Bohnacker, then maybe you should realize that I won't want to tell you, either. And maybe you'd really rather not hear what I have to say."

His upper lip hikes. Even now that he's desperate, pleading with me, his contempt still shows through. "Name your price, Miss Kittering. I need the truth. I'm ready to pay handsomely for it. Dashiell's death wasn't as simple as it seemed, I *know* that. Ever since he died, I've had—I suppose it's only an intuition, but it's an unshakable one. It wasn't merely an accidental overdose. There's something else there. I don't know what it is, but it's haunting me."

I tip my head and smile at him. Everything I look at sparks with the silver fringe around my eyes, and my hand drifts down to rest on my stomach. Something I've learned is that I have to take my chances where I can get them, and this looks like the one I've been needing. "I'll name my price afterward, then."

He waves a hand. Weary acquiescence. It's not exactly comfortable having this conversation out on the street. We're squeezed against the wall of my building by the crowds pushing past on their way to restaurants and clubs. I'm not about to invite him up to my apartment, though. I've had more than enough of hysterical Bohnackers carrying on in there already. And why should this take long? I'll spit out the story and leave.

"Weren't you concerned that Dashiell might have drug debts?" I ask. "After he finally kicked heroin? That he might owe money to, oh, lowlife scum, and not have any way to pay them? Did that cross your mind?"

Dr. Bohnacker pitches from side to side. Now that I'm studying him I think he might be more than drunk. His eyes are glazed as he stares at me. It's like he's seen so much that his pupils have given up on accepting anything more.

"I could have guessed that there might be some trouble of the kind. I didn't know anything specific."

"Because he'd stopped telling you anything," I snap. "So I'll tell you now. Dashiell owed eight thousand dollars to a complete scumbag named Carl. His old dealer. And since you'd removed yourself from the picture, Dr. Bohnacker, who do you think Carl came to, to try and get his money?"

I let him think about that. He has Dashiell's gray eyes, but colder.

"After I'd talked to him a few times, Carl told me he'd accept something *other* than cash. That I could pay off Dashiell's debt in just an hour or two. I hated Carl. Trust me on that. He was a horrible, repellent rat of a man. But there he was, telling me he was in love with me. That he'd do anything to get his hands on me."

"Are you saying Dashiell pimped you?" Dr. Bohnacker leans against the brick wall, his eyes half-shuttered, his face dead white. "Of all the things—Dashiell routinely did things that appalled me, and I could never trust—but I never would have thought he'd stoop to *that*."

"He never would. Dashiell didn't know. I made my deal with Carl behind his back. I thought Dash would understand, finally, how much I loved him, since I'd done something so degrading to help him. I thought he'd be grateful. But afterward, when I told him what had happened—Dash didn't take it well. He was furious. He said, if he'd only known what I was thinking, he could have found another way. He said—awful things to me. It was the worst fight we'd ever had."

"I'm very sorry for what you experienced. But I don't see what bearing all this has on Dashiell's death. I don't—"

But then he does see. The shine in his eyes shrinks to pinpoints and he sits down, hard. Right on the dirty sidewalk. Dr. Bohnacker is one of the most respected neurosurgeons in New York and here he is, slumped on the pavement like any old derelict. I'm standing over him in a brocade hoopskirt and towering shoes. Everyone walking past gawks at us. The juxtaposition must look as grotesque as it feels.

He asked me for the truth, but I doubt he'll ever completely recover from hearing it. I'd say it serves him right.

"It was that night," I say. "Dr. Bohnacker. Dashiell had stayed completely clean until then. I would have known if he hadn't."

"You're telling me that he bought drugs from this man Carl again. That night."

"Yes."

"Knowing full well that Carl was obsessed with you. And

therefore highly motivated to dispense with your boyfriend. It was easy enough for Carl to slip Dashiell a dose that was guaranteed to kill him. And to be confident that no one could ever prove it was murder. Is that correct? That's what you're telling me?"

"I'm telling you that that's the whole reason Dashiell shot up again. I'm telling you he deliberately *chose* to let Carl murder him. If it was only that Dash was craving drugs, we had plenty of friends who knew other dealers. He could have scored at our corner bar in twenty minutes if he'd wanted to, but instead he put his life in the hands of someone he knew would take it from him. So would you say that counts as a suicide, Dr. Bohnacker?"

"But why? I understand, of course, that Dashiell was very upset that night, and he could be quite volatile. But why would he—seek out annihilation?"

"Ask yourself that," I say. I turn my back on him. This is justice, but that doesn't help. It's astounding how bitter justice can be.

"I'm asking you!" All his self-control is gone. His voice is a thin howl behind me. "Miss Kittering, I am asking—begging—you. You seem to think I should understand why my son sought his own murder. I don't understand. I *never* understood. His endless compulsions, his self-destructiveness. None of it made the slightest sense to me. He was a dearly loved child."

I hold up my hand and a cab swings to a halt in front of me. Tonight's party isn't far away, and I would walk if this was a normal night. But once he's heard what I'm about to tell him, I'll have to get out of here in a hurry. Escape the emotional flood. I don't pity him. I can't. But I still glance back at him: an old man in a rumpled gray suit, struggling to his knees.

"Dashiell knew exactly what he was," I say. "He was afraid that—just by being alive, and being himself—he would destroy people he loved. *Corrupt* them." Recognition flashes in Dr. Bohnacker's exhausted face at the word. His mouth slips open. "Maybe knowing that I'd whored for him made that worse. What I did shoved his deepest fears in his face, even though I'd only meant to help. But there was also what you'd said to him. You say *you're* haunted, Dr. Bohnacker? So was Dashiell. He was haunted by the monster you saw in him."

The cab's back door pops open in my hand. There's the usual musty rubber smell. Candy wrappers wedged in the crack of the seat. It's a dark and stinking space, waiting to carry me to yet another room where my only real job is to show that the host is rich enough to afford a cohort of costumed girls in the corners. I don't have to do anything but stand there. I won't even bother to smile.

"Dashiell's come back, Miss Kittering. All the way from death, and regardless of how impossible that is, Dashiell has returned to us. I know it's absolute madness to say it. I couldn't believe it myself at first, not even while he was speaking to me. But now I'm nearly sure it's true. He hasn't tried to see you?"

My God, he's drunk. Completely blitzed. He *has* to be. I get into the cab, pulling the wave of my skirts in after me. Maroon and silver roses rustle as high as my chin.

"My son has come *home*. He held me. He kissed me. He asked me to trust him. He's out there now, trying to save . . . Whatever I did to hurt Dashiell, I know he forgives me."

I slam the door. There's still the question of what he owes me, but since it's something far more serious than money I'd rather talk to him about it once he pulls himself together. And it seems like that could take years, or maybe the rest of his life, which would be more bad luck for me.

Because as sick as I am of these bad-penny Bohnackers, I need something from them. And for that, they'd better be functional.

RUBY SLIPPERS

*　*　*　*

"So who am I talking to this time?" Elena asks when she sees me. She's sitting on Liv's stoop waiting for me; it will be awkward enough, the two of us going in there together, so I can understand why she didn't want to ring the bell alone. "Are you Ruby, or some insane ghost here to talk me into making the worst mistake of my life? I can't believe I'm doing this."

"Right," I snap. "You're missing a *real* party. With all the cool kids. That is just so nice of you!"

Elena has a box from a fancy cupcake shop balanced on her knees. I don't know exactly what's going on at Nathan's tonight, but it definitely doesn't involve cupcakes, or toenail polish, or watching anime. From the rumors I've heard it's probably more like ten kids high on mushrooms rolling around on the floor together, or maybe breaking into an abandoned warehouse to dance in near-perfect darkness with just a few candles propped in jars. I honestly can't believe she's here, either, and it still blows my mind that they invited Everett. Even Everett-not-quite-himself.

Then I realize something: Nathan invited Ever because Elena asked him to.

"I'm here, Ruby. I'm putting myself in serious danger to help your twin brother. So maybe you can drop the sarcasm? You should drop it for your own sake, anyway. It just makes you sound insecure."

I guess it's easy not to be insecure when you're totally full of yourself, I almost say. I smashed that spying cat's head with a branch and kicked its small body into the Gowanus. I *had* to do it, but my nerves are still roaring with the horror of the crack, the sensation of caving bone, the white rings in foul water. I'm not in any mood to listen to Elena telling me how I should behave.

Except that she's right; at least, it's true that she's heading into something terrible for the smallest chance of saving Ever, and maybe she deserves to have me act like I appreciate it. I thought that nothing could surprise me anymore, but Elena being secretly in love with Everett? That still comes as a shock. Of course Dash was the one who saw it first. And of course he was the one who thought of using it.

Everett will never forgive me if anything happens to her tonight, but I'll take him hating me for the chance of saving him.

"Sorry," I mutter without looking at her. My right hand is burrowing under the rosebush and the last shriveled apricot petals plop down on my wrist. What do we do if it's gone?

But there it is, slipped deep among the roots: roughened nubs on a hard swerve of ivory. I extricate it slowly, trying not to damage the rosebush. After that poor cat I can't face doing harm to another living thing.

As the object breaks free of the soil, light recoils from it in a dozen places. It's a human jawbone and the teeth are studded with bright gems: diamonds and aquamarines, emeralds and pale topaz. A single, huge, raspberry pink ruby blots out one entire canine.

"Jesus, that's sick," Elena says, looking over my shoulder. "That's wrong in so many ways I don't know where to start. Like, tacky is the least of its issues."

The gems have nothing to do with why this thing is so valuable. I hurry to hide it in my coat pocket before anyone sees what we're doing. "Dash said the gangster who shot Aloysius hacked off his bottom jaw and kept the bone as some kind of trophy, because his jeweled teeth were so famous and everybody who saw it would recognize it right away. It was only decades later that Aloysius realized it could be dangerous and sent someone to try and get it back. Get rid of it. But whoever he sent botched the job."

Elena stares at me. "Was this what your life was like before you were, ah, possessed? Because you say these things like they're completely normal."

"No," I say. "But they're normal for me now. They have to be. I don't have time to waste on freaking out. And anyway—" *There's something I know now. I didn't understand before, but I should have. I should have realized as soon as I saw Everett with his throat slashed open.*

"Anyway what?" Elena asks. I hadn't really looked at her before, but I do now: her bobbed hair streaked blue and swarming like shadows, her face defined by soft curves of light from passing cars. She must really be crazy about Everett if she's doing this, but it's still hard for me to understand that; Elena could have almost any guy she wanted, so why him? *I* know Ever's awesome, but that's never been obvious to people outside our family. But it hits me now: she sees who Everett really is, and she must have for a long time. Maybe she's seen him more clearly than I did until right this moment. "Anyway what, Ruby? I heard everything your ghost brother said, and I almost believed him. But I still feel like my head is ripping open, trying to understand what the hell is going on here."

"Part of me is in the Land of the Dead," I say. "That's the price of letting Dashiell live inside me. So if I'm split between my life here and death, how can anything seem strange to me?"

"And that's where we're going," Elena says. Her voice is flat but I can sense the fear rippling under it. "The Land of the Dead. There, and to a slumber party."

"Yay, slumber party!" I say, and for a moment there's a flash between us: a bleak smile that wings from her lips to mine and back again. For a moment it feels like we're friends.

"Oh my *God*," Elena raps out in a voice like clacking stones. "Cupcakes!"

She turns to ring the doorbell.

EVERETT

I've pretty much lost my grip on the world now, and I know that's a problem. The darkness isn't still anymore. It's more like I'm caught in a pitching, spinning dizziness where all I can detect are periodic pops of emotion coming from Aloysius. Like, he gets flustered when he reaches the subway turnstiles and finds out they don't take tokens anymore—he really hasn't been back in New York in a while!—and I feel him experiencing that confusion totally clearly. I get the curious, watchful sensation of him observing other people going through with their Metro-Cards, and I know when he finds mine in my jeans.

Then there's the scraping, jagged pain of my broken ribs: that, I feel all the time, but it's like the pain is dislocated. Like it's not in any specific part of my body, but whirling around with no direction. He's probably offloading all the suffering he can onto me, but I can tell that he has to put up with at least some of it, too.

But I can't see or hear anything. I guess I know where we're going, but a guess is all it is, really. So I don't have much to do but think about what Aloysius told me earlier. I'm sure he wouldn't mind lying, but everything he said about Dash felt so true that it raked right through me. Yeah, so Dash was saving his own ass and using us to do it, but he was also looking out for me and Ruby—trying to keep us out of the exact mess I've gotten into now, all by myself. But I went and assumed the absolute worst of him, and I was wrong, and now I get to live with knowing that.

Though probably not for long.

Jesus, Dash. Why didn't you just tell me? But he can't hear me thinking anymore, not now that we've been cut off from each other. And I'm honestly not sure if I would have believed him, not even if he had told me the whole crazy story. He probably knew that my default assumption was that everything he ever said was a lie.

A flash of the street. Wet and moody, with thin trees scraping at the grubby, lamp-stained night. A window full of brightly lit wedding dresses, bone white and hovering over the sidewalk. Spectral skirts and dead arms. Why is he showing this to me?

Because it's the East Village, is why. We're three doors down from Paige's apartment building. I'm helpless to do anything, stop anything, and the realization of what's going to happen is like a tic deep inside me. And every little jump in my stomach squeezes the dread out, farther and farther through my body, until fear has taken the place of every cell I've got.

Paige maybe won't be thrilled to see me, or what she thinks is me, but she won't be afraid, either. She won't run. She'll probably come right up to me and ask me what my problem is, and what the hell do I think I'm doing, stalking her like this.

Miss Kittering didn't respond when you rang her bell, Aloysius thinks at me. *Perhaps she's out painting the town. But she'll be coming home in due course, won't she?*

He curls one fingertip back and forth, stroking the handle of the butcher knife he shoved into the lining of my jacket. Every time that wooden handle slides against my skin there's a tiny propulsive blurt of feeling in me, something between disgust and hot-cold horror.

She won't come home! I tell him. *She'll be out all night with some new boyfriend. You'll be standing here in the drizzle like a complete fool.*

But he knows I'm lying. He knows I wouldn't be so spastic with fear if I believed for one second that what I'm saying is true.

*Oh, that seems unlikely. I don't suppose Miss Kittering is a young lady any self-respecting man would keep in his bed after she's served her purpose. More the sort to whom one hands cab fare, and perhaps something on top. A tumble and then a fistful of gold coins, isn't that right, young Everett? A hasty thank-you for the pleasure of her com*pany, *and show her to the door. I knew demimondaines of her type very well, back in my day.*

Ugh. I don't know if he knows somehow what happened with me and Paige, or if he's just guessing, but I'd like to drag his entrails through the street for talking about her this way— even knowing that every loop of intestine was actually mine.

But that's the problem. The more enraged and sickened I get, the more he enjoys it; that's the whole point of his game. Otherwise he'd just keep me blacked out.

And when she does return? Why, I think I'll keep you bright-eyed and alert. Intimately aware of every detail of our transaction. You might find you relish it rather more than you expect. You might even acquire the taste.

I don't bother answering him anymore. I feel so totally obliterated, as weak as my own smashed bones. I feel so lost, and the maze is my own damned body. I don't know where I am inside it, really, or where it stops or starts, or whether I'm fooling myself when I imagine bashing my way through Aloysius's control again. Disrupting his grip on my hands. I wouldn't need to do it for long. Just a few seconds.

I mean, assuming that I could find the nerve to turn my hand around and slash that knife across my own throat, then that's all the time it would take.

RUBY SLIPPERS

✳   ✳   ✳   ✳

There's a hole at the bottom of my dreams.

I find the crevice where Dash said to look for it: under the bed he slept in as a teenager, before everything went so wrong. Now the sheets are dusk gray and covered completely in ruby-red script just like the writing on his bedroom walls—*No one has injured you except yourself*—except here the letters writhe slightly. They shine with a patchwork glow that brightens and gutters out again. In their dim light I can just make out the ragged edges of the gap between the floorboards, and I crawl through.

It's a thin and twisted passage; Dashiell has been burrowing up through the defenses he built himself. Through slanting barricades made of every material, or none; of flotsam and shipwreck and broken-off rinds from the moon; the fireplace mantel from my mother's London apartment, which I've only seen once; slats from the Coney Island boardwalk dotted with shoes I wore when I was ten. Dash has been busy, working with whatever he can find abandoned here, in this sedimentary layer between waking thought and dreams.

Once I'm almost sure I feel him. Once his warm hand brushes mine as he reaches up from below. Then it's gone again.

He has other tasks to do tonight, I know that; maybe he's gone to loosen a way through for Elena, and that's why he's pulled his hand away before I could see him.

At least, I hope that hand was his. I keep twisting downward, catching at chinks in the debris to pull myself through.

"Ruby? Ruby, are you okay?"

I can barely hear Liv's voice, echoing from *somewhere*. She sounds very distant. Feathers of sound wafting far above.

For a moment I hesitate. I think I can still turn around but soon I'll have gone too deep. I'll lose track of the way back to waking.

"You're getting dressed? Ruby, it's after three in the morning! What—did I say something wrong? Are you upset with me?"

There's a lull, and then I dimly hear myself speaking: *"My dad texted. There's some kind of emergency? I have to get home. Don't worry, Liv, I'll call a cab."*

Dashiell. But he can't imitate my voice nearly as well as he can do Everett's. Liv will notice how wrong I sound, how chirpy and artificial. Maybe, just maybe, she'll think it's because I'm so upset.

There's a bigger problem here, though: where is Dashiell taking my body? What is he planning to do with it? From what I know, our plan doesn't involve me *physically* going anywhere, and I should stay curled up in my sleeping bag on Liv's floor until morning. As far as anyone can guess by looking at me, anyway. I should be part of the jumble of girls on the rug, cupcake frosting dabbed in our hair from the food fight we had earlier.

Dash? I call. I can see my thought rising like red smoke up through the chaos of planks and lost dolls. *Dash-Dot-Dot, what's going on?*

I know he won't answer—and just like I expected, he pretends not to notice me crying out to him. If Liv is still talking I can't tell. All I can hear now is the dull fluting of a draft seeping through the cracks around me: a draft from *below*. I must be almost through, about to step out into the borderlands where I first found him. If I keep going then any moment now I'll find my feet sinking into the spongy mud of the riverbank, but I think it's not too late to turn back.

For a long moment I stay where I am, uncertain. If I crawl out of this dream and back to the surface of my sleeping body then I can at least knock at Dashiell's awareness—I can demand that he hear me. Have we already walked out of Liv's house; are we standing on her stoop in the deep blue night? I can't tell.

But if I turn around any chance that our plan will succeed will be utterly ruined. I know what that failure will mean, for Everett and for me. Because I'm bitterly aware now that Ever was right: Dash won't tolerate the risk my twin poses, both to me and to Dashiell's life inside me.

Dash will try this way first—he'll sincerely try his best, I trust him to do that much—but then he'll move on to *last resorts*. So following Dashiell's instructions now, following them exactly, is my only real hope of saving Everett.

And what will I do, if we fail tonight, if we reach the point where Dashiell will say we have no choice? I don't know. I can't stand to think about it. I can't let myself even imagine what might come next.

So I gather whatever I am in this place: the illusion of breath, the dreamed heart crashing in a chest that aches even though it isn't really there at all. And I keep going down, insinuating my way among my own memories. I only pause once, right at the final edge: I have one last small task to do, before I emerge.

Everything I see belongs to me. Until I touch down on the gray soil of a country that belongs equally to all of us.

The river laps at my toes, and when I glance down I see my crimson patent-leather boots, though I'm sure I wasn't wearing them earlier. They're so bright in this dim place that their color is throbbing.

Ruby slippers for you, my sweet Ruby-Ru.

EVERETT

There she is: a silvery girl in silver feathers and a huge skirt striped silver and dark purplish red. Some kind of crazy necklace that sticks out six inches in all directions and big plumes waving out of her hair. I've been in the dark for so long that at first she's all I see, blazing in the middle of a black fog. It's so cold out, it *has* to be, but she's walking around without a coat. Just some little furry thing wrapped around her shoulders. She's heading away from me, maybe fifteen yards up the street; as far as I can tell she hasn't seen me at all.

All around her the mist is shining. Scintillating. For a second I think the light is coming from her and my heart skips. Every tiny flutter passing through her costume passes through me, too, like my fear is rustling.

I'm sunk so deep in myself that the view of Paige seems like it's being beamed down to me.

And what comes after it is the sense of Aloysius's cold, metallic smirk clanking down here. *Ah, young Everett, even after the long hours you've had for contemplation, you overlooked a certain essential fact. I've never seen the nasty little trollop we're hunting before. That young lady looked to be the right general sort of creature, but I couldn't have been certain of the identification—if only your boyish excitement hadn't given her away.*

Maybe he's telling the truth, or maybe he's just out to mess me up. Either way I won't answer. He's right that I've had plenty of time to think. I'm pretty disoriented, but we must have been pacing this block for hours. I've been thinking as hard as I can the whole time; like, trying to work through the problem logically. Consider all the possibilities, even if everything that occurs to me seems desperate and irrational.

That beam of vision blinks out, and when it comes back we've closed almost half the distance. I can see more of the world now: a blur of shop windows, their light hitting the water droplets in the air like handfuls of flung glitter. It must be really late, because there's no one else on the street that I can see: just Paige with her silvery plumes bending in the wind, and us following her. Her spike heels clack but my sneakers are dead silent. She's passing that shop with the wedding dresses now: almost to her own building.

Darkness again. I wait for the world to flash in on me, knowing that when it does she'll be closer. This time she's like a silvery comet, looming into view. So near that I can see the black fuzz on the back of her neck. And I can't help it, my fear of what's about to happen grows with her, bigger and brighter, until panic starts to blot out all the parts of my mind that are still trying to be reasonable, to find a solution.

The pain in my ribs bursts through me at every step.

When Aloysius attacked my dad I held him off by exploiting my own weakness, and that's what he'll be watching out for now. But realistically he has to have weaknesses too. I just have to find them.

I try to stay with that thought as Paige pauses, maybe just eight feet away, and unzips the miniscule sparkly handbag dangling from her shoulder. She's poking around in it for her keys, but it seems like they're lost.

I try to stay with it—*calm now, calm, there's a way, he's a ghost but so am I now, a ghost in my own body, and I'm haunting him, I'll haunt him all the way to hell*—as his grip tightens on the handle of that knife. *Alive or not, as long as I'm adrift in this nowhere I'm another ghost, like him.*

So think: what can they do? What have I seen Dashiell do, since he's been haunting my body?

Aloysius will be waiting for me to pull the trick with my asthma again. He'll have a good hold on my lungs. And he'll be braced for me to bash up against him. To try to fight my way to the surface. He's strong, and he's ready to swat me back down.

He takes out the knife and slowly turns it in the glow of the streetlamp. He lets a spike of reflected light play over my face, then pivots his hand—no, *my* hand—and sends the shine-blade dancing over the back of Paige's dress, her fur wrap.

Trying to take back my hand was a stupid idea, I can feel it. He's baiting me into attempting that right now so that he can smack me down for fun. He's in complete control, smirking at the thought of me rushing him.

God—there's something here. The clue I need is right here.

And actually I'd better rush him. I'd better give him the satisfaction of seeing me rise to the bait. If I don't, he might start to wonder if I've thought of something else.

Which I have, I think. Maybe, maybe, if I'm not deluding myself—maybe it's worth a try.

So I collect all of my shapeless scraps of self into a boiling mass. All I am, all the energy I can muster, slams up at him at once, wrenching at my fingers and striking at the weight of his mind.

Nothing yields, though. There's a quick shudder in my right hand and he has to make an effort to keep from dropping the knife, but that's it. Bubbles of his silent laughter fizz through the dark.

Paige has finally found her keys and she's fiddling with them. The knife stops twisting around and balances at the level of her heart. I can feel Aloysius getting ready. His intentions squeeze us both, enough that I know he's waiting for the moment her key is in the lock to drive the blade deep between her ribs.

In the course of doing what was necessary to maintain control, I knocked you down—deeper than I'd meant to. That's what Dash told me, pissily, about how we wound up running through the Land of the Dead together. About how we went too deep.

Paige tips forward with the key in her hand. In the glass door her reflection looks like a froth of silvery light. I can feel the muscles in my arm tense for the blow.

"Miss Kittering," Aloysius whispers, and I see her turning, her feathers like trails of glow on the mist. She hasn't seen the knife and she's not scared yet, just confused. Her mouth opens to say something, but I can't stop to listen.

I *will not* let him hurt her. Her eyes are on my face, her expression just starting to sharpen into annoyance, and all I want is to erase every pain she's ever felt, every humiliation. And all at once I feel stronger than I ever knew I *could* feel: I'm a force swirling out of nothingness, and no one is going to hurt Paige while I'm here.

I crash at Aloysius again, madly now, and he shoves me down savagely.

We're vapors, both of us. We're the smear and welter of tangling minds. But even so, even though he's just the *impression* of mass, shoving down that hard gives him a lot of momentum. And down is the one direction I think he's not expecting.

Instead of pushing back I collapse beneath him, then as he stumbles—if you can describe a mind as *stumbling*—I grasp him and plunge.

And—oh, thank God—he's caught completely off guard.

We're dropping in a violent, lashing mass. It's a fight without shapes or limbs, and I can't tell if his mind is wrapped around mine and strangling it, or if I'm rupturing him from inside. But we're falling, and that's all I care about: out of control, out of light.

Out of my body. What will happen to it without anyone left to maneuver it at all? But I can't think about that. All I can do is keep Aloysius wrapped up inextricably, his essence bundled into mine. I feel him like I never have before, his cruelty like cold links chaining my mind and gouging into it. I feel him scrambling for some purchase, some way to stop us from whistling deeper and deeper into the dark.

And I feel his terror. What I thought was the speed of our fall shrilling through me begins to feel more like a scream, too high-pitched to hear.

Or, God, maybe that scream is Paige's after all. Maybe my hand was already driving forward at the same time that my body went haywire and the blade slashed into her, spiraled across her bare skin, opened an artery. Her blood could be fountaining across my face and I wouldn't know, not even if I was choking on it. I'm thrashing in a shapeless mess, trying to get back to her, but it's like I've grown a hundred liquid arms that bubble out and merge again and I'm still going down.

Then the scream gets louder, or somehow my consciousness tunes in on it more, and I can identify Aloysius's fizzly voice with complete certainty. There's some potential danger in the Land of the Dead that sends fear wheeling through him, I know that now. All at once I understand: he hasn't just been possessing me as a way to get back at Dashiell.

He's been on the run. He's been using my body as a hideout. And I didn't know what I was doing, but I've ripped him out of his refuge.

A dim, rattling chime reverberates through here. I'm almost sure it was the sound of the knife blade striking against the pavement, far away from us.

We touch down at the same time as the sound. I know we don't have bodies in this place, not exactly, but hey, at least I have my normal appearance back. I'm separate from him, doubled up on the riverbank and clutching my knees.

"Boy," Aloysius snarls, "have you the faintest conception of how I'll make you suffer for this?"

Uh, what is he now, exactly? That grating voice came from *something* but it's not remotely humanoid. A gray, intestinal tangle on spindly legs—like a flamingo's, maybe. It waddles at me, trying to be menacing.

And I'm so relieved and emptied, so heart-shredded and bewildered all at once, that I just plain crack up laughing at the sight. Even though I'm still in danger. Even though he can still crawl back into my body and go after Paige all over again, and probably Elena too, now. The reality is that all I've accomplished is to maybe buy Paige some time.

No matter what happened, she must have heard the knife drop. She must have seen me doing who knows what, weaving around or spilling face-first onto the pavement. I'm pretty sure now that she wasn't hurt, though, or Aloysius wouldn't be so enraged. Paige will probably have the sense to decide that I'm a homicidal maniac and barricade herself in her apartment. It's horrible but I have to be thankful for it.

I have to be thankful for anything I can get.

I'm laughing in hysterics, halfway sobbing, but it's obvious that Aloysius isn't used to anybody laughing at him at all. It's obvious that he's not sure how to react, at first; I mean, ordering someone not to laugh is only going to make him seem that much more ridiculous.

"Will you be laughing when I carve ribbons of flesh from your Elena, boy? When she watches you twist the knife in her guts, and you hear her screaming?"

"Yeah," I say, but I'm laughing so hard it seems like I might disintegrate at any moment. "Using me to maim and kill has been working out *great* for you. I mean, the greatest."

And now it's really hitting me: as powerful as he is, I've beaten him back twice. He's been completely astounded both times. I'm sure he's used people he possessed to carry out his murders before; I could feel that. But somehow I must be almost a match for him, because nobody has died at my hands. Not yet.

There's a sensation of sudden movement, but I can't tell if I'm plummeting down or being yanked up. But half a second later I feel cold, definite breath coming in shallow bursts through my nose. Pain burns me with every inhalation, smokes its way up to my shoulder.

I'm lying curled on the pavement with my eyes closed. Whatever is wrong with my lungs, it's obviously way worse than my usual asthma. My heart is pattering in this frantic, airy way.

There's enough foggy streetlamp light on my eyelids that I can detect the darkness of someone bending over me. I don't want to look, but I'm pretty sure I know who it is. So he's finally here, and it'll be easy enough for him to pick up that knife. Slide it into me and break the circuit, and then the horror will finally be over.

I can feel the blade above me. Cold steel disrupting the night.

It's how I've died, twice, in the Land of the Dead. It feels right, natural, like I've been practicing for this. And anyway, what's one more?

"Dash?" I say. "It's okay. Really. You can tell Ruby I said so. Just get it over with."

I break out coughing, and the pain is so bad that it wipes out everything else. If he's answering—hell, even if he's stabbing me—my chest is so crowded with saw-toothed stars that I don't think I'd know the difference.

MABEL

* * * * *

Ruby-girl is here and they're all around her, grabbing and poking and rumpling in her clothes, and she makes their heads look like bedrooms with black walls and strange pictures slapped up willy-nilly. Some of them have bright red writing on the black, like squirming threads, but the same lines over and over, like in a copybook from school. Aloysius's guards are men but their faces are empty blocks, all with the same bedroom inside them, and Ruby fights in their arms but she can't get away.

"She doesn't have it," Charlie says. "The boss was positive she would have it, but it's nowhere."

"That's what I've been telling you!" Ruby squeals. "I don't know how—oh, I must have lost it on the way down here." The empty rooms turn at each other: *isittrue isittrue* showing in them, almost the way the letters written on their walls show. *Itbetterbetrue, ifit'snottrue, andwecallhim. Verybad.*

I don't like her to be so upset, with her face scrunched and spotted bright by tears. Hot red in her cheeks. I go running over the lumpy ground—and you see, I knew Ruby was nice, I knew it, because now it's so easy to be pretty as a doll with her looking at me. Nothing is crawling on me and my dress floats like perfect clouds.

"Let her go," I beg. "Please, you have to let her go! Ruby, it's me, it's Mabel, and I'm here to help you! Everett is in big trouble."

They're going to let her go. That's what Aloysius told them to do, but they have to act mad first. "I don't *think* so," Charlie sneers. "Mabel, why would anyone listen to you?"

"Dashiell is about to chop up her brother Everett! Dashiell's got the knife right now, and he's following Everett, but if we take Ruby to her body she can make it stop!"

Aloysius told me. I say exactly what he hissed into my head and made me repeat back until I had it just right, and I remember him saying each word in the instant that I recite it. I say my lessons perfectly and so he can't be mad at me.

The rooms turn to stare into one another; no eyes but they don't need eyes to see here. This time they turn, acting it all out for Ruby.

"And where did you learn that tidbit, Mabel? You don't know anything. You're just making up nonsense."

"But you know I have Old Body!" I yell at them. *Act desperate,* Aloysius told me. *She hasn't the slightest idea you've lost your Old Body, has she? Assuming dear Dashiell has neglected to inform her, which would be perfectly in keeping with his deceitful, low-down character. So she'll have no reason to suspect that what you say is a lie. Act as if monkeys were rending your own mother limb from limb, there's a pet.* "I was following Dashiell—he's in Ruby's body, and I was afraid of what he would do, so I went after him, through the subways and everywhere. And now he's going to kill Everett, and Everett's been so kind to me. I can't let Dashiell do it!"

Ruby's gone the color of bones. She's swaying.

"Oh, God. Everett said this would happen. He warned me and I didn't want to believe it. He *warned* me."

We know all about that already, so Ruby doesn't need to tell us anything. Aloysius was listening inside Everett when Everett said that warning to her, and Aloysius was laughing, laughing where no one could hear him, because it gave him the best idea for how to fool her.

I don't like lying to her. But I have to do it so we can be together. When everything is all better and I'm living in her, I'll confess I was bad and she'll forgive me.

"We have to go right now, Ruby!" I yell. "Please, please let her go! It isn't far away!"

The rooms spin and their curtains wave and I can see boy clothes, black and gray, piled on the floors of their faces.

"Well . . . we can ask Aloysius. We can ask if he thinks it's the proper thing to do. You know it's against policy, Mabel, to let a living person reclaim their body. Even if it is Dashiell Bohnacker we're talking about, it doesn't seem right."

"But there's no time!" I scream, and Ruby drops her face and covers it with her hands. Her back moves like the ocean. "There's no time, because Dashiell's right behind Everett, and as soon as he gets somewhere dark enough, he'll start to stab and stab! But Ruby never said he could use her body that way!"

I told Ruby about the gun that Old Body dreamed for me. I didn't know when I said it what a clever girl I was, but now I know, because I put the thought *gun* in Ruby's head and that made her so nervous she kept thinking it, until her thought put the gun in my pocket. I keep my hand covering it so she won't see the shape bulging in the white lace. I won't be mean to her like I was to Old Body, I promise, I promise I've learned my lesson and I'll be so nice that she'll be happy every day to live with me. She just has to do things my way, that's all.

Charlie sighs, big, like he's on stage. "Teddy, run and find Aloysius. Mabel, I guess we'll have to risk it that the boss might not approve, if he doesn't get here in time. You can escort Ruby to her corpse and explain to her what she has to do to stop Everett from being knifed in cold blood by his own big brother. But you've got to understand, I'm coming too."

I reach up to pull Ruby's hand off her face. "But—what can *I* do to stop Dash? What you're talking about—tell me it won't hurt him!"

"It won't hurt, Ruby, I promise. It will just take him out of you so he can't do anything to Everett where he needs your hands. It doesn't hurt, not even a teeny bit. Not even as much as a pin." I singsong it, croon it to her as sweetly as a little bird. Aloysius didn't give me clear words for this part so I have to make them up by myself, but it's true. It's true that getting knocked out of Ruby won't hurt Dashiell, except for his feelings.

It's what Aloysius will do to Dashiell once he's back here and can't escape that will hurt, hurt and burn and rip until there's not one speck left. No ashes, no potato peels, no silk ribbons, no dust. Finished.

But Ruby mustn't know that. It will make her sad and I want her to *neverever* be sad.

I have her hand in mine and she is soft and fresh and I am pulling her between the shacks that she sees out of nothing. I know where to go. Ruby is stumbling like Old Body used to do late at night after too many spirits, but it is sad-and-worried that is making Ruby drunk. It hurts me to see so I pull her faster, because the sooner she does it the sooner I can live in her and comfort her from inside. *Therethere Rubygirl we'retogethernow,* I'll say, and hold her heart like a lamp.

"Think of Everett," I say, coo and song and chirp in the trees, "your sweet, good brother Everett. Dashiell already had his turn to live, didn't he? And it will be too, too sad if Everett has to lose his only chance to be alive so, so young. He shouldn't lose it just because Dashiell made big mistakes. It wouldn't be fair."

Charlie walking to the side tilts his room-head at me, to let me know I'm doing good, a good job, saying just-right things.

Ruby is so scared and sad that the clouds have sunk down just above us and they have dark mouths that slip and slide and moan. She is staring sad at her red boots and I hope she won't look up and see clouds like that.

"You're talking about—about forcing Dashiell out of me, aren't you? Like what Everett did to him. But if he doesn't have me to live in then we'll lose him again, Mabel! We'll lose him forever this time, and I love him so *much.* I can't go through that a second time."

I don't like hearing her talking this way, and I can tell Charlie doesn't like it either. She's walking with her head spilled toward the ground, but she's still coming with me, letting me lead her through. The maze is here without her, but we just *know* it's there; we can't see or feel anything. Now every open door is a black moon sucking out the light.

No matter what she's saying, she hasn't pulled her hand away. No matter what she's saying, she's still dragging along like me going with my mother to church. So maybe that's her real answer and I shouldn't worry so terribly that she'll say no when we get there?

"But *Everett*," I say, thinking of angels singing hymns. Trying to make it sound that way. "Everett, your good brother, your kind brother. You know how brave he is. You have to do it, to save his life! Ruby, I know! It's very, very terrible to be dead like me. You keep losing everything you loved, all the time, and memories are all you have left instead of the whole world! You can't let Dashiell do that to him. Even Dashiell knows that! He *knows* he's doing a very bad thing now!"

Poor Ruby. She's weeping and tripping over a smooth flat world. She's sobbing like my mother did when the doctor said I'd be dead before morning, not knowing I could hear. All because I'm lying to her, and Charlie nodding secretly where she doesn't see. Nodding: *that'srightMabel, that'sagoodgirl.*

Good girl. I am a good girl when bad men, evil men, tell me to be. I'm sorry, Ruby. I hope you won't be angry at me.

Ruby sobs all the way to the dark door that eats a hole right through the night. "In there, Ruby," I whisper. "You'll see. It's your body that Dashiell drowned. You just have to give it a big hug. If you don't then poor, good Everett will die any minute, so you have to hurry! And then come out. Come back to me."

She's almost falling into the dark. Charlie and I, we let her go on alone. I don't like it but it's what Aloysius said to do. "First introduce the dread and guilt, and then step back. Let them devour her in their own good time."

Just like what Dashiell did to me. You see?

Aloysius has made you promises he can't keep, Mabel, assuming he ever had the slightest intention of trying. I think you know that.

That's what Dashiell said to me, and there's the dread, the thumping secret dread. Maybe Aloysius doesn't mean anything he promised. That might be the reason they aren't saying, that they've run so fast to fetch him, and that Charlie won't stop watching me.

Maybe he'll steal my Ruby from me? And she's much too nice for him!

Footsteps footsteps footsteps. Very softly. But I'm so angry thinking about it, that Aloysius might try to take her from me, that I just tip up my chin. I don't say one word to Charlie, about the footsteps whispering. And now Aloysius is waiting beside him.

EVERETT

✴ ✴   ✴ ✴

Why isn't it finished? The shadow hangs over me, unmoving, while every short, hacking breath tears me apart. Then—*damn him*—he reaches down and strokes my cheek. "Dash, enough already! Just make it stop."

I finally open my eyes, though even that much movement hurts, or maybe it's the random fragments of nighttime light that hurt me. Sure enough, it's Dashiell in Ruby's body, looking at me in a way I can't make out. His expression is blotted into darkness by a streetlamp behind his head—or, right, *Ruby's* head, if there's even a serious distinction between them anymore. I can see the knife in his hand, resting casually on one thigh as he kneels there.

"Never-Ever, I recognize that this isn't an ideal moment for us to talk. But it might be the last opportunity we'll have, so I'd appreciate if you could try to bear with me."

"Why can't we talk *after* you kill me? Being dead didn't shut you up any."

Dashiell laughs at that and ruffles my hair. He's got all the time in the world, I guess; Aloysius probably won't bother taking me over again while I'm in such crappy condition. Why should Dash care that I'm suffering?

"There are some things you should understand, Never. About yourself. For instance, that you truly are brave, and noble, and pure of heart. You're worth five of me, in fact. I'm sure our father knows that, beyond question. And so does our Ruby Slippers, deep down, loath as she'd be to admit it."

Great, so I have to listen to him trying to make himself feel better before he'll finally end this.

"Dash, I really, really don't need your excuses, all right? I already told you I'm okay with it. I mean, I know Aloysius can keep coming back, as long as I live. I'd rather you just cancel me out than have Aloysius make me into a murderer."

He's looking off like he's not listening to me at all, though. His face has turned enough that the light catches it in yellowish curves, and I notice how Ruby's mouth has dropped. There are tears—*Dashiell's* tears?—welling in her green eyes.

"You've had some firsthand experience of being me now, Never. You know what it's like. So treat it as an education and keep the parts of me you can use." He smiles and shrugs and gives me one quick glance: that ultra-Dashiell sly quirk of a smile, that extreme-whatever shrug he does. "Keep what you need, and forget the rest."

Here we go again: Dashiell spinning his oblique phrases at me. Dashiell making me guess what the hell he's going on about. And my body feels like ice, jerking with tremors and stabbed through by pain, and I'm just plain done with asking him what he means. He can say shit that makes sense, or not.

There's a whining noise in the distance. After a few seconds of wobbly confusion I recognize the sound. Sirens. If they're heading this way, that will *force* him to finally slit my throat. I mean, it's now or never.

He stands up, polishing the knife methodically with a fold of Ruby's scarf. He's buffing the fingerprints off, and maybe that will protect Ruby from getting busted for this. Good.

Then he turns away. What is he *doing*? He walks a few paces by the curb, bends.

And chucks the knife down a storm drain. I can hear it clunking away.

"Dash?" I sputter. I'm not sure if the words are even comprehensible. "Dash, what—what are we going to do now?"

"Hush now, Never. The ambulance will be here soon. I expect you have a collapsed lung from those ribs I kicked in, but they can fix that. You've turned a distressing shade of blue. You appear to be going into shock, in fact, but with any luck you'll live through it."

I'm so flummoxed I can't even answer. It's not like I want to die, exactly, but if I live then how will the people I love ever be safe? I'm shaking so hard now that it's stirring up a weird black dust in my vision. I'm falling out of joint with the world.

"You're an entirely different species of man than me, Never. Wherever I'm going, it's safe to say you won't wind up there. We won't be seeing each other again."

Dashiell? I try to say, but I can't tell if there's any sound. Maybe my eyes have closed again, because I don't see anything except red-black mist. The sirens are blasting into my mind now—they must be almost here—and all at once I understand that I have to tell him goodbye. I'm straining as hard as I can to form the words, but all that comes out is a croak.

"Your resentment of me is perfectly valid, Never. I won't try to tell you that it isn't. I'm sure it's been brutally difficult, both Ruby and me overshadowing you in our various ways, and showing so little consideration for your feelings on that score. The ways you trump *us* aren't so nakedly obvious, simply. But if it helps anything, you should know that I love you. More and more, as I've come to appreciate who you are."

I hear his footsteps walking away, and I try to call him back. I try to say whatever it is I *have* to say—because I finally grasp that this is really my last chance. There are things I'll regret forever that I didn't tell him, if I can only remember what they are and then force the sounds out. But I can't.

I can't.

RUBY SLIPPERS

* * * *

The shack encloses me like a cube of smoke-gray velvet. I stagger in with my arms stretched in front of me, feeling at every step like I might fall, and fall forever. How can I do what I *have* to do, even when the situation is so desperate, even though there's no other way? I don't see my body in here anywhere and the walls are spinning. Mabel wouldn't lie about this, but maybe she was confused and there's no drowned corpse in here. No corpse with my face, my dress, my hands greenish and spongy from long submersion.

Then I notice something low in the corner, coming into focus in the lethargic way things sometimes do here; *Everett's* corpse came into my vision with the same slow drift, the delayed understanding. But now it's not my body I'm seeing, not a human form at all. It's oblong and made of glass: a huge, boxy aquarium, filled almost to the brim with muddy water.

An aquarium exactly the same size as a coffin. And in the fog and silt, the dimmest suggestion of a solid form. A nebulous, pale smear like a dead fish half emerges from the gray-brown murk.

It's as if time thickened, and understanding has to fight

its way through it. That pale thing has dark cracks running lengthwise, and after an indefinite moment I realize that it's my own hand and those cracks are the gaps between my fingers, and it's so much worse than it would be if I could see myself clearly in that tank. I know I have to go to it, reach in and lift out my corpse. But I picture that floating hand leading to something much worse than my own dead body, something gray and covered with cartilaginous scales; something that will break into sinuous movement at my touch. I'm almost sure I can see a very subtle fluttering in the depths and I stop where I am, stiff with dread.

There isn't much time. I know that, I know I have to leap forward, to burst through the frozen moment. Any second now it will be too late, and Everett will be destroyed—by me. By what I did and what I failed to do.

I pry my right foot off the dirt floor. I can barely lift it, and when I try to lean into the step I feel like endless midnight-colored towers are toppling and pulling me down with them. Like I'll never find the ground again.

A stirring in the murk. An almost imperceptible splash in the corner of my eye. If that's really my corpse then maybe it's not as dead as it should be.

That, or it's not alone in the tank. Maybe whatever is in there is waiting to twine around my neck and pull me in. Maybe it will drown me all over again with my mouth crushed against my corpse's bloated lips, those wide green eyes inches from mine. The swishing movement comes again, sending delicate eddies through the sediment. I can feel how something in there is waiting for me, the tautness of its anticipation.

My foot finally slaps down and I teeter.

I'll never make it in time, not moving so slowly. I close my eyes so I won't see that soft, anxious swirling, and throw my weight forward so that my legs *have* to move to stop me from pitching headlong onto the floor. I feel the tank's sharp edge hitting me just below the knees and I double over, my left hand smacking the wall and the right sinking into slimy wet.

A cold and slippery *something* wraps itself around my hand and forearm. Or, no: it isn't binding me, but surging through me, a chill substance merging with my flesh, and even though I know this is what I *have* to do, and do now, a scream tears from my throat and I rear back.

As my arm pulls out of the sludge it's too heavy, too long: as if it's grown an extra segment in place of my hand. Then I see a drenched, flowered sleeve rising up where my fingertips should be, followed by a shoulder, an algae-filmed cascade of my own dirty blond hair. My arm has fused into my corpse's arm as high as our elbows. Dead fingers nose from the flesh below my triceps and I'm shrieking so that my throat feels like shredded paper.

I yank back again, struggling to free myself, and the Ruby-corpse heaves into sitting position, but floppily, spilling forward over the tank's brim. She looks slack and her skin is puffy and sodden. Electric green weeds spill from her sagging jaw. I feel the silence in her wide mouth, and somehow it stops me from screaming.

She's sick and pitiful. She's me, though; I have to take her back. I have to fold her into me like a door, and then turn the key.

And lock Dashiell out.

Tiny, pearl-pink fish drop from her hair and dart away into the muddy water.

"You *know* how much I love you, Dash," I say out loud. "You know I'd do anything for you that I could. I'd give my own life for yours, over and over again, if only that was the choice I had to make."

Even as I say it I'm staring into my own vacant eyes, remembering how this poor dead Ruby felt as Dashiell shoved her under the river, how her lungs ballooned with water. How she thrashed for air, but wouldn't fight hard enough to get free because she couldn't bear to hurt him. I feel such piercing compassion for her that I reach forward with my left hand—it's the only hand I have, with my right completely swallowed by her arm—and stroke her cheek. As if I could comfort her.

My hand swims straight into her face. Her skin parts around it like a puddle, and then a heavy suction takes over and we're sliding into each other, our parts all slipping and rearranging until her hands nestle into my hands, her chest in my chest. Her lower body snakes out of the water, pulling into me.

There's a terrible moment when my worst fear comes true and her unbreathing mouth squeezes mine, a kiss of warmth and chill death, and then heat and cold boil into a single pair of lips, gasping with nausea. I feel the cold gel of her eyeballs roiling in mine, and for an instant I'm not sure which of us is crying.

And then I'm panting on the dirt floor. One girl, unified. One heart, so dense with grief that there's no space left in it for the brother I loved beyond everything else in life.

This should be more than enough to finish anyone. But I know it's not, I know there's more I have to do.

As my breathing calms, I become aware that there are figures in the doorway. Dim silhouettes with glints of light in their
eyes, watching me with ravenous longing.

"Ruby, darling," a high-pitched man's voice says. "Are you
feeling better now?"

MABEL

✳ ✳ ✳ ✳ ✳

Charlie yanks my hair back in a big fist and shoves his other fist between my teeth before I can scream, and Aloysius dips one hand to filch the gun from my pocket. He dandles it and gives it a flip and smiles.

"Now, Mabel," Aloysius says with his teeth twisted up like a big bow, "you know very well that Ruby Bohnacker is too rare and delicious a morsel to be wasted on a little bitch like you. Be very grateful that we've excused you for your past naughtiness, and leave it at that, there's a lamb. A single, solitary peep of complaint out of you, and you'll be punished most severely."

Youpromised, youpromised! I can't scream it out with Charlie stuffing my voice down. He promised, and I did everything he said to do, I coaxed and cooed to Ruby just, just so, and he has Everett anyway.

"You'd like to say that I don't require her services, since I already possess her brother? That runt is worse than useless, unfortunately. Ruby will pay me back for my disappointment, though, now that she's so wonderfully unencumbered. Footloose and fancy-free, so to speak. And Mabel, you'll do just as you're told, if you want to keep the barest memories of your old life."

In the dark hut Ruby rolls into herself, arms and legs wriggling from spidery doubling into one girl. Then she lies on the floor and gasps, her face striped bright with tears. When Aloysius calls to her and asks is she better she looks at him, blank and shiny, like nothing and nobody makes sense to her now that Dashiell's shoved out. Charlie lets me go, knocks me down and sideways into the mud. *Don't come, Ruby!* I should scream, but they'll hurt me and hurt me if I do and so I keep quiet.

She gets up and her face is like she's lost, like she's forgotten how to see. And Aloysius stares at her crazy-sharp, because he wants to say, *Come to me,* but not too soon, not until the just-right moment, in case he scares her. Because even now that he has the gun, she has to come toward him. Of her very own free, free will. Or it won't work and Aloysius won't get her.

Ruby looks so dizzy, though, so goggling and empty, and I'm frightened for her. I'm scared she's too blank and sad to understand that she mustn't, mustn't go near him, like she has become the dark woods with no more moon, like she can't imagine that anything can matter. But Ruby, it does, it still does!

And Aloysius sees it too, how snapping herself closed to Dashiell has left her like a forest with no paths going through. "Ruby?" he says, but he keeps his voice easy, like it doesn't matter. "Could you come here for a minute, please?"

Ruby lifts one shiny red boot and stands there with it floating in front of her, but she doesn't put the foot down and Aloysius and Charlie are fixed with no attention left for anything but her, not in the world. It's only Ruby in the dark shack and if she'll keep coming, that's all they know or care about. Like two snakes hypnotized, the way I saw once at a fair.

So they don't hear and they don't see, not what I see, and I keep quiet. Oh, no, not a single peep, just like he told me.

Ruby wavers, drowsy and confused, and her floating red toes dip toward the ground, and there's the quick suck of breath from Aloysius.

I see a little flick in Ruby, like the tiniest possible spark hiding under her lashes, and I want to squeal. But I have to keep very, very still. Because Aloysius mustn't guess that Ruby's not so silly after all. She stops and wobbles and gawks above his head like she's forgetting all about where she is and what she was doing.

"Ruby," he calls. Trying to sound nice, but it's tight with how angry he is, and I want to squeal and laugh at him. "Ruby, darling, just one moment of your time. Step right this way."

Another lift, wobble, tap of her foot. Then one more. So slow and sleepy, like each step is a dream big enough for everybody here.

Is it enough steps forward, yet? She lets her boot go like a leaf into the air, and sail along, and his fingers are so white with readiness to swing the gun at her, but he wants to be sure, *veryverysure*, that she's come to him enough for it to count.

And as he waits the blue-striped girl is silent behind him, getting closer. Almost close enough to reach and touch him, when Ruby's foot taps down.

At the same time the gun is lifting. At the same time Charlie sees the girl in blue satin pajamas and starts yelling. Aloysius is spinning and the bullets flash into the dark; did they hit her? But no, the blue girl is dipping in quick and low, one bullet just wisping through her blue-striped hair, and the colored stars shine on the teeth Aloysius had when he was alive.

But none of us can touch anything that was in our bodies when we were alive. That's what happened to Constance, her mother hugged her wearing part of Constance in a locket, and Constance crumpled up and was gone.

An allergy to our mortal remains, Dashiell said when I told him the story. *An allergy of the most violent kind, from the sound of it.* And he got a look like a shopkeeper who thinks you might pay too much for something.

And now I am laughing, because I see Aloysius's old teeth biting into his neck. The blue girl is shoving the teeth into him, hard. They're sinking into his skin, and he starts to fold up, and the girl jumps back screaming. Aloysius points the gun even as his shoulder wads up like dirty laundry. It's aiming right at her, about to blast her wide open. She came up to him *ofherownfree-will,* and so Aloysius can still escape inside her if he hits her just so.

But Ruby isn't moving like a sleepy leaf anymore. She's running in and toppling Aloysius to the side, so his gun shoots space instead. And the whole time he falls he's creasing into himself, his skin turning into a hundred umbrellas all folding up at once. He looks so shocked that he might not know what's happening to him.

Every bit of his body is sucking inward, draining into flower-shaped holes, all closing. His cheeks pull in and his face pleats smaller. Funnels sink in his neck and chest, spewing breath as they go deeper, pulling him after them. Legs turn into paper lanterns, scrunching in the rain.

Then he sees his teeth, where the blue girl let them drop. Pale and biting up from the ground. Oh, and now he understands how they tricked him. He understands it wasn't enough to worry about Ruby, and if *she* was carrying teeth in her pocket! But it's too late now.

Ruby lets him have eyes, or maybe it's the strange girl who is seeing him that way? A little, creasing monkey of an old man, getting smaller every moment, but with his eyes stretched so huge they dig holes in the air. His mouth has shriveled into a tiny dot but his eyes are still screaming, and we all hear it: a shriek whistling out of his pupils, like high wind through cracks in a wall.

Now Dashiell comes walking right up, in jeans but no shirt and his feet bare on the dirt. He walks swinging and calm, like he's not scared, like he doesn't have lots of enemies here. Aloysius is so bent into his disappearing that he can't even fight when Dashiell opens what's left of his fingers and takes his gun away.

Ruby runs straight to Dashiell and throws her arms around his neck—*Ruby, no! You should know better. Don't trust him!* But she went so quick, before I even realized, and it's too late to shout that. He squeezes her tight and croons to her. "Ruby-Ru, my sweetest, my precious girl. How bravely you've come through."

Then he lifts the gun's nose and presses it to the side of her head.

RUBY

* * * *

I didn't understand how cold I was, cold through my heart and through the quick of my being, until I felt Dashiell's warmth against me. I nestle my face against him, sobbing, and only the muzzle of the gun at my temple remains as an imprint of chill.

Aloysius keeps collapsing on the ground in front of us, a shrill scream piping from the wreckage of what he was. I try not to watch, it's so horrible, but I still see too much from the corners of my eyes. Facets of skin pleat in to meet one another, his body pulled into a slow implosion.

Elena sits on the ground, eyes wide with shock, and hugs herself. She knew what she was doing when we met just at the edge of our tumble into the borderlands, when I passed that jawbone to her. She knew that approaching Aloysius would give him a chance to try and take her, but it's impossible to understand, viscerally, how it will feel to come that close to losing yourself. It was close for me, too, and now that it's over I can't understand how I stayed so perfectly controlled as I walked toward that focused evil, feeling the yawn of its hunger for me.

Mabel is hopping around in excitement, and that thug who dragged me here—Charlie?—is already darting away.

"Softly, Ru-Ru. Everett is safe now, assuming anyway that he pulls through the physical damage he's suffered, which I think he will. But he's safe from Aloysius, forever. He owns himself again, completely, and the shadow-corpse he left here will vanish along with the ghost who created it. Don't cry."

"Did we hurt him, Dash?" I barely hear myself, but Dashiell does.

"Ah, Ru, we did. We hurt him badly. Staved in his ribs and popped a lung, as far as I could tell, all in the interests of hampering Aloysius. But we didn't kill him, and he truly wouldn't have wanted it any other way. A few days in the hospital and he should be all right."

That makes Elena glance up for the first time, and the anger on her face flickers into alarm as she registers the gun in Dashiell's hand.

"Let Ruby go! My God, after everything she's been through tonight, and *because* of you. And you put Everett in the hospital? I don't understand how anyone could be so—"

"Elena!" I need to stop her before she says anything terrible. "It's okay. I wouldn't have gone to Dash if it *wasn't* okay with me. I know what that means, here. If I didn't want him to possess me again, I could have just stayed away."

Dashiell kisses me on the forehead, so gently. And I can't help it: a tremor goes through me at the contrast between the round warmth of his lips and the round cold of the barrel on my bare skin. I tell myself that the pain won't last long; there will be only one quick jolt, and I won't even feel the fall. Dash won't hurt me any more than he has to.

He doesn't know that I thought of holding back, that I almost changed my mind and didn't go to him. Because even now that Everett is saved, I can't forget what Dash was ready to do if he thought he had to. As utterly as I love him, I'm not sure if that's something I can forgive.

"But, Ruby! You just—just a few *minutes* ago, you went through the whole—grabbing your own corpse, pulling it back in? You did that for nothing? Or—"

And then she gets it, and her voice stops on a sharp exhalation.

"I knew Aloysius would be gravely tempted by a chance at our Miss Slippers," Dash explains, and strokes my hair with his free hand. "He wouldn't care to lose face, either, by letting everyone see that a girl he'd marked as his own select prey had escaped his grasp. But I thought he'd be too leery to risk coming near her, knowing what he knew about the object in my possession. Unless he was entirely persuaded that my Ru-Ru had betrayed me. So we planned it this way, Ru and I, though she wasn't sure she was capable of such advanced deceit. Oh, but you did a fine job in the event, didn't you, Miss Slippers?"

"You mean she was fooling me?" Mabel yelps somewhere behind me. "Ruby, you were tricking me, too?"

I don't answer. Mabel set up Everett. We nearly lost him forever because of her. Even if she is a little girl, there's no way I can let that go. She whimpers and tugs on my clothes, and I bury my face in Dashiell's chest. Aloysius's scream is still there, but getting higher and thinner: a broken, babbling stream of sound.

Then it goes out, twisting off into silence.

"Mabel," Dashiell snaps. "Leave us alone, please. Elena, you too, if you don't mind. You've proved you're the one girl brave enough for my brother, and he's the only man you're likely to meet anytime soon who's remotely worthy of *you*. You've rescued him, and you've saved the dead here from a sadistic tyrant into the bargain. But everything that remains now is between me and my Ru. Let us be, and you'll wake up very soon."

"Ruby?" Elena must have dragged herself to her feet, because she curls a hand on my shoulder. "You're seriously planning to spend the rest of your life being half someone else? A walking life-support system for a ghost? Because that's what this comes down to."

"Remember what you said to me?" I say. I don't look at her, because I don't want her to see that I'm crying. I'll be giving up a lot of myself, and a lot of my freedom, to keep Dashiell with us, I know that. And I can't completely forgive him, but I can't abandon him here, either. "I'm not asking your permission."

I don't know where she goes—maybe she wakes up on Liv's floor with her sleeping bag billowing around her? There's some more whining and scuffling from Mabel, but we ignore her until she leaves us, too, screaming names at me as she runs.

Then Dash and I are alone in this gray space, among vague shacks and wiry trees limned in sporadic gold and green. His tangled golden hair covers my eyes and we sway almost imperceptibly together with each breath.

"I'm sorry to be holding the gun to your head, Ru," Dash murmurs after a while. "But it keeps the other ghosts at bay. Aloysius's old lieutenants are watching us from every side. None of them will hassle us, though, not when they can see I have an exit instantly at hand."

"You can go ahead, though, Dash. I'm ready. We can go home."

I try to brace myself for the blast, the sensation of my skull shattering inward. My fists are clenched tight against his naked back and my breath is thick, but the shot just doesn't come.

"Ah, but that's what I have to tell you, Ru. That's why we need our privacy. I won't be coming back with you. I can feel a change in the resistance of this place, if that makes sense. I'm free to go on."

I can't understand this. I can't take it in. I rear back to stare at him and my eyes must be jagged with accusation, because he actually flinches. It's so unlike Dash to flinch at anything that seeing it hurts me even more.

"I'm dead, Ruby-Ru, and hauling me around in your body won't undo that. Let me be dead and gone, then. Let the dead bury the dead."

"Dead and gone where?" The world is warping in my eyes, rippling like light in ice, and I can barely breathe. I know that nothing I can say will help. Who's ever gotten Dash to change his mind—even if I completely want him to? I can't stand to lose him, but at the same time I can't quite open myself to him, can't swell my heart with him, not in the same way that I have all my life. "Dashiell? If you're going on, then where?"

"Where? Hell, presumably, if there's any justice in the universe. But since we all know there isn't, I wouldn't worry too much, sweet Ru." He smiles at me, dabbles with my hair. "Ru, our father was perfectly right. It's better that I died young, truly, much as you'd rather not understand that. If I had lived, I would have always been a danger to you. To other people as well, probably—Paige comes to mind—but to you in particular. That's what you haven't been willing to see, so I thought I'd take this last chance to tell you."

"You were never a *danger* to me! Dash, I loved you more than anything, and I was never really afraid. No matter what you did, I couldn't be afraid of you." *I was only worried for Everett, not for myself,* but I don't say that to him. And anyway, he knows. Dash has always known everything I feel, I recognize that now. He even knows the impulse that passed through me as Aloysius crumpled: to withhold myself from him. To keep myself closed.

"Ah, but there's the difficulty, dearest Ru. You should have been afraid. Because I needed you, much more than you realized. I needed to see myself through your eyes. There were plenty of times when that was the only bearable view. And what I might have done to hold on to your tenderness, as you grew older, as you started to drift away from me . . ." Dashiell shrugs. "I'd have given way to the urge to drag you into whatever mire I happened to be in myself. Do you really suppose I wasn't tempted, Ru-Ru? And you wouldn't have stopped me. I always knew that."

Grief shakes through me, and I can feel that brick wall where Dashiell pinned me again, the wet snow weeping into my face. I know he's thinking of it, too.

"You nearly did, once," I say. "That afternoon in Williamsburg. When I came looking for you."

"I nearly did," Dash confirms. His voice is soft in my hair. "I badly wanted to. And you had just turned fifteen, then. Suppose you'd been a year or two older? But there was still just enough decency left in me that I tried to frighten you instead."

"So is that what you're going to do now, Dash?" I ask, and I can't keep the bitterness from my voice. Even long before I was possessed, Dash and I lived as secrets inside each other, expanded each other like shadows stretched from sinking lights; I know that now. I always felt like his creation, like a miracle he made by seeing something fierce and glorious in me—but he was my creation, too. And he can go off someplace where that won't matter anymore, but I'll have to live on without him to sustain me. "Order me to walk away, and not look back at you?"

"Ah, but I'm the one who'll be walking away, this time." He presses soft kisses on my face. Drinks down my tears. "I have a distinct sense that I'll be disappearing from view in just a few paces. And you'll be going home, to find out who you are without me, and who you can love instead. I think you'll know both those things soon."

He lets me go and steps backward.

He lets the gun fall from his hand.

His face is still there, his gray eyes gazing into me, ironic and sweet and insolent all at once. And it's the face of all the heart I've ever had.

But I don't scream his name.

I don't beg him not to go.

DASHIELL

* * * * *

What is given to the dead? No kind of future, that much is sure. Memory rattles its telescopes sometimes, offers its narrow views, all the more precious here in the borderlands where there's nothing else to see. But in those visions, nothing changes. Ruby sits beside me in the shoe store and tries on her crimson boots again and again, tugging the laces with clockwork delicacy, always precisely the same. Paige turns to meet my eyes for the first time and her rain-blue lips curl into an identical smile; her hair flicks in the same breeze. We have what we have, and no more. Even the shuffling and elaboration of dreams is lost to us.

But as I slip from my boundaries, it's not my own life that blinks in my eyes. A future that isn't mine grants me the mercy of a few home movies, rapid-fire and blazing, and I see:

Everett coming home from the hospital, still weak, but with a new clarity and determination in his look that does wonders for him. Elena's arm steadies him as he climbs our front steps.

My father lowering his face to hide his tears as he rocks my infant son on his lap, there in the nursery they've made from my old room. He's trying to sing a lullaby but grief breaks up his voice. Really, I hope this is a particularly rough day for him, or that those are at least partially tears of happiness.

Paige confusingly dressed in a business suit, looking so much older that I hardly recognize her. She's waiting to board a plane. Ah, I'd have liked to see her face as she read my letter, my final effort to explain and possibly even to console, but evidently that's too much to ask. So many things are, it seems.

And then my Ruby Slippers, perhaps in her mid-twenties, holding a framed photo of me in both hands. Truly a lady of slipping and sliding now, elegant in gray angora. She lifts the photo and softly kisses my image on the forehead, just the way I always kissed her.

Then she opens a drawer and lowers the photo inside, and bites her lower lip.

The drawer slides closed, and all I was spills open.

Read on for a glimpse of
Sarah Porter's next Tor Teen novel

NEVER-CONTENTED THINGS

* * * * * * *

Available September 2018

It was Friday night, it was lush buzzing June, and only a week into summer break. I'd just graduated, along with the rest of the senior class. The gorge's rim should have been thick with kids we knew. I'd been expecting that our friends Lexi and Xand would be there, at least, though maybe Xand was out of town and I'd forgotten, and Lexi wouldn't come out without him.

But there was no candlelight staggered by the tree trunks, no visible slices of sequins or denim. It was silent apart from the rattle of the bugs, and it was blue and banded violet where the gorge opened into midnight, and our faces went a blending-in blue again as we walked along chewing our pizza. Josh stopped and nuzzled his cheek, kittenish, into my shoulder, which is a thing he does and the way he is, especially with me.

"Doesn't anybody want to see us, Kezzer? Doesn't anybody care?" His voice was teasing, but also not. And of course I thought it, too: that there must be something else going on, something better than the usual beers and mason jars radiant with sweating candles, and we'd been left out. Which might be understandable if it was just me, but who doesn't want Josh at a party, to sass and dance and smile, never showing off or getting in the center of things but just softly glimmering in the corners? Who doesn't want the chance to maybe make out with him, right before dawn, behind their parents' hydrangeas? He's a shade chubby, in a sinuous way—it's part of what makes people take him for a girl—and he makes chubby look prettier and sultrier than anyone else can.

That was when we heard sounds coming from a clearing farther along than the one we typically used. Laughing voices and a song that was new to me, dark but piercing, with languid harmonies and scattered bells. That was when our eyes opened wide to take in their lights, still mostly blocked by trees, but with a crystalline sharpness that wasn't like candle flames. Maybe they were rich college kids with some kind of new LED setup. It didn't make a lot of sense that we were only noticing them now, and so out of the blue, but there they were, and we crept closer. I wouldn't have bothered with people I didn't know, but Josh was already smiling. I knew he could follow that smile straight into their circle; even if he was young, he was so unmistakably deft, so ready to be one of them.

And I felt guilty, for no reason at all. I might have been edging toward weariness, I might have preferred to go home and watch a video together, but I knew Josh was eager to play. I felt like I had something to make up to him, though there was nothing I'd actually done. So it seemed like he should go have his fun, and I'd look after him, and get him safely home no matter how late it got or who tried out the softness of his skin.

That was what I thought, but that wasn't what happened.

"Ooh, Kezzer," Josh crooned. "Just look at them!"

Because they were beautiful. Maybe nineteen or twenty kids who looked like high school juniors or seniors, college freshmen at most. Josh and I should have known them at least by sight, but we'd never seen them before. For half a moment I thought they must be models, dancers, on break between takes of a music video, because they had the glitz and seduction of pure images. Most of them were spinning, undulating their arms, but a few perched in intimate pairs on boulders around the edge of the clearing.

There was a girl with blue-black skin and pink dreads past her hips and patterns like neon butterfly wings painted up to her eye-brows, a pale boy in shiny black leather tights and a white billowy jacket like a ship under sail, a milky blonde dressed in surreal Victoriana with a mink head sewn, open-mouthed and snarling, right over her heart. Dripping red poetry was written on her skirt, and I thought she might have used blood. I looked, and looked again, and then gave up trying to take in all the details. It was too much, it scattered and refracted when I looked too hard. All that I could truly see of them was their glamour.

Josh stepped out of the tree-shadows before I could catch his arm, and they pivoted to him.

They smiled knowing, comfortable smiles. I wasn't sure I liked them but I couldn't leave Josh there alone, so I followed, into the ice-blue twinkling of their lights.

"How can I not *know* you?" Josh asked, with a full-on blast of wonder. His tone was beguiling, disarming; I could feel the strangers warming to him. "Unless you're just visiting here?"

"We've met before," the pale boy said. His white jacket caught too much of the light. There was a burning cast to its pallor that made me look off, but I could feel how his stare lanced at us. "I can't believe you've forgotten that . . . Josh."

There was a lilt to the way he said Josh's name, and I was nearly certain of what I'd heard: it was the *ping* of a lucky guess. A long shot, maybe, but I knew that no one who'd met them would forget them. It wasn't possible.

But Josh's eyes widened, then spun searching through the leaves. "That's right! It was here. Was that sometime last spring?"

"Something like that," the pale boy agreed. "We had a thoroughly wonderful time." The pink-dreaded girl shimmied up to Josh and wrapped her arms around him, giggling confidentially, and the pale boy's attention beamed toward me. "You and your brother here stayed up till dawn with us." When I looked at the boy, his smile leaped all over me. Prodded like a dog's claws.

He was waiting for me to introduce myself, but I didn't. We'd never seen them before, I was sure—and *Josh* is common enough that him saying it didn't prove anything. But if he could hit on the name *Ksenia,* I might start to question my own memory.

That, or question if they'd spied on us somehow. Either way, it set me on edge. If part of me thought I should be more open to new people—especially to gorgeous, wild new people—the offness of how they were acting completely killed the impulse.

"I'm sorry, I can't recall your name," the boy said. Too formally, I thought, for a teenager. "It begins with a K, I think? Kelvin?"

"Close," I said. Josh was absorbed in the dark girl's banter but now he glanced at me, and I shot him a look to say *keep your mouth shut.* "It's Keyshaun, actually."

"Keyshaun," the stranger repeated. I felt the tiny slap of his doubt. "I remembered the K, and that it was something a bit unusual."

Josh had been gawking, on the edge of outing me, though it wasn't anything new for us to invent names to match what people thought we were. He didn't like me lying to these brand-new, very old friends of his, but at that he subsided.

"Keyshaun," Josh said, and smiled blissfully. "You remember now, don't you? How much fun we had? You were dancing for hours with . . ." and he scanned the crowd like he was trying to find his own memory out in the night, pick it up and slot it into his brain. "With that guy in the blue."

A boy in blue holographic leather came up to me then. Amber-skinned, deep-eyed. The look of him, the look of all of them, was too perfect, too cutting, but for Josh's sake I didn't shy away when he slipped an arm around me and pulled me into the center of the glade.

The gorge yawned ten yards distant. We were dancing and the music chimed and chattered in a way that made my tongue prickle. Bells seemed to be ringing in my head. The night took on an unctuous gloss that sent me gliding too fast through time.

I watched Josh from the corner of my eye. Pink dreads and white jacket had him in a triangular hug, three faces leaning in together, cheeks touching, and that was how they were dancing. No one had told us their names, I realized, but my thoughts felt slippery and it seemed too late to ask.

I watched them press a drink into Josh's hand; not the usual beer, some kind of moody, earth-smelling wine. He gulped it down. I had a full glass too, and I couldn't remember taking it from anyone. Something in the scent of it bothered me. When I got a chance I set it down on a tree stump, and if anyone noticed they didn't say anything. A girl wearing—what? Silver snail shells?—smiled at me sidelong and reached to run a nail along my cheek.

The night started to feel like the continuation of a story I'd begun and then lost track of somehow. I could see how Josh had believed them, but why had they lied? He swooned backward supported by their crossed arms, his head upside down and his red bangs trailing over the stones. They spun him like that and he laughed.

The boy in blue tugged me back against a tree and kissed me, hard, and the prickling in my mouth got louder, like something was singing in there. It should have been thrilling but I wasn't sure how I felt about it. I thought dawn must be coming soon;

I thought that then I would have an excuse to drag Josh away, though it was clear he'd never choose to leave on his own.

I'd closed my eyes, but I opened them in time to see the pale boy in white and the dark girl streaming pink as they led Josh away into the shadows. He fired me a last round-mouthed *oh my God* face over his shoulder, like he couldn't believe his luck. My muscles flinched with the urge to go after him, pull him back, though it wasn't our way to interfere.

The boy in blue pressed in harder and slid his hands up my shirt, at which point he should have realized that my name probably wasn't Keyshaun. He didn't seem to care.

Because they'd given up on me for the moment, though I didn't understand that then. They'd picked their first target and I just needed to be kept out of the way. The kiss slid down my throat like biting insects, like a prancing thing with too many needle-fine feet.

I was getting dizzy, and I tried to push him off. And then my mind was one big black buzz and I was down on the grass and stones. I could feel the cold lumps digging into my shoulder blades. The ground seemed too chilly, and too unsteady, for June.

There was a fading-away, where I had just enough of my mind to catch the trail of disappearances: voices dialing out in mid-sentence, the music shedding its notes. I remember trying to stand up, even thinking I *was* up, only to feel my body still sucking the cold from the sod. I remember trying to call out for him. It was up to me to keep Josh safe, so I couldn't just pass out. That thought kept blaring at me in anxious bursts. I held onto it—*get up, get up*—and clawed at the ground.

When I woke up, everyone was gone. My bowler hat had rolled away and come to rest in a patch of moss.

ABOUT THE AUTHOR

SARAH PORTER is a writer, artist, and freelance teacher who lives in Brooklyn with her husband and two cats. She is the author of several books for young adults, including *Vassa in the Night*. She has an M.F.A. in creative writing from City College. Look for her online at sarahporterbooks.com, facebook.com/sarahporterauthor, and on Twitter as @sarahporterbook.